I Burned My Tongue in Colorado

M.J. Fox

FoxJam Books

Published by FoxJam Books

FoxJam Books

www.foxjambooks.com

ISBN: 979-8-9924014-5-5 (paperback)

ISBN: 979-8-9924014-4-8 (ebook)

Cover Design by Gowtham Thangaraj

Edited by Janis Ingham

This book is a work of fiction. Names, characters, places, and incidents are the product of the author's imagination or are used fictitiously. Any resemblance to actual events, locales, or persons, living or dead, is coincidental.

Chapter One

"It looks like a penis."

"A penis?"

"Definitely a penis. Penis adjacent at a minimum."

Parker and I stared down at the plate. The croissant was about six inches long, engorged on one end, with a slight bend to the right. The raspberry glaze gave it a pinkish hue.

"What if we rotate it?" Parker nudged the plate counterclockwise. A dribble of vanilla custard oozed from the tip.

"Let's try another angle." I twisted the plate back to its original position, then tilted the tripod twenty degrees.

Nope.

"Maybe if I adjust the lighting." Parker cranked the temperature on the panel lights down from neutral white to warm white, then inserted a light diffuser over the LED bulbs. "Any better?"

I peered through the viewfinder.

A giant penis stared back at me.

Not that I had any recent personal references to draw upon

for a visual comparison. With penises, that is, not pastries. I had plenty of personal references with pastries.

Still staring into the viewfinder, I could have sworn the cream hole winked.

You're probably wondering who the strange woman is taking pictures of a raspberry flavored schlong. Allow me to introduce myself. My name is Samantha Li, but my followers call me Sam. I'm an influencer. Which means that businesses, sponsors as we like to call them, give me stuff and I promote it. Basically, it's like marketing.

Or prostitution, if you ask my mom. But, as I've explained to her six hundred and forty-seven times, yes, it's a real job, and yes, people pay me to do it.

Sometimes quite generously.

Other times ... not.

Parker is my assistant. An up and coming social media star himself. Okay, star may be generous. His parents go to the same church as mine do, so that's how we met. I agreed to share my brilliance and wisdom in exchange for logistical support and manual labor. Like coffee fetching. And moving furniture into my new apartment.

That morning, we were doing a promotion for a new place called the "Golden Bean," the latest, greatest coffee shop in Beverly Hills. So far, other than the phallus shaped pastries, it was ... decent. The air hung thick with vanilla notes and caramelized sugar. Edison bulbs dangled from the ceiling. The playlist was vaguely indie with just the right amount of bass.

Most importantly, one of the baristas had a man-bun and a sleeve of tattoos covering his left arm. Any coffee shop hoping to have a chance of relevance in Los Angeles HAD to have a barista with a man-bun.

"We could use the muffins instead?" Parker pointed to the

display case where a pair of plump strawberry frosted mounds, red cherries perched on top, were framed behind the glass.

I rolled my eyes, making sure Parker could see it. "Clearly, the universe is mocking me."

Man-bun called our order and Parker bounced over to the counter. Parker was what they call a "morning person." Someone who can function before 10:00am. I, on the other hand, was what they call a "normal person." Someone who functions best after noon.

As Parker gathered our drinks, I looked around for other shots I could use. Tech bros hunched over MacBooks. Aspiring screenwriters pecked away at their keyboards. A cluster of yoga enthusiasts in coordinated athleisure sat in the corner.

Parker returned from the counter, placing one of two steaming white mugs on the table. "That one's the lavender pistachio." The image of a swan floated on the surface, fresh froth fizzing.

I snapped a few photos. Luckily, nothing came out looking phallus shaped.

Parker positioned the second mug beside the first. "And that's the turmeric cardamom." A foam tulip bubbled beneath the steam. It sort of reminded me of a vulva, but I took pictures of it, anyway.

When I finished shooting the latte art, I looked up to find Parker staring at me. "What?"

"Aren't you going to eat it?" He bobbed his head toward the croissant. More of the creamy white filling had seeped out at the end.

"I think I'm good."

"Just because it *looks* bad doesn't mean it *tastes* bad." Parker delicately lifted the croissant with two hands. "Looks aren't everything, you know." A glob of custard fell and splattered on the plate.

"Actually, young apprentice, in our business, looks *are* everything. Perception *is* reality. Virtual reality, at least. How something tastes is irrelevant. The only things that matter are likes and views."

As Parker wrangled the thing into his mouth, I contemplated how ironic it was that a twenty-one-year-old Chinese-American man-boy presumed to lecture *me* on life. Apparently, mansplaining wasn't limited to boomer-aged Caucasians.

"Ohh meh gawd," said Parker, mouth full of cream. "Dis es ah-meez-in." His face looked like he was in the middle of having a ... well ... never mind. If I weren't so repulsed, I would have taken a video of the spectacle for my YouTube channel.

"You sure you don't want just a little taste?" Parker offered me the last gooey morsel, smacking his lips.

I waved him off. "I'm sure. Besides, we should start heading over to our LuxeLife interview. I checked the time on my phone. "I want to be early just in case."

"You know, it's only a couple blocks from here," said Parker. "We could walk."

I looked up from checking the engagement metrics on my phone. "Walk?"

Parker pointed out one of the Golden Bean's gold leaf framed windows. "It's beautiful outside. The sky's blue. The sun is shining. You can barely see the smog."

"You know what's even more beautiful than outside?"

Parker shook his head.

"Anything inside." It's true what they sing in that Missing Persons song, "Nobody Walks in L.A." Because nobody *does* walk in L.A. Especially me. Walking, or really any sort of physical activity whatsoever, was NOT something I would ever choose to do willingly.

"Nervous?" Parker's eyes drifted to my fingers, which I

realized were tapping on the table at the pace of a thrash metal song.

"Ehh." I waved him off, careful not to raise my arm too high and reveal the waterfall of stress sweat pouring out of my pits.

I wasn't nervous.

I was terrified.

The LuxeLife contract, if I got it, would become my *SIGNATURE* gig. If I could get in with LuxeLife, my career would blow up faster than a new grumpy cat meme. Watch out Kardashians, here I come!

My foot tapped the floor as if it were at a tryout for *Riverdance*. Maybe a walk to burn off some nervous energy would do me some good. Or a quick sprint to Encino. But that would have involved physical effort. So no.

"Hey Siri, grab me an Uber," I called to my phone.

"Opening YouTube," came the robotic response.

"No, Siri, that's not what I'm looking for."

"Here are the lyrics to U2's 'I Still Haven't Found What I'm Looking For.'"

"No, I need a car to pick me up."

"Setting a reminder. Pick up car from shop," Siri chirped cheerfully.

"Why does everything have to be so difficult?" What happened next would have made Rube Goldberg proud.

I grabbed my phone.

Still locked to the tripod I'd been using to take pictures of the latte art.

The tripod knocked over the light panel.

Which crashed into the turmeric cardamom mug.

Creating a tidal wave of tulip-shaped froth.

Which hurtled across the birchwood tabletop right at me.

Fortunately for me, Parker had cat-like reflexes. He leaped out of his chair, snatched a fistful of napkins from the dispenser, and sopped up the flowing foam just as it reached the edge of the table.

Unfortunately for me, Parker had hippopotamus-like hand-eye coordination. In his heroic efforts to stem the tide of turmeric cardamom, his elbow smacked the pistachio lavender, which tumbled straight into my lap.

Lava-hot latte soaked through my LoveShackFancy miniskirt, hot coffee dripping down my legs. My nether regions felt like they had gotten a bikini wax with a flamethrower.

That's when man-bun intervened.

"I got you!" Super Man-Bun leapt to the rescue, barista towel waving like a superhero cape, lunging toward my crotch. Head between my knees, he froze, realizing the compromising position of where he'd need to dab. His face turned the color of a boob-shaped muffin.

"Thanks." I snatched the towel from his hand. "I got it from here." I tried to mop up the spill, but the coffee soaked through. An unfortunate wet patch now stained my entire pelvic area.

Man-bun and I made eye contact, neither one of us sure how to proceed. I handed back his towel. "Thanks?"

We both looked down at my wet crotch before resuming the awkward eye contact. "You're welcome?"

As Man-Bun slunk back behind the counter, I looked up to find Parker smiling, not at all concerned with my latte scalding.

"Why are you smiling?"

"You know what that was, don't you?"

"A third-degree burn?"

"That was a meet-cute," said Parker, a twinkle in his eye.

"That was not a meet-cute. That was a 'random coffee shop guy with a man-bun invading the personal space of my crotch.' There was nothing cute about it." I grabbed some more napkins and sopped up the espresso that had leaked into my shoe. "And if it was a meet-cute, it was a terrible one. People don't form relationships based on random coffee shop misadventures." When I looked up, Parker's eyes were still twinkling. "You're still smiling. Stop smiling."

"You should get his number."

"So I can send him my dry-cleaning bill? Good idea."

"I'm being serious."

"So am I. This skirt costs almost as much as my monthly rent. If that boutique in Sherman Oaks hadn't sent it to me as part of a promo, I'd never be able to afford something like this on my own."

"He's totally into you," said Parker, ignoring my skirt problems. "Plus, he's kinda cute."

"If I were into man-buns," I said. "Which I am not. Besides, I have no time for dating. And even if I had time to pursue some semblance of a relationship, there isn't a decent guy worth ... relating ... in the entire state. California men are sus. L.A. men especially."

"Ouch." Parker placed his hand on his heart in mock indignation.

* * *

After drying my skirt under the hand dryer in the ladies' restroom (and an apologetic smile to the elderly woman who walked in on me), Parker and I hopped in an Uber, which dropped us in front of the company headquarters of LuxeLife Resorts and Spas. We stared up at the towering fortress of steel and glass for a few moments, calming our nerves. It was where our wildest dreams or deepest nightmares were about to come true.

"Yikes." Parker's jaw hung open.

My mouth joined his. "Yeah. If a bunch of evil supervillains ever got together and built a corporate headquarters, it would look exactly like this."

"You ready?"

I glimpsed my reflection in the mirrored surface. My coffee-stained skirt clung to my thighs like plastic wrap. At least the ruffles partially obscured the stain. "Of course I'm ready." I took a deep breath. Then another one. And finally, a third. "I was born ready. You queued the deck?"

"Locked and loaded." Parker patted his laptop bag. "We've got printouts of all the social metrics spreadsheets, engagement forecasts, and competitor analyses." When he peeked in his bag, it looked like twelve acres of Oregonian forest had valiantly sacrificed themselves just for this presentation.

As we approached the front entrance, the glare from the sun punched right through the tint of my Prada sunglasses, another promotional gift I could never afford on my own. That was another reason the LuxeLife contract was so important. There I was, a professional influencer, supposedly showing people how the better half lives. But the truth was, I wasn't in the better half. Not even the better two-thirds. Maybe the better fifteen-sixteenths? I don't know; fractions were never my specialty. The point is, this was finally my chance to be something real.

* * *

The first-floor lobby of LuxeLife Resorts and Spas stretched before us like a temple. Sunlight knifed through floor-to-ceiling windows. The perfumed air hung cool and still. My heels echoed across the marble floors. The softer I tried to walk, the louder they seemed to get.

Behind the reception desk sat a woman who seemed as

carefully designed as the space itself. "May I help you?" Neither her tone nor her face seemed very helpful.

"Samantha Li and Parker Wang," I said. "We have an appointment."

"Mr. Wiles will be with you shortly. Please have a seat."

The design of the waiting area could have been plucked from the pages of *Architecture Digest*. A massive abstract painting dominated one wall, bold slashes of gold and red. Parker and I perched on the edge of what I assumed was a couch. Or possibly one of those curvy sex chairs, but big enough for an entire orgy.

Ten minutes passed.

"What did you say our latest engagement metrics were again?" I asked, desperate for a distraction.

"Up twelve percent this quarter. The demographics sheet shows we're hitting their target audience dead-center."

I nodded, squirming in my seat. Not just because I was nervous, but also because my butt was going numb. Clearly, the waiting area was not designed for any actual waiting.

Another ten minutes passed.

"And the competitor analysis?"

"A similar influencer worked with Mountain Ridge Resorts last season," said Parker. "None of their posts even broke fifty thousand views."

I smoothed my skirt for the hundredth time. "Maybe we should go through the proposal again," I suggested.

"Right. Good idea." Parker reached into his laptop bag, and, once again, his hippopotamus hand-eye coordination reared its bulbous head. Before I knew what was happening, dozens of meticulously prepared, organized, and sorted proposal documents exploded outward, fluttering through the air and across the marble floor like a flock of startled birds.

"Parker!" My voice ricocheted through the lobby. The

receptionist shot us a look. Parker and I both dropped to our knees, scrambling to collect the scattered papers.

That's when we heard the voice.

A deep voice.

A commanding voice.

A voice that grew louder with every echoing footstep because it was coming our way.

"Absolutely unacceptable!" The voice boomed from somewhere down the hall. "This is precisely why Victoria fired half the marketing department."

My fingers went numb as I snatched papers. Parker's hands transformed into clumsy paddles, knocking over the stack of spreadsheets I'd just gathered.

"I don't have time for excuses," said the voice. I could hear the crescendoing tip-tap of expensive shoes stomping over marble. "When I schedule a meeting, I expect preparation. I expect order."

Parker's elbow inadvertently jabbed me in the nose. My foot accidentally kicked him in the shin. We turned at the same time, both lunging for the same spreadsheet that had somehow slid halfway under the sex sofa. The cracking of skulls filled the lobby with an audible knock. The receptionist glared again.

"Sorry," said both Parker and me at once.

"Sorry? SORRY?" The voice was just around the corner now. "LuxeLife wasn't built on apologies. It's built on precision. Coordination. Discipline."

I jammed a market analysis graph upside down into a folder. Parker stuffed papers back into his laptop bag out of order and backwards.

"When you walk into a meeting with me, you'd better have your shit together," said the voice. "Every document. Every figure. Every contingency planned for."

I spotted my executive summary, the cornerstone of my

entire presentation, lying traitorously behind a potted palm. I lunged for it just as Parker stood abruptly, his hip broadsiding my ribs, sending my balance sideways.

"I'm hanging up now. I have another social media team waiting."

Parker and I froze in our respective contortions, him half-squatting with papers clutched to his chest, and me stretched across the floor like I was mid-stroke in the freestyle lap of a swimming competition.

In a desperate last gasp effort, I snatched the executive summary from behind the palm, Parker hauled me to my feet, and we both spun toward the entrance to the hallway, documents clutched in white-knuckled grips and our faces arranged into what we hoped portrayed calm, confident professionalism.

Marcus Wiles appeared in the archway, his scowl melting into a brilliant smile, eyes lit up with practiced warmth. "Miss Li! Mr. Wang!" said Marcus, voice dripping with sugar. "Sorry to keep you waiting."

"Not at all," I managed, clutching my executive summary to my chest.

When Marcus smiled, his teeth almost blinded me. I had met plenty of super-rich, super-successful people in my line of work. People who had personal chefs, personal trainers, even personal closet organizers. Marcus must have had a personal dentist who bleached his teeth every morning before he came into work.

"Shall we?" He swept his arm toward the elevator banks, much like a medieval executioner might direct condemned prisoners toward the dungeon for a full day of latte crotch burns and sitting on uncomfortable sex furniture.

Chapter Two

We followed Marcus to the executive conference room, where serious looking LuxeLife executives sat around a polished table. Already judging me.

"Please, take a seat." Marcus directed Parker and me toward a pair of empty chairs, then leaned in close. "Oh, and Miss Li, one more thing before we get started." His voice was barely a whisper, low enough that only I could hear. "I'm the one that recommended Victoria consider you." His smile grew wider, his teeth somehow whiter. "So don't fuck this up."

Forcing a smile to my face, I noticed the stain on my skirt had dried into a pattern that looked disturbingly like the state of Florida. "Right."

"So. Marcus," barked a voice entering the room. "Is this the new social media miracle worker you were telling me about?"

Victoria Sterling strode to the head of the table, CEO of LuxeLife Resorts and Spas. The kind of woman who made Cruella DeVille look warm and cuddly. The type who probably kept her skin wrinkle free by drinking the blood of kittens. Everything about her was sharp angles and clean lines. When her Louboutins struck the floor, each click emitted a tiny sonic boom.

"You must be Samantha," she said, extending a hand adorned with a diamond that could single-handedly fund world famine relief. At first, I wasn't sure if I was supposed to shake it or kiss it. I went with shaking.

Victoria took her seat at the head of the table. Looking through the expansive windows, it looked like we were floating in the clouds. "I'm going to be honest with you here, Samantha. Before Marcus showed me your little videos or posts or whatever you call them, I had no idea who you were. But Marcus tells me this is what people pay attention to these days, for whatever reason. And now here we are."

An assistant scurried in to refill Victoria's sparkling water, then disappeared just as fast. Parker and I exchanged a flash of eye contact that communicated an entire conversation.

We're screwed.

Stay calm.

I am calm.

You don't look calm.

I have to pee.

Was that a pelican that flew past the window?

Focus!

Victoria took a sip of her sparkling water, then settled back in her chair. "So go on then, Samantha. Wow me."

This was it. The moment of truth.

Our presentation packets were a hot mess after the lobby explosion, so I shook my head when Parker reached into his bag to pull them out. I was going to have to wow Victoria Sterling and her executive team all on my own. Good thing I had spent the past week of sleepless nights going over the pitch again and again in my head.

I took a deep breath, then looked around the table, meeting

each pair of expectant eyes staring back at me. These weren't just expensive suits. These were the gatekeepers. The key masters standing guard to everything I'd been working toward. Not just the financial security, though that certainly mattered. And not just the subscriber numbers, though those counted too.

No. It was more than that. Much more.

This was about proving I could do more than post pretty pictures and cute captions. This was about proving my parents, my friends, and everyone else who'd been politely waiting for me to "come to my senses" that they were wrong. That their daughter hadn't thrown away a Stanford education and generations of family sacrifice just to take selfies for a living.

Another deep breath. It was time to put up or shut up. Prove it or lose it. Do or die.

"Ms. Sterling, Mr. Wiles, executives of LuxeLife," I began, both relieved and surprised my voice still functioned. "Most people would probably come in here with a bunch of fancy presentations. Dazzle you with the competitor analyses they spent all night stapling together. Wow you with the detailed subscriber trends they spent three hours at the UPS store printing out."

Parker mouthed the word "sorry."

"But I'm not going to do that." I leaned forward, chin held high. "Because I am not your run-of-the-mill corporate presenter. Dependent upon a well-organized series of PowerPoint slides to keep herself from rambling. I don't have a fancy MBA. Actually, I have a partial degree in art history that my parents still haven't forgiven me for. But that's a topic for another day."

A man in an Armani suit was playing with his phone under the table. A woman in a bright pink blazer cleared her throat. Victoria's left eyebrow arched so high it nearly left her forehead.

"What I do have is an authentic connection with real

people. And that's why you're going to hire me." I cued Parker, who'd taken advantage of my brilliant stalling techniques to bluetooth the conference room's Wi-Fi to my phone. I lifted it in the air, like a sword swinging William Wallace signaling a charge.

With all eyes on me, I hit play. The gigantic conference room video display flickered to life, showing a video of a no name hole-in-the-wall taqueria in East Los Angeles.

"This is Doña Maria," I said, my voice louder. Less shaky. On screen, an older Hispanic woman rolled tortillas by hand behind the chipped tile counter. "Before I posted this, she was about to lose her family restaurant. Now she has lines around the block and hired her nieces to manage the social media accounts I set up for her."

Out of the corner of my eye, I saw Parker pecking away at the keys on his laptop. He must have hacked into the room's audio setup because dramatic music started playing over the surround sound speakers.

I swiped to another post. "This is Jin's Bubble Tea in Korea town. He named a special drink after me. The 'Bubble Trouble.' Why he insisted on using the word 'trouble' is not important right now. What is important is that it became his bestseller after I posted about it. Not because I'm polished. But because people trust what I recommend."

I took another deep breath. A few heads were nodding. Armani suit guy stopped playing with his phone. "People don't follow me because I show them a fantasy life," I said. "They follow me because I'm real. I tell them where the bathroom is hidden in Venice Beach. I show them which food truck has the best refried beans even though they're in a sketchy parking lot in the industrial section of Burbank. I warn them when the cute new bistro serves mediocre, overpriced food."

An executive with slicked-back hair leaned forward, a fake

smile fixed on his face. "That's charming, Miss Li, but our clientele isn't interested in food trucks. They want champagne wishes and caviar dreams. They want the fantasy."

"Do they, though? Or is that what you think they want because that's what you've always crammed down their throats?"

Parker, miracle worker that he was, had somehow juxtaposed my gritty, authentic, real content with LuxeLife's corporate website, which was filled with polished photography that looked fake and posed. In my posts, people were smiling, laughing, living their best life. The LuxeLife people looked like actors and models getting paid to flash their pretty teeth.

"Your target demographic isn't just wealthy baby boomers anymore," I pressed. "It's millennials who've finally made it. Despite the odds. GenZ trust fund babies. Tech entrepreneurs who wear hoodies to board meetings. They have money to spend, but they're not impressed by the same things their parents were. Certainly not their grandparents. And not the things you're trying to sell them."

Slicked back hair guy made a snort. Others were whispering and shaking their heads. Marcus leaned over and whispered into Victoria's ear, then glanced toward the door. Probably wondering how long it would take the security guards to rush in and toss us out.

"Actually, you know what," said the pink suited woman. "She has a point."

"I do?" I asked.

"She does?" asked Marcus at exactly the same time.

Pink blazer girl nodded. She was, by far, the youngest one in the room, other than me and Parker. She made cutesy eyes in his direction. "Mind if I take over?"

"Be my guest." Parker's cheeks turned the same color as Pink Blazer girl's wardrobe.

I Burned My Tongue in Colorado

She poked a few swipes on her tablet and took over the screen share, displaying lots of colored lines crossing up and down on a graph. "Our customer research shows exactly that trend. Our demographics have been skewing younger every year."

"To be fair," interjected a man with a voice like he narrated golf tournaments on the side, "Miss Li's background isn't exactly aligned with luxury travel. She said herself she started reviewing hole-in-the-wall Mexican restaurants? That's quite a leap to our five-star properties."

I felt my face flush. Not from embarrassment. From being pissed off. "Is there something wrong with Mexican restaurants?" I asked.

The room fell silent as everyone's attention shifted from me to him. "No, no, of course not," Golf Voice backpedaled. "But it's a different market segment entirely."

"You mean affordable?"

"No. It's just, well, you know ..."

"Or is your problem that my heritage is Chinese, so you find it incongruous that I'd appreciate Mexican cuisine?" It wasn't the first time some suit had made assumptions based on ethnic stereotypes.

Golf Voice's face went the color of undercooked chicken. "I didn't mean ..."

"You know what's funny?" I cut in. "Asian Americans can enjoy Mexican food. Wealthy people can enjoy street tacos. And believe it or not, people who drop a thousand dollars a night on a LuxeLife hotel still want to know where the locals eat."

clap ... clap ... clap

All eyes turned toward the head of the table, where Victoria executed a movie climax worthy slow clap. Or she was summoning the security guards to throw me down the trash chute. Or possibly trying to operate one of those clap activated nightlights they hawk on late-night TV.

Victoria wagged her finger at me. "I like this girl, Marcus. I like her *a lot*. She's got grit."

The executive who'd questioned my background looked like he wanted to melt into his expensive chair. Parker did a little fist bump with himself.

"But..." Victoria leaned over the table, eyes fixed on mine. "LuxeLife does, in fact, sell luxury. It's in our name. Miss Li, how would you reconcile this authenticity with the aspirational lifestyle our brand represents?"

I gathered my wits and my thoughts. "Luxury isn't just about thread counts and infinity pools anymore," I said. "It's about access. Experiences. Stories worth telling. Rich people can go anywhere. But what they can't buy is the local knowledge, the hidden gems, the genuine connections."

Marcus nodded, seeming to warm to the idea. "So you're suggesting exclusive access to authentic experiences."

"Exactly!" I pointed at him like he'd just solved a math equation involving fractions.

Marcus leaned in close to Victoria, whispering in her ear. She nodded, then whispered back. "Miss Li, you're familiar with our portfolio?"

"Like the back of my hand." As soon as we'd gotten the invitation to interview with LuxeLife about their campaign, Parker and I had poured over every piece of information we could find. I had all their top spots memorized. Paris. London. Bali. Hong Kong. There were more places, but not anywhere worth going.

"There's one property in particular where we think you might be a good fit."

Please be Paris, please be Paris, please be Paris.

Or London.

I Burned My Tongue in Colorado

Or Bali.

Or Hong Kong.

"Aster Park," said Marcus.

"Aster Park? As in ... Colorado?"

"It's been bleeding red. Bookings are down despite renovation efforts.

"Expensive renovation efforts," Victoria added. "Do you think you could work a little of your Samantha magic there?"

Aster Park. I knew all about it. I just didn't want to go.

Over the past week, any time I dared to let myself dream of the remote possibility that I could land this job, I always pictured myself nibbling designer macarons in Paris. Taking selfies in front of Kensington Palace. Putting together Instagram reels of my over-water bungalow in Bali.

"Samantha?"

I forced a smile back onto my face. I was a professional after all. "Yes, I can absolutely work my magic there. Of course. Your Aster Park property isn't just a luxury resort. It's a gateway to experiences most people will never have. The best mountain views known only to locals. The small-batch bourbon distillery that doesn't offer public tours but might open its doors for LuxeLife guests who don't mind splurging on craft cocktails."

Victoria tapped a polished nail against her chin. "So authenticity as the new luxury."

"And who better to showcase that than someone who built her entire brand on finding authentic experiences?" I asked the room. "I won't just show your customers the spa treatments and the thread counts. I'll show them the moments in between. The ones that make a vacation unforgettable."

The room had shifted. I could feel it in the air, like the moment at a K-Pop concert when the band is about to debut their new dance moves. Even Golf Voice and Slick Hair seemed to buy it.

Victoria steepled her fingers. All she needed was an eye patch and a hairless cat and she would have been a perfect Austin Powers villain. "And you think you can do this at Aster Park?"

"I know I can," I replied immediately, praying my voice sounded more confident than I was.

Victoria exchanged another long look with Marcus. Some silent communication passed between them.

"The Aster Park team has been pushing for more 'local flavor' in our advertising," said Victoria.

"Local flavor?" asked Parker

"You know, Colorado stuff. Dress up in cowboy boots and take a selfie with a polar bear or something."

"I don't think they have polar bears in Colorado." Parker frowned.

"Whatever. You'll figure it out." Victoria waved her hand as if she was shooing a gnat. "Honestly, I don't care what you do or how you do it as long as you get people to spend their money at my resort. Ship in a polar bear from the South Pole if you have to."

"Technically, polar bears are only found near the North Pole," said Parker, but Victoria wasn't listening.

Marcus was actually nodding now. "That could get them off our backs until their contract runs out." I didn't know "them" and I had no idea what contract he was talking about, but I was too focused on getting my own contract at that moment to give it another thought.

"Two birds with one stone." Victoria smiled, then turned back toward me. "We need to fly you out there as soon as possible.

"Does that mean I got the job?" When I glanced at Parker, he was holding his breath.

"If you can make this luxury authenticity thing happen, then yes. How's tomorrow work?"

"Tomorrow?"

"Bookings are under forecast and we're over budget. I need a quick win to justify the renovation costs for our investors."

Marcus punched out a message on his phone. "I'll have my assistant work out the logistics and text you first thing in the morning."

When Victoria smiled, it almost looked genuine. "I like you, Samantha. If you pull this off, you'll have a bright future with us. You know we just acquired a new property right next to the Seine. You can see the Eiffel Tower from the penthouse. And we're looking at an expansion at our chateau collection in Zurich."

Mentally, I started strategizing an accessory plan for lederhosen. It was the opportunity of a lifetime. I'd always dreamed of traveling the world, but I'd never even been out of the country before, unless you count that disastrous spring break in Tijuana, which most of my brain cells had opted to forget. At least the ones not murdered by the tequila shots.

"Here are the contract terms we're offering." Marcus slid a stack of papers across the table, roughly the page count of the United States tax code, the bible, and *Moby Dick* combined. "I'll just need you to initial the addendum for 'authentic adventures' once our legal team finishes writing it up."

He made quote fingers when he said "authentic adventures," which should have worried me, but I was too busy trying not to hyperventilate when I saw the figure at the bottom of the page. The Aster Park sponsorship was worth more than I made in an entire year. My entire career, actually.

"Oh, and of course, the ethics clause." Marcus handed me another stack of papers. "Can't forget that."

"Ethics clause?"

"Just the standard terms." Marcus flashed his warmest smile. About the temperature of an iceberg. "Nothing that should present any complications, I'm sure."

"We'll also comp all expenses and incidentals." Victoria added. "So make sure to take full advantage of the amenities."

I saluted her. "I absolutely will." In my mind's eye, I saw myself getting a hot stone massage by a lumberjack masseuse while being hand-fed mountain trout caviar by the resort's Michelin-starred chef.

Once we were alone in the elevator, on our way back down to the lobby, Parker asked, "She wasn't really serious about the polar bear, was she?"

"For what they're paying us, I'll take selfies with whatever kind of bear they want me too."

Chapter Three

WEE-ERR-WEE-ERR-WEE-ERR! I bolted awake to a sharp-pitched, earsplitting sound, my phone flashing like it was in a mosh-pit at a rave. At first, I wasn't sure if I was still in bed or trapped in a deep-water submarine dodging torpedoes.

It was a text notification from my phone. "Goddamn it."

My hand fumbled around my nightstand like a drunk octopus, eyes still glued shut.

THUD

Something hit the floor.

THUMP

Probably the jade facial roller one of my sponsors gifted me.

CRASH

Definitely my lucky bergamot orange scent diffuser, which, as it turns out, wasn't so lucky after all.

My fingers finally found my phone, poking and pressing to make the siren noise stop. When the screen lit up, I saw the time.

4:30 am.

"Holy hell." As normal brain functioning oozed back into my cranium, I remembered what the super loud, super annoying red alert sound effect meant. It was a special alert I had set for any text messages from Marcus at LuxeLife.

Realization dawning (unlike the actual dawn, which was still hours away), I went from a state of sleep-deprived-pissed-off to a state of wide-awake-terror in the span of 1.2 seconds. As I scrambled to open my messaging app, second guesses and self-doubts poured through my inner monologue like a horde of teen girls at a Taylor Swift concert.

LuxeLife changed its mind ...

Victoria realized I was a total fraud ...

Golf Voice and Slick Hair staged a corporate coup and made it their life mission to destroy me ...

The text message from Marcus wasn't any of those things.

It was worse.

My phone made more noise. This time, a buzzing sound, an incoming call from Parker.

"Oh my god oh my god oh my god oh my god. Did you see the email? Did you see the text?" Parker's voice was annoyingly alert for pre-sunlight.

"No. I was sleeping. Like a normal person." My voice came out as a croak.

"Well, you better stop sleeping and start moving because you leave for Aster Park Regional Airport in two hours."

4:32am.

I briefly considered the possibility I was still dreaming, or more accurately, nightmaring, but then I rammed my big toe into the crate of arctic glacier detox masks at the foot of my bed and the sharp stab of pain confirmed that I was, indeed, awake.

"Sam, did you hear what I said? You leave in TWO

HOURS." There was a brief pause, then Parker added, "Actually, make that one hour and fifty-seven minutes."

I'd transitioned from sleep-deprived-pissed-off to wide-awake-terror, which now gave way to five-alarm-panic. My torso shot straight up in bed, knocking a jar of sponsor-supplied truffle-infused night cream halfway across the room.

Over the past few years, my downtown pseudo-affordable apartment had transformed into a mixed-use space. Forty-nine percent video studio, forty-nine percent warehouse, and two percent living quarters. With all the free product people sent me for reviews and reveals, I could have opened my own beauty supply store.

"Now one hour and fifty-six minutes," said Parker's voice, now emanating from the nightstand where I'd switched him to speakerphone.

"Call them back!" I ordered. "Tell them to book me on a later flight." When Marcus said his assistant would work out the travel arrangements after our LuxeLife meeting, I had thought it would take a few days to pull everything together, not a few hours. I'd also assumed there would be a step where they checked in with me first before booking me on a flight halfway across the country.

"I already tried," said Parker. "The six thirty was the only flight to Aster Park that still had a seat open in first class." He paused dramatically. "Unless you'd prefer to fly coach."

"I'd rather start flapping my arms and fly there myself."

My phone rang yet again. According to the display, this time, my parents. Somehow, my LA apartment had transformed into Grand Central Station overnight. "What do they want?" I mumbled to myself. "I don't have time for this." I sent their call straight to voicemail.

4:35am.

My mental state shifted back to wide-awake-terror, which

was followed quickly by overwhelming paralysis. The million different things I would have to do to get ready for the trip were engulfed in a battle-royale for my sleep-hampered attention span.

I needed to pee. And eat. And shower, I confirmed after a quick sniff.

Or should I shower, then eat, then pee? And then pack and get dressed. Or get dressed and then pack. Or pack and then eat? But did I even have time to shower? Did I even have time to pee?

Some people are good with surprises. Emergency room surgeons. Navy Seals. Kindergarten teachers.

I was not.

One time, when I was seven, my parents threw me a surprise birthday party with all my friends, and when Dad opened the door and everyone yelled "surprise," I grabbed the piñata bat and hit a home run in his crotch.

4:36am.

I ripped off the Britney Spears concert t-shirt I used for a sleep shirt like it was on fire and jumped out of bed. To be fair, the word "jump" in this case was more of a trip, a flop and a stumble.

As soon as my feet hit the floor, I banged my knee on a box of sea kelp-based facial creams that a new cosmetic brand had sent me for an upcoming giveaway.

I decided packing was at the top of the priority list (peeing came in a close second). I foraged through my closet for appropriate travel clothes, still mired in a sleep-deprived fog. "What do people wear in Colorado?" I asked Parker, who was still on speaker mode.

"Mountain leisure," said Parker's voice from across the room. I was pretty sure that was NOT a thing. "You should definitely bring comfortable hiking shoes."

"Why would I bring hiking shoes?"

"For hiking?"

"I will not be doing any hiking," I shouted from inside my closet.

"Bring a waterproof bag too."

"Why would I need a waterproof bag?"

"For the fishing and the camping."

"I won't be doing any fishing or camping either, so I think I'm good."

"What if you fall out of a canoe?"

"I won't be falling out of a canoe because I won't be getting inside a canoe, I can promise you that."

"Weren't you the one pitching authenticity?" asked Parker.

"Technically, that was Victoria. I just took her idea and ran with it."

I grabbed a few pairs of cotton leggings and some flow blouses, then glanced at my closet full of designer heels. None of them were comfortable enough to walk any distance in, and I highly doubted any of them were waterproof.

"You know my grandpa used to take me fishing," said Parker over the speakerphone. "It was fun."

I made a face, even though Parker couldn't see me. "Well, the closest I'll ever get to fishing is choosing a can of tuna from the market."

With an armful of random articles of clothing, I realized I needed something to put them in. I pulled my Louis Vuitton suitcase off the top shelf of my closet and laid it open on the bed. To be clear, it was a piece of luggage I could never have afforded on my own. A travel agent gave it to me in exchange for a series of Instagram posts.

4:56am

After hanging up with Parker, I took care of the pee and shower items on my to-do list. I'd have been dressed too, but all my underwear (the ones without holes in them) was still in the washer, a soggy mass of delicate fabrics that smelled faintly of mildew. Laundry management was not at the top of my skills list.

I had just tossed them in the dryer when my phone rang. AGAIN. It was my parents. AGAIN.

Parker must have tipped them off about the LuxeLife trip, because that is exactly what he would do if he thought I was stressing out about it, which, of course I was, and now Mom was calling to lecture me on travel safety procedures. The last thing I needed was lessons about preventative bed bug techniques, or the dangers of hitchhiking with strangers. Which I literally did every day. We just didn't call it hitchhiking any more. We called it Uber.

5:12am

My eyes darted to the pile of unopened PR packages in the corner of my bedroom. One of the boxes was stamped with the logo for 'Brief Encounters', a new online intimate-wear company that had been hounding me for a campaign for months. I maneuvered through the stack of boxes like I was playing Jenga, pulling the Brief Encounters box out of the stack. Miraculously, the whole thing didn't topple over and smother me.

Dropping my towel on the floor, I tore open the box. As soon as I got back from Colorado, I'd shoot an official unboxing reveal and post it on my streams, but at that moment, it was more important to cover my naked butt.

Which ... the thing I held in my hand was definitely NOT going to do. It looked like a piece of cherry-red dental floss.

Holding the thin strip of silk up to the light, I tried to figure out which side was the front and which side was the back. Both sides promised extreme discomfort no matter which part of my body they wedged into. At least the matching push-up bra looked straightforward. Surely the rhinestones went on the outside of the nipples.

I threaded one leg through what I thought was an opening in the red silk, then pulled them up over my hips. That's when I realized the panties weren't just wafer-thin and translucent; they were also crotchless.

5:18am

My phone rang again.

Parents.

Decline.

Then came the doorbell. Once. Twice. The third time nearly made my head explode. LuxeLife must have sent a driver to take me to the airport, and they were early.

Walking bowlegged and cursing, I ambled into the living room where a mountain of colorful boxes were strewn about like the aftermath of a tornado. The latest Korean sheet masks spilled from a holographic box onto my kitchen table. A rainbow of nail polishes lined the countertop.

Dodging packages like they were landmines, I got close enough for the driver to hear me through the door. "I'm not ready yet! I just woke up!"

Ding Dong

"Holy hell," I grumbled.

As far as mornings went, I'd had better. I set my feet in front of the locked door, fists planted on my silk-stringed hips. I took a deep breath, winding up to tell the driver exactly where he could go and what he could do with himself while I finished getting ready.

What happened next went in slow motion.

The lock clicked.

The knob TURNED.

THE DOOR SWUNG OPEN!

Leaving me face to face with a middle-aged Chinese American couple standing on the threshold.

My parents.

"Holy fuck!" At first, I wasn't sure if I had said it out loud, or only in my head. By the look of horror on Mom's face, I assumed it was out loud. Before the image of my half-naked body could imprint itself on Dad's brain, I slammed the door in their faces.

"Fuck fuck fuck fuck FUUUUUUCK!"

5:23am

It was hard to decide which part of the past ten seconds had been most horrible.

The part where Mom and Dad saw me wearing a red crotchless G-string?

The part where I yelled 'holy fuck' at them?

Or the part where I slammed the door in their faces?

Glancing back toward my bedroom, I briefly considered jumping out the window and then fleeing the country. I was only ten stories up. Maybe I could aim my flailing body toward a trash-bag-packed dumpster.

Instead, I grabbed a semi-damp towel from my bathroom floor, wrapped it around my body, then tugged open the door.

My parents stood in the exact same place, with the exact same look of shock and awe glued to their faces.

"Sorry. I ... ah ..."

Mom's eyebrow twitched. Dad's mouth hung open.

"What are you doing here anyway?" I asked at last.

"Parker said you needed a ride to the airport," said Mom.

"We also brought breakfast." Dad looked everywhere but at me.

"We figured you wouldn't have time to eat." Mom held up a pink box, and my saliva gland's rate of drool production went from puddling to flash flood. The scent of sesame, cinnamon, and butter filled my tiny apartment.

"It's huajuan," said Dad, still not making eye contact.

Huajuan, pronounced hwa-jwahn (as if that makes it any easier), is a traditional Chinese pastry where light fluffy dough is rolled and steamed. The ones in the box Mom held were smeared with sesame paste and dusted with cinnamon and powdered sugar. Best of all, they didn't resemble any part of the male anatomy.

"Edgar sent them," announced Mom. *Of course, he did.* Mom's face reminded me of a very cunning but also very evil fox who had just tricked a crow into dropping her hunk of cheese. I'm the crow, by the way, in this scenario.

"He told me to tell you hi." *Of course he did.* "So, hi," Mom continued. Then she waved.

My mother and Edgar's mother had been trying to get the two of us together for years.

Edgar was the type of son that every Chinese American parent dreamed about. He studied hard in school, never got caught smoking pot in his parent's gazebo, and got a full ride to Stanford where he got his MBA and graduated Magna Cum Laude. Heck, if I were my mother, I'd try to force me into an arranged marriage with Edgar too.

But while Edgar was every Chinese American parent's dream child, I was the type of daughter that haunted every Chinese American parent's nightmares. My grade point average in high school rhymed with the word "shoe." Not only did I get caught smoking pot (yes, in my parents' gazebo), I also totaled their Honda Odyssey two days after I got my license, dyed my hair pink for prom, and dated a black guy when I was twenty-three. Just to clarify, the fact that he was black wasn't the problem. They took issue with the fact that he was majoring in Film Studies, which they felt would inevitably lead to a life of perpetual unemployment (which, of course, is true).

Basically, I'd become the cautionary tale parents used to scare their children into compliance. The whispered warning at family gatherings. You don't want to end up like Samantha, do you? All that potential and now she takes pictures of fancy things for strangers.

On the plus side, I did end up going to Stanford, but I dropped out once my influencing gigs took off, and the only MBA I ever got was a Masters in Binging Alcohol. Pina coladas specifically, with a minor is smoking pot.

To be clear, I didn't resent Edgar for being perfect. I resented him for making my imperfection so visible by comparison. He'd taken the path everyone else thought I was supposed to take and walked it flawlessly, which made my departure from that path feel less like brave independence and more like elaborate self-sabotage.

"You know, Samantha, Edgar runs his family's bakery now."

"Yes, Mom, I know." I knew because Mom had mentioned it twenty-five million times, along with Edgar's interviews in LA food blogs, his recent expansion into organic sourdough, and his decision to modernize the family recipes while still honoring tradition.

"At least he put his Stanford education to good use," Dad added, twisting the knife deeper into my spinal cord. I braced for the inevitable. You see, despite the fact that my father was born and raised in Southern California, English was still effectively a second language. At home growing up, we almost exclusively spoke Cantonese. However, despite this, my father was a world-class master linguist when it came to referencing the fact that he was still making payments on my student loans, which he could literally work into any and all conversations.

"That reminds me," said Dad, right on schedule. "I still need last quarter's loan payment invoice so I can give it to my accountant." *See?*

"That's okay, darling." Mom patted Dad on the shoulder with the patient smile of someone who'd perfected the art of loving disappointment. "I'm sure Samantha will go back and finish her schooling once she gets bored with the silly chat snapping."

"It's called Snapchat, Mom. I told you."

"Tickingtalking, Instatube, Facepage, it's all just a fad." Mom snorted and shook her head.

"Then *you* can take over *your* family's business." Much like my mother's continuous efforts to pimp me out to Edgar, my father's personal life quest was to convince me, his only child, to take over our family business so he could retire. "It's what your great-great-great-grandfather always wanted."

"Right." This was also a story I'd heard a million times before. According to family legend, my great-great-great grand-father traversed six thousand nautical miles of shark-infested waters to start a new life in America, just so one day, his great-great-great granddaughter could serve broth-covered dumplings to tourists.

"We can come with you to Colorado if you want," Mom said, causing me to choke on a bite of huajuan. "Your father and I are always happy to support you." My parents considered a constant flow of constructive criticism support.

"Absolutely not," I sputtered, still coughing. "You may not have realized it yet, but I'm actually NOT a toddler anymore. I don't need chaperones."

"Are you sure?" Mom looked around my apartment, taking in the chaos of unopened packages, discarded takeout containers, and a half-eaten breakfast burrito still on the counter from yesterday. "Because it looks like you might."

I followed her gaze, seeing my carefully curated life through her eyes. To my legions of followers, I was the picture of put-together millennial success. Artfully arranged coffee cups. Motivational quotes over tasteful decor. Morning routine videos that definitely didn't feature yesterday's underwear still damp in the dryer. But Mom saw the truth. I was a master of surfaces, a disaster of depths.

"I'm twenty-six years old," I reminded them. "I've been living on my own for years. Mostly."

"And yet you still can't do laundry," Mom observed, eyeing my towel-covered body. "You get dressed. Your father and I will take care of everything else.

Chapter Four

The drive to LAX was a nonstop lecture on the dangers of Colorado, interspersed with thinly veiled suggestions that I might want to consider a more stable career path. The unspoken subtext hung in the air thicker than LA smog. If this trip failed, it wouldn't just be professional embarrassment. It would be confirmation that all their multitudes of parental investments had been a waste. Proof that I should have listened to them from the beginning.

"I put in some vitamin C packets and Pepto-Bismol," said Mom, peeking back at me through the rear-view mirror. "You know how sensitive your tummy is."

"Yes, Mom."

"You know they have mountains there Samantha," said Dad. "The roads twist." He made a twisting motion with his hand, nearly broadsiding a semi trailer truck in the process.

"Remember that summer you visited Aunt Francis in Big Bear?" Mom mimed a violent vomiting episode.

"Yes, Mom."

"And don't underestimate the pollen from the trees," said

Dad, checking his side mirror for the seventh time before changing lanes. His blinker had been on for the past ten minutes. "Your allergies."

They were acting as if I were going backcountry camping in the untamed wilderness. But I wasn't going to Colorado to live off the land. I was going to Colorado to be pampered like a princess and get paid a king's ransom to do it. "I'll grab Benadryl and Dramamine when I get there," I said. If nothing else, I would sleep well.

"And don't exert yourself," said Mom. "The elevation will make you dizzy."

"No worries there."

"Do you want your father to stop and buy you a bottle of water? You have to stay hydrated."

"I'm pretty sure they have water there."

"And watch out for the meese." said Dad. "So many meese in Colorado."

"They're called moose."

"One moose, lots of meese," Mom countered.

"It's still moose," I insisted. "Moose is singular and plural."

"What about goose and geese?" asked Dad.

"That's different."

"Why is that different?" Mom asked.

"It just is."

"What do you know about mooses, anyway?" Mom gave another snort of dismissal.

"Nothing Mom. I don't know anything about moose. Or mooses. Or meese. You realize I'm staying at a luxury resort, right? Not camping in the wilderness." Unless they had a moose working the reception desk of the full-service spa, I had no intention of putting myself in a situation where I would be anywhere near the things.

I Burned My Tongue in Colorado

* * *

After my parents dropped me off at the curb, I raced through Los Angeles International Airport without a minute to spare. I didn't even have time to stop for coffee.

When I got to the gate, doubled-over, out of breath, waiting for the aneurysm, I didn't see any people lined up. I asked the gate attendant if the flight had already finished boarding. She gave me her corporately trained smile, one that conveyed 'oh you poor dear' and 'you're fucked' simultaneously. "I'm afraid there's been a slight delay."

By slight, she meant four hours. Apparently, some poor seagull kamikazed into an engine intake valve. The bird had lost, obviously, but the plane didn't exactly win either. While I waited, I developed an encyclopedic knowledge of the duty-free shop's perfume selection and memorized every ceiling tile in Gate B23.

Once on board, first class did its best to compensate. I'd nursed two perfectly chilled mimosas before we even left California airspace. By the time I finished the third, watching Bachelorette Season 21 (the one where Brittany dates the secret billionaire disguised as a plumber), my blood alcohol content had reached the sweet spot where my anxiety started to blur.

"Ladies and gentlemen, we're beginning our descent into Aster Park Regional Airport," the pilot announced, his voice crackling over the speakers. "Current temperature is 68 degrees, clear skies, and light winds."

I returned my seat and tray table to their upright and locked positions as the flight attendant, Tiffany, collected my empty mimosa glass. "First time to Aster Park?" she asked.

"Yes," I replied, squirming in my seat in a futile attempt to dislodge the silk thong that had spent the last two hours trying to bisect me. "Work trip."

Tiffany's face went from cheerful to sympathetic. She gave my shoulder a gentle pat, then leaned over and whispered. "I'll get you one more mimosa before we land."

* * *

The plane touched down with a bounce that sent my stomach into my throat, then rolled to a stop on what appeared to be a glorified country road. Complete with pot holes. I looked out the window. "Oh boy."

Aster Park Regional Airport was, and I use this term very loosely, "quaint." No jetways here, just a patch of tarmac in the middle of an empty field, surrounded by mountains and pine trees.

The moment I stepped onto the portable metal stairs, the Colorado air slapped me across the face, thin, sharp, and crisp. It smelled clean in a way that made me wonder if we landed on another planet. Notes of pine, wildflowers, and something earthy. My lungs, accustomed to the smog of Los Angeles, momentarily forgot how to function. I clutched the railing as a wave of light-headedness washed over me.

"Is this what oxygen poisoning feels like?" I asked the woman behind me. She made a funny face and frowned.

"Holy sunshine." I fumbled for my Prada sunglasses, a sample pair for an Instagram reel I'd done when I first started influencing. Even with the tinted lenses, the world was technicolor-bright. The sky above wasn't just blue, it was aggressively azure, a shade so intense it looked Photoshopped.

Luckily, I didn't see any moose. No polar bears either.

As I descended the portable stairs, the tiny terminal building appeared to be constructed of rough hewn timber and wishful thinking. It had all the architectural sophistication of a Lincoln Log set.

I Burned My Tongue in Colorado

While my fellow passengers shuffled toward the spot where the crew was unloading luggage, I scanned the nearly empty parking lot for my "luxury transportation." Marcus promised me that LuxeLife would send a proper car, something sleek and luxurious, with leather seats and a driver.

What I saw instead was the vehicular equivalent of road-kill. Parked at the edge of the lot was a Jeep that looked like it had gone ten rounds with the Rocky Mountains. And lost. The once-red paint had faded to the color of a bad sunburn, with patches that suggested a lifelong battle with ultraviolet radiation and acid rain. The tires were massive, mud-caked monuments, its driver clearly overcompensating for something. And was that … duct tape holding part of the bumper on?

I pulled out my phone to text Marcus's assistant. Instead of 5G, a "No Service" message mocked me, the digital equivalent of flicking me the bird.

"Perfect," I muttered, shoving my phone back into my pocket. "Just perfect."

* * *

I dragged my suitcase through what an overhead sign generously called a "concourse." What the Aster Park Regional Airport lacked in size, it made up for in … let's call it … "rustic charm." Vintage ski posters announced events from decades past. Hand-carved wooden bears stood frozen in eternal waves. Ten different scents of potpourri waged olfactory warfare. It was like someone had liquefied a Yankee Candle store and crop-dusted the entire building.

Making my way deeper into the terminal, it looked like a taxidermy museum had a one-night stand with a hunting lodge, then birthed a carnival of the macabre. Every few feet, another dead-eyed woodland creature stared at me from its mounted perch, glass eyes following my progress in anticipation. Anticipating what, I wasn't sure.

I continued searching for my driver, projecting positivity into the universe.

There's going to be a sign that says Samantha.

There's going to be a sign that says Samantha.

There's going to be a sign that says Samantha.

I didn't see a sign that said Samantha. Or anyone even close to resembling a chauffeur. In fact, every third person I passed appeared to be auditioning for a lumberjack calendar.

If I had had a small brown terrier with me named Toto, I would have knelt down and whispered, "I have a feeling we're not in Los Angeles anymore." Instead, I just adjusted my Prada sunglasses and tried to look like someone who knew what a "switchback" was.

The blessed sight of a coffee shop was like seeing an oasis in the desert. If I had to wait for my chauffeured luxury transportation a little longer, I might as well treat myself to something resembling civilization.

I made my way across the main hallway, narrowly avoiding a family of five, all dressed in matching camouflage. In case of an emergency, they were clearly prepared to disappear into the airport's wood paneling at a moment's notice.

Just before the coffee shop, I spotted a newsstand, but instead of *US Weekly* and *Vogue*, the magazine rack displayed titles like *Trophy Buck Monthly* and *Wilderness Survival Review*. Behind the counter, a man wearing both camouflage and flannel was arranging an abundant supply of reindeer jerky in flavors ranging from "Original" to "Spicy Maple."

I couldn't help but wonder what Aster Park's parents told their children around Christmas. "Sorry, Suzie, Santa can't make it this year. Uncle Joey turned all Santa's reindeer into chemically preserved meat sticks."

I Burned My Tongue in Colorado

Just when I thought I couldn't be any more grossed out, I spotted a burger joint next to the newsstand called "Moe's Mountain Eats." Every menu item seemed to involve a creature that had previously starred in a Disney film. Elk burgers. Bison burgers. And something called a "Mountain Man Special" that promised to include three different animals in one bun. A hand-painted sign featured a cartoon elk giving a thumbs-up to its own consumption.

I began to wonder if maybe, perhaps, somewhere mid-flight, my plane had accidentally flown through a multidimensional wormhole and transported me to a parallel universe where people enthusiastically consumed nothing but cute, fuzzy forest creatures.

Shaking the thought from my head, I made my way to the coffee shop. The chalkboard menu listed the standard coffee shop fare, though each item had been given a mountain-themed name. Avalanche Americano. Lumberjack Latte. Backpacker's Brew. I was relieved not to see "Moose Milk" or "Elk Cream" among the milk alternatives.

"What can I getcha?" asked the barista, pouring clear liquid into an ice filled glass from a bottle labeled "Mountain Moonshine." Her braided hair fell to her shoulders, and her outfit suggested she was an L.L. Bean reward club member. Her name tag read "Brie."

"I'll have a double shot oat milk cappuccino with three pumps of vanilla and one pump of caramel," I said, figuring I needed as much caffeine and sugar as possible.

Brie gestured toward an impressive display of liquor bottles behind her. "You want a shot of Kahlua in that?" Her eyes scanned me over, head to toe. "Looks like you've had a day."

"You have no idea."

Brie gave me a genuine smile, suggesting she did. She

pointed to the glass on the counter. "Got some local moonshine too, if you're feeling adventurous."

I checked my watch. It was 4:13pm Mountain Time, which made alcohol both a terrible idea and a brilliant one simultaneously. At least now I knew how people in Aster Park survived living in the middle of nowhere.

"I better pass," I said, my eyes lingering on the bottle of Mountain Moonshine. "But ask me again later if my driver doesn't show."

"Suit yourself." Brie shrugged, turning back to her espresso machine. "What's your name?"

"Samantha," I answered. "But my friends call me Sam."

"Nice to meet you, Sam." Brie hit a button and the espresso machine hissed like a river boat. A gurgling stream of scalding hot liquid pitter pattered into the paper cup. "First time in Aster Park?"

"Is it that obvious?" I asked, finally remembering to take my Prada sunglasses off, which I slipped inside my Louis Vuitton.

Brie smiled the kind of smile that suggested she'd seen my type before. Probably scraped off the side of a mountain. "Well, let's see. You're wearing fancy white shoes in an area where the sidewalks are optional. Your suitcase probably costs more than my car. And you didn't immediately say yes to alcohol." She poured oat milk into a stainless steel pitcher. "Around here, that's practically hanging a sign around your neck that says, I'm from out of town, please tell me bear safety tips."

"Bear safety tips?" I asked, my pitch rising.

"Rule number one. You don't need to outrun the bear." Brie dunked the steam wand into the oat milk. "You just need to outrun your hiking buddy." Brie winked, nodding toward the card reader. "That'll be $7.50." I touched my American Express to the card reader, mentally calculating how much of my credit limit I would need to preserve for all the therapy I'd be needing.

While Brie finished steaming the oat milk, I watched a man in a "Buck Wild" shirt buy three sticks of jerky and a magazine called *Extreme Ice Fishing* from the newsstand. Looking around, I still didn't see any black-suited chauffeur with a little sign reading "Samantha." The only sign I did see was the one advertising a BOGO deal on alpaca hair mittens.

"It's okay," I said to myself. LuxeLife was a luxury brand. Like Marcus said, it was in the name. Any minute now, some sleek town car would pull up outside, a uniformed driver would apologize profusely for the delay, and I'd be whisked away to a five-star mountain paradise with bottomless champagne.

Any minute now, civilization would arrive.

Any minute.

"You're all set," said Brie, sliding my drink across the counter. Lifting it toward my lips, I stared into the shapeless white mound of foam floating on top. No tulip. No rosette. Not even an artistically crafted swan that made you feel guilty about drinking it. Just a blob. Like a miniature avalanche. Perhaps inspired by the local geography.

"Just be careful when you take a sip," said Brie. "We just got our espresso machine serviced and everything has been coming out super hot."

I appreciated the warning. I would have appreciated it even more if she had told me two seconds earlier, before I took a giant sip.

It was like one of those scenes in a cartoon when billows of steam shoot out of the character's ears. The liquid hit my tongue with the thermal impact of molten lava. Now I'd never personally consumed anything from an active volcano, but it had to be a close approximation.

My eyes watered.

My nostrils flared.

My tongue blistered.

My mouth wasn't just on fire, it was experiencing its own personal supernova. Time slowed down as my taste buds screamed in unison, each one writing its own individual last will and testament. Sucker punched with pain, my short-circuited brain could only form one functioning command.

GET. IT. OUT.

Mouth full of coffee and body acting on the survival instinct of a cornered animal, I spun to my right, desperate to spit the boiling liquid anywhere that wasn't inside my mouth.

I didn't see the person standing beside me.

I didn't see anything until I sprayed a mouthful of scalding hot cappuccino across what appeared to be another flannel shirt.

Stretched over a set of impressively defined pectoral muscles.

Beneath a sharply lined beard-stubbled chin.

"What the fuh ..." a deep voice started.

But I wasn't done making a first impression. Mouth still burning with the intensity of a thousand suns, I snatched the nearest drink I could find, downing the entire thing in one gulp.

It took point two seconds for my taste buds to send the message to my brain. A message that went something like, "Hey dumbass, that stuff you just chugged wasn't water."

Moonshine hit my scorched mouth like a chemical weapon, burning in a completely different but equally apocalyptic way. I did a 180 to my left and ejected the drink with the force and trajectory of a pressurized fire hose.

Directly into the face of the coffee-dampened stranger.

Same flannel. Same pecs. Same beard-stubbled chin.

He'd circled around behind me to grab napkins from the counter.

I Burned My Tongue in Colorado

I froze, mouth agape, staring at the dripping face of the most devastatingly handsome man I'd ever assaulted with bodily fluids. Droplets of coffee and moonshine slid down his chiseled jaw, collecting in the stubble of his beard before falling onto his now drenched flannel shirt. His blue eyes, the color of a high mountain lake, narrowed into dangerous slits. His broad shoulders tensed, their girth suggesting a personal relationship with chopping wood.

"I ... um ..." Mortification washed over me in waves hot enough to rival the coffee.

"I see you've met Samantha." Brie came to the rescue with a stack of napkins, eyes wide with the kind of fascinated horror usually reserved for *Love Island* eliminations. She dabbed over the man's face and chest.

"My friends call me, Sam."

"Samantha." Mountain Man said my name like a curse. Coffee dripped from his nose.

Brie strategically placed her body between us, reaching over to snatch another fistful of napkins from the counter. "Sam, this is Noah. Noah Barrett. He's my brother."

Chapter Five

B rie's brother, *Noah Barrett*, and I stared at each other for a solid thirty-seven seconds without blinking while Brie sopped up the spills. Eventually, she had to step away to grab more napkins, leaving the two of us alone.

Still staring.

Not blinking.

With a mind of their own, my eyes took a scenic detour over his perfectly shaped lips, framed by that stubbled jaw carved out of mountain granite. Even wrapped in flannel, I could tell his biceps were roughly the same size as my thighs.

"Is there anything else you'd like to spit on me?" Noah asked, his voice low and controlled. A muscle in his jaw twitched. The rhythm of it was so precise I wondered if it was practicing Morse code.

"I'm so sorry."

I gave him a smile.

He gave me a frown.

"I thought that was water." I glanced down at the empty glass clutched in my hand like a smoking gun. "It wasn't water.

I Burned My Tongue in Colorado

Can I at least get you a drink to make it up to you?" I asked. "On me, of course. As opposed to the first one, which was on you. Get it? *On* you. As in ..." I gestured to his wet clothes.

I gave him another smile.

He gave me another frown.

Brie returned with more napkins and looked at me as if I'd just kicked a hornet's nest barefooted, then punched a moose in the balls.

"Sam just came in from Los Angeles," said Brie extra cheerfully, trying to change the subject.

"Los Angeles?" Finally, Noah blinked. "Wait ... did Luxe-Life send you?" He said the word LuxeLife as if it were a rancid lemon on his tongue.

"LuxeLife! Yes!" I held my breath as his impossibly blue eyes cataloged every inch of me. "I was just grabbing a coffee while I waited for my uniformed chauffeur. You haven't seen anyone in a black suit holding up a little sign that says 'Samantha,' have you?"

"You mean like this?" Noah reached into the back pocket of his faded blue jeans, then pulled out a wad of tattered paper. He unfolded it to reveal a name.

My name.

"Samantha" was handwritten in black marker

"Shit." I didn't mean to say it out loud.

Staring at my wrinkled name on the crumpled paper, I immediately noticed two things. The first thing was Noah's hands. They had the texture of artisanal leather, aged in a barrel of distilled testosterone for twenty years. There were scrapes on his knuckles and a bruise on his thumb.

Probably from bar fights. Or bear wrestling.

The second thing I noticed was some sort of sticky, red goo smeared on the paper. Like blood.

Probably from bar fights. Or bear wrestling.

"What is that?" I pointed to the blood-like substance.

"Ketchup."

"Ketchup?"

"Ketchup."

"Why is there ketchup on my name sign?"

"You want to know why there's ketchup on your name sign?"

"Yes, I want to know why there's ketchup on my name sign." The muscles in his neck clenched. They appeared to be made of petrified wood.

"The reason there is ketchup on your name sign is that the person whose name is on the name sign was late. So the person who was holding the name sign got something to eat while he waited." Noah cleared his throat. "And then may have run out of napkins."

"Let me guess." I glanced over at the burger joint next to the coffee shop, Moe's Mountain Eats. "You had an elk burger?"

"With reindeer bacon." Noah's eyes got even squintier. "How'd you know?"

"Lucky guess." At least now I knew what kind of Neanderthal ate elk and reindeer. An obnoxiously gorgeous one with shoulders broad enough to land small aircraft.

"Okay, my turn," said Noah. "The last thing *you* ate was some sort of California kale, spinach thing." He said the word California the same way he said the word LuxeLife.

"How'd *you* know?"

"Lucky guess. Plus, you've got a chunk of green stuff in your teeth."

It was true. Back in Los Angeles, I'd had a protein smoothie while my flight was delayed. After picking out an embarrassingly large wad of greenery, we stood there eye to eye again, scowl to scowl, facing off like two MMA street fighters in a bare-knuckle brawl.

"And for the record," said Noah. "I wasn't even the one who was supposed to be here. Your fancy LuxeLife chauffeur, whose name is Bob, by the way, and has never worn a suit in his life, had to get his kid to her chorus concert. So I told him I would cover for him and pick you up."

"Such a gentleman."

"Oh, I'm not a gentleman."

"Gee, I'm shocked."

Brie stepped back in the middle, handing each of us a glass of iced liquid. "Just water, I promise."

"Good," I said.

"Darn," said Noah at the same time.

"Figured everybody could cool off." She gave her brother a pointed look.

Looking again at the crumpled up, ketchup-stained paper with my name on it, the realization hit me like a splash of moonshine to the face. "Wait. So, does that mean I'm supposed to ride all the way over to the resort with you?"

"She's a little slow, isn't she?" Noah asked Brie.

"Noah, be nice."

I scanned the departures board for the first flight back to Los Angeles. Unfortunately, there were none. Just a blinking "WELCOME TO ASTER PARK" message that felt more like a threat than a greeting.

"It'll be dark in a few hours. We should go." Noah stomped toward the exit without waiting for a response. He didn't offer to take my Louis Vuitton luggage. He didn't even check to see if I was keeping up. He stalked toward the door like a man on a mission to get as far away from me as possible.

"Sorry about him," said Brie. "He's usually not so ... actually, never mind. He *is* always so grumpy. But if it makes you feel any better, it's not personal. Not entirely. He hates everyone at LuxeLife."

"Why would your brother hate everyone at LuxeLife?"

"Long story." Brie pointed toward her rapidly retreating brother. "You'd better hurry if you want to catch up. He's not only grumpy; he's also impatient."

Tripping over my suitcase in boots that were not made for scurrying, I caught up to Noah just as he pushed through the airport's main doors, the mountain air reminding me once again what real breathing felt like.

"You weren't going to wait for me?" I called to Noah's muscled back.

"I already did," he replied, without slowing or turning. "For about four hours."

"You could at least offer to help carry my bag."

"I could," he admitted. He kept walking.

"Oh, my God!" I screeched to a halt, stopping dead in my tracks.

"What now?" Noah scowled as he spun around.

I pointed. "Whoo ..."

"Whoo?"

I wiggled my finger, pointing behind him. "Whuuh ..."

"Whuuh?"

"Whoo ... whuuh ... wolf," I whispered, poking my finger over his shoulder as I hid behind his back.

Noah turned back, now face-to-face with a monstrous beast. It had thick fur in streaks of grey and white. Its crystal blue eyes were both wild and cunning. And its teeth ... big teeth. Sharp teeth. Teeth dripping with slobber.

Noah looked at the wolf, then back at me. He started crying.

W.T.F.

I couldn't believe what I was seeing. The big tough mountain man was driven to tears when confronted with something bigger and badder than he was. Clearly, I had misjudged him.

But then I realized he wasn't crying.

He was laughing.

And then he was crying.

Crying because he was laughing so hard.

"You're laughing? Why are you laughing?" That's when I realized he wasn't just laughing, he was laughing at ME. "What the hell is so funny? We're about to get eaten by a WOLF!" I pointed at the ferocious beast, right in front of us, just in case Noah hadn't seen it.

Ignoring me, Noah exhaled sharply, creating a loud whistle through his teeth. At first, I thought maybe it was some sort of advanced mountain man wildlife deterrence technique. But instead of deterring the wolf, Noah's whistle did the opposite. It prompted the beast to charge.

As I cowered behind Noah's broad, muscle-laden body, hoping the wolf wasn't planning a *Little Red Riding Hood* reenactment with my face, I remembered Brie's bear tip, hoping it applied to wolves too. I didn't have to outrun the thing; I just had to outrun Noah. I wasn't entirely sure of Colorado etiquette in wild animal attack scenarios, but I assumed, like in Los Angeles, it was an "every woman for herself" type situation.

But before I could even move, the wolf lunged. Noah fell to his knees, and the wolf began devouring his head. Its tongue slobbered all over Noah's face. One of its massive paws perched on one of Noah's massive shoulders as its tongue licked his neck.

But instead of screaming in terror, Noah was ... laughing?

And instead of fighting for his life, Noah was ... petting it?

W.T.F.

Noah stood up and patted the head of the creature, which

miraculously sat calmly at his feet without ripping his hand off. The animal, which was roughly the size of a small horse, looked at me with intelligent eyes that seemed to calculate how many calories I contained if it consumed me.

"You and the wolf are friends?"

"Yeti's not a wolf. She's a Siberian Husky, German Shepherd mix."

"Her name is Yeti?"

"Yup."

"Seems to fit," I said.

"Want to pet her?" Noah was getting far too much joy out of my terror.

"I think I'm good."

Yeti looked me straight in the eye and licked her lips, a move that seemed more like a threat than a moisturizing technique.

"So the airport people just let that thing hang out here?"

Noah patted the wolf's ... I mean the dog's ... head. "Well, they tried to stop her once, but she ate them."

It took me a moment to realize he was joking. For the first time since I spit coffee all over him, then moonshine, Noah smiled. An *actual* smile. Of course, his smile was at my expense. "Colorado is very pet friendly," he said, as if that explained why no one stopped him from bringing a barely domesticated wolf-beast onto public property.

Yeti was still staring at me like I was a pile of chopped liver. She licked her lips again. Then smiled. It felt like an intimidation tactic.

"I don't think she likes me."

"Hmm." Noah rubbed his stubbled, chiseled chin. "And she's usually such a good judge of character." He gave Yeti another pat. "You know, the key with animals is not to show fear."

I Burned My Tongue in Colorado

"I literally just cowered in fear. Actual cowering."

Noah smirked. "I'm over there."

I followed Noah toward the parking lot, keeping one eye on the wolf dog. He fished his keys out of his pocket as he approached ... *oh crap* ... the piece-of-shit Jeep I saw when my plane landed. The one that looked like it got kicked down the side of a mountain.

"Oh, no. Absolutely not." I planted my boots on the pavement.

Noah didn't hear me, or he didn't care. He held his hand out for my bag. "Need to strap it to the roof or she'll slobber all over it."

Yeti batted her eyes innocently.

Now that I was closer, I could see the Jeep lacked a separate trunk area for proper luggage storage. It also didn't have proper doors. Or any doors, period. There were only two seats, and judging by the amount of dog hair, one of them belonged to Yeti.

"I'm not getting into that deathtrap. I'd rather walk."

Noah's expression suggested I'd just proposed something either incredibly amusing or incredibly idiotic. Probably both. He pointed at one of the snow-capped mountains in the distance. "The *resort* is twenty-five miles that way. Better hurry, though. You don't want to get caught out here after dark."

I rolled my eyes and scoffed. "Let me guess, that's when all the polar bears come out."

"I was talking about the mountain lions," said Noah. "Only bear out here is black bear. Not that I'd want to tangle with one of them either."

"I guess we have a problem, then." Sticking out my bottom lip, I called his bluff with the confidence of someone who had no clue how poker worked.

"*We* don't have a problem. *You* have a problem."

53

But I caught something in his peripheral vision — a quick glance toward my abandoned suitcase, then back to me. It lasted maybe half a second, but there was something almost protective in that glance. Like he was cataloging my vulnerability and filing it away for later consideration.

Noah pointed to the passenger seat. "Yeti, come." The wolf-dog didn't move at first, alternating glances between the two humans.

Noah got in on the driver's side and put the key in the ignition. The jeep rumbled to life with a sound like logs fed to a wood chipper. "Now, Yeti. Let's go." The wolf-dog leapt inside the Jeep, tail wagging anxiously and head cocked like she was trying to assess what was wrong.

"I'll tell Victoria Sterling!" I played what I thought was my trump card, wielding the LuxeLife executive's name like a corporate get-out-of-jail-free card.

"While you're at it, I've got a few other things you can tell Victoria." Noah stomped his foot on the clutch and yanked the transmission into reverse. "And if she's got a problem with any of them, instead of sending one of her LuxeLife lackeys, tell her to come up here herself so I can tell them to her face."

"LuxeLife lackey? I'm not a LuxeLife lackey."

Noah raised an eyebrow. "You said you worked for them, right?".

"Well, yes, technically. But ..."

He pressed his foot to the accelerator, the Jeep lurching backward, and the mud splattered tires kicking up dust.

"Wait, what are you doing?" It didn't seem like the way bluffs were supposed to work.

Noah jammed the gearshift into drive, the Jeep emitting a sound like a bowling ball falling down a full flight of stairs.

"You can't just leave me here." I said, raising my voice over the clunking of the engine.

I Burned My Tongue in Colorado

For a split second, Noah's hands stilled on the steering wheel, and something flickered across his face. His jaw muscle ticked, and I caught the way his knuckles went white against the worn steering wheel, like he was gripping it to steady his resolve. But then his shoulders straightened, and Mr. Mountain Mc'Grumpypants returned. "Oh yeah? Watch me."

I did.

And he did. Leave me, that is. His foot punched down on the accelerator, and the Jeep took off down the road.

Open-mouthed, I stared after him as the Jeep disappeared around a bend, leaving me stranded with nothing but my coffee-scorched tongue. But even after one minute ... two minutes ... five minutes ... I held out hope. Because as Noah was driving away, I caught him checking the rearview mirror. Not once, but three times in the first hundred yards, like he was fighting the urge to turn around.

Yeti's head was turned backward too, looking toward me out the back with what I could have sworn was canine confusion.

"He'll come back," I said to no one in particular, my voice swallowed up by the empty parking lot.

He didn't.

Chapter Six

With the cloud of dust settled and the roar of the Jeep's engine long gone, I realized with growing horror that Noah wasn't coming back. I was stranded in the middle of nowhere. With no cell service. No transportation. And a Louis Vuitton suitcase that suddenly seemed about as useful as a giant paperweight. Staring off into the empty distance, I wondered if travel insurance covered being left to die in the wilderness.

"Well, this is it," I said to the curious bird watching me from a lamppost. "This is the moment Dad will reference for the rest of my life. Remember when you were abandoned at that airport in Colorado? Send me the receipt for the return flight to California."

I could already hear Mom on the phone with her friends, voice heavy with loving disappointment. Our daughter, the social media failure? Oh, she'll be fine. Just learning some hard lessons about following dreams instead of listening to her parents.

The bird looked at me with what I assumed was avian

empathy. Or it was deciding which eyeball to peck out after the mountain lions were done with me.

The worst part was, my parents wouldn't even be wrong. I'd flown all the way out here to represent a luxury brand, and I couldn't even handle basic transportation logistics. So much for proving I was more than just pretty pictures and cute captions.

But even as I spiraled into self-pity, part of my brain kept replaying those last few moments in the Jeep. The way Noah's hands had hesitated on the wheel. The way he'd avoided eye contact. The way he'd checked that rearview mirror ...

I'd grown up reading people's micro-expressions in my parents' restaurant. Figuring out which customers were going to be difficult, which ones hid disappointment, which ones were putting on a show for their companions. And Noah Barrett's micro-expressions suggested ... I had no idea.

Other than the fact that he hated me. Obviously. Too bad I'd never see him again to find out more.

Looking across the empty parking lot, I realized I had two options at that point. Option one, I could take the next flight home to Los Angeles, admit to Mom and Dad my influencing career was a failure, and then submit myself to a life of dumpling folding.

Or, option two, I could wait outside and let the Colorado mountain lions eat me.

Pretty much a coin flip, really.

Dragging my Louis Vuitton with one hand and my collapsing mental stability with the other, I trudged back into the terminal. The stuffed moose head mounted over the information desk seemed to look down at me with smug satisfaction, as if to say, "I knew you'd be back."

I briefly considered going back to Gate 3 so I could take Brie up on her offer to pour me a moonshine. Then I saw the sign that said, "Transportation."

* * *

"You like pancakes?" asked Al, his eyes never leaving the road. Al was the driver of the faded yellow taxi I'd found parked at the curb. He'd been asking me random questions for the past twenty minutes, ever since we left the airport.

"Yes," I answered. "I do like pancakes."

"Hmm." Al nodded sagely, as if I'd confirmed an important philosophical point.

I stared out the window, looking at nothing but dense forest and an empty road. The air streaming through the partially open window carried the scent of pine trees. We must have been miles from civilization, because for a long stretch, we were the only car on the road.

"Whadda bout waffles? You like them too?"

"Yes." I wondered if I'd somehow stumbled into an episode of *Twin Peaks.* "I like waffles too."

Another five minutes passed. Maybe ten minutes. Maybe ten thousand.

"How do you feel about French toast?"

"French toast is good too."

"Hmm." Al made another noise that might have been approval. Or disapproval. Or something in the middle.

"I'm more of a flapjack man myself."

Eventually, the taxi climbed a winding road that snaked up the mountainside, switchbacks twisting like a roller coaster. My stomach felt like I'd been trapped on the spinning teacup ride at Disneyland for three weeks straight.

"Now, your store-bought syrup is mostly corn syrup with flavoring," said Al, navigating a hairpin turn. "Real maple syrup comes in grades. I prefer the dark robust. More mineral notes." He whipped around sharp corners as if they were lined with feather pillows instead of a treacherous plunge off a cliff.

I Burned My Tongue in Colorado

It's a good thing I didn't get in that Jeep with Noah, I thought to myself. Since the Jeep didn't have doors, I would have been thrown out the side and bounced into a gorge. Plus, we would have been stuck together for the entire ride with him glaring at me and rolling his eyes the whole time. Literally next to each other. With nothing but a wolf dog between us.

My traitorous mind drifted back to Noah's impossibly blue eyes and the way his flannel shirt had stretched across his shoulders. Even soaked in moonshine and coffee, he'd been gorgeous. Which made it all the more infuriating that he'd just tossed me aside.

Noah.

The guy who looked like a model on a protein powder canister and ate elk burgers. Like he didn't have enough testosterone already.

Noah.

The guy who drove a doorless death trap and kept a wolf as a pet. Sure, I'd spit coffee and moonshine all over the guy, but that hardly warranted stranding someone in the middle of nowhere.

Noah.

The guy who accused me of being a LuxeLife lackey. What did that even mean? They were paying me to do a job. A job I intended to do. Because they were paying me. Which, okay, fine, technically made me a lackey if you were following the strict definition of the word.

But the way he said it. Such ... disdain. Like I was just another cog in the corporate machine. A machine he clearly despised for some reason.

I gave my head a small shake. Altitude sickness. That's all this was. Lack of oxygen to the brain, creating self-doubts and making me think absurd thoughts about flannel-wearing, beast-befriending jerks with perfect jawlines.

Noah and I weren't just opposites; we were opposing species. I was homo sapiens influencerus, and he was whatever scientific classification covers "grumpy wilderness dweller who abandons women at airports." Hopefully, I would never have to see him again, and clearly, the feeling was mutual. Good riddance.

I gripped the door handle as Al took another turn, my stomach jumping up into my throat. "...and that's why birch syrup has more complexity," finished Al, completely unaware of my mental detour. "Takes about a hundred gallons of birch sap to make one gallon of syrup, compared to forty for maple. More labor-intensive, but the flavor profile makes it all worth it. Notes of balsamic, with a minerality that maple just can't achieve on its own."

I nodded, having given up on contributing to the conversation long ago. The adrenaline from our white-knuckle ride had worn off, leaving me with nothing but exhaustion and an encyclopedic knowledge of batter-based breakfast foods.

"Course, there's black walnut syrup, too. More of an acquired taste. But nothing beats a good birch syrup on a sourdough flapjack."

By the time we finally turned onto a narrow, unmarked road, the sun had started to settle over the mountains. Crawling down the road through the trees, the taxi's headlights swept across a wooden sign planted in a clump of brush, so weathered I could barely make out the carved letters: "Pine Ridge Lodge."

Someone had nailed a smaller, much newer sign beneath it that read "Now Aster Park Mountain Resort & Spa" in elegant script, complete with a gold logo that looked out of place against the rustic wood.

Al drove the taxi toward a large log building nestled among towering pines. Warm light spilled from the windows onto a wide porch, which wrapped around the entire building. It wasn't the modern luxury hotel I'd expected. It looked like ... a giant log cabin. Something you might see on the label of birch syrup.

"Here we are," Al announced, bringing the taxi to a stop in a small gravel parking area. I checked the map on my phone. My blue dot was in the middle of a green blob.

"You sure this is it?"

"This is the address you gave me." I double-checked against the address from Marcus's email. It checked out.

I paid Al and climbed out of the car, where the fresh mountain air smacked me in the nose again. Crisp. Clean. Pine scented.

I grabbed my Louis Vuitton from the back seat and stood staring at what was supposed to be my luxury mountain getaway. It looked more like the set of *The Colorado Chainsaw Massacre.*

"You know," Al said through the open window, "if you go into town, you should try the flapjacks at Mabel's Diner. You won't regret it."

"I'll keep that in mind."

The taxi retreated down the gravel drive, its taillights disappearing into the trees. Left alone in the diminishing light, I had a growing sense that I had made a terrible, terrible mistake. Maybe spending the rest of my life cleaning wok grease out of my hair and listening to Mom's lectures wasn't such a bad life after all.

"Hello?"

No one answered. And on a positive note, nothing growled.

The silence of the forest was profound, broken only by the gentle rustle of wind through the trees and the distant call of a bird. Hopefully, the non-flesh eating kind. No traffic. No sirens. Just nature.

Creepy.

"Welcome to Colorado," I whispered to the trees. I couldn't make it out exactly, but I think they whispered back.

Turning my attention to the weathered wooden building in front of me, I was certain my altitude-addled brain was playing tricks on me. Where were the panoramic windows? The grand stone entrance with hand-carved beams? All I saw was a tired-looking barn-like structure that seemed one harsh winter away from collapsing. And the scent wafting toward me wasn't from a gourmet restaurant. It was distinctly livestock-related, with firm notes of hay and manure.

"Can I help you?"

I nearly jumped out of my skin at the sound of the voice behind me. A woman in mud-splattered boots and well-worn jeans approached, brown-blonde hair pulled back in a practical braid. Her skin bore the rich tan of someone who lived permanently outdoors.

"Ah ... I'm looking for the Aster Park Mountain Resort and Spa?"

"You're the girl LuxeLife sent from California." It was a statement, not a question, and she said the word California the same way Noah did. With derision and loathing.

"You want the main lobby."

"This isn't the main lobby?" I pointed to a wooden sign that clearly read, "Main Lobby," at the edge of the gravel, right behind a clump of shrubs. "It says Main Lobby right there."

The woman walked over to the sign and pulled away the branch obscuring the bottom half. Beneath the words "Main Lobby" was an arrow pointing straight up the mountain.

"This is the Adventure Center," she explained, gesturing toward the barn-like structure. "Part of the original property from 1910. The map apps bring people here all the time. The main resort's on up the road." She said the word "resort," like Noah did, and made the same quote fingers, too. "Name's Jenn, by the way. I'd shake your hand, but..." She held up her gloved hands. "Just finished mucking out the stalls."

I pulled my hand back out of shaking distance. "I'm Samantha Li. My friends call me Sam."

Jenn smiled, but her eyes weren't exactly friendly. She leaned on her pitchfork, looked me up and down. "Well, Samantha, seems like you're in the wrong place at the wrong time. It's about to get dark around here. Real dark."

I invoked my super influencer powers. "Any chance you could give me a ride?"

Jenn held up her gloved hands.

"Right. The muck. From the stalls."

"You know how to ride a horse?" asked Jenn, extra cheerful.

"I'll just call the front desk to have somebody fetch me." I pulled out my phone to make the call, but once again, the screen mocked me with zero bars.

"Yeah, service is sketchy down here," said Jenn. "It comes and it goes. Like Californians."

"Oh, you have a lot of California visitors that come and go?"

"I meant the sketchy part."

"Oh."

It was like I was in one of those indie horror films where everyone in the quirky little town has a dark secret, and then, the unsuspecting Asian-American girl from Los Angeles gets sacrificed by a cult.

My shoulders slumped, and my boots sank into what I desperately prayed was just mud. "Well, at least my day can't get any worse."

"You'd be surprised," said Jenn.

"Maybe I should have just taken the ride with Noah," I grumbled.

"Wait, Noah?" Jenn pushed off from her pitchfork. "Tall

guy? Messy hair, never shaves? Impossibly blue eyes, but kind of full of himself?"

"Yes, that's the one." I crossed my arms, ignoring the little flutter in my stomach at the mention of those impossibly blue eyes. "Plus, he had some sort of wolf-dog with him."

"And Noah was going to give *you* a ride from the airport?"

"He was going to ... but then he abandoned me. Because he hates me."

Jenn chuckled, shaking her head. "His customer service skills are admittedly lacking."

"Lacking? Try nonexistent."

Jenn paused, with a twinkle in her eye. "I can call him if you want. Have *him* drive you to the lobby?"

"No." I stopped her short. "I'd rather walk." Staring up the road, I noticed the temperature dropped when the sun dipped under the mountain tops, making my pink Lululemon pullover feel like tissue paper.

"Well, you better get moving then," said Jenn, glancing at the darkening sky. "You don't really want to be out here by yourself after dark."

"Yeah, Noah told me. Mountain lions." The memory brought a fresh wave of irritation. If he hadn't abandoned me, I wouldn't be facing this death march through predator-infested woods.

"Well, yeah, those, sure. But you also have to watch out for the coyotes. Bobcats, bears, rattlesnakes."

"Rattlesnakes?"

"Oh, and moose."

"You really have moose?" Despite my parents' warnings, I'd half-convinced myself the moose thing was an elaborate prank played on tourists.

"All over the place."

"What is this, Jurassic Park?" I glanced nervously at the

surrounding forest, now transforming into a labyrinth of danger-filled shadows.

"Every once in a while, we even get a rabid beaver." Jenn seemed to be enjoying herself.

"I get the picture, thanks." The only predators I ever had to worry about in Los Angeles were bartenders serving overpriced cocktails and guys in clubs claiming to be lingerie photographers. At least *they* didn't come with fangs.

"How do I get up to the resort?" I asked.

Jenn pointed to the trail leading up the mountain. "Just follow the path. You can't miss it." Jenn was severely underestimating my ability to get lost. "I would offer to help you with your bag, but, well, you know." She held up her muck-covered gloves.

"I think I'm good." I wasn't good. I was about to hike through moose-infested wilderness, hauling designer luggage with no cell service.

As I began trudging up the hill, Jenn called after me. "Oh, and Samantha."

I turned.

"Don't worry about Noah. I'm sure he doesn't hate you specifically. He just hates everyone from LuxeLife."

I was beginning to feel like an extra in a supervillain origin story, *The Tale of Super Mountain Grumpy Face*. "Why does Noah hate everyone from LuxeLife?" I called back down the trail.

"Long story!"

I was about to press further, but Jenn had already turned back toward the stables, leaving me alone with my questions and my dread.

"Wonderful," I mumbled to the empty woods. At least I hoped they were empty.

Chapter Seven

Gravel crunched under my heels as I dragged my Louis Vuitton up the steep path, its wheels collecting pine needles and small rocks along the way. Every rustle in the bushes sent waves of panic through my body. Was that a mountain lion? A bear? A rabid beaver with a taste for human flesh?

As I climbed higher, my thoughts returned to Noah, which only fueled my frustration. His piercing blue eyes kept materializing in my mind, along with those broad shoulders and the stubble that somehow looked deliberate rather than lazy.

"What kind of person just abandons someone at an airport?" I asked myself for the ten thousandth time. Clearly, Noah had some sort of problem with LuxeLife, but that didn't give him the right to take it out on me. Did he hate LuxeLife that much? Did he hate *me* that much? We'd barely exchanged ten sentences before he decided I wasn't worth his precious mountain-man time.

Nobody could be that much of a jerk.

Nobody.

Except, apparently, for him.

One of the wheels on my Louis Vuitton got caught on a root, and when I tried to yank it loose, the whole suitcase tipped over like a helpless turtle. Which I assumed they didn't have in Colorado. And if they did, it would probably be the flesh-eating kind.

As I struggled to reorient both myself and my luggage, my mind drifted once again to those blue eyes and broad shoulders. *Jerk. Stupid jerk face. Stupid jerky jerk jerk ... jerk.* I was too exhausted to even come up with a proper insult.

After what felt like an eternity of climbing, I reached a fork in the road. "Left or right?" I muttered.

Neither direction had any signs, because why would a luxury resort want to help its guests avoid getting eaten? The right path looked slightly more worn, so I took it, hoping "worn" meant "frequently used by resort guests" and not "preferred hunting route for hungry bears."

The trail curved through thick stands of pine trees, branches creating a canopy that filtered the remaining light into eerie patterns across the ground. My phone flashlight barely penetrated the shadows.

If I had been a character in one of those dark romantasy books, it would have been a good time for the hot werewolf to pop out and ravage me. But there was no hot werewolf. Only a grumpy mountain man with a pet wolf. And there certainly wouldn't be any ravaging with him.

"Yikes!" Distracted by thoughts of Noah, I nearly plummeted to my death as the path opened suddenly onto a rocky overlook.

Below me stretched a mirror-smooth lake. Mountain peaks rose on all sides, their snow-capped tops tinged blue and grey.

"Well, this doesn't suck." It was a view that would get millions of likes ... if I had any phone service to post it. I took a few pictures anyway. Maybe if I survived, I could post them later.

Turning around and doubling back, I made my way back to the intersection and took the left path. The trail grew steeper, and the forest grew denser, trees closing in on all sides. The only sounds were the labored breathing from my out-of-shape body and the occasional snap of a twig beneath my stumbling feet. Until ...

Crack

I froze, heart thundering, oxygen-starved lungs clamping tight.

Rustle. Crack. Shuffle.

Something moved in the undergrowth. Just beyond my flashlight's beam. "Hello?" My voice got swallowed by the dark.

RUSTLE ... RUSTLE ... RUSTLE

The rustling grew louder, accompanied by what sounded like ... scratching? Clawing? My mind conjured images of razor-sharp talons and glistening fangs.

I held my breath, frozen in place as the undergrowth parted. A shape emerged, low to the ground, moving with jerky motions, like something out of a horror movie. My phone slipped out of my sweat-slicked palm, the flashlight beam bouncing wildly on the ground.

"Stay back!" I brandished my Louis Vuitton like a shield.

The shape made a strange, gurgling sound that sent a chill up my spine, then emerged from the trees.

It was a bird.

A very strange bird.

A very ugly bird.

About the size of a chicken, but with mottled brown and white feathers, it had a distinctive white breast and what looked like weird spiky feathers standing up on its head. Its yellow eyes fixed on me with equal parts confusion and judgment.

"What the hell?"

The creature strutted across the path with the confidence of a runway model, its head bobbing forward and backward with every step. It made that bizarre gurgling sound again, followed by a series of pops like someone slowly opening bottles of champagne.

"Nice chicken," I said, still clutching my suitcase in front of me. "Please don't be a rabid chicken."

The bird paid me no attention, continuing its strange dance, inflating what I now noticed were bizarre yellowish sacs on either side of its neck. It was simultaneously the most ridiculous and the most terrifying thing I'd seen all day, which, given my encounter with Noah and Yeti, was saying a lot.

After what felt like an eternity of this bizarre mating dance, which may or may not have been directed at me, the creature suddenly vanished back into the underbrush, leaving me alone on the path, heart still pounding.

"Noah probably planned this," I muttered, picking my phone off the ground and shining it all around me. Once I was sure the bird was gone, I continued my trek toward the Luxe-Life main lobby, looking over my shoulder just in case. "Sent his demon bird friend to finish me off."

Dragging both my body and my luggage up the trail, I eventually saw lights through the trees. Buoyed by newfound hope, I pushed forward, quickening my pace despite my battered legs, calves, and feet.

The dirt-packed trail emerged onto a wide paved driveway, and I finally got my first look at the real Aster Park Mountain Resort & Spa. The grand log-and-stone structure rose from the landscape like a mirage, its windows gleaming from the interior lights. A massive stone chimney pierced the sky, wisps of smoke curling into the crisp mountain air.

Just as I took my first step toward civilization, my phone vibrated so violently in my pocket my entire body nearly bounced back down the mountain.

"Guess I got service." The screen lit up with notifications, hours' worth of missed messages coming all at once.

MARCUS WILES:

Your driver will be waiting when you land

Look for the name sign that says, Samantha

Enjoy the champagne and caviar! 🍾

VICTORIA STERLING:

Try the mountain berry welcome cocktail when you arrive 🍸

And the black truffle honey in the welcome basket 🍯

And the custom Alpine Meadow bath salts waiting in your suite 🛁 They're hand made by an aromatherapist from Sweden

PARKER:

TSA vibrator story is CRUSHING IT. 22k shares in 2 hrs 😂✈️

Stranded LAX saga is gold! 🙏 for Sam's 📱 is trending

Engagement rate +47%. Keep posting EVERYTHING 🔥😍💚

I didn't remember posting that many updates, but it appeared my misfortune resonated with my followers. At least something good was coming from my suffering. Then another wave of messages flooded my screen.

I Burned My Tongue in Colorado

MOM&DAD:

SAMANTHA. ITS MOM. WHY ARE YOU
IGNORING US.

its dad your mother is worried about the
meese

I READ MOUNTAIN LIONS ARE MOST
ACTIVE AT NIGHT

TEXT ME BACK.

ITS MOM

AGAIN

its dad your mother is worried about
mountain lions

ARE YOU HYDRATING SAMANTHA

its dad your mother said there's an avalanche
warning

WE FOUND A FLIGHT TO COLORADO THAT
LEAVES FIRST THING IN THE MORNING

WAIT HERES ONE THAT LEAVES TONIGHT

WAIT THAT GOES TO UTAH

HOW CLOSE ARE YOU TO MONTANA

its dad your mother is looking up flights

My thumbs flew across the screen in panic, texting Mom and Dad back.

I'M ALIVE!

Just got cell service.

At resort now.

Everything fine.

DO NOT COME TO COLORADO.

I cycled through the other conversations, quickly administering damage control.

(TO MARCUS):

Ride to the resort was ... something I'll never forget.

(TO VICTORIA):

Can't wait to try everything

(TO PARKER):

OMG WTF TTYL

Approaching the front entrance, I must have looked like some kind of swamp creature emerging from the woods, because the valet jumped when he saw me. For a moment, he looked like he was trying to decide if he should call security or the National Enquirer.

"Samantha Li," I announced, standing up straight and lifting my chin. "I have a reservation."

"Miss Li?" He checked his logs. "Oh yes, of course. We've been expecting you." The look on his face made it clear I was definitely NOT what he was expecting.

"Is the bar still open?"

The valet peeled my death grip off the Louis Vuitton handle. "The Aspen Lounge is open until midnight. I'll bring your key as soon as your room is ready."

I nodded gratefully and limped toward the bar, leaving a trail of pine needles across the polished hardwood floor.

Hobbling inside, the Aspen Lounge was exactly what I needed, all leather chairs and mood lighting, with a massive stone fireplace on one wall. I collapsed onto a barstool, my feet screaming in relief.

The bartender eyed my disheveled appearance. "Rough day?"

I Burned My Tongue in Colorado

"You have no idea." I glanced at the cocktail menu propped open on the bar. "I'll take the Mountain Sunset Martini."

"Coming right up." He started mixing the drink, pouring liquids in a fluid dance that was almost hypnotic. He slid the martini in front of me, a gorgeous gradient from deep purple to orange, garnished with a twist of lemon peel. "On the house." His eyes lingered on my head. "May I?"

"May you what?"

He reached over and plucked a leaf out of my hair, holding it up with a sympathetic smile.

"Thanks." I took a long sip of my Mountain Sunset Martini, letting the combination of vodka and mountain berry liqueur wash away the trauma of my trek through the wilderness. The sweet-tart flavor bubbled over my tongue. "You're my new favorite person."

"Name's Steve," said the bartender.

"Nice to meet you, Steve." I couldn't help but notice that Steve was kind of cute. And wasn't wearing flannel. And didn't have a wild animal as a pet. And best of all, didn't have R.G.F.

Resting Grumpy Face.

As I turned around on my stool to see if the valet had made any progress with my room key, a woman wearing a hastily pulled on business suit, who looked like she'd just woken up, attempted to sprint in high heels.

"Miss Li! I'm so sorry about the transportation mix-up." As she got close, I saw she missed a button on her blouse, and one earring was missing. She covered her mouth in a failed attempt to hide a yawn. Only one of her eyes had eyeliner.

"I'm Maya Rodriguez, the resort manager." She reached over and picked another leaf out of my hair, then handed over my room key. "I had your bag delivered to your suite after the staff scraped the mud off." She glanced at the nearly empty drink in my hand. "Can I get you another cocktail?" Her eyes wandered over my stained and rumpled outfit. "Or arrange some dry cleaning? And maybe the earliest appointment at our in-house salon?"

"Yes to everything." I tried to laugh, but it came out more like a wheeze.

Maya held up two fingers, and Steve mixed another pair of drinks. Once he handed them over, Maya guided me to a table in the corner, away from the other guests.

"I can't apologize enough for the transportation mix-up," said Maya, downing almost half her martini in one gulp. "We pride ourselves on five-star service, and I can assure you that what happened today was not up to our usual standards."

"You don't usually strand your guests at the airport?" I knew I was being a smart ass, but in my defense, it had been one hell of a day. "Sorry."

"No, no, you're right. Bob, our normal driver, had to leave when your flight was delayed, and, well, Noah was there visiting his sister anyway, so ..."

I held up my hand to stop her. "It's fine. Really."

Maya downed the rest of her drink, then waved down Steve for another.

"So what does Noah do around here, anyway?" I casually glanced around the bar, feigning disinterest. "Hopefully nothing that involves people."

Maya snickered as Steve brought her drink. "Noah's not a resort employee."

"He's not?"

"It's complicated." She leaned in closer after Steve returned to the bar. "To be honest, we try to keep him away from the resort guests as much as possible."

Thinking back on my very brief and very irritating encounter with Noah, he certainly didn't seem like any resort employee I'd ever met. He wasn't wearing a uniform. He didn't have a name tag. Truth be told, I wasn't entirely sure he had even showered that day. Not that he smelled bad. The opposite, in fact. He smelled of fresh air and pine trees, with undertones of something earthy and masculine.

"Are you okay?" I looked up to find Maya staring at me. "Sometimes the altitude makes people a little loopy when they first get here."

I waved her off. "I'm fine." But was I fine? For some strange reason, Noah's scent was now stuck in my brain. And for some even stranger reason, I wanted to smell more of him. *What was wrong with me?*

Maya looked across the table, concern on her face. She reached out. I thought she was going to pat me on the shoulder to comfort me, but instead, she pulled another leaf out of my hair. "Looks like your room is ready."

The bellhop waved from the lobby.

"Let's get you up to your suite so you can rest," Maya continued. "We can start fresh in the morning. I'll give you the grand tour, and you can post everything. Show the entire world what Aster Park Mountain Resort and Spa is all about." Maya leaned in conspiratorially. She picked another leaf from my hair, then whispered, "How does Crab Benedict sound?"

"Crab Benedict sounds delightful," I replied. Just the mention of food made my stomach growl like a mountain lion stalking an unsuspecting Californian.

"Our chef makes the hollandaise sauce from scratch. The eggs come from one of our chicken coops on the property, and the cayenne pepper comes straight from our greenhouse."

"I don't suppose I could get some room service sent up to my suite so I can have a snack after I shower? I haven't had anything to eat since that spinach smoothie in Los Angeles."

"Oh, I was wondering what that was." Maya pointed to my teeth, where I scraped out another wad of vegetation.

A smile stretched over Maya's face. "But the room service is already taken care of. And to make it up to you for what happened earlier today with Noah, I sent up a bottle of wine from our private cellar. You like Chardonnay?"

"I love Chardonnay."

"I had a 2014 Peter Michael 'La Carrière' that's a-maz-ing."

"It sounds amazing." Anything with alcohol sounded amazing.

As Maya escorted me toward the elevator, she stopped and pulled me aside. "Look, Samantha."

"Call me Sam, please."

"Sam, I was hoping we could keep what happened at the airport with Noah between the two of us, okay? No need to get Marcus and Victoria all worked up."

"Sure," I said. "No problem."

"What happens in Colorado stays in Colorado?"

"What happens in Colorado stays in Colorado," I agreed.

Chapter Eight

The elevator dinged open on the top floor. I stumbled as I stepped out, the Mountain Sunset Martini swimming through my bloodstream.

"Last door on the right," Maya had instructed, handing me a key card embossed with the LuxeLife logo. "The Aspen Penthouse. Best suite in the house."

The hallway stretched before me, illuminated by wall sconces that cast pools of warm amber light against textured wallpaper that resembled birch bark. I found my door, a massive slab of polished wood, and pressed the card against the sensor. A soft green light blinked, followed by the whisper-click of the lock disengaging.

I pushed the door open and froze on the threshold. The penthouse suite was the most spectacular thing I'd ever seen.

"Holy shit."

My exhaustion whooshed away like smog in a Santa Ana wind gust.

A stone fireplace covered one wall, flames already dancing over logs that crackled and popped. The furniture looked rustic *and* expensive. Cashmere throws draped over armchairs. A coffee table hewn from a massive tree trunk, polished to a gleam that reflected the firelight.

The bottle of Chardonnay Maya promised bathed in an ice bucket on the dining table, alongside a covered silver tray filled with snacks.

I floated across the room to peer out the floor-to-ceiling windows, framing the most beautiful view I'd ever seen. The night sky sprawled above snow-dusted mountain peaks, studded with every star in the galaxy. The moon hung low and full, illuminating a river that wound through the valley like a ribbon of liquid metal.

"Now this is worth posting," I said, suddenly wide awake. My thumb flew across my phone as I took more and more pictures, the custom millwork around doorframes, hand-painted tiles in the kitchen backsplash, the throw pillows embroidered with wildlife motifs.

The captions practically wrote themselves:

"Midnight in the mountains. Worth a moose encounter to wake up to this view. #LuxeLifeColorado #MidnightLuxury"

The post went live, and within seconds, despite the late hour, likes began accumulating like snowflakes in a blizzard.

"Heaven is a place in Colorado," commented @TravelDreamerXO.

"I would literally die for that view," added @LuxuryListings.

"Is that the new LuxeLife resort? BOOKING NOW," declared @LifestyleGoals22.

I Burned My Tongue in Colorado

The validation hit my system like another martini, warming me from the inside out. Social proof that what I did mattered.

I continued my exploration, pushing open doors to discover a powder room with a copper sink, a media room with a projection system, and finally, the bedroom.

"Oh. My. God."

The king-size four-poster bed sat against the far wall, each post carved from what appeared to be entire tree trunks. The sheets gleamed in the low light, promising a thread count that exceeded my credit score. Another fireplace, smaller than the one in the living room but no less impressive, crackled in the corner. More windows showcased the star-filled sky.

I approached the bed, pressing my hand against the mattress. "Well, aren't you cozy?" It yielded beneath my touch like a cloud, all but begging me to dive face-first into its downy embrace. But my mud-streaked body and leaf-filled hair reminded me that I wasn't exactly in pristine condition.

"Hygiene first." Though it pained me to delay my reunion with horizontal surfaces.

I pushed open the bathroom door and gasped out loud. "Holy mother of bathrooms." The marble-clad space was larger than my entire bedroom back home, maybe my entire apartment, illuminated by the soft glow of backlit mirrors and crystal light fixtures.

A deep soaking tub was positioned directly beneath a skylight, framing the star-studded heavens. The entire Milky Way had assembled specifically for my bathing entertainment.

I twisted the taps, and water gushed forth, steam rising in lazy spirals that caught the moonlight. "I'm never leaving here. Ever. And I'm totally serious."

A collection of bath products waited on a wooden caddy, salts, oils, bubbles. I selected a bottle labeled "Mountain Bliss," pouring a generous amount under the running water. The scent bloomed in the steam, wildflowers and pine, with undertones of vanilla and amber.

While the tub filled, I returned to the dining area to investigate my late-night snacks. Lifting the silver dome, I discovered an artfully arranged plate of what the accompanying card described as "Colorado Harvest," a locally sourced artisanal cheese board with huckleberry reduction, wild mushroom risotto, and roasted root vegetables. A second, smaller dome concealed a dessert, dark chocolate tart with sea salt and candied pine nuts.

"Maya, I could kiss you." But then I did a breath test on the back of my hand and decided that was probably a bad idea for multiple reasons.

My stomach growled, reminding me that terror, hiking, and alcohol made for a potent appetite-stimulating combination. I carried the plate and the wine back to the bathroom, setting them on a convenient shelf near the tub.

As the water continued to rise in the tub, the bathroom mirror revealed the full extent of my dishevelment, hair tangled with twigs and leaves, smudges of dirt across my cheek, eyes bright from a combination of exhaustion and martini.

"Yikes." I looked like I'd been dragged upside down and backward across the mountain.

I peeled off my travel-stained clothes, letting them drop to the heated marble floor, then stepped into the tub, a moan escaping my lips as the hot water enveloped my aching body. I sank deeper, the scented water lapping at my collarbone, my muscles surrendering to the heat.

The starlight above, combined with the room's dim illumination, created a dreamlike atmosphere. I found myself wondering if Noah was looking up at the same stars right now. Maybe in a sleeping bag in a tent. Or a dark cave. His wolf-dog curled at his feet.

I Burned My Tongue in Colorado

"Guess who got the laugh last now, Mr. Grumpy Frumpy Mumpy Man," I called out to the stars.

Sinking deeper into the tub, I took a sip of the Chardonnay, a perfect balance of rich and crisp. My stomach growled, reminding me that wine alone wasn't going to be enough. I hadn't been that hungry since that one time in college when my roommate, Trish, guilted me into joining Weight Watchers with her. It was the most torturous three hours of my life.

I followed the sip of Chardonnay with a bite of aged cheese. "Oh my God, are you magic cheese?" The flavors burst across my tongue, the huckleberry sauce adding a sweet-tart counterpoint.

As I floated in botanical-infused bliss, I couldn't help but think of Noah again, an occurrence that was becoming both more frequent and alarming. What would Mr. Mountain Man make of all this luxury? Would he scoff at the heated floors? Laugh at the designer soaps? Silently judge me?

Definitely judge me. Definitely not silent judgment either.

A master of illusion. A swindler of substance.

"Stop it," I told myself. "Stop thinking about the jerk who abandoned you at an airport."

I sank even lower in the tub, letting the water lap at my chin. Tomorrow, I'd focus on my assignment. I'd dazzle Maya and Marcus and Victoria with my content creation skills. I'd explore every inch of LuxeLife's mountain paradise and translate it into engagement and likes. Fulfill my contract, prove the haters wrong ... pay off the late charges multiplying all over my credit card statements like horny jackrabbits.

And I would absolutely, definitely, one hundred percent not think about Noah. Or his irritatingly perfect blue eyes. Or his stubbled chin.

The lie tasted sweeter than the wine.

I reached for my phone with fingers like sun-dried raisins,

angling for one last shot, the steam rising from the bath, stars visible through the skylight, my bare legs extending from a blanket of bubbles.

"Midnight soak under Colorado stars. I could get used to this mountain lifestyle. #LuxeLifeAfterDark #SelfCare"

The post went live just as my eyelids grew heavy; the combination of exhaustion, alcohol, and hot water finally overcame my second wind. Steam rose in hypnotic swirls as my eyelids grew heavier, the weight of the day finally claiming victory over my stubborn determination to remain conscious. The bath's lavender scent wrapped around me like a spell, pulling me down ...

Down ...

Down ...

Into the darkness ...

Knock. Knock. Knock.

The sound floated toward me as if traveling through water, distant yet distinct. My limbs felt impossibly heavy, weighted with lingering exhaustion and silky bathwater.

KNOCK. KNOCK. KNOCK.

More insistent this time, the rhythm drummed against the edges of my consciousness.

"Just five more minutes," I mumbled, inhaling fumes from the lavender-scented water. The jets had switched off while I'd dozed, leaving the bathroom in peaceful silence broken only by the soft drip of condensation from the faucet.

Click

It was the sound of the door opening.

My eyes fluttered open. Maya was probably just being proactive, checking if I needed anything else after my rough arrival.

I Burned My Tongue in Colorado

I held my breath, not making a sound. The bathwater had cooled, but enough bubbles remained to preserve my modesty, creating a shimmering film across the surface.

Footsteps echoed through the suite, each one slightly distorted, as if I were hearing them from underwater ... in outer space.

I slid down until just my nose and eyes remained above the waterline, letting the foam cover everything else.

The footsteps drew closer to the bathroom, unhurried yet purposeful. A shadow appeared in the gap beneath the door, larger than it should be, stretching impossibly across the marble floor.

My breath caught as the bathroom door opened with dreamlike slowness. Through the steam, Noah's tall frame filled the doorway, his broad shoulders blocking the light from the bedroom. He seemed taller than I remembered, his presence filling the room completely. The moonlight streaming through the skylight illuminated him from behind, creating a halo effect around his tousled hair.

"What are you doing here?" My voice sounded breathless, uncertain.

Noah's eyes locked with mine, impossibly blue even in the dimness, like alpine lakes reflecting a summer sky. He ran a hand through his already-disheveled hair, the movement fluid and mesmerizing. "I wanted to make it up to you. For what happened at the airport."

The bathwater swirled around me as I shifted. The bubbles that had been clinging to the water's surface began to disappear. They didn't simply pop; they dissolved into the air like wisps of vapor, one by one, in silent surrender. "And how do you intend to make it up to me?" The words flowed from my lips unbidden.

Noah took a step closer, his boots silent now on the marble

floor. The corner of his mouth curved up in a half-smile that sent liquid heat racing through my veins, pooling low in my belly. "Let me show you."

The water suddenly surged forward, rising over my face and covering my entire head. I gasped, inhaling bathwater instead of air. Panic clawed at my chest as I realized I'd slipped beneath the surface, the dream shattered by the harsh reality of lavender-scented water shooting up my nose.

"Aagh!" My head breached the surface, water splashing over the edges of the tub as I bolted upright, coughing and sputtering. Lavender bath salts burned my nasal passages, my lungs heaving as I choked up bath water.

Once I was sure I wasn't drowning, I blinked rapidly, disoriented, searching for any other presence in my room. But the bathroom was empty, steam still hanging in the air. No Noah. No footsteps. Just the echo of my racing heart and the now-tepid bathwater lapping against the sides of the tub.

"What the actual hell?" I gasped between coughs, horrified by the vivid dream my exhausted brain had conjured. "Bad brain! Bad!"

I scrambled out of the tub on shaky legs, grabbing a towel to wrap around myself as if Noah might materialize again if I didn't cover up quickly. My skin was pruned from the extended soak, my limbs heavy with fatigue despite my racing heart.

"No more lavender bath products," I lectured myself as I dried off, trying to ignore the lingering sensations ghosting across my skin. "Clearly, they're hallucinogenic."

Stumbling into the suite's bedroom, the bed called to me like a siren song. Not bothering with pajamas, I collapsed onto the mattress. But as I sank into the feather-soft sheets, I couldn't help but trace my lips with my fingertips, wondering what it would have felt like if the dream had continued for just a few seconds more.

"Damn it, Sam. Get it together."

With a groan, I buried my face in the pillow, determined to sleep dreamlessly until morning. I had a job to do, after all, and it didn't involve grumpy mountain men, no matter what my subconscious might want to focus on.

Tomorrow would be strictly professional. No thoughts of Noah. None at all.

* * *

RING RING RING.

I pried one eye open. Morning light streamed through the windows, transforming the penthouse suite into a sun-drenched paradise. The mountains in the distance looked like they'd been painted into place, impossibly majestic against a backdrop of pristine blue sky.

For one blissful moment, I forgot about my travel ordeals, and my late night bath dream about a certain blue-eyed mountain man who had somehow worked himself into my regular dreams too.

RING RING RING.

"Alright, alright." I squinted at the phone screen. It was Mom and Dad, of course. "Hello?"

"Samantha! Are you alive? I saw on the news that a hiker got lost in Montana and had to be rescued by helicopter!"

In the background, I could hear Dad clarifying the geographic locations of Western states. It was their morning routine: Mom catastrophizing, Dad attempting to de-catastrophize.

"I'm fine, Mom," I said, forcing myself upright. My head throbbed slightly, a souvenir from last night's Mountain Sunset Martinis. "Totally fine. Not lost. Not helicoptered anywhere. And I'm nowhere near Montana. I think."

"See?" I could hear Dad's voice in the background. "Put her on speaker."

There was a fumbling sound, followed by Dad's voice. "Have you seen any mooses yet?"

"No *moose* yet," I answered, padding toward the panoramic windows in my luxurious LuxeLife robe. "But I did see a wolf-dog."

"A wolf-dog?" Mom's voice ratcheted up several notches. "Do they have rabies shots in Colorado?"

"It belonged to the guy who was supposed to pick me up from the airport." My mood darkened at the memory. "Why do the good-looking ones always have to be so obnoxious?"

Silence fell on the line.

"Fuck fuck fuck fuck fuck fuck fuck," I hissed, holding my hand over my phone speaker. Too late, I realized I'd said out loud what I meant to keep in my head.

"The man was good-looking?" Mom's voice perked with interest, probably already calculating wedding guest lists in her head.

I closed my eyes, mentally kicking myself. "Well, I mean, I suppose. If you're into those kinds of things."

"What things?"

"I don't know. Things."

"What *kinds* of things?" Mom repeated. She'd spent the past decade trying to orchestrate my love life. No way in Colorado she'd be deterred now.

"Well, let's see." I mentally went through the checklist. Bulging forearms. Chiseled jawline. Eyes the color of alpine lakes. Shoulders that could probably carry fallen timber. Not that I would admit any of that to Mom.

"Mountain man things," I said. "Flannel. Beards. Whatever."

"He sounds very practical," Mom said approvingly. "Have you met his mother yet?"

I simply shook my head.

"Send your dad and me a picture," Mom demanded. She never pretended to be subtle.

"What makes you think I have a picture?"

"Because you take pictures of everything. Especially if they're good-looking."

With a resigned sigh, I navigated to my photo library. Nestled between shots of airport coffee shops and elk burger signs was a quick snap of Noah, with Yeti outside the airport. I'd taken it surreptitiously, for evidence, in case I ended up as a statistic on a true crime podcast.

I texted the photo to my parents, knowing I'd regret it immediately.

Three ...

Two ...

One ...

"Ooooohhh!" Mom's squeal almost shattered every window in the room. "He IS good-looking! VERY good-looking. What did you say his name was?"

"I didn't. But it's Noah."

"Like with the ark?"

"I'm pretty sure he doesn't have an ark."

"You should wear that red underwear you had on when we came over," said Mom. "Then he'd show you his ark for sure." Dad groaned in the background.

"I don't think you're using the word 'ark' properly. And I'm definitely not showing Noah my underwear anytime soon, or ever, thank you very much."

Mom must have lowered the phone, but I could still hear her and Dad arguing about the need for her to insert herself into facilitating my sex life for the next several minutes. It was unclear who the winner was, but the clear loser was me.

Mercifully, Dad changed the subject. He lifted the phone back up. "Maybe if this LuxeLife place likes what you do there, they'll send you to Copenhagen."

I frowned, surprised. "How do you know LuxeLife has a resort in Copenhagen?"

"I looked it up." I could picture Mom rolling her eyes. Dad had been trying to convince her to take a trip to Denmark for as long as I could remember, because that's where they invented Lego. My father, pushing sixty, still maintained a passionate love affair with interlocking plastic bricks. I'd caught him once constructing an entire medieval village on the dining room table while Mom was visiting her cousin in Boise.

As they bickered about Dad's unhealthy Lego obsession versus his appreciation for architectural ingenuity in miniature, I made my way to the glass-enclosed shower, where a digital display controlled multiple shower heads. I set it to "Mountain Mist."

Interrupting a spirited discussion about how much space old Lego boxes were consuming in the garage, I shouted, "Okay, love you both. Promise I'll text. I'll also make sure to watch out for moose. And avoid grumpy mountain men!"

I hung up before they could respond.

Chapter Nine

I strolled into the resort's restaurant at precisely 8:00 AM, my mood improved with the promise of a full day of pampered luxury.

The dining room was a masterpiece of rustic-chic design. Soaring timber beams crisscrossed the ceiling. Glass walls framed the mountains like works of art. Maya waved enthusiastically from a corner table.

"I took the liberty of ordering for us both," Maya said as I slid into the chair across from her. She gestured at the spread before us, an Instagram-worthy feast that looked like it had been styled by a food photographer. "Hope you don't mind."

"Mind? This looks perfect." My camera was already out, capturing the perfectly poached eggs draped in sunshine-yellow hollandaise, perched atop fresh lump crabmeat and house-made English muffins. Sliced avocado fanned artfully along one side of the plate, sprinkled with micro greens and what appeared to be edible mountain flowers.

A smaller plate held a geometric arrangement of berries, so perfectly ripe they glistened. Beside that sat a glass of fresh-pressed juice in a gradient from deep orange to sunny yellow, garnished with a sprig of mint.

"The berries came from a local farm about twenty minutes away," said Maya, clearly pleased by the smile stretched across my face.

I took a sip of the coffee Maya poured for me, somehow managing not to spit, splash, or spill it all over her. As soon as I lifted the cup to my nose, the heavenly aroma of dark roast with hints of chocolate and caramel made my mouth water.

"We try to source as much as we can locally."

I adjusted my camera angle to catch how the light played through the fresh-pressed juice, transforming it into liquid amber. "The lighting in here is perfect. Did you design it specifically for photo shoots?"

"Actually, I wouldn't be surprised. Victoria was personally involved in every detail of the renovations. She's very hands-on. And specific. And insistent." Maya leaned in slightly. "Pretty sure she's never heard the word no."

"Renovations?" I asked, cutting into my eggs to capture yolk-porn for my followers. "Sorry, had to get that money shot." I continued taking video as the yolk spilled over the crabmeat in a perfect golden cascade. "This isn't how the lodge originally looked?"

"Oh God, no." Maya shook her head. "You wouldn't recognize this place from a year ago. It used to be geared toward hunting and fishing. Think mounted trophy bass and plaid everything." Maya waved her hand to encompass the room. "The bones of the old lodge are still here, but LuxeLife completely reimagined it. We're sitting in what used to be the tackle shop."

I glanced around, trying to imagine fishing rods and bait boxes where now there were white tablecloths and silver service. "That's quite a transformation."

"Night and day," Maya agreed. "The renovation costs are ..." She let out a low whistle. "That's why there's been such a push on the marketing front. Victoria needs to recoup the investment. Heard some big shareholders are making some noise."

Maya took a sip of coffee while I popped a raspberry into my mouth. It may have been the best thing I'd ever eaten.

"How's your suite? Everything to your liking?"

"Like it? I'm considering moving in permanently." I nibbled a blackberry. "I must have taken fifty pictures just from my window."

"I'm glad," said Maya. "And I want to apologize again for yesterday's transportation ... mix-up."

I held up my hand. "You can make it up to me by never mentioning it again. In fact, let's make a pact never to mention the name Noah Barrett ever again."

Just saying his name sent an unwelcome flash of last night's dream coursing through me, which I promptly squashed with another raspberry.

"Deal. No more mention of ... that person." Maya pulled out an iPad from a sleek leather portfolio. "Speaking of making it up to you, wait until you see what I've got planned for today."

She flipped the screen around to show me a meticulously crafted itinerary that made my influencer heart sing. "Full property tour first, the spa, fitness center, indoor and outdoor pools. We've scheduled treatments for you this afternoon, a signature massage, facial, the works. For lunch, our executive chef from our farm to table restaurant will be curating a special tasting menu. Then this evening, we have a private cocktail mixing class with our executive mixologist, followed by a sunset stroll to our private overlook where we'll have champagne and charcuterie set up."

My eyes widened with each new thing. This was influencer

nirvana, exclusive experiences, photogenic settings, and luxury treatments, all carefully packaged for maximum social media impact. Everything I'd been hoping for from this trip and more.

And the best part? No cantankerous mountain men with stupidly blue eyes and wolf-dogs.

I began planning my captions and hashtags. After yesterday's travel fiasco, it felt good to be back in my element. This was what I did best. Finding the perfect angles, the most flattering light, turning ordinary moments into something extraordinary.

"So, are you ready to get started?" Maya looked at me expectantly.

I tucked my phone into my pocket and drained the last of my coffee. "Lead the way."

* * *

"Our signature scent is a blend of sage and mountain lavender," Maya explained as we stepped through the double glass doors of the spa entrance.

I inhaled deeply, letting the fragrance wrap around me like a blanket. It was mountain wilderness distilled into perfume form, minus the sweat smell from hiking and terror.

"It's intoxicating," I said, holding my phone up to capture the delicate tendrils of steam rising from hot stones in a copper bowl. The vapor caught the morning light streaming through the skylights, creating ethereal wisps that danced in the air.

"Each amenity is designed to bring the outside in," Maya continued, offering me a cucumber-infused water from a dispenser. "We want guests to feel connected to the mountain environment, but cocooned in luxury."

"Cocooned in luxury is good." Vaulted ceilings soared overhead. A wall of water trickled over slate, creating a gentle soundtrack. "My followers are going to lose their minds over this." I leaned in close, my camera capturing everything.

"Just wait," Maya said with a knowing smile. "Follow me."

She guided me down a corridor as the floor transitioned from stone to cedar. "This is our flagship treatment space."

My jaw dropped as we entered one of the circular rooms. The glass ceiling offered an unobstructed view of the mountain sky. Aspens surrounded the perimeter, their white trunks and golden leaves creating a natural privacy screen.

"During the winter, guests can watch the snow fall while getting a hot stone massage," said Maya.

I crouched down to capture the perfect angle. A beam of light had pierced through the aspen leaves at just the right moment, illuminating the aromatherapy diffuser and creating a mystical haze that filled the room.

"The massage tables are heated with volcanic rock from Iceland," Maya continued. "And these sheets are made from organic bamboo."

"This is all incredible." I ran my hand across the polished wooden surface of the nearest table.

"After the tour, you're welcome to come back and indulge in whatever you'd like."

My mind raced with tantalizing possibilities: hot stone massages, aromatherapy wraps, botanical facials. I could practically feel imaginary hands working expert pressure into the knot that had taken up residence between my shoulder blades.

Noah induced stress, probably. I ignored the brief flash of blue eyes that snuck into my brain.

The fitness center was next on our tour, and while I avoided exercise at all costs, even I had to admit this was a gym worth documenting.

"Our equipment's all top of the line." Maya gestured toward the rows of gleaming machines. "Peloton bikes, Hydrow rowers, and we just got these new AI-powered strength training systems."

I filmed a smooth pan across the gym, capturing how the natural light glinted off chrome surfaces. Through the massive windows, the mountains provided a backdrop that made even treadmills look appealing. Almost.

"What's that room back there?"

"That's our movement studio. We offer everything from sunrise yoga to HIIT classes." Maya pointed at the schedule on the wall. "This week we have sound bath meditation, mountain flow yoga, and our sip and stretch. Basically, it's Pilates with wine afterwards."

"Count me in on the wine part."

I could already visualize the content. Time-lapse videos of sunrise salutations as alpenglow painted the peaks pink. Sped-up footage of clouds rolling past while I pretended to know how to hold warrior pose without falling on my butt.

"Over here we have our recovery zone." Maya pointed to the massage chairs that looked advanced enough to apply for their own medical licenses. Then she walked me past the smoothie bar, stocked with organic protein powders in glass jars and fresh fruit arranged in a rainbow.

"All our post-workout drinks are customized for altitude adjustment. The Mountain Berry Blast is my personal favorite. Helps with oxygen absorption."

I zoomed in on the menu board, capturing the artisanal chalk lettering and illustrated mountain motifs.

"And of course, just like with all our spa treatments, you're more than welcome to partake in any fitness classes or use the exercise machines whenever you want. Your room key allows access twenty-four seven."

I looked around at the fitness fanatics already working up a sweat. A woman on a Peloton was pedaling like she was fleeing from bears, while a man with shoulders wider than my torso grunted as he hoisted weights that could anchor a small yacht.

"Yeah, I think I'm good."

I followed Maya through another set of glass doors, revealing what had to be the most spectacular pool area I'd ever seen. A series of cascading waterfalls created intimate grottos between multiple hot tubs, each one perfectly positioned to frame a different mountain vista. Steam rose from the water's surface, catching the morning light and creating an ethereal mist that softened the boundaries between water, air, and stone.

"Each hot tub is set to a different temperature," Maya explained, leading me along a path of smooth river rocks embedded in cedar decking. "The minerals from the springs are excellent for muscle recovery and relaxation."

"This is incredible."

"Wait until you see the grotto bar."

Maya led me through a cave-like passage, where the rough stone walls opened into a hidden oasis. A swim-up bar curved along one edge of a lagoon-like pool. Hanging plants cascaded from the ceiling. Lighting integrated into the rock walls created the impression of being inside a bioluminescent cave.

"Our mixologists created a specialty cocktail menu inspired by mountain streams." Maya picked up a leather-bound menu from a nearby table. "The Glacier Melt is our most popular, local gin, blue curaçao, and elderflower liqueur topped with sparkling wine and edible silver flakes."

As if on cue, a bartender in a fitted black shirt began crafting one, his movements fluid and precise. I filmed the entire process, from the theatrical pour of electric-blue liqueur to the final sprinkle of silver flakes that swirled through the cocktail like metallic snowflakes in a winter storm.

The bartender offered me the drink, but I waved him off.

"Maybe later. Actually, definitely later. I'll be back." I did my best Arnold Schwarzenegger impression, but both the bartender and Maya just looked at me like I was crazy.

"You know, *Terminator*."

More blank stares.

"My parents grew up in the eighties, so I've sorta been brainwashed. You know how GenXers are."

Maya smiled politely.

Beyond the grotto, the infinity pool seemed to spill right into the mountain lake below, the boundaries between man-made and natural blurred to the point of invisibility. The water reflected the clouds overhead, creating a perfect mirror image.

I captured everything. Boomerangs of the spa's waterfall features. Slow-motion videos of water cascading over polished river rocks. Panoramas of the mountains reflecting in still pool surfaces. Each post generated immediate engagement, comments rolling in faster than I could read them.

"OMG that view! 😍 🏔️ 🌲"

"Booking my stay ASAP 🤍 🏨"

"Got to try those drinks! ALL of them! 🍸 🍹 🍎 🍷"

I wrapped up my Instagram stories with a sweeping pan of the grotto, feeling the familiar satisfaction that came from creating content I knew would perform well.

"Stay tuned, everyone! This is just the beginning of our mountain adventure. Wait until you see what we have planned next! #LuxeLifeMountains #AsterParksFinest #sponsored"

I Burned My Tongue in Colorado

The entire space was a content creator's dream, the interplay of light and water, the contrast of rough stone and smooth glass, the incredible views and colors. At this rate, Marcus and Victoria were going to be booked solid until the next ice age. Maybe Dad would get his Copenhagen Lego pilgrimage after all.

For the rest of the morning, Maya showed me the 10,000-bottle wine cellar, a collection that would make a sommelier weep. Next was the library, with first editions behind glass, and a game room filled with billiards tables and chess sets carved by local artisans.

The grand finale was the farm-to-table restaurant, where the executive chef, a serious-looking woman with intricate sleeve tattoos, prepared a special tasting menu curated specifically for my posts.

Each dish was a miniature work of art. Locally foraged mushrooms presented on slate tiles. Microgreens arranged in precise patterns atop purees that swooped across white porcelain. Edible flowers provided pops of color so vibrant they looked like digital art.

It was the kind of content that would have made even casual scrollers zoom in to appreciate the details. Then click subscribe and share.

"This is all just ..." Words failed me, forcing me to capture everything on my phone. Even though I'd consumed enough fresh berries at breakfast to send a grizzly bear into hibernation, my stomach growled louder than an avalanche with the introduction of each new dish.

"Can we eat it now?"

The chef nodded. "Go right ahead."

I was about to reach for one of the lobster-stuffed mushrooms when a pair of waiters appeared out of nowhere, whisking the entire spread away.

"Wait, what?"

I stared at the now-empty table, my hand still outstretched.

When I looked over at Maya, her ever-present smile was gone and her phone was clutched in hand. "I'm afraid there's been a slight change of plans."

"Change?"

"Marcus, set up a Zoom call." The look on her face didn't help ease my concern. "Looks like we'll be having a working lunch in the business center this afternoon."

Something told me a working lunch on a Zoom call would not involve lobster stuffed mushrooms. Probably those gross little triangle sandwiches instead.

"Is everything okay?" I asked. "I mean, a few of my posts are already trending. Which is ... good. Right?"

Maya shrugged, looking as confused as I did. "I guess you and I are about to find out together."

Chapter Ten

I followed Maya through the west wing of the resort, my mind racing through everything I'd posted. "Do you think maybe I used the wrong filter on the spa content? Maybe my caption for the infinity pool was too generic."

"I think the infinity pool posts were fine." Maya gave me a smile that was supposed to be reassuring, but felt like pity.

"Did Marcus say anything else?" I scurried faster to catch up. "Anything specific?"

"Apparently, Victoria has some notes."

"Notes?" I'd thought my content was performing beautifully, but clearly I'd made some sort of mistake.

Maya forced a smile. "I'm sure it's nothing major."

It was definitely something major.

"Maybe the engagement isn't high enough. I can adjust my posting schedule to hit the algorithm sweet spots. I can focus more on the aesthetics. Or less on the aesthetics."

"The numbers are great, I'm sure. Victoria can be particular. Just because something is successful doesn't mean ..." Maya paused, considering her words carefully.

"Doesn't mean what?"

"Doesn't mean it's what she had in mind." Maya stopped to take a breath, forcing me to take one too. She pointed across the hall to a section of the resort that was clearly mid-renovation, though they'd attempted to disguise it with temporary walls painted to match the rest of the decor.

"See that room there?"

"Yes."

"It's the third time we're redoing it."

The partitioned barricade couldn't fully conceal the sounds of construction, drills whirring, hammers pounding, men shouting instructions. I caught a glimpse of a massive stone fireplace being dismantled piece by piece.

"Part of the original lodge," said Maya when she saw the question on my face. "Victoria thought it was too rustic." She paused, but only for a moment, watching through the break in the barricade as more workers unceremoniously stacked decades-old woodwork like discarded kindling. "God forbid LuxeLife preserves any bit of the history of this place." Maya seemed to catch herself. "Sorry," she blurted. "It's just ... sometimes things are never good enough."

"Yeah, I know how that is." No matter how great I thought a post was, some people always had to be critics. "Did you work here before?" I asked. "I mean before LuxeLife took over."

"No," said Maya. "But I grew up just outside Denver. My parents used to take my brother and I here when we were kids." A distant look settled in her eyes. "But now my parents are gone, and, well, my brother is a tax attorney who lives in Miami with his wife and kids. So that's that."

Maya blinked her eyes and shuddered, as if waking from a trance. "The new space will be a champagne and caviar bar. This time with ice sculptures and ceiling lights meant to evoke the Northern Lights."

I Burned My Tongue in Colorado

"Sounds great," I replied. "Because nothing says authentic Colorado mountain experience like imported fish eggs and artificial auroras."

Maya chuckled before catching herself.

"I just thought of something," I said. "If I'm going to defend myself and my content to Marcus and Victoria, I need to be both camera ready and articulate. Do I have time to grab a quick coffee?"

Maya checked her watch. "I'll cover for you. But just promise you won't abandon me, okay? I need all the friends I can get."

"Never." I smiled. Maya smiled back. "You want me to get you anything?"

"I could really use another Mountain Sunset Martini, but that would probably be a bad idea. Just get me whatever you're having. I trust you."

Following Maya's directions, I wandered past a collection of curated boutique shops toward the main atrium, each more expensive than the last.

I scrolled through my recent posts as I walked, frantically searching for anything that might have rubbed Victoria the wrong way. The rational part of my brain knew my content was solid, better than solid, exceptional. But the perfectionist in me was already mentally rehearsing how I'd defend my creative choices without sounding defensive.

The coffee shop came into view, along with the aroma of freshly ground artisanal beans. The scent drew me forward like a cartoon character floating on visible tendrils of fragrance.

I squared my shoulders and marched through the cafe doors, ready to order whatever concoction would best fortify both me and my new ally Maya for the impending Zoom call of doom.

The interior design of "Alpine Brews" was a masterclass in

rustic-luxe. Antler chandeliers cast a honeyed glow over leather armchairs, artfully distressed to look vintage. A mounted elk head watched from above the fireplace, wearing what looked like a hand-knitted scarf. I couldn't help but wonder what happened to the rest of it. Probably transformed into elk burgers.

The menu board, written in chalk calligraphy, listed drinks like "Mountain Mocha", "Powder Day Pour-Over," and "Wilderness Cold Brew." A handwritten sign proclaimed that all the beans were single-origin and ethically sourced.

"Two Alpine Peak Lattes to go, please."

"Excellent choice," said the barista, as if I'd selected a fine wine rather than an overpriced coffee.

She turned to the gleaming copper espresso machine that looked like it belonged in a steampunk laboratory. As she worked her barista magic, I surveyed the room, taking in the cafe's clientele, the type of people Victoria hired *me* to impress.

A couple in matching Patagonia fleece cuddled on the loveseat. The woman wore a diamond ring so massive it nearly blinded me. Another pair in brand new hiking gear pored over a trail map. A woman browsed a novel with a cover featuring a shirtless cowboy.

The seeds of doubt planted during Marcus's surprise Zoom call took root and bloomed. Maybe it wasn't the content I was posting that Victoria had concerns about. Maybe it was me. Looking around, it was clear I didn't belong there. I didn't fit in.

"It feels like I walked into a Norman Rockwell painting," I mumbled to myself. At any moment, someone was going to turn around, spot the impostor, and an angry mob would chase me away with locally forged pitchforks.

"Two Alpine Peak Lattes for Samantha!"

I snapped out of my spiral of insecurity and grabbed the pair of drinks, momentarily distracted by the work of art the barista created in the foam. An intricate mountain range rose from one side of the cups, complete with tiny pine trees and what appeared to be a soaring eagle. She'd even dusted them with what looked like edible gold flakes.

"That's ... wow." I pulled out my phone, adjusting the angle to catch both the latte art and the cozy fireplace in the background. "This is incredible."

"We take our craft seriously here." The barista beamed with pride.

I was about to take a taste when I remembered the scorching lesson from the airport. Parts of my tongue were still seared from my last latte lament. Steam poured from the liquid surfaces like miniature geysers.

"You have any plastic lids?" I looked along the counter but didn't see any.

"We're eco-friendly here," said the barista. Eco-aggressive seemed more descriptive.

Glancing at my phone, I realized the time. If I were going to make it to the Zoom call on time, I needed to get moving.

Balancing two full lattes, I power-walked through the resort's winding hallways. Was it right at the antique ski display or left at the vintage snowshoes wall? "Past the stone fireplace ..." I said to myself. "There are at least three hundred stone fireplaces in this resort."

I rounded a corner at full speed.

THUD.

SPLASH

I ran straight into a brick wall, or rather, the human equivalent of one. Both lattes exploded as scalding liquid splashed across a familiar broad chest.

Beneath a familiar beard stubbled chin.

Accompanied by the scream of a familiar voice.

"Jesus fucking Christ!" Noah jumped backward, then

yanked the soaked shirt over his head in one fluid motion, muscles rippling beneath tanned skin. An angry red patch flared across his chest where coffee had singed a light dusting of chest hair.

I stood frozen, two empty cups still in hand, mouth agape as I stared at Noah's now bare torso. My brain, apparently having abandoned all professional and social protocols, helpfully noted that what remained of his non-burned chest hair formed a perfect V pointing down past his belt buckle like a biological arrow saying, "Right this way!"

"Oh, my God. I am SO sorry." I hadn't been this mortified since, well, the day before when I spilled coffee all over him.

"Do you make a habit of assaulting people with hot beverages?" Noah pressed his wadded-up shirt against his chest, wincing as he dabbed at the red mark. "What the hell was that?"

"Two Alpine Peak lattes." I said, eyes searching for the nearest emergency exit route. "I was trying to find the business center and got turned around and ..." When I looked back up, into Noah's narrowed eyes, my cheeks burned even hotter than the coffee I just splattered all over him.

"Well, if you're looking for the business center, you're going the wrong way." He gestured behind him with his free hand, the movement causing his shoulder muscles to ripple. "Business center's back there. First right past the elk head."

"Which elk head? This place has a concerning number of dead animals on the walls."

It wasn't quite a smile, but his mouth moved in a less frowny direction. "The one wearing the beanie."

"I thought it was wearing a scarf?"

Noah's eyes narrowed, the blue somehow more intense without a shirt to compete with them. "That's a different elk."

My eyes involuntarily drifted again to his chest, which

looked like it had been sculpted by an artist. I would have bet you could grate artisanal mountain cheese on those abs. Or use them as a washboard for laundering elk head accessories. Like beanies and scarves.

"Why are you looking for the business center?" Noah used his shirt to dry some of the coffee that had dripped into his pants. My eyes took careful note of his drying technique.

Noah cleared his throat, the sound snapping me back to the present moment where I was, in fact, still staring at his naked torso like I was taking mental measurements for a custom-fit suit.

"Maya's making me go to some Zoom call."

"That sounds ... horrible."

"What are you doing here?" I asked. "Maya said you weren't even a resort employee, so what are you doing in the *resort?*" I mimicked the way he'd said the word at the airport, just to mess with him.

"Yes, as everyone keeps reminding me." Noah walked over to a clearance display outside the clothing boutique, grabbed a t-shirt off the rack. "I'm just here to pick up a tour group." He pulled the t-shirt over his head, but it looked at least a size too small. The lines of his arms and shoulder stretched the cotton to its limit.

I held my hand to my face, trying to muffle a giggle.

"What's so funny?" Noah glared.

"Nothing." My eyes flicked back to his shirt. It read "Mountain Man" in bold font across the chest. I suppressed another giggle. "What kind of tour?" I asked, not really interested, but looking for a distraction.

"Hiking tour."

"That sounds ... horrible."

We did our whole glaring and glowering thing.

"I thought you said you had a Zoom call," said Noah,

clearly done with our conversation. "You need help getting there or something?"

"Is that a question or an offer?" The words tumbled out before my brain could stop them, landing between us with all the subtlety of a falling piano. They seemed to surprise him even more than me.

"Um ..." Noah's eyebrows shot up. His cheeks were now as red as his scalded chest.

"Actually, it's fine. I'm sure I can find it all by myself." Before he could respond, I brushed forcefully past him, ignoring the electric sensation when my arm accidentally grazed his bare skin. I dumped the now-empty cups in the nearest bin and marched down the hall, refusing to look back even as I felt his eyes boring into the back of my skull.

As I passed under the elk head wearing the beanie, not its scarf-wearing cousin, the frozen smirk on its taxidermied lips seemed to be laughing at me.

I spotted a sign with an arrow that said "Business Center" and nearly broke into a run. I was actually looking forward to the Zoom call now. Anything to distract me from what I'd just done. Taking the steps two at a time, I clung to one last desperate hope: that I would never see Mr. Mountain Shirt Grumpy Muscles ever again.

Chapter Eleven

"Hello? Hello? Can you hear us?" Maya shouted toward the gigantic black screen on the wall, then pressed a button on and off again, for the hundredth time. "How about now?"

Recessed lighting cast a muted glow over the polished mahogany table, where a silver speakerphone sat like a metallic spaceship. Maya fiddled with more settings on a control pad. I wouldn't have been surprised if somewhere, rockets launched into space.

After a swift smack of the remote control on the table, the massive wall-mounted screen flickered to life, splitting into three empty rectangles.

"Can you hear me now?" called a disembodied voice from one of the voids.

In another, a close-up of someone's nostrils appeared. The third remained stubbornly dark. Like a black hole consuming the universe.

"Hello? Is anyone there?" Marcus's voice crackled from the speakerphone, though his face was nowhere to be seen.

"We can hear you, Marcus, but we can't see you." Maya leaned forward and yelled into the box.

A harsh static blared from the speakerphone as a fourth square appeared, showing Victoria's face frozen in an unflattering mid-blink, her mouth open mid-word, one that looked like it rhymed with "luck." Eventually, her lips started moving, but no sound emerged.

"Victoria, you need to unmute yourself," Marcus shouted, as if the increased volume of his voice could somehow solve a mute button problem.

After another fifteen minutes of technological incompetence, a couple of IT guys intervened and our Zoom call got underway.

"Finally," said Victoria, smoothing her perfectly coiffed hair as if the technical difficulties had somehow physically mussed it. "Shall we begin?"

Maya cleared her throat. "While we have everyone here, I just want to mention how awesome Sam's content has been performing. I think she's really outdone herself."

I gave her a quick smile of gratitude. It was nice knowing at least someone had my back.

"Her shots of the grotto bar alone generated more buzz than our entire spring campaign. And don't even get me started on her Instagram stories from the spa tour," Maya continued. "We've already had three booking inquiries just this morning."

"Only three?" asked Marcus.

"The engagement metrics are off the charts," said Parker, finally appearing in the fourth square of the Zoom grid. *Make that two people who had my back.* "We're seeing a 42% increase in profile visits and a 28% boost in saved posts."

"Yes," said Victoria, leaning toward her camera until her face filled her entire square on the giant monitor, like a goddess looking down from the heavens to pick out the next victim for her lightning bolt tossing practice. "Our marketing team ran some preliminary analytics on the initial content, and I must say that I'm incredibly ..."

Maya and I leaned forward in our chairs, both holding our breath.

I'm incredibly pleased?
I'm incredibly impressed?
I'm incredibly ecstatic?

"I'm incredibly disappointed," Victoria finished.

Maya and I both deflated faster than a balloon arch at a porcupine gender reveal.

"The numbers are good, sure," said Victoria, her giant-sized manicured fingers waving across the screen. "But they're just numbers."

Marcus shared his screen; the conference room monitor now filled with spreadsheets and charts. "We ran the user comments through our generative AI tools, then compiled comparative analytics with our other properties around the globe."

More charts and figures appeared. Engagement rates. Click-throughs. Sentiment analysis scores.

"I haven't been this confused since trigonometry," I whispered to Maya, who muted our phone so Marcus wouldn't hear us.

"Look at this heat map." He circled his cursor over a bright red blob that could have been user engagement data or possibly a weather radar showing an approaching hurricane. "The engagement pattern is identical to our Maldives resort launch. And these sentiment clusters?" He switched to a word cloud where "stunning," "luxury," and "goals" floated in various sizes. "They mirror our Tuscany property almost exactly.

I started nodding my head. Then realized everyone else was shaking their heads. So I did that instead.

"And that's ... a bad thing?" I asked genuinely confused. I glanced at Maya, who was furiously scribbling notes, her knuckles white around her pen.

"The metrics are strong," Marcus continued, pulling up another chart. "But there's nothing that says 'Colorado.' Nothing that makes Aster Park unique. It could be any luxury resort anywhere in the world. Paris. Stockholm. Hong Kong."

Victoria's voice cut through the speakers. "Look, Samantha, the bottom line is there isn't enough of that local flavor we talked about. I can get my nethers waxed with locally sourced beeswax in Ipanema. I can get my naked body rubbed on a massage table in Bora Bora." Victoria froze on her screen again, falling silent. Either she was having technical difficulties ... or still thinking about Bora Bora.

"Are we still talking about resort properties?" I whispered.

Maya nodded tentatively. "I think so."

Victoria snapped back to life on the screen, picking up where she left off. "I can get hibiscus-scented spring water shot up my ass while sitting on a bidet in the South of France."

I was pretty sure I hadn't posted any content involving water shooting up anyone's ass, but nodded along and smiled, anyway.

Victoria leaned into the camera again, her pores like moon craters on the oversized monitor. "It was your idea to focus on authenticity, Samantha, remember?"

"Look, Samantha," said Marcus. "We didn't fly you out to Colorado to do the same thing everyone else does. We need you to capture the soul of the place. We need differentiation."

I opened my mouth to defend myself, to refocus on how well the engagement numbers were trending, but the words died in my throat. They were right. My posts were beautiful, polished, technically flawless.

And completely interchangeable with every other high-end

resort ever featured on social media. I could have taken the exact same photos anywhere with a pretty mountain view. I'd captured the luxury but missed the location. The polish, but not the place.

I'd done exactly what they'd asked for in our initial briefing, focusing on the amenities and experiences that justified the eye-watering room rates, but somehow I'd missed the point entirely.

Victoria's face still loomed large on the screen. "You promised *authenticity*, Samantha."

"You're right," I admitted. "I did."

Maya hit mute. "This coming from a woman who insisted we rip out ancient hand-carved beams and stone fireplaces to install champagne bars."

"And where decapitated elk heads wore scarves and beanies," I added.

"Samantha." Victoria's voice grabbed my attention back by the nape of its neck. "I thought you were going to show everyone what makes Colorado special. Instead, you've given us run-of-the-mill ... luxury porn."

"Luxury porn?" Scrolling back through my pictures, I realized she was right. I'd captured nothing uniquely Colorado. The amenities could exist anywhere in the world, just with different views out the windows. "I can fix this," I said, looking directly into the camera.

Maya mouthed the word, "How?"

I mouthed, "I have no idea."

"You realize you two are on video and we can see you, right?" Marcus frowned.

"I have an idea," said Parker from his video square. "I'll share my screen."

Marcus's charts and graphs disappeared and Parker's desktop took their place, a chaotic landscape of editing software, a Minecraft game, and thirty-seven open browser tabs of Pokemon card auctions on eBay.

"I've been tracking everything related to Sam's trip. Including where she's tagged." Parker double-clicked. The giant monitor switched to a screenshot of a new post.

A picture of a grumpy mountain man who looked very familiar.

And VERY irritating.

To my complete and utter horror, the picture I took of Noah and Yeti now filled the conference room wall. It was the candid shot I'd snapped at the airport when I thought I might need evidence for a future police investigation into my own disappearance.

"Wait a second," I said. "I didn't upload that. That's not my post. I swear I didn't post that." Frantic, I searched every face on screen for validation, but nobody was looking at me. They were all looking at Noah, transfixed by his windswept hair, piercing blue eyes, and the half-smile playing at the corner of his mouth as Yeti drooled beside him. It was hard to tell through the speakerphone's distortion, but I was pretty sure I heard Victoria whistle.

"I didn't post that ..." I repeated weakly.

"No, you're right, it's not your post, Sam," Parker confirmed. "But you're tagged in it."

"What? How?" Then I saw the username above Noah's photograph. My jaw dropped.

IT. WAS. MY. MOTHER.

If someone had handed me a genie-filled lamp in that moment, my first wish would have been to wish I was adopted.

"Now that's what I'm talking about," Victoria purred, leaning so close to her camera that her face threatened to burst through the screen. "Can't get any more authentic than *that*."

"Wait," Marcus interrupted. "Are those numbers right?"

I Burned My Tongue in Colorado

"Yup," Parker highlighted the statistics and zoomed in for a close-up. "And the post only went up this morning. The numbers are still climbing." He scrolled through the comments while the rest of us processed what we were seeing.

"OMG who is this mountain man? 😍 🔥"

"That dog is literally a wolf and I'm here for it! 🐺"

"Finally some REAL Colorado content! Not another lame fancy spa treatment shot that no one can afford!"

I stared at Noah's giant image on screen. Mom had captioned it, "Mountain Man and Wolf-Dog," tagging my personal account along with every single one of my business hashtags, effectively hijacking my professional brand to broadcast her shameless matchmaking agenda to the world.

"Wait, scroll back up," Victoria commanded. "What was that one about authentic content?"

Parker obliged, and there it was — another comment on Mom's post.

"This is what AUTHENTIC Colorado looks like! Not those fake marketing posts!"

My cheeks burned as I sank deeper into my chair, which suddenly felt less like a luxury office accessory and more like a witness stand. The contrast between my carefully curated resort photos and this candid shot of Noah, his authentic ruggedness, that barely there smile, Yeti looking wolf-like instead of a planted prop, was painfully obvious.

Marcus's marketing brain was visibly recalculating. "Those numbers are higher than all of Samantha's other posts."

Wonderful. My own mother was better at my job than I was. And she still had an AOL email address and shared the same phone with Dad.

"That's EXACTLY what I need," said Victoria. As the rest of us stared at her, Victoria sat up straight and cleared her throat. "What I meant was, that's exactly what Samantha needs." All eyes shifted from Victoria to me.

"What I need?"

"Yes, you, Sam," said Victoria. "He is exactly what YOU need. What this campaign needs. Luxury *and* authenticity. You said it yourself. And what better way to achieve both those objectives than you and Noah working together?"

Everyone began talking over each other all at once. "Me and Noah together?" I asked through the bedlam.

"Yes, yes," said Marcus, throwing more charts and graphs on the screen. "The potential for crossover synergies is inspired."

"Look at these demographics," added Parker, moving his cursor over a pie chart on the screen share. "We're hitting both the adventure-seeking millennials and the luxury-loving boomers. It's cross-generational appeal."

"Urban sophistication meets mountain expertise." Marcus smiled for the first time since the Zoom call started. "I like it. I like it a lot."

"Well, I LOVE it." It was clear from the look in her eyes that when Victoria said, "I love it," what she meant was, you better find a way to make this work or else.

For the next several minutes, Victoria, Marcus, and Parker brainstormed strategies and workshopped logistics while I tried to contain a full-blown panic attack. Mixed with a mental breakdown. Topped with an emotional outburst.

Obviously, there was no way such a crazy idea would ever work. Noah and I working together? It was preposterous. Ludicrous. An impossibility. Noah hated me. I mean, he couldn't stand me so much that he stranded me at the airport.

Not to mention the fact that *I* also hated *him*.

"Aren't you all forgetting one thing?" I raised my hand tentatively, like a student who didn't want to be called on, but felt obligated to point out that the classroom was on fire and we were all about to die.

The excited energy on screen sputtered to a halt.

"Noah hates me," I pointed out. "There's no way he would ever agree to this."

Victoria smiled. Slowly, she shook her head. "Samantha. Dear sweet, Samantha. That's ridiculous. Noah doesn't hate you." She stared into the camera. "Noah hates me. Not that it matters who Noah hates. Because we have all the leverage. Isn't that right, Maya?"

Maya stared down at the table. Her shoulders slumped, but she nodded.

"He'll play ball," said Marcus, his smile carrying all the warmth of a collections telemarketer. "If he wants to save his job and the jobs of his friends."

"Sam's right," said Maya, her voice strained. "There's no way Noah would agree to this."

"Just make him an offer he can't refuse," said Victoria.

"What is this, a *Godfather* movie?" I waited for Marcus to suggest putting one of the severed elk heads in Noah's bed.

"Honestly, Maya, Samantha, I don't care how you get him to do it, just get it done. What could possibly go wrong?"

Chapter Twelve

"**N**O. FUCKING. WAY."

Noah crossed his arms, biceps popping out of his flannel sleeves like granite boulders. His steel-blue eyes bore into us like we'd just propositioned him for a threesome. Which, to be honest, would have been a lot less awkward and intimidating.

As soon as Maya and I hung up from the Zoom call, she'd let it all out. She told me how Noah and his crew ran the Adventure Center, the log cabin barn-like structure where Al dropped me off my first night. It was part of the original lodge, she explained, and handled all the "authentic Colorado" guest experiences. Hiking, rafting, horseback riding, the works.

Needless to say, it didn't quite fit the LuxeLife brand. So once their contract was up ... bye-bye Adventure Center. And apparently Noah and his friends would go bye-bye with it.

"This was Victoria's idea?"

"Actually, it was Sam's," Maya shot back.

Thanks Maya. Sure, I deserved partial blame for the whole authenticity angle, but getting up close and personal with Mr.

I Burned My Tongue in Colorado

Mc'Grumpy Flannel Frump was definitely not part of my vision. Unless you count the vision I had in the tub. And the dreams I had after getting out of the tub. And several dozen random imagination malfunctions since.

Noah glared over at me again.

"Just hear me out." Maya held up her hands, either as a pleading gesture, or because she was trying to stop Noah from tackling me. "This is your chance. Show Victoria that this place still has value. Generate interest. Grow bookings. Increase revenue."

I kept my mouth shut. Before we borrowed one of the resort's pimped-out four-wheel-drive golf carts and drove down there, Maya and I agreed that she would do all the talking. My job was simply to stand there and keep quiet. And I fully intended to execute my half of the plan flawlessly. Plus, Yeti was staring at me and drooling, so I didn't want to make any sudden movements and set her off.

"I think this could really be helpful for everyone," Maya pleaded. "It's not as bad as it sounds."

"No?" Noah spun his boot in the gravel. "Cause it sounds like the worst idea I've ever heard."

Maya leveled her index finger at my nose. "She's on our side. Sam wants to show real Colorado experiences, not that crap they're peddling up at the resort."

"You mean the crap Victoria hired her to promote?" Noah glared at me like I was personally responsible for LuxeLife screwing him over. "Whatever *Samantha* thinks she wants, she won't find it here."

"Noah, please." Maya chased after him as he stomped toward his hunk-of-junk Jeep.

From across the parking lot, I watched Noah and Maya angry-whisper, clearly about me. Every couple of words,

Noah's face would get red, and he'd jerk his arm in my direction like he was chopping wood.

"You're back," said a woman's voice behind me. I turned and saw Jenn come out of the log building. Luckily, muck-free.

A wilderness-y looking Latino dude joined her. He wore half a wetsuit, the top half peeled back over his torso like a banana. Even from a distance, I could tell he smelled like river mud.

"That her?" asked wetsuit dude.

"That's the one." Jenn's lips twisted into a smirk.

"Doesn't look very influential to me."

They walked over, studying every inch of me along the way.

"New shoes?" asked Jenn.

"Yes, they are," I said, flashing my best influencer smile. Noah already hated me, so I was determined not to make enemies of his friends. "Maya let me pick them from the boutique."

"Boutique?" asked wetsuit dude.

"Yes, at the resort."

"The resort. Right." Wetsuit dude was now the third person who'd pronounced "resort" like "bear-poop-on-the-bottom-of-my-shoe."

I stuck one of my legs out and twisted my foot back and forth so Jenn could see the colored pattern on the laces. They really drew out the orchid purple color of my puffy vest. And the red matched my lip gloss perfectly.

Nothing bonds two women faster than new footwear.

Except in Colorado, apparently.

"Nice." Jenn's tone didn't match the word. "This is Diego." She jabbed her thumb at wetsuit dude. "Diego, this is Samantha.".

"My friends call me Sam."

I Burned My Tongue in Colorado

"I'm sure they do, Samantha" said Diego.

Across the parking lot, Maya and Noah were still engaged in robust conversation, with more grumpy looks and wood-chopping-esqe finger pointing. The three of us watched the back and forth like a high stakes tennis match, where the losing player would be forced to watch more tennis.

"So." I said, pulling their attention back to me. "LuxeLife wants me to get some content of all the stuff you all do." If Noah wasn't going to cooperate, I'd just have to go around him.

"Content?" asked Diego.

"Stuff?" asked Jenn.

"You know, like ..." I gestured at Diego's half on, half off wetsuit, and the still dripping life vest in his hand. "Videos of river whatchahoosies. And photos of horsey thingamabobs."

"River whatchahoosies?" asked Diego.

"Horsey thingamabobs?" asked Jenn.

I reapplied my most influential influencer smile. "Maybe while Noah and Maya are sorting out the details, the two of you could show me around."

"The only details those two are working out is which one of you Noah is going to drop off the mountain first," said Diego. "Besides, I've got a river whatchahoosie I need to get to." Diego headed for a truck attached to a trailer filled with rafts.

"And I'd rather go shovel out some more horse thingam-abobs." Jenn headed around the back of the Adventure Center, toward the stables.

"Well, that went better than expected," I said to Yeti.

Woof.

"Good wolf-dog. Nice wolf-dog." I said, pulling out my influencer smile again. I hoped it worked on wild creatures. "Noah didn't tell you to eat me, did he?"

WOOF!

"That sounded like a yes."

"Hey!" Noah whistled one of his mountain-man calls to get our attention. "Stop scaring her and get over here."

"Yeah, Yeti." I wagged my finger at Noah's pet. "It's not nice to scare people."

"I wasn't talking to the dog," Noah growled. "I was talking to you."

As soon as I stepped inside, I saw Maya wasn't kidding when she said the Adventure Center didn't fit the LuxeLife brand. It looked like a dusty, moldy, grime-covered barn. Because it was. The air smelled like wet dog and burnt coffee.

"Well, this is quaint." Legitimately, though, the place was a content goldmine, not because it was aesthetically pleasing. Or pleasing in any other way. But because it was real. Authentic. The very thing Victoria kept harping about.

Faded photographs of smiling tourists lined the unpainted walls, holding up fish or paddling on the river. Mismatched chairs surrounded a table spread with laminated maps. Brochures, pamphlets, and gear piled up on the counter. It was basically the mountain barn version of my apartment.

"Can I take some pictures?" At least there weren't any decapitated animal heads wearing ski goggles on the wall.

"Better do it quick," said Noah. "Before you help LuxeLife destroy it all."

"Noah Barrett, stop." Maya helped herself to a cup of coffee, then propped an elbow on the counter. She seemed right at home here. "This isn't Sam's fault, and you know it."

Noah crossed his arms again, his go-to power pose, apparently. "Right. Just following orders." Yeti flopped down near his feet, eyeing my new boots as if she had plans for them later.

I pulled out my phone and started documenting the space, ignoring Noah's eyes as they followed my every move. I captured a shot of an ancient fishing rod mounted on the wall. A collection of river stones labeled with dates stretching back decades. A wall of Polaroids showing what must have been regular customers returning year after year.

"There's some petrified bear scat in one of the classrooms in back. You want to take a picture of that too?"

"It would certainly capture the essence of the place, so sure."

Maya cleared her throat. "Okay enough. Both of you. Noah, let's just cut the shit, okay? Your contract with LuxeLife is just about over. When it ends, Victoria's gonna come in here with a bulldozer and level this place to the ground. Probably to make room for a salt cave and an oxygen bar."

"Sounds about right." Noah's face got even grumpier, which I didn't think was physically possible.

"But ..." Maya made sure he was looking at her.

"But what?"

"Victoria said I could make a deal."

"What kind of deal?"

"A deal to save your Adventure Center."

"Victoria agreed to that? Because the one and only time she walked in here, she said this was, and I quote, 'a tired old relic that reeks of mediocrity and boy scout energy.' Or something like that."

"Yeah, that was pretty much it, exactly." Maya nodded.

"That sounds like Victoria," I agreed.

Noah shot me another glare.

"I think I can convince her to reconsider another contract renewal," said Maya.

"You think."

"If this works. If you play nice."

"Sounds like a deal with the devil."

"Victoria isn't the devil," I interrupted. "She's just a smart businesswoman who recognizes a good opportunity when she sees it."

"I wasn't talking about Victoria." Noah redirected his glare back to me. But I could see the gears turning in his head. Was it possible? Was he actually considering this insane idea?

"Fuck." Noah ran a calloused hand through his hair, which somehow ended up looking even better than before. "What would I have to do with this thing, anyway? If I agreed to it. Which, to be clear, I have not."

Recognizing the crack in Noah's shield of stubbornness, Maya grabbed the bull by the horns. Or, in this case, the grumpy mountain man by the flannel. "You and Sam would collaborate on an Authentic Colorado Adventure series. Hiking, climbing, rafting, the works."

"The works?," I asked. "Um ... I don't remember agreeing to the works."

Maya shushed me. "Showcase what makes the Adventure Center special. Through Sam's platforms."

"Platforms?"

"Her social media channels. TikTok, Instagram, YouTube."

Noah looked like we were trying to communicate with him in Chinese.

"Sam gets to keep her job. Victoria gets her authentic Colorado content. You get to keep the Adventure Center. It's a win, win, win."

"What the hell are you doing?"

I looked up to find Noah talking to me.

"And better yet, what the hell are you wearing?"

"Oh, this?" I pulled the fluffy purple pom-pom beanie back off my head. "I found it in the gift shop at the resort. It matches my puffy vest." I put the beanie back on my head. "See?"

I smiled.

Noah didn't.

"And as far as what I was doing ..." I pulled out my phone, angling it upward and reversing my camera. I snapped a photo.

"I was taking a snow shoe selfie for my feed." I posed in front of the pair of vintage snowshoes hanging on the wall, then took another picture.

Noah looked back over at Maya, though he still pointed directly at me. "Seriously? She wouldn't last ten seconds on a real trail."

"Oh come on now," I shot back. "I've got a good twenty seconds in me at least."

Noah didn't find that funny, either.

"Seriously, though, I did hike all the way up to the resort yesterday. In the dark. Through mountain lion infested woods. Where I was almost attacked by some weird disco chicken thing."

"Disco chicken thing?" Noah and Maya both frowned.

I mimicked the bizarre mating dance of the creature I'd encountered.

"Are you having a seizure?" asked Noah. He turned to Maya. "If she passes out, I'm not the one doing mouth-to-mouth."

"Ew. Gross," I agreed. "I'd rather get slobbered on by Yeti."

"That can be arranged," said Noah. In the corner, Yeti cocked her ear.

"The point is," I said. "I can do this. I don't want to do this, but I can do this. Probably. I think."

"Don't you see Noah? That's the spin. The naïve, inexperienced city girl sampling authentic Colorado experiences. The uninformed outsider making a fool of herself for everyone to see."

"Whose side are you on, exactly, anyway?" I asked.

"Whoever's side I need to be on to make this work." Maya pointed at my purple pom-pom beanie. "That's exactly what this whole video series would be about."

"That and my reputation being dragged through the mud when she hooks herself with a fishing line."

I adjusted my beanie in the window's reflection, pulling it lower on my ears. "I don't know why everyone has such a problem with my accessorizing today," I muttered.

"Or when she falls off a horse. Or gets swept down a river rapid."

"I can hear you, you know," I reminded him.

"Good."

Maya took a deep breath, rubbed at her temples. "Look, I know you don't want to work with us."

"With LuxeLife," he corrected. "Nothing personal against you, Maya. Everything you've done for me, my crew, that's the only reason we're even talking about this."

"I wouldn't be here if I didn't think it could work. And it might be the last chance I get to help save what you've built here."

Noah ran another hand through his perpetually disheveled hair. In one single swipe, he somehow made an entire head of hair look perfect, not a single strand out of place. His head dropped slightly, followed by his shoulders. "What's the catch then? What aren't you telling me?"

"Victoria's going to want tangible results. Occupancy rates. Revenue increases. Repeat booking trends. Things won't magically improve overnight.

"She's setting us up to fail."

"Not necessarily" I said, stuffing the beanie back in my pocket. "I did a campaign for a budget hotel chain last year. Increased their bookings by thirty percent. In just three months."

"That's ... incredible Sam." At least Maya seemed impressed. Noah ... eh.

"I'm actually good at my job, Noah. And that was for a

place that had bedbugs in half the rooms. We just didn't mention those in the posts."

For the first time, Noah seemed to really look at me. Non-judgementally. Well, okay, it was still judgmental, but ... more curiosity than contempt.

"Something tells me your usual audience isn't our target demographic." Noah gestured around the room. "How many of your fans own hiking boots that have actually touched dirt?"

"Followers. They're called followers." I made a conscious effort not to look down at my new pair of pristine white boots. I'd been carefully avoiding all dirt-related surfaces since Maya had let me pick them out from the mountain leisure boutique at the resort.

"That's really the whole point," said Maya. "Sam exposes your adventures to people who wouldn't normally consider them. Make the wilderness accessible and appealing to a wider audience. Show them that an authentic Colorado experience is worth getting their boots dirty for."

"And if I say no?" he asked.

Maya's professional smile faltered. "Then the Adventure Center closes as scheduled. Jenn goes back to Alaska. Diego goes back to Florida. I check my 401k balance every couple of hours until I can retire. And you ... you go do whatever it is that you do."

Noah's jaw tightened as he looked around the room, taking in all the history, the memories, the life that had been built there. I found myself following his gaze, seeing the place through his eyes, not just as an old, repurposed barn, but as a legacy. One worth fighting for.

"So that's it? I either play tour guide to Insta-whatever, Face-thingy Princess here, or lose everything?"

"Hey, I'm not exactly thrilled about this arrangement

either," I snapped. "I didn't sign up to be dragged through the wilderness by Mr. Mountain Man Grumpy Face."

"Mr. Mountain Man Grumpy Face?"

"You heard me."

Maya shrugged. "She's got a point."

"See, that face right there." I pointed at his scowl.

For a moment, Noah and I stared each other down. Then, unexpectedly, the corner of his mouth twitched. His smile formed slowly, a twinkle in his eye. "You really want to do this?"

"Do I want to do this? No. But it seems that neither one of us has a choice."

"Okay."

"Okay?" Maya and I shared a hopeful look. Had our plan actually worked?

"But we start tomorrow, first thing."

"So what, like ten, eleven?"

"Well, the trip's called Dawn Patrol, so ..." Noah's smile stretched wider still.

Chapter Thirteen

The next morning, Noah met me in the resort lobby at 4:00am. Although the term "morning" is debatable. Technically, since the sun hadn't even come up, as far as I was concerned, it was still the middle of the night.

Noah grimaced like he was looking at a giant pile of moose dung as soon as he saw me. "What are you wearing?"

"Clothes?" I stared down at my outfit, the outfit Maya let me pick out from the boutique where I got my beanie and my boots.

"We're going for a hike, not a photo shoot." Noah scanned me again, then shook his head.

I'd chosen a heathered gray Patagonia fleece pullover, some stretchy black Lululemon yoga pants that made my butt look a-maz-ing, and a pair of baby-blue merino wool socks that embraced my feet in a hug. I was going for an "I'm an outdoorsy person who definitely knows what she's doing and wants to look good doing it" vibe, even if it wasn't remotely true.

"Follow me." Noah's tone suggested he was going to escort

me to the principal's office where he would bend me over his knee and spank me for being naughty. Which I guess I must have been okay with because I fell in line behind him without fussing, an extra spring in my step.

We made our way outside to the main driveway. Even in the darkness, Noah's Jeep looked like a pile of something Bigfoot left in the woods.

"So let me guess, we're taking that ... thing."

"Smart girl."

"Smart ass," I said back.

"Yeti, move." Noah snapped his fingers, and the wolf-dog moved from the passenger seat to the back.

"Great, you brought your wolf-dog, too."

"Might want to brush the seat off first. Wouldn't want to get dog hair all over your fancy yoga pants." Noah still wore a scowl on his lips, but I was pretty sure his eyes were smiling.

"Hey, look, you have doors now." Sure enough, the piece of Bigfoot dung Jeep did indeed have doors, even though it didn't have them at the airport.

"Put 'em on this morning," said Noah. "These roads can get pretty rough. Can't have you bouncing down the mountain."

"Aww, so sweet."

"My survival depends on your survival now, so I figured I better keep you alive."

"Gee, thanks."

"Just to be clear, I'm not opening the door for you." Noah marched directly to the passenger-side door and yanked on the handle until it popped open.

"That's literally what you just did," I pointed out.

"But not in a gentlemanly way." Noah left the door hanging open.

"Don't worry, I would never accuse you of being a gentleman."

"Good." Noah circled around the Jeep to the driver's side.

"Good." Climbing in required more upper body strength than I expected. Taking my seat, I tried to find a position where my new clothes weren't touching anything mud-covered.

It was mathematically impossible.

"We'll stop by the shop first so I can get you some proper clothes," said Noah, settling in behind the wheel. "What size are you?"

"That's a little personal, don't you think?"

"You want me to get you clothes that fit?" He jammed the key into the ignition. "Or you want me to wing it?"

If Noah thought his glare was scary, he'd never seen mine after being forced to wear misfit clothing. Mom used to make me wear my older cousin's hand-me-downs instead of taking me on a proper back-to-school shopping trip when times were tight. I'd been scarred ever since.

"Six," I answered, just to make him stop looking at my waist.

He looked at me like he was counting how many of the resort's house-baked white chocolate, macadamia nut cookies I had before bed. For the record, it was the same number as my pant size. "If you say so."

"What's that supposed to mean?"

"Nothing. I just said, "If you say so.'"

"You said 'if you say so' like you have an opinion about what I said."

Noah shrugged. "I used to take Brie clothes shopping all the time."

For the life of me, I couldn't imagine Mr. Grumpy Mountain Grouchy Face sitting outside a waiting room in a department store while his sister tried on clothes. "Why would *you* take your sister clothes shopping?"

"That's not important. What is important is that I know a

size seven when I see one. I just want you to be comfortable during our hike."

Noah turned the key in the ignition. The engine wheezed to life.

If I were going to be forced to go on a stupid hike, and be forced out of bed before dawn, the last thing I wanted to do was compound my misery by squeezing into tight pants. "Okay, fine. Maybe I'm a seven. But that's only because I've been doing a lot of food promotions lately. As soon as I get back to Los Angeles, I'm going on a diet."

"If you say so."

"I do say so."

"So now it's been said." Noah pointed to the mud-caked strap. "Seatbelt."

I fumbled with the complicated harness system that appeared to be designed for extreme racing sports rather than basic transportation. "Is all this really necessary?" Hopefully, he didn't notice how I had to give the lap belt a little extra slack to fit it around my waist.

"Only if you want to remain inside the vehicle when we hit the switchbacks."

"The what?"

Noah jerked the stick shift into drive, and it sounded like the entire engine fell out the bottom. He punched his foot on the accelerator and the rear tires spit gravel.

As we eased onto the main road, I turned to face him. "What's wrong with the clothes I'm wearing, anyway?

"Well, let's see, where should we start?" Noah lifted his foot off the clutch at a bend and the Jeep lurched forward around the curve. "First off, that fleece?" Noah gestured at my pullover without taking his eyes off the dark mountain road. "It'll snag on every branch we pass. One good catch and you'll have a hole the size of Boulder. The city, not the rock."

I Burned My Tongue in Colorado

"This is a three hundred dollar sweater."

"Then you might not want to wear it in the woods. That sweater really cost three hundred dollars?"

"Well, I didn't pay three hundred dollars for it. That's like my entire grocery budget for the month. LuxeLife is paying the expense tab. Maya said I could pick out whatever I want."

"Hmm."

I sensed judgment in his hmm, but was too tired to get into it. I strained my eyes to see through the mud-splattered windshield, wondering if Noah was secretly a Jedi Knight. Force powers were the only thing I could think of that would enable him to see where we were going in the pitch dark, considering the headlights were mostly covered by splattered mud. "Shouldn't you maybe slow down just a bit?"

"And those pants?" He continued as if he hadn't heard me.

"What's wrong with my pants?"

"They're going to get soaked the second we cross the stream. Then you'll be hiking in wet synthetics that'll chafe worse than sandpaper. Better hope that fancy resort shop of yours sells diaper rash cream."

I shifted in my seat. Not by choice. A pothole jostled me airborne. "There's a stream crossing?"

"Two actually. Though one of them is more of a river." Noah downshifted and whipped around another hairpin turn. "And those socks?" Noah snorted. "Merino wool in summer? Your feet are gonna cook. Then blister. Then probably fall off. And just in case you were wondering, at no point will I be carrying you."

"Well, on that point we can agree," I said.

"But the real problem?" Noah pulled into the gravel lot in front of the Adventure Center. "Those shoes."

I glanced down at my new white boots. I'd paid extra for the custom memory foam inserts. Well, technically, LuxeLife paid extra. "What's wrong with my boots? They're Canada Goose."

"Please. A goose wouldn't be caught dead in those things. Canadian, or otherwise."

"It's a clothing brand. Not an actual ... goose."

Noah chuckled.

"You're fucking with me, aren't you?"

"Only in your dreams." Noah hopped out of the Jeep and came over to my side.

I tried to think of a snappy comeback, but he was right. Literally. The previous night, Dream Noah had once again invaded my sleep, leaving me tossing and turning for hours. The jerk was not only tormenting my day life; he plagued my night life too.

Noah jiggled the handle, then yanked open my door. "Really, though, those shoes have zero ankle support. And the laces are going to come untied every ten steps."

Yeti hopped out the back, and the three of us headed toward the Adventure Center's front door, giving Noah more time to criticize my footwear.

"And those soles are about as grippy as bowling shoes on ice. One wrong step on wet rock and you're taking a header off the mountain. Which reminds me, another thing I won't be doing is rappelling down a cliff to dig you out of a ravine."

"I thought this was supposed to be an easy hike."

"Dawn Patrol isn't just a hike. It's a scramble."

"As in eggs?" I asked hopefully.

"Nope."

* * *

Noah flicked on the lights inside the Adventure Center, and the fluorescents hummed to life, casting harsh shadows across the equipment-lined walls. Yeti found a napping spot in a corner and closed her eyes. I was immediately envious.

"Take off your clothes."

I nearly choked. "Excuse me?"

"Can't put on new clothes if you're still wearing the old ones."

I glanced around the wide-open space as Noah started pulling things from shelves. "Is there a changing room then?"

Noah's laugh echoed off the high ceiling. "This isn't Barney's, princess."

"What would you know about Barney's anyway?"

Noah shrugged. "My parents took Brie and I to New York City once when we were kids."

"And you went shopping at Barney's? You realized it had nothing to do with the purple dinosaur, right?"

Something smile-like crept over Noah's face. "Our mom saw a dress she liked in a window display. Probably cost almost as much as that getup you're wearing. More than our dad made in a month." He set the stack of clothes he picked out on the counter. "Let me guess, you shop at Barney's all the time."

"Actually, Barney's went bankrupt. They don't even exist anymore."

"Oh, no?" Noah stopped in his tracks. For some strange reason, the tough guy mountain man seemed almost disappointed. "What happened to it?"

"Trends change. Tastes change. That's why people like me are employed. Somebody's got to try to keep up with it all."

Noah stuffed the clothes in my arms. "Anyway, this is a working gear shop, not Michigan Avenue. No fancy fitting rooms."

"Then where exactly am I supposed to change?"

"Behind the rain jackets works for most people." He gestured to a corner of the shop. "Unless you'd prefer to strip right here in the middle?" The teasing glint in his eye made my stomach do a little flip.

Hidden behind the rack of rain jackets, I peeled off my designer mountain leisure wear and pulled on the sturdy hiking pants Noah had picked out for me. They were surprisingly comfortable, if not exactly Instagram-worthy.

"So you went to New York as a kid?" I called out, trying to break the awkwardness of being half naked with nothing but a rack of weather wear to protect me. "What else did you do there besides shopping at Barneys?"

"Tourist stuff."

I tugged the moisture-wicking shirt over my head. It felt soft against my skin. "Your parents sound nice. Taking you and your sister all the way to New York just to see the sights."

"Yeah." His voice got quiet.

"You ever go back? To New York, I mean?

"That was the first and last time I left Colorado."

I peeked around the rack. Noah stood with his back to me, organizing gear on a shelf, never looking over his shoulder.

"Don't you like to travel?"

"My whole life is here. Got no reason to go anywhere else."

A picture on the wall behind me caught my eye. In it, a boy and his younger sister stood in front of a cliff face with their parents, decked out in climbing gear. The boy looked like a smaller, younger version of Noah.

I stepped out from behind the raincoats. Cleared my throat so Noah could turn around and inspect me.

He nodded at my feet. "Double knot them. Last thing we need is you tripping on the trail because you don't know how to tie shoes properly." And just like that, Grumpy Noah was back, his mountain man wall as high and as thick as ever.

"I know how to tie shoes, you know."

"If you say so."

I Burned My Tongue in Colorado

* * *

The headlights carved through the darkness, illuminating scraggly pine trees and massive boulders. The Jeep bounced over another rut in the dirt road; the pre-dawn darkness made every bump feel like a potential cliff edge. I had to grab the door handle to keep from smacking my head against the roll bar.

"You could slow down a little," I said through gritted teeth.

"This is slow." Noah handled the steering wheel as if he were racing down the 405 during rush hour. "I would have had the LuxeLife limousine pick you up, but the trail's only accessible by four-wheel drive."

"Ha ha," I said. "Smart ass," I mumbled under my breath.

"I heard that."

"Good."

Yeti barked. I think she was agreeing with me.

The dirt road was like driving on the surface of Mars. The Jeep hit another bump, and the headrest nearly gave me a concussion.

"You hit that one on purpose."

"Whoops."

"I don't remember reading anything about backwoods death traps in the resort brochure."

"That's why you should always read the fine print."

Yeti's head popped up between our seats, her warm breath tickling my ear. At least someone in this vehicle was friendly. And slobbery. She smeared a puddle of drool on my sleeve.

"Your breath smells like bear farts," I said.

"Don't listen to her, Yeti."

"I wasn't talking to Yeti. I was talking to you."

We hit another bump, and I yelped, drawing another eye

roll from Noah. "Relax. I've driven this road hundreds of times."

"In the dark?"

"Best time to do it. That way you can't see how far down it is to the bottom." He downshifted, the engine growling as we climbed higher. "Plus, Dawn Patrol means getting there before dawn. Hence the name."

I wanted to snap back with something witty, but my stomach lurched as we rounded another hairpin turn. The headlights briefly swept across empty space before finding the road again.

"How much further?" I asked, trying to keep the tremor out of my voice. And last night's cookies from climbing back up my throat.

"Ten minutes to the trailhead." Noah glanced over. "You're not going to throw up, are you? Because if you are, let me know now so I can slow down and push you out."

"I'm fine." I wasn't fine. But I'd rather have died than admit weakness.

The Jeep continued crawling upward, suspension creaking. Through the windshield, I caught glimpses of stars scattered across the sky. No light pollution out here to dim their brilliance. Despite my churning stomach, I had to admit it was beautiful.

"Seriously though, I can stop if you want me to. I got some water in the back."

When I looked over, the look of actual concern on his face surprised me. "I'll be fine. We have to get there before dawn, right?"

Noah put his foot back down on the accelerator, and we continued on our way. A few minutes later, the Jeep lurched to a stop in a small clearing. My phone's clock read 5:15AM. It was still pitch black.

I Burned My Tongue in Colorado

Noah hopped out and opened the back, pulling out two backpacks and what looked like ski poles. "Here."

I staggered under the weight of the backpack. "What's in here, bowling balls?"

"First aid kit, emergency blanket, satellite phone, flares."

"Flares? Are you expecting we'll need a rescue?"

He adjusted the straps on my pack. "Had a guest break her ankle last month. Two miles from the nearest access point."

"That's not reassuring." Noah tightened another strap, squeezing most of the air out of my lungs. "Did you carry *her*?"

Noah shrugged. "Her? Yes. But she was really a size six."

"Very funny."

Yeti barked.

"She thought so." Noah patted his wolf-dog on the head.

I shifted the weight on my back, trying to find a position that didn't make it feel like my spine was warping. "Is it really worth this kind of joint trauma?"

"Better safe than sorry. You never know when somebody's gonna come down with altitude sickness, dehydration, hypothermia, a broken bone, animal encounters that go sideways ... severe inner thigh chafing ..."

"Okay, all dangers noted. You can stop now."

"Lightning strikes, rockslides, mudslides, poison oak, poison ivy ..."

I held up my hand. "Seriously. I get it."

"Bee stings. Hornet stings. Fire ant bites. Surprise skunk spraying."

"A fist to the face from a malcontent hiking companion," I added.

"Cute."

Yeti barked.

"She thought so." I patted Yeti on the head.

Noah grinned as he handed me one of the ski poles. Which

made little sense since it wasn't snowing. Unless, of course it was a surprise he was saving for later.

"These are trekking poles."

"Are those anything like *Star Trek* fans from Poland?"

Not even Yeti barked at that one.

"My dad took me to a *Star Trek* convention in San Diego once. Bought me Spock ears and everything." I made the split-finger Spock hand thing. "Live long and prosper."

Noah looked at me like I was the dumbest person on Earth, then handed me a set of poles.

"You hold it here, and plant it into the ground like this." Noah demonstrated proper pole placement and adjusted my set to fit me. "They'll help with balance and take pressure off your knees. You'll thank me later."

"If I survive that long." I fumbled with the poles, feeling like a baby giraffe on a deep-sea crabbing boat in the middle of a tsunami.

"The pack also has bear spray. That's essential out here. The other day, Jenn saw a mother black bear and three cubs. Last thing you ever want to do is get between a momma and her baby."

"I'll keep that in mind."

Chapter Fourteen

I huffed and I puffed up the trail, my legs already burning and a cramp pinching a muscle in my back. And my legs. And my butt. The saddest part? We'd only been hiking for ten minutes.

Meanwhile, Noah moved like a mountain goat ahead of me, not even breaking a sweat. I caught myself watching the way his shoulders moved under his shirt, the effortless way he navigated the trail's obstacles. Any second now, I figured he would start skipping up the trail and yodeling.

"Let me guess," I called ahead of me. "You and your parents and Brie did stuff like this all the time."

He nodded. "I grew up on these trails."

"If my parents had made me go on a hike when I was a kid, I would have called child services."

He started moving again.

"Can you hold on a second? I need to get some establishing shots for my posts." Actually, it was an excuse to take a break before I keeled over from a heart attack.

I leaned my trekking poles against a tree and pulled out my

phone, squinting at the screen in the darkness. "Just need to adjust my settings real quick for dark mode."

"We're running out of time." Noah's voice carried an edge of impatience I was becoming all too familiar with.

"What time is it?"

"Time to hike."

"This'll only take a minute." I switched to pro mode, tweaking the ISO and shutter speed. "Can't post grainy content. My followers expect quality."

"Your followers can wait."

I ignored him, checking my phone for a signal. Service had been coming and going all morning, depending on how many mountains were between me and civilization. I had a few bars at the moment, so decided to live stream.

"Hey everyone!" I spoke in my signature upbeat tone. "Coming to you live from ..." I hit pause. "Where are we exactly?"

"Big Tree Trail." Noah crossed his arms.

"A little on the nose, don't you think?"

"I guess the early settlers who first traversed the Rocky Mountains in covered wagons were too busy worrying about starving to death and cholera to come up with a clever name for you to hashtag."

"Like you even know what a hashtag is."

"I heard Diego say it once."

The sarcasm was so thick I could have used it as trail mix. But as I looked around at the towering pines, their names suddenly seemed perfectly logical. Sometimes the obvious choice was obvious because it was right.

"Fair point," I admitted, lowering my phone. "Though I bet they would've been influencer gold. #CoveredWagonLife #PioneerVibes #WestwardBoundBabe."

Noah stared at me as if I'd started speaking in Cantonese. "Do you ever turn it off?"

"Turn what off?"

"The performance. The constant need to translate everything into content."

I thought a moment, tapping on my chin. "Um ... no." I angled my phone to catch the starlit sky behind me, then hit record again. "It's dawn patrol time in Colorado! We're about to experience a gorgeous sunrise from ..." I glanced at Noah. "How high up are we going?"

He just stared at me.

"Anyway, we're going up! Way up! And I've got the amazing Noah Barrett as my guide." I turned the camera toward him.

Noah showed several thousand livestream viewers his extended middle finger.

"He's a little camera shy." I quickly switched back to selfie mode. "But look at this amazing gear he got me!" I struck a pose, making sure to capture my new hiking outfit. "Who says outdoor adventure can't be both functional and stylish?"

I crouched down for a better angle of my face, looking up at the star-filled sky when Yeti photobombed my shot, her tongue streaking across my cheek. She pressed in cheek to cheek with me until her snout filled the entire viewing angle.

"At least someone knows how to work a camera." I scratched behind her ears. "Unlike her grumpy human." I flashed the camera back to Noah quickly, which drew a steady stream of grumpy face emojis from my followers. "Folks, this is my new friend Yeti, part dog, part wolf, all badass. Say hi to all your fans, Yeti." She barked, and the heart emojis started rolling in.

"You too, Yeti?" said a grumpy voice offscreen.

Yeti barked, then licked my cheek again.

"Traitor." Noah checked his watch for the tenth time. "Are you done yet?"

"Almost." I snapped a few more angles, trying to capture the ethereal pre-dawn light. "Just need to check the lighting one more ..."

Noah started walking up the trail, Yeti trotting back over to walk beside him.

"Hey! Wait up!" I scrambled to stuff my phone in my pocket, nearly tripping over my trekking poles. "I was thinking I could shoot you giving some trail safety rules with that mountain over there in the backdrop."

"Rule number one," Noah called over his shoulder without turning around. "Keep up."

The trail narrowed as we climbed further; the path turning from packed dirt to loose rock that shifted treacherously. I was thankful I'd taken Noah's advice and changed my boots. The ones he gave me gripped the trail like they had little suction cups on the bottom.

The higher we went, the prettier the view. But I'd given up trying to film anything. Both hands were needed just to keep my balance and my dignity intact. I was grateful Noah had insisted on bringing the hiking poles. Without them, my knees would have disintegrated into bone powder.

"Watch your step here." Noah pointed to a section where the path dropped off sharply on one side, exposing a view of treetops far below. "The rain washed out part of the trail last week."

I eyed the steep slope beside us, my stomach lurching at the drop. "You're joking, right?"

"Just stay close to the inside wall." As if to show how simple it was to defy death, Yeti trotted past the drop-off like she was strolling through a dog park.

I took a tentative step forward, and a chunk of dirt crumbled under my foot, disappearing over the edge. "Aaagh!" I froze, heart hammering against my ribs.

"Here." Noah reached back, hand extended. "Take my hand."

I hesitated for a split second before grabbing it. His palm was warm and calloused, fingers wrapping securely around mine. The simple touch sent tingles racing up my arm.

"I've got you," he said. "Just follow my lead."

We inched forward, my other hand trailing along the rock face for additional security. Noah's grip remained steady, grounding me as we picked our way across the narrow section. Despite the chill mountain air, heat bloomed where our skin touched.

"Almost there," Noah murmured. His thumb brushed across my knuckles, sending another wave of goosebumps dancing up my arms.

I was grateful he was focused on the trail ahead and couldn't see my reaction. This was ridiculous. I was a grown woman; an accidental touch shouldn't have affected me like that. But something about the quiet confidence in his movements, the gentle strength in his grip ...

"A few more steps."

Noah pulled me to wider ground, but he didn't immediately let go. For one suspended moment, we stood connected, my pulse thrumming in my ears.

"Why are you looking at me like that?" I asked, my voice barely audible over the rustling leaves.

Noah's eyes were wolf-like. Not wolf-dog like, I mean full-on wolf. Like a predator, intense and penetrating.

"I'm not looking at you. I'm looking above you." His piercing blue eyes angled over my head. "Turn around." He pointed toward a tree branch.

"See it?" asked Noah, reverent like we were in church. "It's a Northern Goshawk. They're incredibly rare in this area."

I squinted up at the branch, making out what looked like ... well, a bird. Brown. Feathery. Basically identical to every other bird I'd ever seen. By that point, my feet ached, my hair was plastered to my neck with sweat, and I couldn't muster the enthusiasm for any nature appreciation.

"Cute." I pulled out my phone and snapped a few pictures, zooming in as close as I could. "I think I'll call it Kevin."

Noah's expression shifted from delight to disbelief as I began typing into my phone. "You're naming it?"

"Of course."

Then, from disbelief to disgust.

"To be a social media sensation, it has to have a name. Have you ever seen all those Grumpy Cat videos?" Noah made a face. "That's the one." I typed into my phone some more. "Nobody cares about a random bird. Everybody loves Kevin."

"It's a protected species," said Noah, jaw clenched. "But sure, let's call it Kevin."

"What, so you're the only one who gets to name animals around here?" I asked, still typing.

"No. Yes. What are you even talking about?"

I pointed at the wolf-dog. "You named that particular animal Yeti."

"She's a dog."

"So?"

"So?"

"So wolf dogs get names but birds don't?"

"She's not a wolf dog, she's a dog dog."

"You're trying to change the subject."

"I don't even know what the subject is!"

"The subject is our friend Kevin, the Northern Goshawk." I held up my phone, turning the screen around so Noah could see it. "Kevin now has his own TikTok account, Instagram page, YouTube channel, and ..." I turned my phone back around so I could read the numbers. "Two hundred and seventy-two dollars in donations to the Northern Goshawk Conservation Fund, thanks to his GoFundMe."

Noah opened his lips to say something, then snapped his mouth shut. He spun on his heels and stomped down the trail.

Waving toward the distant tree, I yelled, "Bye, Kevin!" I made sure to yell it loudly enough for Noah to hear me.

* * *

More hiking.

Then, more after that.

And finally ... more hiking.

When we took a quick break to sip some water, Yeti took off into the woods to chase a squirrel or something.

"Is she going to be okay?" I asked. "Taking off on her own?"

Noah watched as she disappeared into the trees. "She knows these mountains better than I do. But she always comes back when I need her."

We'd stopped on a part of the trail where there was a break in the trees. A long-range mountain view stretched out in front of me. "Since we're stopped, I might as well grab some more authentic Colorado content."

I began executing my tried-and-true arsenal of selfie poses, nailing the perfect casual-yet-adventurous vibe. In the reflection of my phone screen, I caught Noah studying me. His expression sat somewhere between fascination and dismay. More-so dismay.

"You know, if you want to capture the authentic Colorado, maybe you should take more pictures of actual Colorado instead of pictures of yourself all the time. You're not the only pretty thing to look at around here."

I looked up from my phone, surprised. "You think I'm pretty?"

Noah frowned, realizing what he'd said. His expression closed like a steel trap. "I didn't say that."

"So you don't think I'm pretty?"

"I didn't say that either." A flush of color spread across his cheekbones like a sunrise over the mountains. Noah Barrett was BLUSHING!

"Am I not mountainy enough for you?"

"What? No."

"Is it because I wax my underarms?"

"No."

"Is it because I *don't* wax my underarms when I don't have to go anywhere?"

"NO."

"I know. It's because I don't wear enough flannel."

"If you're trying to annoy the shit out of me, you can stop now, because it worked."

I decided to let him off the hook, though I admit it was tempting to keep going. "Fine. Since you're the authentic Colorado expert, what else did you have in mind?"

"Well ..." Noah scanned the surrounding wilderness, his eyes looking everywhere except at me. Lighting up, he crouched beside a cluster of yellow flowers that looked like miniature sunbursts. "This is Arnica Montana. Native healers used it for centuries before it became commercialized."

"So to highlight the beauty of the state of Colorado, you want me to feature a flower named after the state of Montana?"

Noah ignored my brilliant observation, crouching down beside a clump of purple petals. "This is wild bergamot. The bees love it." His voice was less gruff, more animated. Almost like he was ... human. "The entire ecosystem depends on these native species." He gestured at various plants with the enthusiasm of a little boy showing off his favorite toys. "This yarrow here can ..."

"Wait, did you say yarrow? As in the stuff they put in face creams?"

"Face creams?"

"This is perfect." I dropped into a crouch beside him, the soreness in my legs temporarily forgotten. "Clean beauty is huge right now." I started framing shots of the delicate white flowers, their lacy patterns forming perfect geometric clusters. "I love the whole ancient wisdom meets modern beauty angle. That's good." I waggled my finger at him. "You're good."

Noah's eyebrows drew together like storm clouds. "These aren't ingredients for beauty products. They're vital parts of a complex ecosystem."

"Right, right, of course. Vital. Ecosystem. Got it." I took a selfie with the yarrow, giving my followers a thumbs up and a wink.

Noah sighed loudly, then started back up the trail. I finished another selfie, then scurried to catch up.

We hiked some more; the trail getting steeper and the elevation gain taking its toll. It wasn't long before my lungs were on fire. My feet were on fire. My glutes were on fire. *Maybe Noah would rub them for me.* Great, now my libido was on fire too.

"Remind me ..." I gasped, struggling to catch up. "Remind me to restart my Pilates membership when I get back home to Los Angeles."

Noah glanced back. "Pilates?" It was the first word he'd said to me since the yarrow incident.

"Yeah, I know."

"I thought exercise wasn't really your thing."

"It isn't. Really, any physical activity whatsoever. My thing is watching reality television on my couch and eating pistachio ice cream."

"Sounds about right." Noah paused, allowing me to catch up. "How'd *you* end up in a Pilates class?"

"It was a birthday gift from my boyfriend." I stopped, hands on my knees, most bodily functions failing. "Should've ... *huff* ... kept it ... *puff* ... up."

"Your boyfriend gave you Pilates classes for your birthday?"

"Real thoughtful, right?" I wiped sweat from my forehead. "Pretty sure he just wanted me to lose weight."

"Your boyfriend sounds like an ass."

"Oh, he is totally. Called me 'fluffy' once. Complained when I ordered dessert. Said my food posts were enabling unhealthy habits."

Noah's face was a blank slate. I wondered what was going on behind those bright blue eyes. "No wonder you didn't bring him along on your little mountain adventure."

"Hard to bring someone who's too busy boning their new girlfriend." I tried to laugh, but it came out more like a wheeze.

"New girlfriend? As in, not you?"

"Not me, no. Definitely not me."

"What happened? I mean, besides the Pilates thing."

"I brought chicken noodle soup over to his apartment."

"He hates chicken soup that much?" Noah's face looked like he was trying to calculate an algebra equation. Or figure out why people like Benson Boone songs.

"Long story." I managed to get my torso upright. "The important thing is I made a commitment never to make another commitment again." I whacked a small rock with my hiking stick, allowing myself a brief moment of joy by visualizing the rock as my ex's head. "Dating is overrated anyway. Like hiking. Shouldn't we get going? I'm sure you have better things to do than hear about my tragic and traumatic love life." Reminiscing with Grumpy Mountain Flannel Pants about my past was not something I wanted to do. Even if it meant more hiking.

"I'm just trying to connect the dots between chicken soup and declaring a life of celibacy."

"You really want to know?" I braced myself for a snide comment or another insult.

Instead, Noah simply said, "Yes."

I relaxed my grip on my trekking poles. "We were supposed to go see a limited showing of my favorite movie, *Titanic*, but he said he was coming down with something and wasn't up for it. So, me being the daughter of my mom, decided to fix everything with chicken soup." I kicked another rock down a cliff, imagining my ex's screams as if it'd been him. "When I walked into his apartment ... well, I guess he was up for other things, apparently."

"He was with someone else?"

"With someone ... that's one way to put it."

For once, the grumpy look on Noah's face didn't seem to be directed at me. His eyes narrowed. There was tenseness in his jaw. "Good thing he didn't come with you."

"Why do you say that?"

"Cause he'd be hanging off the edge of a cliff right about now. Or Yeti would have eaten him." Right on cue, the wolf-dog emerged from the woods, prancing back over to join us. "Here." He reached for my backpack straps.

"What are you doing?" I clutched them tighter.

"We need to move faster if we're going to catch the sunrise." He gently pulled the pack from my shoulders. "It's not much further anyway."

"I can carry my own ..."

"Samantha. Sam." His voice was firm, but not unkind.

"You're going to want to get set up and have your phone ready before the sun pops up over the mountains. Trust me."

I released my grip on the straps, watching as he slung my pack over his shoulder like it was stuffed with feathers.

"So, *Titanic,* huh?"

"Mass tragedy seems to resonate with me. That, and Leonardo DiCaprio."

"It's Brie's favorite too. She made me watch it like a thousand times."

"Wow. Were you going for some sort of Brother of the Year nomination or something? Clothes shopping and movie watching with your little sister?"

"Something like that." Noah smiled, but it didn't quite reach his eyes. "You ready?"

"Ready as I'll ever be."

"Then let's go get your first good look at authentic Colorado."

Chapter Fifteen

W e emerged from the treeline into an open clearing, and I froze. The sky blazed with streaks of amber and rose as the first rays of sunlight crept over the jagged edge of the horizon. My hands trembled as I fumbled for my phone.

"Oh my God," I whispered, peering through my phone's viewfinder to make sure I was capturing it all. The mountains stretched endlessly, snow-capped peaks catching fire in the light of dawn. Wisps of clouds turned to spun gold, and the valley below us filled with a purple haze. "Stay right there," I said, backing up a few steps.

This time, Noah didn't dodge away when I pointed the camera in his direction. He stood at the edge of the clearing, Yeti sitting proudly beside him, both of them silhouetted against the blazing sky.

I captured dozens of photos, then switched to video. The sun continued its slow climb, painting everything in impossible colors, as if cast from a wizard's spell. The mountains stretched endlessly, each peak wearing a different crown of clouds.

"Victoria wanted authentic content? Wait until she sees this," I said. "She's going to lose her mind."

I couldn't even believe what I was seeing through my camera lens. I began calculating the number of likes and shares in my head.

"You're missing it, you know," said Noah.

I looked at him through my viewfinder. "Missing what?"

"The actual view." Noah walked over and gently nudged my phone down out of my face. He put both hands on my shoulders and turned me around. "See?"

I did see. Looking at everything in front of me, unfiltered, took things to a whole other level.

"What do you think?"

"This is ..." All I could manage was a nod, rendered speechless by mountains and sky bigger than any post could capture, more beautiful than any caption could describe.

"Beautiful." Noah finished, his voice soft beside me.

"Yeah," I said simply. "This might be the most beautiful thing I've ever seen."

"Worth getting up at four AM?" Noah asked, finally pulling his hands away from my shoulders.

"Totally." Even though they'd only been there a few seconds, the absence of his touch was like missing a limb.

We just stood there for a moment, side by side.

Not talking. Barely breathing.

Just soaking up the scene.

Placing my hand over my eyes to shield them from the sun, I saw something in the distance. "What's that?" It looked like a small wooden structure on the side of a mountain, nestled amongst the trees. "People live out here?"

"That's an old fishing cabin. There's a bunch of them scattered all over the mountain."

"I bet the view with your morning coffee doesn't suck. People rent them out?"

"Used to. They were part of the original lodge before Luxe-Life shut 'em all down."

"Why would they shut them down?"

"No gourmet kitchen," he quipped. "Also, no running water. Victoria didn't think her LuxeLife clientele would appreciate roughing it."

The parallel between the old cabins and the Adventure Center hung in the brisk mountain air between us. Noah didn't say anything. But he didn't have to. It was a good reminder of why we were even out there to begin with.

The sun fully crested the mountain ridge, bathing everything in golden light. I couldn't stop staring at the way it caught the edges of the clouds, turning them into floating rivers of fire.

"I better get some more pictures."

"Good idea."

When Noah stepped away, I was suddenly very much aware of the altitude. It felt like all the oxygen got sucked right off the top of the mountain. It took all my mental fortitude to pull my eyes away when he knelt down on the ground beside his backpack. You know, so I wouldn't accidentally *on purpose* stare at his perfectly shaped butt.

While I grabbed more content, Noah rustled through his backpack, pulling out a collapsible bowl and filling it with water for Yeti. The wolf-dog lapped it up enthusiastically, spraying water in every direction. When she was finished, she bounded back into the trees, presumably patrolling our perimeter for squirrels. Or chipmunks. Or disco chickens.

"What about you, you thirsty? Hungry?" Noah pulled a black and red plaid blanket from his pack.

"Starving, actually." My stomach growled at the thought, a rumble fierce enough to give Yeti a run for her money.

Noah spread the blanket on a relatively flat patch of ground, then pulled several foil-wrapped bundles from the depths of his backpack. I caught the scent of fresh herbs and warm butter.

"Did you get those from the resort?" I asked as he laid out what looked like breakfast burritos and fresh fruit.

"Nope. I made them fresh this morning."

"You made these?" They looked even better than they smelled. Crispy toasted tortillas on the outside, gooey melted cheese oozing from the middle.

"Can't hike on an empty stomach." Noah kept a careful distance as he unscrewed a thermos. "Coffee?"

"God, yes." I reached for it, but he pulled back.

He shook his head. "I like these hiking boots too much to risk them."

"That was one time ..."

"Three times actually."

Noah poured the steaming liquid into a metal cup, maintaining a safe distance as he handed it over. "Better blow on it first. It's hot."

"I'm not completely helpless, you know." But I blew on it a couple of times anyway, the rich aroma making my mouth water.

Noah sat at one end of the blanket, pouring himself a cup of coffee from the thermos, and I sat at the opposite corner.

"I have to admit, this sure beats my usual breakfasts," I said, taking a sip. The coffee was still hot, but not so hot that I felt the urge to spit it on him.

"Your fancy LA restaurants don't do sunrise picnics?"

"Usually just avocado toast with microgreens, or carefully arranged açai bowls." I unwrapped the burrito, taking a small bite that turned into a bigger one. The eggs were perfectly seasoned, spicy, but not too spicy, and chunks of potato mixed with green chilies, black beans, and salsa. The symphony of flavors exploded on my taste buds.

"This is incredible," I said between bites. "Who are you, Gordon Ramsey? Or did you get the recipe from TikTok?"

"It was my mom's recipe, actually."

"Well, tell her I approve."

Noah only smiled, taking another bite of his food.

"Most guys I know can barely make instant ramen. Although Parker makes a mean ramen mac and cheese."

As Noah looked off into the distance, the morning light caught his profile, highlighting the sharp line of his jaw. He had a small scar near his temple I hadn't noticed before. Somehow, it made his rugged look even more rugged.

"I'm not giving you the rest of mine if that's why you're staring at me."

"I'm not staring."

"Mm-hmm."

I stuffed my mouth with burrito, a brilliant maneuver to avoid coming up with an excuse for staring at him again.

"Save room for dessert?" Noah asked.

"I always have room for dessert," I said, mouth still full.

Noah reached in his backpack, pulled out two tightly wrapped mounds. He handed one to me, and I caught the slightest hesitation, not uncertainty about giving it to me, but something that looked almost like anticipation.

I peeled back the foil to discover a perfectly baked muffin, light and fluffy on the inside with a sugar-crusted top, bursting with bluish - purple berries. The smell was life-altering.

"Blueberry?"

"Huckleberry." Noah pointed into the distance. "Picked from the side of that mountain right over there."

I took a bite and the spongy deliciousness melted on my

tongue. The flavor was complex, tart, and sweet all at once. "This is incredible."

"Wild berry flavors are more intense, so I balance the tartness with maple syrup and orange zest."

"You bake and you zest?" He wasn't just throwing ingredients together; he actually knew what he was doing.

"I guess I'm full of surprises." He poured more coffee into my cup, his movements precise and careful. When his fingers brushed mine for a split second, he didn't pull away immediately. The touch lingered just long enough to send a jolt through my arm that had nothing to do with the caffeine.

"So," I ventured, watching him over the rim of my cup. "Does someone special ever buy you Pilates lessons? Because these muffins suggest hidden depths."

His shoulders stiffened beneath his flannel, fingers tightening around the wrapper. "Nope."

"Come on, a guy who can cook and bake like that? There must be a story."

"There isn't." But one look into those blue eyes of his and I could tell that there was.

"If you say so."

"I do say so."

"So now it's been said." That made him smile. Almost.

We sat in silence. Eating muffins. Drinking coffee. I saw small signs I'd missed before. The way Noah checked my reaction to each bite. The way his jaw relaxed slightly when I smiled.

"Why are you being nice to me?"

"I'm not being nice."

"In most civilized societies, baking muffins for someone is generally considered an act of niceness."

"Act of niceness? That's not even a thing." He took another sip of coffee and looked off into the trees.

I Burned My Tongue in Colorado

I whipped out my phone, fingers tapping across the screen. Noah watched me out of the corner of his eye. "There. 'Act of niceness.' Now it's a thing." I showed him my phone — a picture of a muffin-holding Noah with the hashtag #actofniceness.

"Incredible."

"Thank you."

"I meant it in a bad way."

"What? Does doing something nice go against your Grumpy Mountain Man Code?"

"I'm just here to do my job. A job you forced me into, by the way."

"So, then you make breakfast for all your hiking companions?"

"This whole thing was Maya's idea, remember?" Storm clouds gathered in his eyes.

"So Maya made you be nice."

"Did you think you were special?" He flinched. Almost as if the words had been as much of a surprise to him as they were to me.

"Of course not."

It seemed like it came out harsher than he was expecting, but, nevertheless, Noah doubled down. "You and I have a business arrangement. I help you. You help me. End of story." It was like he wasn't just reminding me; he was reminding himself.

"Noah, wait. I didn't mean ..."

But he was already moving, stuffing the trash into a carry-out bag. Screwing the top back on the thermos with enough elbow grease to seal it permanently. "We should head back." He practically yanked the end of the blanket out from under me, stuffing it back into his pack. "The trail gets busy later in the morning, and we don't want to be stuck out here any longer than we have to.

"Noah ..."

"I'm sure you've got better things to do. I know I do."

My heart sank as he whistled for Yeti, his wolf-dog happily frolicking after a butterfly. For a moment there, I thought we were actually getting along. No coffee was spilled. No one had been stranded. Maybe, possibly, something even more than just "getting along."

I sat there for a moment wondering what I had done wrong. Noah didn't even look back as he slung his pack over his shoulder and headed back down the trail. Just like that, Grumpy Noah was back and grumpier than ever.

The rest of the hike stretched in silence, broken only by our footsteps and Yeti's occasional snuffling in the underbrush. Just as eager to get back as he was, I matched Noah's pace, despite the aches and pains. At least the descent felt easier with the sun warming my shoulders and the wind at my back.

When the Jeep finally appeared through the trees, Noah still hadn't spoken another word to me. Clearly, I'd stepped on a landmine I hadn't known existed in our conversational battlefield.

I headed for the passenger door handle, but Noah beat me to it, stopping me in my tracks with another glare.

"I know, I know, you're not being a gentleman."

"It sticks," he grunted, throwing his shoulder into the metal. The door groaned in protest before popping open with a screech that sounded like bear claws on a chalkboard. "There."

"Charming vehicle you've got here. You do know you can buy a new one of these, right?"

"New doesn't mean better." Noah stepped aside so I could wiggle into my seat, another feat of strength and skill that would have benefited from continued Pilates lessons.

Yeti jumped into the back, and Noah slid behind the wheel, stabbing his key into the ignition like a knife. He turned it. The engine made a sad whirring sound.

"Shit."

Another turn had the same result.

"Shit, shit, shit."

After the third time, the whirring was followed by a loud CLICK that seemed to echo through the forest.

Noah closed his eyes. Perhaps praying. Probably cursing.

"Come on, girl." He tried one more time. More whirring, more clicking, then the solemn silence of mechanical betrayal.

I looked over. "That doesn't sound good."

Noah threw me a look that could have flash frozen a mountain river.

"When's the last time you had this thing serviced? Or is this part of your normal client hiking experience, too?"

"Must have jarred a wire loose when we hit one of those bumps." He popped the hood and jumped out.

While Noah checked the engine, I checked my phone. No bars again. "Great."

Yeti leaned forward into the front half of the Jeep, tail wagging, slobber drooling, as Noah messed under the hood. He muttered words I couldn't hear but could definitely categorize.

"Try it now!" he called.

I pushed Yeti's face out of the way and slid over to the driver's seat. I turned the key. Nothing.

"Again!"

Click.

Click.

Click.

The sound of imminent doom.

Noah slammed the hood shut. "Battery's dead. You turned the light off when you finished looking in the mirror, right?"

"Um..." Before our hike, I'd asked Noah if I could turn on the interior light to check my makeup in the mirror. "I thought it turned off automatically?"

"Does this vehicle look like it has automatic anything?"

I couldn't post selfies with an imperfect face, could I? I made the wise choice not to say that part out loud. "Good thing you brought those flares with you, huh?" I mimed a flare shot, or at least my imagining of what shooting off a flare would look like, since I'd never actually done it.

Noah's eyebrows sank even lower. "We're not using the flares."

"Satellite phone then?"

Noah came around to my side of the Jeep and yanked the door back open, the metal protesting like it was being summoned from the dead. "We're not calling for help either."

"Air lift it is."

Noah pointed to an opening in the trees, a narrow path barely visible through the undergrowth. "We walk."

"Great. More hiking." To say Noah was unsympathetic would have been generous.

"Come on, Yeti." The wolf-dog sprang from the back of the Jeep as if she'd been waiting for this opportunity her entire life. She plunged down the path, a wolf-dog on a mission.

Noah grabbed both backpacks from the rear, slinging them over one shoulder. "Good thing you changed those shoes."

Chapter Sixteen

You know those movies where the hero and heroine hack their way through the dense jungle with a machete, dodging spiders, bouncing witty banter back and forth, the sexual tension rising all along the way?

It was nothing like that.

First, we didn't have a machete, which meant random branches kept whacking me in the face. Next, there was no banter, witty or otherwise. And sexual tension? Please. We didn't even act the part of a hero and heroine. Noah did a lot of grumping. I mostly whined.

The spider part though? That was spot-on.

"Are we there yet?" Another branch jabbed me in the leg.

Noah didn't answer. He'd stopped responding after the tenth time I'd asked the same thing.

Foot-tripping roots and ankle-busting stumps peppered the tangled underbrush as we made our way further down the overgrown trail. Mosquitoes swarmed over me like dark clouds of miniature vampires. Somewhere in the distance, a woodpecker drummed against a tree, searching for lunch. Or it was telling its bear friends where to find us in Morse code.

I stopped to pick a thorn out of my sock. "You know that poem they make you read in English class? The one about taking the road less traveled?"

Noah smacked a mosquito off his cheek. "Robert Frost."

"Yeah. That one."

Noah cleared his throat. His poetry voice was deep and sexy. "Two roads diverged in a wood, and I took the one less traveled by, and that has made all the difference."

"Yeah. That guy was full of shit." I ducked under a fallen log, making sure there wasn't a snake waiting to jump on my head first.

Noah flicked another mosquito off his ear. "For once, we can agree."

Eventually, the less-traveled road merged onto something more traveled. The ground was even, and you didn't have to step over a log every couple of steps. We even started seeing other people.

"Are you having some sort of medical emergency?" Noah stopped when he heard me grunting. "I'm not giving you mouth-to-mouth."

"I'd rather choke than let you give me mouth-to-mouth."

"Choking is the Heimlich. Where you grab the person and squeeze."

"Well, I'd rather choke than let you grab me or squeeze me." I thrashed back and forth, trying to reach the spot on my back where it felt like my skin caught on fire. "Something's biting me!" I ripped my shirt off over my head, then used it to flay myself.

Thwack ... Thwack

"For Christ's sake. Here, let me see."

Noah grabbed my shoulders and spun me around. I was so

freaked out by whatever was burrowing into my flesh, probably to lay its larvae or something, the fact that he now had a close-up view of my purple sports bra didn't even bother me.

"Oh, oh." His hands dropped from my shoulders.

"Oh, oh? Oh, oh what? What is it? What do you see?" I twisted around but couldn't see anything.

"It's fine. I just need you to stay calm and stay still." I heard him unzip his backpack.

"Wait. What is it? What's back there?"

"Like I said, just stay calm."

"Don't you know if you want somebody to stay calm, the last thing you say to them is 'stay calm?'"

Noah pulled out a knife. It was one of those big knives, with one side that looked like shark teeth. I yelped, taking a step backward and holding my hands up in surrender.

"If I wanted to stab you, I would have done it by now. Hold still."

Before I could even protest, Noah turned me back around and pressed the blunt edge of the blade against my back. He scraped along my skin.

"There."

The burning spot didn't burn as much. "You got it? What was it?"

"Nothing to worry about. Probably."

"Again, if you don't want someone to worry, don't tell them 'nothing to worry about.'" I whipped back around. "Show it to me."

Noah held up the blade of the knife. "Rocky Mountain wood tick. See?" It looked like a small, reddish-brown speck. "Hey maybe you should name it?" At least he was grinning again.

"How about Noah? Since it's so irritating and obnoxious."

"Don't forget blood sucking."

"Oh, he definitely sucks."

Noah's grin got a little wider. "Okay. I guess I deserved that one. Turn back around and I'll patch you up."

I did, and he did, pulling the first aid kit out of his backpack.

"Bet you're glad we brought our emergency supplies now." His touch was gentle as he dabbed a bead of salve on the itchy spot, then placed a bandage over the bite. As his fingers traced over the surface of my skin, the electric jolts zapping through my nerves made me forget all about the tick attack. "Better?"

"Better." When I turned around, we were standing face to face. His lips were inches from mine.

Those lake-blue eyes flicked downward, toward the place where my sports bra hugged my breasts, sweat slick on my skin. The look was so quick it was almost as if it didn't happen. But it did.

Noah's teeth dug into his bottom lip. "You should probably put your shirt back on."

"Probably."

Neither of us moved.

"Wouldn't want you to get another tick."

"That would suck."

"I'd have to pull it off you again."

"Really suck."

Still, we didn't move.

"Everything okay here?" A woman's concerned voice made us jump. A family of four marched down the trail, decked out in serious hiking gear. Trekking poles, backpacks, the works.

The mom and the dad fixed their eyes on Noah's knife, still poised in front of me. The two kids, who looked about the same age as my cousin's six-year-old, both stared at my bra.

"Mom, she's not wearing her shirt," hissed the little girl.

The boy just kept staring.

I quickly pulled my hiking shirt back over my torso, and Noah sheathed his knife.

"You okay, miss?" asked the father.

"I'm fine," I told them. "It's not what it looks like. I'm not exactly sure what this looks like. But it's not that."

The mom and dad looked unconvinced.

Noah reached out and snatched my hand, squeezing it tight. "Just a happy couple," he explained. "In love." Noah leaned over and kissed my cheek.

"Oh. Yes. Right," I said, squeezing his hand harder. "My boyfriend was just showing off his big knife. Probably overcompensating for something." I looked at the mom. "Am I right?"

The mom raised an eyebrow.

The little boy kept staring at my chest.

"Come on, kids, let's let these two lovebirds get back to their ..." The dad couldn't seem to come up with the right word to finish. He corralled his wife and two children, then scurried down the trail.

As soon as they were gone, I immediately flung Noah's hand away and repeatedly wiped the spot where he'd kissed me with the back of my hand.

"You slobber worse than Yeti."

"For someone whose job it is to promote skin stuff, I figured your cheek would have been softer." Noah scooped up the backpacks and started back down the trail.

"By the way, your breath smells worse than Yeti's, too," I called after him.

* * *

The Adventure Center's timber roof came into view, and if I'd had any energy left, I would have done one of those little jumps in the air where you tap your heels together in celebration. Like in a freeze frame at the end of a movie. But I didn't have any energy left, so I simply followed Yeti and Noah into the parking lot.

"Last chance to carry me," I called to Noah's retreating backside.

He stopped and turned, face as grumpy as ever. "You managed to hike almost four miles. I think you can handle another twenty feet."

"My feet have turned into bloody stumps."

Noah dug into the backpack. "Here." He tossed me the first-aid kit. When I didn't make any effort to catch it, it clattered on the ground.

"Just in case you were wondering, I'm giving you a one-star review on every mountain man travel app I can find," I called after him.

"You know, the longer you stay like that, the stiffer you're gonna get," he called back.

"Is that a medical opinion? Because I'm pretty sure the only cure for this level of exhaustion is being carried."

Ignoring my dire state, Noah walked back into the building, his effortless stride showing no sign of the fact that we'd basically just duplicated Lewis and Clark's entire trek to the Pacific and back.

Eventually, I dragged myself through the Adventure Center's doors on my own two feet.

Jenn glanced up from her paperwork at the front desk with a smile.

Diego paused in sorting a pile of life jackets when he saw me. "Damn it." He stomped over and slapped a twenty-dollar bill in front of Jenn.

"What was that for?"

"Nothing," both Jenn and Diego said together.

I Burned My Tongue in Colorado

"Well, look who survived Dawn Patrol." Maya emerged from the back.

"Barely." I slumped against the counter. "Noah tried to murder me in at least seven different ways."

"Only seven?" Jenn returned to her paperwork. "Noah must be going soft."

"Seriously, how'd it go?" Maya asked, wincing at my worn appearance.

"Well, first, Noah made me climb what had to be the steepest mountain in Colorado. Then he forced me to carry this massive backpack that weighed more than my entire luggage collection." I ticked off each offense on my fingers. "He wouldn't let me rest, rushed me through my content creation, and made me trek through tick-infested wilderness."

"Yeah, those things are nasty," said Diego. "Whatever you do, don't let them on you. They carry all kinds of diseases."

"They do? What kind of diseases?"

"Well, there's Colorado tick fever," said Jenn.

"Rocky Mountain Spotted Fever," added Diego.

"Don't forget tick paralysis," said Maya.

"Tick paralysis?" I tested my limb function.

"Don't listen to them. You're fine." Noah dropped his pack by the desk with a thud. "Probably."

"And don't even get me started on the death march shortcut through the woods after YOUR Jeep broke down." I turned back to Jenn. "Which, by the way, was absolutely not my fault."

"The interior light you left on would disagree," Noah muttered.

"See what I have to deal with?" I thumbed at Noah over my shoulder. "Pure evil in flannel and hiking boots."

Diego laughed, abandoning his gear sorting completely. "Sounds like a typical Noah morning to me."

"At least the muffins were good. Almost made the whole thing worth it. Almost."

"Wait," Jenn said, her pen freezing mid-air. "Muffins? What muffins?"

"He said they were huckleberry." I turned to Maya. "Huckleberries aren't poisonous, are they?" She shook her head.

"Noah baked you his huckleberry muffins?" Jenn's and Diego's eyes both snapped to Noah with synchronized precision.

Noah pointed at Maya. "That was her idea. She was the one who suggested I give her the full experience."

"Mmm-hmm." Jenn's smile only grew wider.

"If you say so." Diego smiled with her.

"It was her idea." Noah pointed at Maya. "Tell them."

Maya held up her hands innocently. "All I did was suggest he might want to bring some snacks in case Sam didn't get a chance to eat breakfast first. Which I thought was a pretty safe bet since they left at 4:00am."

Maya, Jenn, and Diego all smiled at Noah, while he scowled at all of them.

"Well, I appreciated the gesture, even if it was Maya's idea," I said. "I would come over there and thank you properly, but I can't feel my legs. Tomorrow, we should take a break from mountain adventuring so I can recover. I'll just spend the day thoroughly documenting the spa."

"Excellent idea," said Noah. "I can spend the day recovering my sanity."

"Yeah, that's not happening," said Maya, a dangerous gleam in her eyes. "Victoria wants authentic Colorado content, and that's exactly what you're going to give her."

"But I don't think I'll be able to walk tomorrow. Seriously. In fact, I may be crippled for life."

"No problem," said Noah. "I know an authentic Colorado

adventure you can take, and you won't have to walk a single step."

A sense of dread washed over me as the hint of a smile crept over Noah's face. "Why not?"

"Because tomorrow you'll be rafting all day."

"You're taking me rafting?" My eyes widened in horror.

"I'm not taking you anywhere. You'll be in Diego's very capable hands from here."

Diego waved, his expression far too cheerful for someone about to expose themselves to glacier cold river water. "I hope you're a strong swimmer."

I turned back to Noah. "You're not going?" For some reason, the thought of Noah not being there left me feeling strangely disappointed.

"My role in this little authentic Colorado adventure is done. Jenn and Diego will take it from here." Noah started heading out the door. "Come on, Yeti." The wolf-dog padded after him.

"Where are you going?"

"Got to grab my toolkit and go fix the Jeep. Then I've got another tour group after lunch. People who actually appreciate a little outdoor adventure."

"And what am I supposed to do the rest of the day?"

"I don't know. Probably something that involves putting cucumbers on your face." He turned back around and was gone.

"So he really made you muffins?" asked Jenn.

"They were actually delicious," I confessed. "He even used orange zest."

Jenn and Diego exchanged another look, conveying an entire conversation with just their eyes.

Diego leaned forward. "He made you the ones with the orange zest?"

"Yes," I said again. "Why? Doesn't he make muffins for all of his morning tours?"

Jenn nearly spit out her sip of coffee, then started choking.

Diego only shook his head.

"Well, still. Maya made him do it."

Maya shrugged. "Honestly? I figured he'd just bring a couple of stale granola bars."

Chapter Seventeen

Defying the laws of vehicular physics, the resort's activity shuttle wound down a dirt road that grew narrower with every hairpin turn.

"Last stop for river adventures, miss." The shuttle driver pulled into a clearing alongside what I could only assume was the River Styx, where the damned, the doomed, and the dead were ferried off to hell. "Enjoy your float."

"Enjoy my float?" As the shuttle started back down the road, I wondered if it was too late to chase it down and bribe the driver to shuttle me back to California. The only way I was ever going to enjoy any "float" was if it was accompanied by a margarita on a lazy river in Palm Springs.

I smoothed down my brand-new sea foam-colored Lululemon ensemble, a matching sports shirt and leggings combo that had looked perfect in the resort boutique mirror. Then made my way down to the river.

Clear water tumbled over smooth stones, creating a symphony of gurgles and splashes. Towering pines lined both banks, their branches swaying in the morning breeze. Patches of sunlight dappled the water's surface. It was the kind of scene Instagram filters were made for.

"Looking good, Sports Illustrated."

I nearly dropped my phone in the river as Diego came up behind me.

"Too bad no one's going to see it." He held up what appeared to be a black rubber S&M gimp costume, which dripped water and smelled like gym socks.

"What is that?" I wrinkled my nose as Diego thrust the dripping monstrosity toward me.

"Your wetsuit. Unless you prefer hypothermia as your next authentic Colorado adventure. The river runs at about forty-five degrees year-round thanks to the snow melt."

I took the wetsuit between two reluctant fingers, holding it at arm's length. "You do realize we're trying to get people to want to visit this place, not run screaming in the opposite direction?"

Diego waved his hand at my Lululemon ensemble. "That might work for a poolside photo shoot, but the river requires something a bit more ..." He paused, searching for the right word. "Functional."

He handed me a faded orange life jacket that looked like it had been gnawed on by river otters. "Safety first, style second."

Just then, a familiar mechanical death rattle echoed through the canyon. Noah's beat-up Jeep limped into the parking lot, kicking up dust clouds and scarring the retinas of any small woodland creatures within eyesight.

Yeti bounded out first, making a beeline for the river. Noah climbed out after her, his jaw set in that stubborn way I was starting to recognize all too well. A gray henley stretched across his broad chest, and his hair stuck up like he'd been running his hands through it in frustration all morning.

I Burned My Tongue in Colorado

"What are you doing here?" I crossed my arms over my chest. "I thought Diego was leading today's adventure."

"Victoria's orders. Apparently." It may have been Victoria who ordered him to be there, but the tone of his voice made it clear that Noah definitely blamed me.

He grabbed an oar from the back of his Jeep, and for a split second, I thought he was going to whack me over the head with it. Judging from the look on his face, he at least considered it. That's when I noticed a kayak strapped to the roof.

"I guess this makes more sense now." I pulled out my phone and showed him Victoria's text from the middle of the night:

VICTORIA STERLING:

More Mountain Man! 🔥 ⛰️ 🪓 😍 🪓 👻

"Looks like you've got a fan club starting, Hermano."

Noah's face darkened like storm clouds rolling over the mountains. "I'm not here to be anyone's social media prop."

"Could've fooled me." I gestured at his wild hair and grey henley. "Apparently, the whole grumpy mountain man thing is really working for our engagement metrics."

"This isn't a performance." Noah brushed past me as he began unloading his kayak. "This is my life." He wrestled his boat to the ground. "Don't fuck it up."

"So here's the deal," Diego said, pulling a massive two-person kayak off the trailer he and Jenn had brought down earlier that morning. It looked like a bright yellow banana that had spent too much time at the gym. "You'll be riding tandem with me, while Noah follows behind as safety."

"Tandem? As in ... sharing?"

"Unless you think you can navigate Class III rapids all by yourself." Diego patted the yellow plastic beast with affection. "You'll sit in front; I'll steer from the back."

I glanced between the kayak and Noah, who was adjusting

his life vest with sharp, irritated jerks. Great. Not only would I be trapped in a floating banana with Diego, but I'd also have Noah's judgmental stare burning into my back the whole time.

Yeti flopped down on the riverbank, her tongue lolling out in what looked suspiciously like laughter.

"You wanted real Colorado, right?" Diego grinned. "Things are about to get real. Unless you'd rather ride with Noah."

"No," we both said at once.

As I attempted to slither into the unfashionable and clingy wetsuit, pulling it over the top of my easy-fitting and fashionable clothes, I saw Noah fastening a red life vest around Yeti's chest. I pulled out my phone, knowing my followers would devour this content faster than I'd inhaled Noah's huckleberry muffins. "Yeti has her own life jacket? That's adorable."

"Safety first," Noah said, without looking up.

I zoomed in as Noah adjusted the straps with surprising gentleness, making sure they were secure but not too tight, and didn't catch on her fur. His rough, capable hands handled the dog with such care that I felt something squeeze inside my chest. It was another glimpse of an actual human being under the grumpy mountain man exterior.

"Yeti, can you smile for the camera?"

Yeti's mouth dropped open in a happy dog grin, her head cocked and tongue lolling out to one side.

"Perfect!" I snapped several shots. "Such a natural. A much better model than some people." I looked pointedly at Noah, who snorted in return.

"I hope that thing's waterproof."

"Why?" I turned back to Diego. "We're not going to get wet, are we?"

Diego exchanged a look with Noah, and they both erupted into laughter, the sound echoing across the river. He pointed at my rubber suit. "You do realize they call it a wetsuit for a reason."

"Here." Noah stepped over and handed me a clear plastic bag with a seal and a latch on top. "Put it in there, and it'll be fine." His fingers brushed mine during the handoff, sending an electric jolt up my arm.

I considered pointing out that the plastic bag would affect the picture quality, but realized the only person who would care was me.

"Actually, you know what would work better?" Diego tapped his chin. "Noah should take your phone while he follows in the safety kayak. He'll get the best angles of us from the water."

I clutched my phone tighter against my chest. "What? No." The thought of Noah handling my precious lifeline, and primary work tool, made my pulse skyrocket.

"Victoria wants authentic Colorado content, right? Can't get more authentic than shooting from river-level. And that way, your followers get to see the real you. The *authentic* you."

"Can't exactly film while you're paddling," said Noah, surprisingly going along with the crazy idea.

"Why can't Diego do it?"

"Diego needs to focus on steering," Noah pointed out.

I bit my lip. They had a point. And the footage would be incredible, assuming my phone survived. And I survived. "Why don't you just use your phone?" I asked Noah.

Noah dug in his pocket and pulled out what looked like a prehistoric flip phone, the kind used by cavemen right after they evolved from drawing dinosaurs on cave walls. It was wrapped in a plastic baggie and sealed with a rubber band. "You mean this?" It was hard to tell through the plastic, but it looked like duct tape might have been involved.

"Fine," I said, stuffing my not-yet-paid-off iPhone into Noah's outstretched hand. "Just remember, safety first."

"Let's talk hip control." Diego planted his feet shoulder-width apart on the rocky shore. "The key to not flipping is all in the hips." Diego launched into what had to be the most morti-fying safety demonstration of all time, swaying his hips back and forth like he was auditioning for *Magic Mike: Colorado Edition*. Like something best performed on a stripper pole, wearing a crotchless g-string. Which, as you know, I had.

"You'll want to feel the motion of the river," Diego contin-ued, rotating his pelvis in ways that would make Elvis blush. "Work with it, not against it."

Mercifully, Diego stopped thrusting, then looked at me expectantly. "Now you try."

"Me?"

"I need to make sure you're not going to flip us." Handing me the paddle, Diego said, "Don't worry. No one's judging you."

Noah leaned leisurely against a pine tree, arms crossed over his broad chest. He was definitely judging me.

I tried to imitate Diego's stance and movements, feeling like I was having some sort of neurological event rather than preparing for water sports. Every time I shook, Diego's frown deepened. Every time I tried to shimmy, Diego looked like he'd sniffed a rotten egg.

"Your angle's still off," Noah called out. "The movement's gotta come from your core."

I thought I detected a hint of a smile on his lips. If I hadn't known better, I'd have thought he was enjoying this. It seemed the grumpy, grouchy mountain man had a sense of humor. It just happened to run on my humiliation.

"Here." Diego grabbed my shoulders. "Pretend you're dancing. Just go with the flow."

I Burned My Tongue in Colorado

"I don't dance."

"Everybody dances," said Diego.

"I don't," said Noah from the tree.

"I have an idea." Diego reached into his pocket and pulled out his phone. After a few swipes, Ricky Martin's "Livin' La Vida Loca" began blasting across the riverbank.

"Are you serious?"

"Safety first," said Diego, swaying his hips to the beat with alarming enthusiasm.

I looked at Noah for help, but he provided the opposite. "Safety first," he called.

"The music will help you find the right rhythm." Diego moved around behind me, hands poised just above my hips. "May I?"

I sighed, shoulders slumped in defeat. "Fine." If being able to salsa dance were the key to not drowning, I figured I would play along.

Just before Diego wrapped his hands around my waist, he stopped and pulled back. "Actually, you know what? This stuff is too good not to film. What's more authentically Colorado than salsa dancing?"

"I'm guessing many, many things?"

"Your followers will love it." Diego started a selfie video, salsa dancing around me like a caffeinated flamingo.

"You're messing with me on purpose."

"Me?" Diego feigned affront. "Never."

"We can't have you flipping the kayak just because you didn't practice your hip rotations," agreed Noah.

"Well, at least now I know you care about my well-being." I gave Noah a fake smile.

"Actually, I was more concerned about the kayak."

I gripped my paddle tighter as I resumed wiggling my hips,

calculating the distance between it and Noah's smug face. One quick swing ...

"Less rigid," Diego instructed, still dancing around me. "Loosen up. Feel the flow."

"I'm flowing, I'm flowing," I muttered through clenched teeth, wiggling faster while plotting Noah's watery demise.

"Noah, you come show her." Diego's grin only widened as he panned the camera to Noah. "She needs a hands-on demonstration."

Noah's eyes widened with alarm. "Me? Why me?"

"Because I'm filming."

At first, I thought Noah was going to stomp off into the wilderness, never to be seen again. But instead, he pushed off the tree and started toward us.

"Safety first," Diego sing-songed, while continuing to video the kayak-paddling-salsa lesson.

My heart beat faster with each closing step, breath catching as Noah approached. The morning sun caught the edges of his dark hair, turning them almost golden. My skin tingled with anticipation as I imagined his firm hands settling on my hips, showing me exactly how to move.

Guiding me.

Commanding me.

His long legs ate up the distance between us in seconds. I could almost feel the heat of his body, smell that mix of coffee and pine that seemed to follow him everywhere. My heart hammered against my ribs as he got closer.

Closer ...

But instead of stepping behind me and taking me in his arms, Noah's arm shot out past my shoulder. He snatched Diego's phone with surprising speed, then shoved it back into Diego's front shirt pocket.

I Burned My Tongue in Colorado

"We're burning daylight," Noah growled. "Some of us have real work to do."

All the breath escaped my lungs at once, and my body felt oddly hollow. Which was ridiculous, because I never wanted Noah's hands on me, anyway. In fact, the only thing I wanted from Noah Barrett was for him to stop looking at me like I was something stuck to the bottom of his hiking boot.

"Well," said Diego, clearing his throat. "I guess the dance lesson's over." He hit stop and the muffled music playing from his shirt pocket ended, replaced by the rush of the river.

"Ready to hit the water?"

With the way the various girl parts inside my body were still tingling, perhaps being doused with ice cold water would do me some good. "Ready as I'll ever be."

Chapter Eighteen

The gentle swoosh of our paddles cutting through the water settled into a peaceful rhythm, the tandem kayak gliding over the river's surface. With Diego guiding our movements from behind, I'd somehow managed not to flip us.

"Not bad," Diego called from the back. "You're getting the hang of it."

The air felt impossibly crisp, carrying scents of wild roses from the riverbank. In the distance, a fish jumped, leaving perfect concentric ripples in its wake that would have looked amazing on video feed. If I had my phone. Which I didn't. Because Noah did.

Noah's kayak drifted alongside us. I tried not to notice how his muscles flexed with each paddle stroke, his wetsuit leaving absolutely nothing to the imagination. Water droplets rolled down his forearms, clinging to his skin. I forced myself to look downstream before he caught me staring.

"Look!" Diego pointed skyward where two birds swooped

overhead, diving and wheeling. "Those are ospreys. Fish eagles. See how they hover before diving for prey?"

"They're beautiful." One bird plunged toward the water in a perfect dive. "It looked like they were dancing together in the air."

"Probably a mated pair," said Diego. "They mate for life, returning to the same nest year after year."

The birds wheeled away downstream, and we followed their path along the river's gentle current. The steady rhythm of paddling became almost meditative, my anxiety temporarily forgotten in the unexpected peace of the moment.

"Coming up on our first set of rapids," Noah called from beside us, pulling out my phone to record.

"Just a little baby one to get warmed up," added Diego.

"Define baby." My knuckles whitened on the paddle.

"Super chill. Like barely a ripple. We call it the practice rapid."

The roar of rushing water grew louder. My heart beat faster as we rounded the bend. What appeared ahead did NOT look like practice anything.

"Those are not ripples!" White foam churned over rocks, creating a series of waves that looked decidedly un-chill. "Those are definitely not ..."

The kayak nose dipped into the first wave, and ice-cold water sprayed across my face. I screamed, the sound echoing off the canyon walls like I was auditioning for a horror movie.

"Lean forward!" Diego shouted over my shrieking. "Work with the waves!"

Ricky Martin started playing in my head as I shimmied my hips.

"No, forward, not side to side!"

"But you said ..."

Another splash hit me square in the mouth. I sputtered and coughed, certain we were about to capsize.

A flash of red caught my eye as Noah glided past us, making the waves look like little more than inconvenient speed bumps. He had one hand on his paddle while the other casually held my phone out over the side of his boat. His expression contained the nonchalance of someone watching paint dry rather than navigating what was clearly a death trap.

"Safety first!" I yelled between screams as we bounced through another wave.

Yeti barked happily from Noah's kayak, her tongue flapping in the wind like a victory flag.

"See?" Diego called. "Nothing to it!"

"Everything to it!" The terror in my voice sent a nearby bird airborne. "Everything to ... oh God, another one!"

Water crashed over us again. Through my panic, I caught Noah watching us, that irritating half-smile playing on his lips as he floated backwards. *Backwards!* Like this was a Sunday stroll through the park.

I wiped water from my face, heart still racing from the so-called "practice" rapid. My wetsuit clung to me like plastic wrap, and my hair plastered all over my face.

"I feel like maybe we skipped practice, and you just threw me straight into the deep end," I shouted back at Diego.

"Speaking of deep." Diego's laugh rumbled behind me. "Thunder Drop is coming up next, one of our signature rapids. Class III on a good day."

"Class III?" The numbers meant nothing to me, but 'Thunder' and 'Drop' were not words I wanted to hear in the same sentence while trapped in a floating banana. "That sounds like a ride at Six Flags that makes people throw up."

"Don't worry, I've run these hundreds of times." Diego adjusted our angle with a few quick paddle strokes. "Just remember what we practiced. Lean forward, brace with your knees, and ..."

"Kiss my ass goodbye?" My lungs temporarily forgot to breathe as I spotted the white water churning between massive boulders. The river seemed to disappear completely at one point, dropping away into nothing like one of those infinity pools, except instead of a luxurious view of the mountains, there was just liquid oblivion.

"Oh no. No, no, no." I gripped my paddle so tight my fingers went numb.

"Paddle hard!" Diego shouted. "Keep it steady!"

Noah shot past us again, this time his expression focused and with two hands on the paddle as he charged toward the rapids. Yeti's tail wagged with excitement as they disappeared over the edge.

"Oh, my God."

The current grabbed our kayak and we picked up speed, racing toward certain death. The thunder of falling water grew deafening.

"I changed my mind!" I screamed. "I want to go back to the practice one!"

The roar of rushing water drowned out my words as we approached what looked like a wall of white foam.

"Okay!" Diego's voice carried over the noise. "When I say draw, paddle forward on the right!"

"What?" I twisted around to look at him. The kayak wobbled like a drunk person trying to walk a straight line.

"Eyes front! Draw! Draw!"

I dug my paddle into the left side of the kayak, and we veered sideways toward a boulder that looked suspiciously like a tombstone.

"Other side! Other side!"

I switched, but now we were heading straight for a rock.

The current picked up speed like a roller coaster reaching the top of its track.

"BRACE!"

"What does that even mean?" I shrieked, lifting my paddle high above my head like I was surrendering to the river gods.

"No, no! Down! Put it ..." Diego's instructions cut off as we spun in a complete circle. Water splashed over the sides, soaking my face. I sputtered and blinked rapidly, mascara surely streaming down my cheeks along with my tears. "Focus!" Diego called. "We need to ..." Another spin. "... straighten out!"

I caught glimpses of shore, river, shore, river as we twirled through the white water. My stomach somersaulted with each rotation, my breakfast threatening a dramatic reappearance.

"Just tell me what to do in English!"

"Put your paddle in the water and LEAN. DOWN. STREAM!"

Everything was a blur of motion and cold spray. The kayak slammed into something hard. My world flipped upside down as I hit the freezing water. The current yanked me under, tumbling me like a sock in a washing machine.

River water rushed up my nose, tasting like dirt and fish. My lungs burned. *Which way was up?* The churning water tossed me around like I was trapped inside a tornado in the middle of a hurricane.

"Help!"

My life jacket jerked me toward the surface. I gasped for air, only to get another mouthful of muddy water. Another wave crashed over my head. This was it. I was a goner for sure.

But then through the spray, I glimpsed Noah's red kayak cutting through the rapids. Faster than a charging moose. More powerful than a grizzly bear. Able to leap over tall waves in a single oar stroke.

I Burned My Tongue in Colorado

"Grab the rope!" Noah's steady, deep voice sliced through the roar of the water.

Something slapped against my arm. I clutched the rescue line, and Noah yanked me through the current with smooth, practiced motions. The rough rope burned my palms, but I held on like my life depended on it. Because it did.

Noah guided me to a calm eddy behind a large boulder. His strong hands gripped my life jacket, hauling me up onto his kayak. I sprawled across the bow, coughing up what felt like half the river and possibly a small fish.

"Are you okay?" Noah's face hovered close to mine. Gone was the grumpy mountain man facade. Instead, his brows furrowed with ... what was that ... concern?

His hands steadied me. I could feel their warmth, even through the cold, damp wetsuit. "Sam, are you okay?"

I looked up. We were face to face. Eyes locked. Our mouths, our lips mere inches apart. For a wild moment, I considered telling him I needed mouth-to-mouth resuscitation. I must have hit my head on a river boulder and suffered a concussion.

Suddenly, Yeti's enormous head burst between us, her tongue sweeping across my face.

"Ugh, Yeti!" I sputtered, pushing her furry face away. "I don't know what tastes worse, fish pee or dog slobber."

"Based on personal experience, I'm going to have to go with the dog slobber." Noah's smile lingered, transforming his face completely. It was like someone had flipped a switch, turning the grumpy mountain man into someone who could model for outdoor magazine covers. "Let's get you on solid ground."

Noah paddled us toward the riverbank, a steady hand securing me across the bow of his boat. Diego waited with the recovered tandem kayak. My teeth chattered despite the summer heat, and my designer "water-resistant" mascara turned me into a raccoon with hypothermia.

Noah steadied the kayak against the rocky shore. "Here, let me help you." His hands wrapped around my waist, lifting me as if I weighed next to nothing. My legs wobbled as I touched ground, threatening to collapse.

"I'm f-fine," I stammered, hugging myself for warmth. "Just cold and humiliated."

Noah unzipped his dry bag and pulled out a frayed but dry towel. "Let's get you out of that wetsuit."

My frozen fingers fumbled with the zipper until Noah stepped behind me. "Here." His breath warmed my neck as he helped peel the clingy neoprene down. I tried not to think about how Noah was literally stripping me out of my clothes, or how his hands moved with careful gentleness.

Noah wrapped the towel around my shoulders. Water dripped from his dark hair, and his wet shirt clung to his chest in a way that made my mouth go dry despite my river-drinking experience.

I looked down at my pruned fingers to distract myself, still trembling from the wet and the cold. "Maybe for the rest of our authentic Colorado adventure series we should stick to things that are less adventurous," I said. "Like basket weaving. Or extreme napping."

Just as I was warming up, Yeti trotted over and gave an enthusiastic full-body shake, spraying a fresh wave of river water and wet dog smell.

"Good girl." Noah patted her head like he had trained the beast to do it on purpose.

"Jenn's on her way," Diego called out, pulling the tandem further up the bank. "We'll drop off the kayaks and then she'll take you back to the resort."

Part of me was desperate to get back to civilization. Take a long hot shower, savor a ten-course meal at the resort's gourmet restaurant, then book one of every deluxe massage package down at the spa. And then for the rest of my assignment, maybe Victoria wouldn't notice if I just lay in bed posting stock photos of mountains with inspirational quotes.

But then another part of me didn't want to leave. I was cold. I was wet. I was shivering. But I was also surrounded by beautiful mountains. Standing under a brilliant blue sky. Breathing in the fresh air from the trees. And despite almost dying, I felt alive ... fulfilled.

Noah had nothing to do with it, of course.

Nothing.

Not a thing.

* * *

A cloud of dust announced Jenn's arrival in an ancient pickup truck, which rattled over the dirt road like it was Noah's Jeep's twin. She hopped out, keys jangling against her belt.

"Ready to load up?" She stopped short, eyes darting between my bedraggled state, Noah's protective hovering, and Diego's barely concealed grin. "What the hell happened?"

"Sam had an impromptu swimming lesson," Diego said, throwing the oars into the bed of the truck.

"I hit a rock." I tried to sound nonchalant despite my chattering teeth. "Or maybe the rock hit me. The details are fuzzy."

"And then Noah fished her out," Diego added, exchanging the same look with Jenn they'd had when I told them Noah baked muffins. Maybe the Adventure Center staff developed their own secret language of significant glances.

"Don't sweat it, Sam," said Jenn, patting my shoulder.

"Water was way too cold for any sweating," I reassured her.

"Sometimes the river's got to humble you before it can

teach you anything worth knowing." She turned to Diego. "Come on, let's get the trailer. These boats won't load themselves."

They climbed into the truck, leaving me alone with Noah. The silence stretched between us, broken only by another Yeti shake that sprayed cold droplets in a twenty-foot radius.

"Thank you," I said. "For pulling me out."

"I'm trying to save the Adventure Center, not kill it. Drownings are bad for business."

"Yeah. Those rarely make the brochure."

"You might want to delete all that." Noah handed me back my phone, still dripping from its waterproof plastic bag.

"Oh, trust me, I'm deleting every second." I swiped the screen open, ready to erase any evidence of my river humiliation. The camera app showed the latest recordings, and my stomach dropped. "Oh no. No, no, no."

Noah raised an eyebrow. "What?"

"You left it live streaming." My voice came out as a gasp.

"Live streaming? What's live streaming? All I did was press that red button and point."

"The whole time. Everything." I scrolled through my notifications, watching the numbers climb higher than any of my previous posts in weeks. "Two hundred thousand views. And climbing."

"That's ... good?" Noah's brow furrowed, creating little lines between his eyebrows.

"No, that's terrible. Thousands of people just watched me fail spectacularly at the exact thing I'm trying to promote!"

"It *was* pretty spectacular."

"This isn't funny."

"Kinda funny."

"NOT. FUNNY."

"Then you need to watch it again."

I Burned My Tongue in Colorado

"I can't believe this." I buried my face in the towel. "Luxe-Life hired me to make their resort look luxurious, not recreate America's Funniest Home Videos, Wilderness Edition."

Meanwhile, the comments kept rolling in.

@MountainMomma84: "OMG I'm dying!! 😂💀 Most authentic travel content I've seen in YEARS! That tour guide can rescue me from ANY DAY 🔥😍"

@AdventureJunkie: "You totally face-planted and GOT BACK UP! 🙌 Real influencers show the messy parts too. Who is Mountain Man and does he have Instagram? Asking for a friend 👀"

@TravelBloggerBecca: "Girl your SCREAM when you hit that rapid 😂😂 I just woke up my boyfriend laughing so hard! But that rescue was super impressive. More REAL content like this please! 💯🖤"

Noah pointed at my screen. "They seem to like it."

"They seem to like you."

"What's not to like?" A smug grin crossed his face.

"Where should I start?"

"You said Victoria wanted authentic, right?"

"Authentically disastrous." I groaned as notifications kept popping.

"Well, look on the bright side," said Noah. "You can always redeem yourself tomorrow."

"Tomorrow?" My head snapped up from the avalanche of comments, a drip of water rolling off my nose. "What's tomorrow?"

"You'll see." Noah gave me a reassuring wink. Which, for the record, was not at all reassuring.

Chapter Nineteen

Guitar strumming drifted through the Adventure Center when I arrived the next morning. It came to a sudden halt at the sound of a brass bell on the front doors. Noah appeared from one of the back rooms moments later.

I couldn't help but notice there wasn't a tray of freshly baked muffins in his hands.

"No muffins today?" I peered around Noah's workbench, dramatically sniffing the air like a bloodhound.

"We're climbing today," said Noah. "Not having a tea party." Without even saying good morning, he grabbed a climbing harness from the wall, the worn leather creaking in his hands.

"Somebody woke up on the wrong side of the bed this morning," I noted.

Jenn emerged from the back as well, pouring herself a fresh cup of stale coffee from the stained carafe. "Noah's bed only has wrong sides."

"Come here." Noah waved me over.

I Burned My Tongue in Colorado

"I heard music when I came in. You a guitar player?" I asked Noah, eyeing the intimidating rock wall that stretched up to the barn's rafters. It was peppered with multicolored plastic holds, little nubs, and protrusions that looked about as supportive as a Facebook comment section.

"No." His tone made it clear that was the end of that topic. I caught a glimpse of Jenn and Diego exchanging another one of their looks. "We're climbing Devil's Ridge today," Noah said, completely dismissing my guitar question.

"Devil's Ridge? That sounds ... horrible."

"It's a Class 5 formation that tops out at about ten thousand feet." Noah patted the barn wall like it was his wolf-dog rather than an instrument of torture. "But before that, we'll get you on the practice wall until you're comfortable with the basics."

"Define comfortable."

Noah stepped in close, wrapping the harness around my waist. "It's a beginner route," he explained, fingers working the straps with practiced efficiency.

"Define beginner."

"Perfect friction, solid holds, and a nice gentle angle."

"Gentle like a baby tiger is gentle," Diego chimed in, spinning a carabiner around his finger. "Still has teeth."

"Stop scaring her," Jenn scolded.

"Didn't you fall the first time you tried that route?" asked Diego

"I caught her, didn't I?" said Noah.

"Yeah, after a thirty-foot free fall, before the line caught." Jenn rubbed the back of her neck as if remembering the whiplash.

"Not helping," I told the room, wondering if it was too late to fake a sudden case of altitude sickness. Or amnesia. Or a Bigfoot kidnapping.

"The route we're taking follows a classic granite face."

Noah's fingers brushed my waist as he tightened a strap, sending a paralyzing shiver up my spine. "There's a nasty crack system about halfway up."

"Is that a good thing or a bad thing?"

He tugged another strap, pulling me slightly off balance. "The exposure gets intense after the first pitch."

I had to steady myself against his chest. "We can forget about the whole climbing thing and go back to the resort. They have muffins there. And mimosas."

Noah's hands stilled on my thigh straps, looking up. "Are you even listening? This is serious."

"I'd listen better with muffins." I tugged at the straps over my shoulders, which were definitely tighter than they needed to be. "Just saying."

When he straightened, his face was inches from mine, close enough that I could see the flecks of darker blue in his irises. The tiny scar above his left eyebrow. The way his breathing slowed.

"One wrong move up there ..."

"Could kill me. Got it." I met his gaze directly, not wilting under the intensity of his attention. "But here's the thing, Noah. My parents didn't raise their daughter to back down from a challenge. So let's stop talking and do this."

"Okay then." The transformation in Noah's expression was like watching a wall crack. He didn't smile exactly, but there was a flicker in his eyes. Noah strapped himself into his own harness, the muscles in his forearms flexing as he adjusted the buckles. His worn jeans hugged his thighs.

"We're not leaving this practice wall until you get to the top." Noah handed me the rope he was threading through my belay loop.

"Consider it done."

Another crack formed in Noah's wall as I stared up at the

physical one in front of me. The chalk marks left by previous climbers traced ghostly paths upward.

"First rule of climbing, maintain three points of contact with the wall at all times," he instructed, clipping a carabiner to his belt with the confidence of a man who actually knew how to both spell and pronounce car-a-bin-er.

"Like Spiderman?"

Noah frowned. "More like ..." He splayed himself against the wall.

"So, like Spiderman."

His frown deepened. "Just watch."

Noah positioned himself on the climbing wall, one hand on a yellow plastic hold, his other on a blue one. He propped his foot on a red nub barely big enough to balance his little toe. "Once you have your three contact points, you just propel forward, letting your momentum carry you upward."

"Propel. Momentum. Upward." I gave him a thumbs-up. "You know, if you'd just embrace the Spiderman thing, I bet I could get you even more TikTok followers than Kevin."

Ignoring me, Noah took his position. With fluid grace that made it look ridiculously easy, he scaled the entire wall as if gravity were merely a suggestion. His movements were both economical and precise, each reach and step calculated for maximum efficiency.

Once at the top, he pushed off with both legs and let the cable attached to his waist slowly lower him back down to the floor. He landed with barely a sound. "See?"

"So exactly like Spiderman. How'd you learn to climb like that?"

"Practice." Noah unhooked himself from the safety line.

"He's just being modest," said Diego.

"Noah started climbing when he was six," added Jenn. "Ever since his parents built this place from scratch."

At the mention of his parents, Noah's hands went still. For a split second, his carefully maintained mask slipped, and I saw something raw flicker across his face.

"So, this is your parents' place?"

Noah didn't look up, his undivided attention on the rope. "Was." Apparently, the circumference of his rope coil wasn't quite precise enough because he let it fall loose and started coiling all over again.

"They started with just a couple of wooden kayaks and some climbing gear," said Jenn. "So it's kinda in his blood."

My stomach twisted as the pieces clicked into place. I glanced at Noah, who was still very focused on coiling that rope, his shoulders tense.

"So, your parents ..."

"Not here anymore." The words fell like boulders from a cliff.

"Which means this place is all his now," said Jenn, walking over to join us. "All the dreams, all the responsibility."

"All the corporate vultures circling overhead," added Noah, looking directly at me.

That's when it clicked. This wasn't just some fancy resort amenities package; this was Noah's entire world. His entire life. Built by hand. Maintained by love. And now threatened by exactly the kind of luxury development I'd been hired to promote. Threatened by LuxeLife. Threatened by me.

"Surely there's something you can do?"

"The problem is Noah owns the business, but LuxeLife owns the land," said Diego.

"So once the lease expires ..."

"Corporate revitalization," said Jenn.

"Market rate improvements," said Diego. "I'm guessing oxygen bars and salt caves have better profit margins than a climbing wall."

I Burned My Tongue in Colorado

The faded pictures on the walls told stories I hadn't bothered to read. Decades of guided climbs, of teaching nervous beginners to trust their own strength, of sharing wilderness magic with city folks and helping families make memories together.

No wonder Noah and I got off on the wrong foot. My job, literally, was to help make his job go away. But not just his job. His family's legacy. His childhood. Noah's entire life purpose. Built from wooden kayaks and determination. And there I was, the face of everything threatening to destroy it.

"Turns out I'm a better climber than businessman." Noah's hands finally stilled on the rope.

I thought about my own family's story. The year of the pandemic. Customers stopped eating out. Tourists stayed in their homes. Supply shortages. Workers getting sick. A family business that took generations to build almost fell apart in an instant. If it hadn't been for the support of the community and the kindness of strangers ...

"No," I said.

"No?" Jenn frowned.

"This isn't happening. Not on my watch."

"What are you talking about, Sam?" Diego looked as confused as Jenn did.

"Maya gave us a lifeline. And I, for one, am not going to let it go. We can fix this. We can turn this thing around. Victoria's not some monster trying to destroy this place just for fun. She's a businesswoman. A smart one. A successful one. If we can prove authentic Colorado is what people really want ... more importantly, what people will pay for, she won't turn her back on a good thing."

"Speaking of lifelines." Noah handed me the climbing rope. "Before we show people more authentic Colorado, you need to show me I won't have to rappel down a mountain and haul your carcass out of a ravine."

"Wow, that's very specific."

"Stick 'em in." Noah opened the bag of chalk and motioned for me to stick my hands inside.

"This isn't going to mess up my manicure, is it?" I stuck my hands in the bag.

"It's definitely going to mess up your manicure."

When I pulled my hands out of the sack, they were covered in chalk, the fine powder coating my fingers like ghostly gloves. "Good. That gives me an excuse to get another one at the spa later. What about you, Jenn, care to join me?"

"Is LuxeLife paying?"

"Absolutely."

"Then count me in."

Diego dropped the life vest he was patching and came over to join us. "You know, I've had a lot of tension in my shoulders lately." He winced as he rubbed the back of his neck. "I could really use a massage."

"You're invited too, Diego." He gave me a grin.

"Probably all the stress of working with Noah," noted Jenn.

"Wait a second. I thought she was the bad guy? When did I become the bad guy?"

"When she bribed us with spa services," Diego explained.

Noah shook his head. "Well, the three of you will have to finish planning your little spa date later, cause right now it's time to stop fucking around and get back to work."

"See what I mean?" Jenn returned to her paperwork. Diego went back to the life vests.

Which left me alone again with Noah.

He pointed at the wall. "Let's go, Miss Li. Up and at 'em." He put firm hands on my shoulders and spun me back around. His hands moved over my harness again, testing each connection point, yanking straps and slapping buckles for what felt like the hundredth time. His chest pressed against my back. His breath felt warm on my neck.

Standing there with his hands all over me, I realized I was basically at his mercy. Beholden to his every whim. For some demented reason, that book about the billionaire with all the sex fetish stuff popped into my head.

"You're not secretly a billionaire, are you?" I asked before I could stop myself.

"Huh?" Noah paused, his hands on my waist.

"Never mind," I muttered, heat creeping up my neck.

It seemed Noah's only whim was to make me climb up tiny plastic rocks. He guided my hands to the right spots, the chalk on his fingers leaving dusty prints on my arms like evidence at a crime scene.

"Left foot there," he said, tapping my ankle with his boot. "Now, reach up with your right hand."

I stretched toward the hold he'd indicated, but my arms felt like overcooked noodles after yesterday's paddling. "I can't ..."

"Yes, you can." His hand settled on my hip, steadying me. "Push with your legs, not your arms. Climbing is all in the lower body."

From across the room, I caught Diego elbowing Jenn, both of them wearing knowing smirks. Jenn whispered something that made Diego snort-laugh.

"Focus," Noah said, still way too close. "Keep your hips close to the wall."

"That's what she said," Diego muttered, earning a smack from Jenn.

I tried to concentrate on the holds in front of me, but Noah's proximity was scrambling my brain cells faster than a high-speed blender. His breath tickled my neck as he adjusted my grip on a particularly sketchy hold.

"Better," he said. "Now shift your weight to the left."

I followed his instructions, hyperaware of his hand still resting on my hip. When I glanced over, Diego was making exaggerated kissing faces at Jenn.

"Eyes on the wall," Noah commanded, completely oblivious to our audience's silent comedy show. "Trust your feet."

I shifted my weight, finding my balance without Noah's support. My fingers curled around the next hold, legs pushing just like he'd shown me. One move at a time, I climbed a few feet up the wall.

"Look at that, you're a natural," Noah said, his voice carrying a note of surprise. He stepped back, letting out the rope. "Time to fly solo. Show us what you've got."

My stomach clenched as I looked up at the ceiling. The wall stretched above me like a skyscraper. I reached for the next hold, found my footing, and pulled myself higher.

Halfway up, my arms started shaking. Sweat trickled down my back, making my shirt cling like flypaper. The holds seemed to shrink with each movement. My fingers ached from gripping the tiny edges.

"I don't know." My voice cracked.

"You're doing great," Noah called up. "If you make it to the top, maybe I'll bake you another batch of muffins."

I groaned. "They were good, but not that good." But even as I complained, my arms kept moving, finding the next hold. This wasn't about muffins or proving Noah wrong. I was determined to help them.

My muscles burned with each move. The top anchor seemed impossibly far away, but I continued making progress. Slow. Steady. But I was doing it. I was actually *doing* it.

"Come on, Sam!" Diego shouted. "Show that wall who's boss!"

Just when I started to believe that I could actually make it, the taste of muffin already forming on my tongue, my foot slipped on a hold slick with chalk and sweat.

Next thing I knew, I was falling.

The wall rushed past as I plummeted, the rope jerking tight around my waist. A scream tore from my throat as I twisted in the harness, my shoulder slamming against the wall with a thud that pulsed through my entire body.

"Sam!" Noah's voice cut through the darkness as everything started spinning.

Chapter Twenty

The safety line caught, pulled taut, swinging me in a slow arc, my body tangled in the rope. Pain shot through my shoulder and hip where I'd hit the wall. I dangled like a broken puppet, trying to right myself but only making the spinning worse.

"Stop moving," Noah commanded, climbing up to meet me. His hands found my waist, steadying me. "I've got you."

I grabbed his shoulders, fingers digging into solid muscle. The room tilted and spun as he carefully untangled the ropes from my legs.

"Ow," I whimpered as he lowered me the last few feet. My shoulder throbbed where it'd smashed against the wall.

"You okay?" Noah seemed as shaken as I was.

"I think so."

I looked back up at the wall, the frustration burning hotter than my throbbing shoulder. The chalk marks from my failed attempt still traced a pathetic path halfway up, evidence of exactly how far I'd made it before gravity reminded me who was boss.

"Let me take a look at it." Noah's fingers probed gently at my shoulder, his touch delicate.

I rotated my arm, wincing. "I'm fine." The tears in my eyes said otherwise, but damned if I was going to cry in front of him.

"You don't look fine," Jenn appeared with an ice pack.

"That's going to leave a mark." Diego handed me some water.

Even Yeti came over, giving me a lick on the hand.

I wiped my eyes with the back of my hand, leaving chalky streaks on my cheeks. "I want to try again."

The words surprised everyone. Everyone but me.

"Li's always get back up." It was something Dad said. Though usually in the context of a bad restaurant review.

"No. Absolutely not," said Noah. "You hit that wall hard."

"I'm bruised, not broken." I stepped back toward the wall, ignoring the protests from both Noah and my shoulder. "I'm not leaving here until I get to the top."

"Sam, you just fell fifteen feet. You don't have to prove anything. That was a nasty fall."

"I'm not trying to prove anything." I flexed my fingers, testing my grip. "This is my job, remember? Can't exactly post about the amazing climbing experience if I quit after one fall."

"We could head over to the lake instead." Diego pointed to a pair of fishing poles next to the rain jackets. "Get some content there. I've seen some mountain trout that are pretty Instagram-worthy."

"Or we could grab some of the four-wheelers," said Jenn. "Take you out to the elk viewing area. The herd's been hanging around the north meadow."

Noah let out a long, tired breath. "Maybe we should just ..."

"Maybe we should just what? Wrap me up in bubble wrap and send me back to Los Angeles? Look, I get it. I'm the city girl who doesn't belong here. I'm the corporate lackey threatening everything you care about. But I wasn't raised to be a quitter. At least give me credit for that."

The silence that followed was broken only by the sound of chalk dust settling.

"Besides," I added. "If I die climbing your wall, that's going to be terrible for LuxeLife's star rating. So, in advance, you're welcome."

Noah shook his head. But it seemed more of a contemplation than a rejection. "You sure you're okay?"

"I'm sure. Or the head bump knocked all the sense out of me."

"That would imply you had any sense to begin with."

"Fair point."

Noah let out another long sigh, as if genuinely considering it.

"Just hurry up and let her climb already. These neck muscles aren't going to massage themselves."

"Okay," Noah said finally. "If your shoulder starts hurting though, we're done."

"Deal." I chalked my hands again, the fine powder coating my scraped palms. "But I'm holding you to those muffins."

I stared up at the wall, mapping out a different route. I put one hand on the first rock, my other hand on a second. My foot found a hold. Three points of contact.

I channeled my inner Spider Woman.

And for the first time since arriving in Colorado, I caught Noah Barrett looking at me like I might be worth the trouble, after all.

That's when Jenn's phone rang.

Her expression shifted from casual to concerned as she listened to what was being said on the other end. Her shoulders tensed, and she began pacing.

Whatever was happening, it wasn't good.

I Burned My Tongue in Colorado

* * *

The lake came into view through a break in the pines, a perfect mirror reflecting mountains and sky. A small crowd gathered at the edge of the water.

"Follow my lead," said Noah, the muscles in his forearm tensed as he twisted the steering wheel. "Trapped animals can be aggressive." Noah angled the Jeep toward the group assembled near the shoreline. "Could get real ugly, real fast."

The call Jenn got was a report of an osprey tangled in a fishing line. As soon as Noah declared he was the one going down to the lake to handle it, I declared I was the one going with him.

"No getting close unless I say it's safe." Noah pulled the Jeep in as close as he could to the water. He jumped out, grabbing his climbing gear and a fully stocked first aid kit. I followed on his heels, the adrenaline numbing the lingering pain in my shoulder.

Since there was another animal involved, Noah made Yeti stay back at the Adventure Center with Diego and Jenn. Apparently, there had been a recent opossum incident no one really wanted to talk about, and she was still grounded.

The group of onlookers parted as we approached, all eyes turned upward.

As soon as I saw it, my heart stopped.

About twenty feet up, tangled in fishing line wrapped around a dead branch, an osprey hung suspended over the water. Its magnificent wings were splayed at awkward angles. Though it still moved, its struggles were weak and sporadic. The once-proud raptor looked defeated, its head drooping.

"Oh God." The words caught in my throat. I'd seen the pair of ospreys on the river, diving gracefully for fish or soaring overhead, but this was different. This was wrong. All that majesty reduced to helpless struggling against something that never should have been there in the first place. Someone else's carelessness had created this crisis, and now it was paying the price.

Noah assessed the situation instantly, his jaw tight enough to crack boulders. "Line's wrapped around its wing and leg. Bird's exhausted itself, fighting to get out."

"We need to call 9-1-1 or wildlife rescue or something, right?" I reached for my phone.

"Nearest rescue team is too far out." Noah shook his head. "Bird won't last that long in this state. The stress can do more damage than the injury. If we don't get it down soon ..." He didn't finish the sentence. He didn't need to.

"This is what happens when people don't clean up after themselves." Noah's jaw ticked, his eyes narrowed. "People come out here, snap their lines, leave them hanging in the trees. They don't think about what happens after. These birds see the glint, think it's a fish."

I watched the osprey's wings twitch feebly, thinking about the pair we'd seen on our river trip. The way Diego had described them, mates for life, returning to the same nest year after year. Was this one of a pair? Was its partner somewhere nearby, wondering why it hadn't returned? Maybe there were baby ospreys back at the nest, crying for their mommy or daddy.

"There has to be something we can do."

Noah studied the dead branch, the angle of the line, the distance to the water. His expression shifted from concerned to determined, like someone who'd made calculations and arrived at a solution.

"It's not going to be easy." The look on Noah's face made me think "not being easy" wasn't the worst of it.

"And?" I asked, waiting for the other shoe to drop.

Noah's jaw set. "It's a two-person job."

I Burned My Tongue in Colorado

While the osprey pathetically struggled and the spectators gawked, Noah and I returned to the Jeep to gather supplies, the familiar climbing gear I'd just been learning to use now being repurposed for wildlife rescue.

Back at the shoreline, Noah pointed to the dead branch. "One person needs to get up there, cut the line. The other person has to catch the bird when it drops."

I stared at the osprey, my stomach churning. "Won't it fight when someone grabs it?"

"That's why we need a towel. Cover its head, keep it calm." Noah glanced at the water below the tree. "Catching from the water will be easier, but if you've never handled an injured animal before ..."

"I'll climb."

"No, Sam. I wasn't suggesting you have to do either." Noah pulled out his duct-taped flip phone. "I'll call Diego. He can ..."

I put my hand on Noah's arm, feeling the tense muscle. "You said yourself it doesn't have much time. It's got to be me. I can help. I *want* to help."

It seemed Noah wasn't sure if he believed me, phone still in hand.

The osprey, hopelessly snared and dangling on the fishing line, gave another half-hearted lurch. "Besides, I'm lighter than you and Diego. That branch looks ready to snap."

Before Noah could protest, I reached out and took the climbing harness from his arms. "My grandmother Gigi had this gigantic oak tree in her backyard growing up. I used to climb that thing all the time."

I wasn't trying to be brave. The truth was, the tree wasn't all that intimidating. The main trunk was huge, with a gradual lean out over the water. Sprawling branches sprang out in all directions about ten to fifteen feet up. Climbing it would be a lot easier than climbing the rock wall.

Noah looked at the tree again, as if he were actually considering my proposal. "If I throw a rope up over that branch there, I can pull you most of the way up." Noah pointed at the tree where the first big branch twisted away from the trunk. "From there, it's fairly level." Noah nodded, beginning to see how it could work. "Worst case, just wrap both legs around the branch and scoot."

"Noah, I can do this."

"Okay."

I stepped into the harness, trying to remember which strap went where from our practice session. Noah's hands were suddenly everywhere, adjusting straps around my thighs, checking the fit at my waist, tugging the buckles snug.

"I'll pull you up as far as I can," said Noah. "Then stay on the main trunk until you reach the branch with the fishing line."

Once my harness was secure, Noah pulled out his knife with the edge that looked like shark teeth. He slipped it back into a leather sheath, then strapped it onto the harness so it would be easy to reach. "Cut the line as close to the bird as you can manage. I'll be right below it with the towel. And Sam ..." Noah's voice made me pause. "Please. Just be careful."

His eyes locked on mine, a mix of emotions making my breath catch. For once, I didn't have a witty comeback.

Noah pulled his shirt over his head, and it took every ounce of willpower to stay focused on the task at hand. I'd seen shirtless men before. I'd even dated a CrossFit instructor once.

But Noah ...

Lean muscle rippled across his shoulders as he kicked off his boots. Mountain-man strength that came from actual work. A scattering of freckles dusted his collarbone. A thin white scar curved along his ribs.

Noah grabbed a large towel from his Jeep in nothing but a

pair of tight black shorts. I forced myself to look away, checking the knife strapped to my harness as a distraction. "Ready?" Noah asked.

"Yep!" I shook my head, trying to clear it.

Bird.

Focus on the bird.

I followed Noah to the edge of the lake, watching as he waded into waist-deep water with the towel draped over his neck. He wrapped his end of the rope in his fists while I took my position beside the tree.

"On three," Noah called up, looping the rope in his hands. "Ready?"

"Ready."

"One ..." Noah set his feet, biceps taut as he braced.

"You can do this, Sam."

"Two ..."

"Just like Gigi's tree."

"Three!"

The ground fell away as Noah hoisted me skyward. The rope creaked against the branch as he adjusted his grip, and I swayed in mid-air like a spinning piñata.

"Grab the branch!"

I reached for it. Pulling myself up, I swung one leg over the branch, straddling it between my legs. The bark bit into my palms, rough and jagged, but I barely noticed. Testing my weight before moving further, I inched closer to the trapped osprey.

Water lapped below as Noah waded deeper into the lake, holding the towel above his head. The osprey's wings fluttered weakly, the tangled line glinting in the sunlight.

"Keep your center-of-gravity close to the trunk," Noah called up.

"I got this!" I yelled back. I was already shifting my weight, finding the sweet spot between momentum and control. Left foot wedged against a knot in the bark. Right hand gripped a smaller branch above. Push up, reach out, find the next hold.

The branch groaned under my weight, and I froze, heart racing, beads of sweat forming on my forehead. The fishing line was just ahead, wrapped around a branch that jutted over the water.

Below, Noah stood ready with the towel, water up to his chest. Our eyes met briefly, his quiet confidence steadying my nerves.

The osprey's dark eyes watched me, too exhausted to struggle.

Just a little further ...

My fingers closed around the branch. Bark crumbled under my grip. Suddenly, the branch beneath my foot gave way with a sharp crack.

My gut dropped as I dropped. Fingers scraping, I caught myself on a lower branch, legs dangling, the harness digging into my thighs.

"Sam!" Noah's shout echoed across the water, raw panic in his voice.

"I'm okay," I called down, steadying myself.

Noah didn't seem too sure. "We can find another way."

"No." I pulled myself up, ignoring the sting of scraped palms. "I can do this."

I reached for the next branch, stronger this time. The osprey needed help.

"Moving up," I announced, finding my rhythm again. Noah watched every move, barely breathing, as I closed the distance to the fishing line.

The line was within reach now. I pulled out the knife, its weight heavy in my palm. The osprey's eyes followed my movements, too exhausted to resist.

I Burned My Tongue in Colorado

"Almost there," I whispered, more to myself than the bird.

Snip

The osprey dropped.

My breath caught, but Noah was there, like he'd done this a hundred times before. The towel cradled the bird as it fell, Noah's arms wrapping securely but gently around its wings.

Noah lifted the wounded osprey clear of the water, then he was moving, keeping the bird's shivering body above the surface as he backed toward shallower water. We hadn't exchanged a single word, yet somehow we'd moved in perfect sync, like we'd rehearsed it all in advance.

A cheer went up from the shoreline. I'd forgotten about our audience, hikers and fisherman, tourists and families enjoying the outdoors. Their applause echoed across the lake, genuine and immediate in a way that no number of heart emojis could ever match. No filters, no careful framing, no strategic hashtags. Just real people celebrating a real moment.

Chapter Twenty-One

As Noah and I stepped out of the Aster Park veterinary clinic and into the late afternoon sun, I felt like someone had lifted the weight of a full-grown moose off my shoulders. The osprey would make it. No broken bones, no permanent damage. Just exhaustion and some minor scrapes that would heal over time. In a couple of days, they planned to move her to a local bird of prey rehabilitation center. She'd be good as new in no time.

I named her Vera.

"Thank you for letting me come," I said, falling into step beside Noah as we headed back toward the Jeep. His hands were shoved deep in his pockets, shoulders relaxed.

"You helped save it," said Noah, his voice missing its usual mountain-flavored grumpiness. "Couldn't have done it alone." He glanced at the sky, reading the sun like a clock. "Too late to climb Devil's Ridge now. Guess I should get you back to the resort."

"Guess so."

Music drifted down the street, the lilting strains of a fiddle weaving through the mountain air. The town square bustled with activity. Colorful banners stretched between lampposts. Food trucks lined the street, windows open to release aromas of grilled BBQ and sweet corn. Kids chased each other through the crowd, faces painted like woodland creatures, foxes, raccoons, and chipmunks.

"What's going on over there?" I asked, drawn by the cheerful sounds of acoustic guitar and children's laughter.

"Mountain Heritage Festival." Noah pointed to a flyer taped to a lamppost. "There's a new festival here every week. Locals try to make the most of the tourist season during the summer. Music. Food. Games. Whole town turns out for them."

"I like music, food, and games."

"Want to check it out?" Noah asked, a new bounce in his tone. "Authentic Colorado is more than just mountains and rivers."

"Is it now?" I raised an eyebrow, trying not to show how intrigued I was by this version of Noah, the one who rescued birds and apparently enjoyed local festivals.

"Follow me."

The festival transformed Aster Park's town square into a labyrinth of stalls and tents, each one packed with local artisans showing off their crafts. Quilts with intricate mountain patterns hung at one booth. Another displayed hand-carved wooden animals. Noah navigated through the crowd with easy familiarity while I trailed behind, taking in the sights, sounds, and smells.

"These guys make the best elk sausage in Colorado," said Noah. "Ever try elk?"

I made a face. "No. I prefer my food not to contain my favorite Disney characters."

Noah laughed. "They make a Disney character safe option

too." He steered me toward a food truck painted with mountain scenes in vibrant blues and greens. "Local mushrooms and herbs, wild rice, some secret ingredients they won't tell anyone."

The aroma of roasted garlic and caramelized onions wafted toward us, making my mouth water. "That actually sounds amazing. So you actually eat food that didn't once have antlers?"

"Don't judge a book by its cover."

Under a nearby tent, a local author set up shop. The book propped up on the table featured what looked like Bigfoot and a scantily clad mountain woman, bosom bursting from her blouse. Noah pointed to it. "Except that one. I read Charlene's latest, and that pretty much sums it up."

"Hey, Noah," said the author, batting her eyes at him.

"Hey Charlene," Noah replied.

"You're just full of surprises, aren't you?" I asked.

"What, that I enjoy a wide variety of fine literature?"

"No," I said. "That you know how to read."

"You might be surprised at some of the things I know how to do."

Luckily, we hadn't started eating our sausages yet because if we had, I definitely would have choked. A flood of heat blossomed inside me like I'd just submerged the lower half of my body in a thermal pool.

I followed Noah to the food truck, where he flashed two fingers at the bearded, flanneled man behind the counter. "All the fixings."

The man placed two plump, herb-flecked sausages on a grill that hissed and popped. The smell intensified, earthy and aromatic with hints of sage and thyme. He nestled each sausage in a toasted pretzel bun, then piled on grilled peppers and onions before drizzling everything with a spicy maple aioli.

I Burned My Tongue in Colorado

I reached for my wallet, but Noah waved me off.

"My treat." He handed over the cash. "Consider it payment for your osprey rescue services."

We found a spot at the edge of the square, sitting on a low stone wall beneath an aspen tree. Golden leaves fluttered in the breeze. I took a tentative bite of the sausage, flavor exploding across my tongue.

"This is amazing," I admitted, taking another, bigger bite. A glob of maple aioli oozed onto my shirt. "Whoops."

"Here." Before I could even move, Noah reached over with a napkin, dabbing at the stain. Our eyes met, and he pulled back quickly, clearing his throat.

The silence stretched from uncomfortable to awkward.

I could tell Noah had something to say, but he wasn't sure if he should say it. I had to remind myself to breathe.

"It really is good," I said again, just to fill the void.

"You doubted me?" Noah's eyes crinkled at the corners.

"Lately, I've been reviewing trendy fusion restaurants where they serve tiny portions on oversized plates and charge eighty dollars for the privilege."

"Yeah, I bet," said Noah. "You've come a long way from reviewing those tiny hole-in-the-wall taquerías."

"Wait. What? How do you know about that? I haven't posted one of those videos in years."

Noah looked like I'd just caught him with his hand in the mountain trail mix jar. He spent a long time staring down at his half-eaten sausage. "So," he began.

"So?"

He wadded up the napkin, avoiding my gaze. "I have a confession to make."

"A confession?" My brain pin-balled through the possibilities. Noah actually hated flannel. Noah was actually allergic to mountains. Noah secretly liked to dress up in a Bigfoot costume and ravish scantily clad, big-bosomed mountain women.

"I looked you up before meeting you at the airport."

"You did?"

"Well, since your flight was late, I had a lot of time to kill. Brie let me borrow her phone, and I scrolled through some of your posts."

I was still holding my sausage up in front of my face, eyes wide, frozen mid-bite.

"Actually, a lot of your posts. Maybe ... most of them."

Slowly, I lowered my sausage. "Wow." It was the best I could manage.

"I mean, I had a lot of time to kill. And I wanted to see what I was up against."

"Up against? Noah, I didn't come here to ..."

He held up his hand, stopping me. "I know, I know. I mean, I know that now. But at the time ..."

"No wonder you left me at the airport."

Noah chewed his bottom lip, tilting his head slightly so he could look over at me without quite meeting my eyes. "Yeah. So I have a confession about that too."

"Another confession?" I braced myself for the big Bigfoot reveal.

"I didn't actually leave you at the airport." Noah took another bite, redirecting all his focus to chewing.

"Um ... I'm pretty sure you did leave me at the airport. Remember? I was there. You drove off into the sunset."

Noah shifted uncomfortably. "Actually, I drove around the corner, waited a bit, then came back. But you were gone. I figured you went back inside, so I parked and went inside myself. Searched everywhere. Brie's coffee shop, the gift shop, even sweet-talked my way past security to check inside the terminal."

I Burned My Tongue in Colorado

My stomach did a weird little flip, and not from the sausage. "You really came back for me?" The circumstances of our first interaction had haunted me ever since. Now, a wave of relief washed over me as powerful as the relief I felt when we found out Vera the Osprey was going to be okay. Noah had misjudged me. But I had misjudged him too.

"I'm sorry, Sam. It was stupid, and I wasn't thinking. I was pissed at LuxeLife and ... doesn't matter. It wasn't my best moment, and I shouldn't have taken it out on you."

"I did kinda provoke you," I admitted.

"I guess a part of me just wanted to prove you weren't the one in charge. Which, for the record, you still aren't."

"Oh, I'm totally in charge," I said. "I just let you think you are."

"Well, technically, I guess Victoria's the one in charge. She's the one holding the purse strings."

"You can say that again." We continued eating, with me reflecting on everything Noah had said. If he hadn't actually left me ... it sorta changed everything. Didn't it?

"We must have just missed each other." His expression softened. "How'd you get over to the resort, anyway?"

"I took a taxi."

"You drove with Al?"

The taxi ride to the resort with Al would forever remain seared in memory. "Yeah. How'd you know?"

"Aster Park has limited transportation options."

"That tracks."

"Did he talk to you about flapjacks?"

"Yes. A lot. Like, really a lot."

"Birch syrup?"

"That, too."

"Damn. Now I'm really sorry." Noah shook his head. "I

might have to make you a batch of my birch syrup glazed pecan scones to make it up to you."

"Might have to? Try definitely have to. In fact, maybe we should go straight back to your place and ..." I stopped, realizing what I'd said. "I mean ..."

"You still have a lot of authentic Colorado to see first," said Noah, rescuing me from my tangle of words just as surely as he'd rescued me from the tangled ropes on the climbing wall. "Ready to see the rest of the festival?"

"After you."

Noah helped me to my feet, and we strolled deeper into the festival. Under a striped tent, a teenage girl demonstrated how to make something called chokecherry syrup while her grandmother explained the traditional ways to use it.

I pulled out my phone to capture the scene. Kids with sticky faces eating kettle corn. Elderly couples holding hands.

"There's Lewis," Noah nodded toward a gray-haired man selling honey jars, each one labeled with the type of flower the bees made it from. "Best beekeeper in the valley. And over there's Rita. She makes soap from goat's milk."

Across from us, a band started up on the gazebo stage, a fiddle, a banjo, and what looked like a washboard. The music they played defied categorization, bluegrass meets rap meets poetry, fused with classic rock. Couples spun across a makeshift dance floor to the hypnotic beat.

"There's more to our small little mountain town than you thought, huh?" Noah asked, reading my expression.

"Yeah. A lot more," I admitted, surprising myself with how much I meant it.

Noah led me past storefronts with hand-painted signs and window displays that belonged in a Hallmark movie. He greeted passersby by name, fist-bumped kids, and paused to scratch dogs behind their ears. Oddly, I found myself wishing Yeti were there with us.

As Noah stopped to introduce me to his former first grade school teacher, who he still called Mrs. Harrison, I thought to myself, this wasn't the gruff mountain man who I thought abandoned me.

"And that ..." said Noah, recapturing my attention. He pointed to a weathered wooden stand. "That is my berry supplier, Mrs. Miller."

I grabbed his arm without thinking, his biceps firm beneath my hand. "We're stopping. Immediately." If I had to wait for birch syrup glazed pecan scones ... back at Noah's place ... the least he could do was woo me with more muffins.

An older woman with silver hair lit up like a Christmas tree at the sight of Noah. "Noah Barrett, about time you showed up."

"Hey, Mrs. Miller." Noah leaned over to kiss her cheek. "This is Sam."

Mrs. Miller's eyes sparkled with suspicion. "So you're the one he's been baking for."

Before I could respond, or process what that might mean, she plucked a fat berry from one of the wooden baskets on the counter and held it out to me. "Try this, dear." The berry was almost the size of a ping-pong ball.

I popped the berry into my mouth, and it burst across my tongue. Sweet, tart, and complex in a way that made the imported berries I bought in LA taste like plastic imitations. "Oh, wow."

"Different from the sad grocery store ones, aren't they?" Mrs. Miller picked up another basket. "These grow wild on the mountainside. The altitude, the soil, the way the morning sun hits. It all matters. Plus, I know exactly where and when to pick 'em. Been in the berry business since this one was knee high." She patted Noah's arm with affection.

"You knew Noah when he was a little boy?" I asked, fascinated by this glimpse into his past.

"Know him?" Mrs. Miller's laugh rang out across the festival grounds. "He spent almost as much time at my farm as he did in the woods. Should've seen him the first time I caught him raiding my berry supply. Must've been what, ten?" She nudged Noah with her elbow.

Noah crossed his arms, assuming his grumpy persona. "Raiding seems like a strong word."

"Face and hands stained purple. Tried to tell me he hadn't touched a thing, but that mouth of his gave him away."

"Something tells me Noah's mouth gets him in trouble a lot," I said, unable to resist.

"Sam, my dear, you have no idea." Mrs. Miller shook her head, still grinning. "His daddy marched him right back up to my farm the next morning. Had Noah doing farm chores every Saturday all summer to make it up to me." Mrs. Miller sorted through her baskets. "Turned out to be the best helper I ever had. Worked harder than any of the farmhands on the actual payroll, so I hired him to work the next couple of summers after too."

"We should probably keep moving if you want to see the rest of the festival," said Noah. He'd clearly had enough talk about his backstory, even though I found it fascinating.

"You two go on," Mrs. Miller said, handing me a small basket of berries. "On the house. Consider it payment for putting up with this grump."

Beyond the berry stand, cheers erupted from a row of wooden targets. I stretched up on my toes, trying to see past the crowd.

I Burned My Tongue in Colorado

"Want to check out the games?" Noah nodded toward the commotion.

"Sure," I said, popping another berry in my mouth. The juice stained my fingers purple, but it matched my nail polish, so it was all good.

"Might want to get your camera ready."

We wandered past kids tossing rings onto bottles and teens shooting BB guns at metal ducks. A group of burly men in flannel shirts hurled horseshoes with deadly accuracy, metal ringing against metal with sharp clangs.

"Well?" Noah arched an eyebrow.

"Pretty much what I expected," I said, gesturing around us. "Except I don't see any lumberjacks doing that log balancing thing."

"Over there." Noah pointed over my shoulder. Sure enough, there they were, two flannel-clad beefcakes dancing on a spinning log floating in a stock tank full of water. One lost his balance and plunged in, the resulting splash sending kids running for cover.

"You should try something," Noah said. "For research purposes. Show your followers a authentic Colorado experience."

I raised an eyebrow. "What exactly are you suggesting?"

"Your pick." He swept an arm over the row of game stations. "Just try not to hurt yourself."

"Fine." I planted my hands on my hips. "But only if you play, too. It's not authentic unless a local demonstrates."

"Deal." Noah smirked. "What'll it be?"

My eyes landed on a station where contestants were throwing axes at wooden targets. Most of them were missing spectacularly, the axes clattering to the ground or bouncing off handle-first.

"That one." I pointed.

Noah's eyebrows shot up. "Axe throwing?"

"What's wrong? Afraid I'll show you up?" I grabbed his sleeve and tugged him toward the line. "Come on, mountain man. Show me how it's done."

Noah slapped a twenty on the wooden counter. "Two rounds."

A bearded man in a red and black buffalo check shirt handed us each a gleaming axe. "Three throws per person. Blue ring's one point, red's three. Bullseye gets five points. Keep your feet behind the line, and for God's sake, don't let go on the backswing."

I tested the weight of the axe in my hand. It was heavier than I expected, the wooden handle smooth from countless throws. The blade glinted in the early evening sun.

"We can always do that one if you prefer." Noah bobbed his head toward the kid version, where the axes were made of foam and stuck to the target using Velcro.

"No, I think I'm good." I hefted the axe onto my shoulder. "Want to make this more interesting?"

"What do you mean, interesting?"

"Winner picks what we do next."

"And what exactly would you pick?"

I gave him my best mysterious smile. "Lose and find out."

Chapter Twenty-Two

Noah spun his axe in his palm, a practiced movement that was totally badass and sexy all at once. His jaw tightened. "Ladies first?"

"That's something a gentleman would do. And since we've already established you're not a gentleman, you go first, hotshot." I stepped back from the line.

Noah smirked, then took his position. The axe spun once in his grip before he brought it up in a fluid arc. It rotated perfectly through the air, embedding itself in the red ring with a satisfying thunk, just a blade's width from the bullseye. A three-point throw.

"Not bad," I conceded, lining up my throw. I mimicked his stance, pretending I was Scarlett Johansen in one of her action movies.

Deep breath. Focus. Release.

The axe flew straight and true, sticking in the target just a few inches outside of his. It wasn't as good as Noah's throw, but it was way better than anybody expected from me, judging by the surprised murmurs from the gathering crowd.

Noah frowned. "Where'd you learn to throw like that?"

"YouTube." I winked.

We traded another series of throws; the crowd grew with each solid hit. Noah edged ahead in the first round with a bullseye on his last throw, but the margin was razor thin.

For round two, I stepped up first. As I forced myself to relax, my throws felt stronger, more controlled. The axe became an extension of my arm rather than an awkward weight. Still, Noah matched me point for point.

The crowd pressed closer as I took my last throw. The axe spun beautifully, striking just a hair's breadth from dead center. Bullseye. A collective "ooh" rose from the onlookers, along with scattered applause.

But Noah was well ahead, so he just needed to hit the target anywhere to win. He took his stance. Muscles tensed beneath his flannel shirt. The axe left his hand in a perfect arc … and sailed completely wide of the target, clattering against the backdrop.

The crowd erupted in cheers. I threw my arms up in victory as Noah bowed his head in defeat.

"What happened there, mountain man?" I nudged his shoulder. "Performance anxiety?"

"Must've been distracted." He shook his head, but I caught a hint of a smile. "Something tells me you've done this before."

I grinned. "Funny you should mention that. Urban Axe House in LA is one of my sponsors."

"You're kidding."

"Nope. They've got an amazing setup: exposed brick walls, craft beer on tap, and vintage logging equipment everywhere. It's like a hipster lumberjack paradise. They even have league nights where tech bros compete in flannel shirts with team names on them." Before I could stop myself, I added, "We should go sometime." But when I saw Noah's smile drop, I quickly added, "I mean, you know, if you ever find yourself in Los Angeles. Not that you ever would."

Noah ran a hand through his hair, then mercifully changed the subject. "You know, your having an ax-throwing sponsorship feels like cheating. I mean, you're basically a professional."

"A deal's a deal." I poked his chest. "Besides, you let me win. It was obvious."

"It was?"

"That last throw? Please." I crossed my arms. "You just wanted to know what I'd pick."

Noah's lips twitched. "So what'll it be?"

"Well, obviously ..." I drew out the moment, enjoying the anticipation on his face. "Muffins."

His face broke into another smile, the kind that made my tummy feel like it was pumped full of butterflies. "Muffins, huh?" He glanced at the setting sun, its golden light casting long shadows across the festival grounds. "I know just the spot."

Noah's hand bumped mine as we navigated through the thickening festival crowd, the accidental brush sending zaps of lightning up my arm and a whirlwind of butterflies in my tummy. In the distance, the band struck up a slower tune, fiddle notes hanging in the air.

Noah steered me toward another line of tents at the far edge of the square, where a rustic wooden table had a hand-painted sign reading "Coffee." The rich aroma of freshly ground beans hit me as Brie leaned over and waved, smiling ear to ear.

"Brie's here? At the festival?"

"She sets up shop every weekend while one of her other baristas covers the airport location. A lot more foot traffic here."

"So I get muffins and coffee!" I clapped my hands like I had just won the grand prize on a game show.

"Well, well, well," said Brie as we approached. Her gaze

alternated between us with undisguised interest. "If it isn't my big brother and the big-city influencer. Together. Without visible injuries."

"We've called a temporary truce," I said.

"Only for the sake of authentic Colorado content," Noah added.

"I'm just glad he doesn't still hate me," I said, hoping it was true.

"I never hated you," said Noah. "I just disliked you. Strongly."

I was afraid to ask my next question, but asked it anyway. "Do you still dislike me strongly?"

"Actually, you're kind of growing on me. Like a foot fungus after hiking all day in wet boots."

"So what can I get you two?" Brie asked, still smiling.

"Two of your special light roasts," said Noah. "The one you roasted last week."

"Coming right up." Brie was still grinning.

"And Noah promised me muffins," I said, getting straight down to business. "However, while I'm sure your muffins are wonderful, Brie, I highly doubt they taste better than Noah's."

Brie laughed so hard she almost choked. "Where do you think I get all my muffins from?"

"Wait, what?" I turned to Noah. "You make muffins for your sister's coffee shop?"

"Noah's baked goods are the reason our morning rush is insane," said Brie. "Between the airport location and the festivals, I can't keep them in stock."

"Oh no, you're out?"

"Well ..." She held up one finger, then disappeared beneath the table. She popped back up with a small, misshapen mound. "This is the only one I have left."

She peeled back the layer of plastic wrap, revealing a

mushed-up muffin spotted with smears of purple. "I accidentally sat on it while I was setting up shop this morning. Figured it was too ugly to sell."

"I don't care what it looks like, as long as it tastes like the one Noah made for our hike."

"Wait." Brie looked confused, her gaze bouncing between Noah and me. "My brother made you muffins for a hike?"

"Yes," I said, breaking off a piece of the mashed muffin and popping it into my mouth. The flavor hit exactly the same complex notes as before, that perfect balance that spoke of someone who truly understood baking as both art and science. "He made us a breakfast picnic on top of the mountain."

"My brother made you a picnic?" Brie looked like I'd just told her that her brother could walk on water. And levitate. And fly.

"Maya's orders," said Noah, but his deflection sounded of surrender.

"Mmm-hmm. Just following orders. Because you're such a rule follower, Noah." Brie's grin only widened.

Noah's face was now the color of the setting sun in the Colorado sky, reddish-pink, which seemed to delight Brie even more.

"Let me grab those coffees so you can wash down your muffin." When Brie returned, she poured two steaming mugs. The coffee smelled like heaven condensed into liquid form. "This is my Sunrise Blend," Brie explained. "Costa Rican beans I get directly from a little family farm in the mountains, then slow-roasted to bring out the natural chocolate notes."

I took a cautious sip, making extra sure it wasn't too hot first. Hints of dark chocolate, a whisper of berries, and something nutty and complex that lingered after I swallowed.

"Holy caffeine gods," I spent the next two minutes gluttonously devouring nibbles of muffin and slurps of perfectly roasted coffee. "This is why you sell out so fast," I mumbled, crumbs rolling down my chin. "You must clean up at these festivals."

Brie nodded, wiping crumbs off her counter while Noah gently brushed them off me. "All the local vendors do. It's what keeps us in business." She gestured around the square. "We're all out here every week. Well, except next week." Brie's expression fell; her usual cheerfulness dimmed.

"What's going on next week?" Noah asked, tensing at his sister's shift in mood.

"Food festival over in Denver," said Brie. "All the food trucks from here to Boulder will be over there, so the town council nixed ours. Said Aster Park can't exactly have a festival without feeding people."

We stayed to talk with Brie a bit longer, then helped her close up shop when the sun dipped behind the mountaintops. She joined us as we returned to Main Street, the strings of lights overhead transforming the town square into something magical. The festival had shifted from its daytime energy to an evening buzz.

"They've got the Wayward Sons playing tonight," Brie said, linking her arm through mine like we were old friends. "Local favorites. They do an amazing cover of 'Sweet Home Colorado' that gets everyone dancing."

Noah rolled his eyes. "That's because half the town is related to someone in the band."

Music drifted through the cooling air, a mix of guitar, fiddle, and something that might have been a banjo. We followed the sound to the town square, where couples spun and twirled on a makeshift dance floor.

"You going to play ..." Brie started to ask.

"No," Noah cut her off before she could finish. "I'm sure Sam is eager to get back. It's been a long day."

I Burned My Tongue in Colorado

"Actually, I'd like to stay a little longer," I said, pulling out my phone again. "This is nothing like the nightlife in Los Angeles." I took a video of a grey-haired couple gliding past. The woman's skirt swished as her partner spun her around, both of them grinning like teenagers.

"Better or worse?" asked Brie.

The band shifted into a slower song, the fiddle drawing out long, sweet notes that seemed to echo off the mountains. Fairy lights twinkled in the trees around the square, catching the sparkle in people's eyes.

"Just different," I answered. "It's all good when people are having fun and enjoying themselves."

A cluster of pre-teen girls in matching t-shirts spotted Noah and descended on him like a pack of wolves.

"Mr. Barrett! Mr. Barrett! Dance with us!" They tugged at his sleeves, practically pulling him off his feet. Noah's usual stoic expression melted. "Ladies, you're supposed to be selling cookies, not harassing people."

"We already sold out!" One girl with braids announced proudly. "Now you have to dance with us."

"Girl Scouts," Brie explained, leaning close to me. "Noah helps them with their outdoor projects from time to time."

I watched as Noah let himself get dragged onto the dance floor by three determined twelve-year-olds. "Noah volunteers with girl scouts?"

Brie's eyes followed her brother as he attempted to teach the proper dance steps to his giggling entourage. "Last summer they built a boardwalk with a wheelchair ramp down by Mirror Lake. So people with disabilities could enjoy the view."

Brie and I watched in amusement as the girl scouts formed a circle around Noah. To my complete shock, he actually knew how to dance. Not just awkward swaying, but genuine rhythm and footwork. His boots tapped against the wooden platform in perfect time with the music as he spun his young dance partner in a circle.

"Okay, who taught mountain man how to dance?" I asked Brie.

"Mom insisted we both take lessons growing up. Said it was a life skill." Brie grinned. "Though I think Noah secretly enjoyed it more than he let on."

Noah twirled another scout under his arm with gentleness and grace, then caught our eyes over the crowd. His expression shifted to mild panic as more girls joined the circle. He mouthed "help me" toward Brie with pleading eyes.

"Looks like your brother needs backup," I said, expecting Brie to be the one to go do the rescuing.

But before I could protest, Brie grabbed my hand and pulled me into the fray. "Come on!" The scouts cheered as we joined their circle, but Brie had other plans. She smoothly maneuvered through the group, then gave me an unexpected push that sent me stumbling right into Noah.

"Your turn!" Brie announced, sweeping several disappointed scouts away with her. "Let's give them some space, girls!"

Noah's hands caught my waist to steady me, and suddenly we were standing chest to chest in the middle of the dance floor. The band transitioned into a slower song, as if on cue.

"Sorry about my sister," Noah said, but didn't let go. "She thinks she's clever."

"Well, you did ask for help." I placed my hand on his shoulder, falling into the proper dance position without thinking. "Though I'm not sure this counts as a rescue."

Noah's arm curved around my waist as we fell into step with the music, the singer's voice carrying across the square with a slight country twang.

My breath caught as Noah drew me closer, his other hand

warm against mine. The calluses on his palm brushed my fingers, reminding me of the strength hidden beneath his gentle touch. He moved with the same fluid grace he showed on mountain trails and climbing walls, leading me through the steps without hesitation.

"You really are full of surprises," I said, looking up at him. The string lights cast a soft glow across his features, softening the usual sharp angles of his face.

"Could say the same about you." His voice dropped low, meant only for me. "I thought you said you couldn't dance?"

"When did I say that?"

"At the river. When Diego was trying to get you to salsa."

"I didn't say I can't dance; I said I don't dance. You're not the only one with a mother who insisted on dance lessons."

The now-familiar scent of pine and coffee clung to his shirt. Noah adjusted his grip, thumb brushing the small of my back. His touch sent electricity down my spine, and I found myself leaning into him without meaning to.

As the music swelled, Noah spun me in a perfect turn before pulling me back. When I returned to his arms, we were even closer than before. His eyes met mine, deep blue in the twilight, and the rest of the festival seemed to fade away.

The music slowed, and the final notes of the song hung in the air between us. Noah's hand slid up my back, steady and sure. My heart thundered against my ribs as he bent his head toward mine, close enough that I could feel his breath ghost across my lips.

Everything else fell away.

Just Noah and I.

Face to face.

He leaned closer still ...

Buzzzz ... Buzzzz ... Buzzzz ...

My phone vibrated in my pocket. I ignored it, lost in the

magnetic pull of Noah's gaze. His fingers traced a path up my spine that made me shiver despite the warmth of his embrace.

The phone buzzed again. And again. The persistence of it shattering the perfect moment like a pickaxe on an icy lake.

"You should probably get that," Noah said, his lips still close enough that I could feel his breath on my cheek.

I pulled back just enough to fish out my phone, already regretting the movement. Marcus's name flashed across the screen, along with three missed calls and an urgent text:

MARCUS WILES:

VICTORIA NEEDS TO TALK

CALL IMMEDIATELY.

The screen's harsh blue light illuminated Noah's face as he read the message upside down. Something shuttered behind his eyes, with the familiar wall coming back up brick by brick. His hands fell away from my waist, leaving cold spots where his warmth had been.

"Duty calls." Noah's voice had lost its softness.

"Yeah." I shoved my phone back in my pocket without responding to the calls. "LuxeLife can wait."

Noah took a step back, the physical distance between us expanding into something more significant.

"It's getting late. We should head back so we can take another run at Devil's Ridge tomorrow. It will be good content for Victoria. So she can sell her resort, and I can hopefully keep my life together."

"Right."

"Plus, the sooner we finish this, the sooner you can get back to Los Angeles. Where you belong."

When I looked back up at him, his eyes were empty, his

face hard. It was a stark reminder of what I was really there to do. I was there to *create* content ... not get cozy with it.

"You'll need your rest," said Noah.

"Right. More authentic adventures." The edge in Noah's tone must have been contagious, because it had infected my voice, too.

Chapter Twenty-Three

T he lobby was eerily quiet after Noah dropped me off, the eyes of the mounted elk heads following me as I made my way through. The other guests were still out at the festival or tucked away in their rooms. After saying goodbye to Brie, the walk back to his Jeep had stretched longer than it had earlier, the comfortable silence replaced by something heavy and awkward.

The elevator hummed softly as it carried me to the penthouse floor, giving me exactly thirty-two seconds to contemplate the near-miss of whatever had almost happened with Noah on that dance floor.

My suite welcomed me with its perfectly curated luxury; the fireplace automatically flickered to life as I entered. It all felt hollow somehow, the Egyptian cotton sheets, the heated marble floors, the yarrow-infused night cream waiting on my bedside table.

I wrapped my arms around myself, already missing the warmth of Noah's embrace, wondering how we'd gone from almost kissing to ...

I Burned My Tongue in Colorado

I kicked off my shoes and flopped face-first onto the bed.

My phone vibrated again. With a groan, I rolled over and pulled it out. Now seven missed calls from Marcus. Four from Parker. And one text from Victoria.

VICTORIA STERLING:

CALL ME! NOW!

I pulled a pillow over my head. Whatever crisis they were having could wait until morning. My brain was too full of huckleberry muffins and fiddle music and the ghost sensation of Noah's hands on my waist.

The phone rang again, puncturing through the pillow barrier.

It was Victoria. Again. She wasn't the kind of person who gave up.

With a resigned sigh, I reached for my phone. "Hello?"

"What the hell do you think you're doing?" Victoria's voice sliced through the receiver, sharp as a stiletto. "I hired you to promote luxury travel, not turn into some goddamn wildlife rescuer. Since when are you Jane Goodall with an Instagram account?"

I sat up, confusion replacing exhaustion. "I'm sorry, what?"

"Don't play dumb with me, Samantha. The bird video. It's everywhere."

"Bird video?" I repeated, my brain struggling to connect the dots. "You mean the osprey rescue?"

"Yes, the osprey rescue." Her voice dripped with sarcasm. "Very heroic. Very touching. Very much the opposite of what I'm paying you to do."

I swung my legs over the side of the bed, fully alert now. "How do you even know about that? It just happened this afternoon." I thought back to earlier that day, the entire episode replaying in my brain. "And I never filmed anything. I didn't even pull out my phone. Once." It was true. The entire time I'd been so focused on saving the osprey, it had never even occurred to me to pull out my phone.

"Some tourist captured the whole thing and posted it online. Tagged Noah and the Adventure Center. Then someone recognized you and tagged you too."

Another text message from Parker popped onto my screen. It was a link to the video.

PARKER:

Over two million views in three hours!!!!

It's gone completely viral!!!!

Victoria's not going to be happy.

No shit, I thought to myself.

I scrambled for my laptop, pulling up Instagram while keeping the phone pressed to my ear. Sure enough, there it was, filling my notifications feed. Tags, comments, shares. Hundreds of them. No, thousands.

The video was surprisingly well-shot for an amateur, capturing the entire rescue from the moment Noah entered the lake. The camera followed me as I climbed the tree, focused on my face as I carefully navigated the branches. It caught my momentary fall, Noah's panicked reaction, then the successful rescue as Noah cradled the injured osprey. The final shot showed us walking away together, the bird safely wrapped in a towel against Noah's bare chest.

Another person had shared it and added a soundtrack, a rendition of "Somewhere Over the Rainbow." The whole thing played like a scene from a movie.

"It's actually really good," I murmured, forgetting Victoria was still on the line.

"Good?" Her voice rose an octave. "*GOOD?* Have you read

the comments? People are using this to attack LuxeLife directly."

I scrolled down to the comment section, and my stomach dropped. Not because of the criticism, but because of how right it was.

@WildernessDefender: "Maybe if luxury resorts stopped destroying natural habitats, wildlife wouldn't need rescuing in the first place. #SaveAsterPark"

@MountainMama42: "Big corporations like LuxeLife are why these birds are endangered. Stop building on protected land! #NoMoreResorts"

@ColoradoNative: "This is what happens when you prioritize profit over planet."

"Oh," I said, eloquence eluding me as I realized the uncomfortable truth. Usually, I was the creator, curating the content, spinning illusions that made the aspirational seem real. This time I was the content itself. Real content. Content that exposed exactly the kind of corporate destruction I'd been hired to spin.

"Oh? That's all you have to say?" Victoria's voice had gone dangerously quiet. "Let me be clear, Samantha. You were hired to promote our resort, not make us look like the bad guy. FIX. THIS. NOW."

"But how am I supposed to fix this?"

"That's literally your job!" Victoria snapped. "You're the influencer. Influence! Post about how LuxeLife practices eco-conscious luxury."

"Eco-conscious luxury?"

"How we're actually helping the environment."

"You literally have the severed heads of innocent animals on your wall," I said after putting the phone on mute.

"I don't care what you say, just change the narrative," barked Victoria.

I stared at the video, watching myself stretch toward the fishing line, determination etched on my face. For once in my social media career, I'd done something that actually mattered. Something real.

"These comments aren't entirely wrong, you know," I said quietly.

"Excuse me?"

"That fishing line didn't appear by magic. It was left there by people. Tourists, probably. Just like the ones who stay at your resort."

There was a long, dangerous silence on the other end of the line.

"Let me remind you of something, Samantha." Victoria's voice had dropped to a glacial whisper. "Your contract has strict performance metrics. Metrics I expect you to meet. I hired you to produce content that portrays LuxeLife as a facilitator of extraordinary experiences, not play grab-ass with some scruffy, small-town mountain man and his pet wolf."

"His name is Noah. And Yeti's a dog, not a wolf."

Victoria's voice was softer when she spoke again, but infinitely more deadly. "I can tell that you care about him, you know. It's obvious when you watch the video. The way you looked at him. The way he looked at you."

"Noah and I are simply business associates," I reassured her. "The only reason we're even working together is because it was your idea to make authentic Colorado adventure content."

"Mmm-hmm. If you say so, Samantha. But just in case saving your own ass isn't enough motivation, let me be clear. If you fail to deliver, Noah's little Adventure Center goes bye-bye forever."

"Is that a threat?"

"A threat? No, Samantha. It's not a threat. It's a promise."

The osprey's dark eyes flashed in my memory, followed by the image of Noah's face when he'd talked about his parents building the center from nothing.

"I expect you to get back on message starting tomorrow. No more wildlife rescues, no more local festival coverage, unless it somehow involves booking a deluxe spa package at my resort. I want authentic local content, but I want luxurious authentic."

"Luxurious authentic?" Was that even a thing?

"Aspirational authentic," said Victoria. "*Expensive* authentic."

"Yes, Ms. Sterling."

"You'll send Marcus all drafts of your posts before they go live going forward."

"But ..."

"No more surprises." The line went dead before I could respond.

I tossed my phone aside and stared at the paused video of the osprey rescue on my laptop, the freeze-frame capturing the exact moment Noah and I locked eyes after the osprey was safe.

"Grab-ass?" I watched the video again. Clearly, no asses were being grabbed. *Where did Victoria even come up with that nonsense?* But there was something in the look in both of our eyes. Relief. Accomplishment. A connection that no filter or caption could ever reproduce.

My laptop pinged with another notification. Parker was calling.

With a sigh, I accepted. His face appeared on the screen, hair sticking up like he'd been pulling at it for days.

"Finally!" He looked both frantic and exhilarated. "Have you seen what's happening? The osprey video is blowing up! It's getting picked up everywhere. News outlets, conservation groups, even National Geographic just shared it!"

"Victoria's furious," I said, cutting his enthusiasm off at the knees.

"She is?" Parker scrunched up his face. "But Sam, this is huge. The numbers are off the charts. And people are feeling things. Like genuine things. Like you're actually making a difference kinds of things. Isn't that pretty amazing?"

I glanced back at the video. "Yeah. It is. It's just too bad the person paying my bills doesn't think so."

"So what's the plan then?" asked Parker. "How are we spinning this?"

I flopped back on the bed, my mind spinning instead.

"Victoria wants me to bury this, to return to posting filtered photos of infinity pools and champagne flutes against mountain backdrops."

The safe, sterile version of Colorado that would drive people to book rooms at LuxeLife. But there was another Colorado. The one with huckleberry muffins and fiddle music and people who rescued ospreys without thinking of how it would play on social media. The one where every vendor knew every other vendor by name, and Girl Scouts built wheelchair ramps so everyone could enjoy the view.

"Sam?" Parker's voice pulled me back to reality.

Victoria's warning played back in my head. *If you fail to deliver, Noah's little Adventure Center goes bye-bye forever.*

"Sam? What do you want to do?" Parker asked again.

I thought long and hard. It was decision time. Keep playing grab-ass, as Victoria put it, with a sexy mountain man who made me feel like I was alive, or do the job I was hired to do, saving Noah's job as well as my own. In the end, there was really only one choice to make.

"One more," I said into the phone.

"Huh?"

"One more authentic adventure with Noah tomorrow, then I'll tell him it would be best if we went our separate ways. I'll stick to the resort for the rest of my trip. Shove pictures of spa treatments and gourmet meals down people's throats until they want to hurl."

Parker was quiet for a long time. For a moment, I thought maybe he had hung up. "Are you sure about this, Sam?"

"Yes." *No.* "I'm sure." *Not sure.* "Positive." *Not even a little bit.*

"You might be able to do both?"

"Look, Parker, it's getting late, and I need to think. I'll ping you tomorrow." I disconnected the call before my conscience could stop me.

Victoria was right about one thing for sure, though. I'd been hired to do a job. A job that, if I did it successfully, would not only catapult my career but save Noah's too.

A couple of days ago, it would have been a no-brainer. Enjoy the luxurious experiences of an all expenses paid trip to a world-class resort. Take pictures of myself doing it. Post to my feeds. Then rinse and repeat, rinse and repeat. Had things really changed that much?

The answer was no.

Reality check, Sam. Put your big-girl panties on and woman up.

Setting my phone aside, I settled into the plush armchair by the window, staring out at the sky full of stars. Back in LA, you could barely see anything through the smog and the light pollution. Here, the stars blanketed the sky like diamonds scattered across black velvet.

Followers. Like. Shares. Subscribers. Those numbers used to mean something to me. Used to make me feel important, powerful even. Mom and Dad thought I would always struggle to make ends meet with my "little internet hobby." They had no idea. The LuxeLife contract made me more money in a week than their restaurant did in an entire month.

But staring up at that vast expanse of sky, those countless points of light, I felt microscopic. What was the point of it all? Pretending to eat a fancy dinner for people I'd never meet. Wearing clothes I didn't actually shop for and could never afford on my own. Creating perfect moments for strangers who didn't know me. The real me.

When was the last time I'd shared a real meal with someone? Not for content, not for networking, just ... because?

It was breakfast.

On top of a mountain.

With Noah Barrett.

The mountains loomed dark and massive beyond my window, ancient and unmoved by all my carefully curated posts and stories. They'd been here long before social media existed, and they'd be here long after it was gone.

A shooting star streaked across the sky. In LA, I would have immediately grabbed my phone to capture it. Instead, I just watched it fade away, feeling smaller than ever.

* * *

The next morning, I walked into the Adventure Center and once again heard the strummed melody of an acoustic guitar. This time, instead of letting the bell ring when the door slammed shut, I closed the door gently so it wouldn't make a noise.

I Burned My Tongue in Colorado

"Anybody home?" My whisper echoed through the empty space. Noah, Diego, and Jenn were nowhere to be seen.

The wall of climbing gear stood untouched, ropes coiled neatly on their hooks. Yesterday's chalk marks still dusted the practice wall.

Behind the desk, next to a laminated map, there was a large day calendar tacked to the wall. A thick red Sharpie circled the last day of the month. I didn't need anyone to tell me why. The end of the lease. The day LuxeLife closed the Adventure Center for good.

Unless, of course, Noah and I were successful. Prove that authenticity was still a suitable business model. Show Victoria and the entire world that authentic Colorado adventures were worth taking.

The guitar continued playing, joined by a burst of laughter, which drifted in through an open window facing out back. I followed the sound, weaving past the desk with its scattered trail maps, then down a hallway and out a screen door onto the deck.

The morning sun hit me full force as I stepped outside. Diego and Jenn lounged in Adirondack chairs around a cozy fire pit, coffee mugs in hand. Yeti looked up and smiled, tail thumping against the deck boards.

Noah's fingers screeched to a hard stop on the strings of the guitar as soon as he saw me. The instrument made a sound equivalent to a grand piano being dropped out of a seven-story window.

"You do play the guitar," I said from the doorway.

"No. I don't." He set the guitar aside as if he'd never seen it before in his life.

"There's our osprey whisperer," Diego called out, raising his mug in greeting.

Jenn propped her feet on a log. "Want some coffee? Brie dropped off a sample of her latest roast."

I hesitated in the doorway, thrown off by the casual scene. "Absolutely. But aren't we supposed to be gearing up for Devil's Ridge?"

Noah stayed quiet, the morning light catching the stubble along his jaw. His expression was unreadable, nothing like the man who'd held me close under festival lights the night before. Jenn and Diego, on the other hand, both stared at me with matching grins.

Something was up.

"Why is everyone smiling?"

"Noah's not smiling," Diego pointed out.

"Noah never smiles," Jenn countered.

"Good point."

"Why doesn't it look like anyone is getting ready to go climbing?" This time, I directed my question directly at Noah.

"Change of plans." Noah took a slow sip of his coffee. "There's a small chance of a storm system moving in later tonight. Can't risk getting caught up there when the rocks are wet."

Jenn and Diego were still smiling suspiciously.

"What aren't you telling me?" I planted my hands on my hips. "You're all acting weird."

"Weird?" Diego pressed a hand to his chest in mock offense. "Us?"

"We would never," Jenn added with an exaggerated shake of her head that only confirmed my suspicions.

"Well, I can't afford to take a day off," I said. "I have a job to do, remember? Victoria ripped me a new one last night. Luxe-Life is expecting authentic Colorado content that's luxurious, aspirational, and expensive. So whatever you have planned, I better look good doing it."

I Burned My Tongue in Colorado

Noah set down his coffee mug. "So that's what your friend Victoria wanted?"

"She thinks I've strayed a little too far off-brand."

"Then they're really not going to like the content you're going to be getting today." Jenn's smile grew even wider. Diego chuckled.

"What content?" I crossed my arms. I didn't like where this was going. Not one bit. "It's not more hiking, is it?"

Diego and Jenn exchanged another one of those knowing looks that made me want to scream. Jenn's smile grew wider still. "You won't have to take a single step."

Chapter Twenty-Four

"Oh no. No, no, no." I slowed my pace as Jenn led us toward the stables, the scent of hay and horse already making my nose twitch. "I don't do animals."

Yeti barked, as if to remind me she was there and could hear me.

"Except you, Yeti. You don't smell. As much."

As soon as I stepped into the stable, a massive brown head poked out over one of the stall doors, lips flapping as the horse nickered. I jumped back, bumping into Noah's chest. After he steadied me, I quickly stepped away, trying to keep up with Jenn as she walked down the aisle.

"This big fellow here is Duke." Jenn patted the brown horse's neck. "He's our gentle giant. Used to be a show horse in Denver until he got too old and his owner abandoned him."

Duke's liquid brown eyes fixed on me as he stretched his neck out, nostrils flaring.

"He's just saying hello," Jenn chuckled. "Here. Let him smell your hand."

I Burned My Tongue in Colorado

I shot Noah a panicked look, but he just crossed his arms, face still neutral. Taking a deep breath, I held my hand out. Duke's whiskers tickled my palm.

"Over here we have Pepper." Jenn moved to a dappled grey horse. "She's got attitude, but knows these trails better than anyone. And this is Scout. He's our newest addition. Former ranch horse who needed a quieter life."

We stopped at a stall housing a copper-colored horse with a white stripe down its face. He had his head hung low, dozing in the afternoon sun.

"And this is Biscuit. He's steady, patient, and smooth as butter on the trails." Biscuit lifted his head, ears pricked forward with interest. Unlike Duke's overwhelming size or Pepper's sharp gaze, something about Biscuit's gentle demeanor put me at ease.

"He won't bite?" I asked.

"Biscuit? He's more likely to fall asleep on the trail than cause any trouble," said Jenn. "Been teaching kids to ride for years."

Biscuit took a few steps forward, stretching his neck to sniff at my shoulder. His breath was warm against my neck, and I found myself reaching up to touch his soft nose before I could stop myself.

"I think he likes you," said Jenn. "And he's perfect for beginners."

"I'm not a beginner. I'm a never-er. I've never been on a horse, and I don't plan to start now."

"Well, too bad for you, because you don't really have a choice," said Noah, his grumpiness dialed back up to a ten. "You weren't the only one who got a call from Victoria, apparently."

"What's he talking about?"

The smile slipped from Jenn's face. She walked over to a

soft-sided cooler waiting on a hay bale. There was a LuxeLife logo embroidered on the side in fancy gold lettering. "Maya dropped this off this morning."

"What are we supposed to do with that?" I asked.

Jenn patted the cooler bag. "There's a very expensive-looking bottle of champagne in there. Seems you and Noah are expected to do a LuxeLife toast when you get to the top of the mountain." She wrinkled her nose. "When Maya dropped it off, she made it clear it wasn't optional."

"A LuxeLife toast? To what exactly?"

"Their dedicated stewardship of the natural environment. Marcus emailed a script and everything."

Across the stable, Noah scoffed. One look at his face was all it took to see how he felt about the arrangement.

"You actually agreed to this?" I asked.

Jenn answered for him. "Noah's agreed to play nice until Victoria renews his contract. *Our* contract. Isn't that right, Noah?"

Noah only grunted, then spun on his boots and marched out of the stable.

"You sure he's going to be okay with this?" I asked Jenn.

"If you pull this off and save his family's business, he will be. Let's get you saddled up."

Jenn led Biscuit out of his stall and into the grassy clearing in front of the stable. "First rule, you've got to be chill. Horses can sense fear." She adjusted my stance as I stood next to Biscuit. "So take a deep breath and relax those shoulders."

"You expect me to relax?" My shoulders crept back up toward my ears as soon as Biscuit shifted toward me.

"Second rule, always approach from the left side." Jenn demonstrated, running her hand along Biscuit's neck. "Let him see you coming. No sudden movements."

Across the clearing, Noah led Duke to a grassy area, Yeti at their heels ... or hooves, rather. Noah scratched the monster horse behind the ears, then flung the LuxeLife branded cooler bag over the back of the saddle.

"When you're in the saddle, you need to use your legs to communicate," continued Jenn. "Squeeze with both legs to go forward, pull back on the reins to stop."

I nodded, my throat dry. Biscuit stood perfectly still, probably wondering why this nervous city girl was taking so long to learn the basics.

"The most important thing is to trust your horse," Jenn continued. "Biscuit knows these trails better than any of us. He'll take care of you if you let him."

"Right." I swallowed hard. "Trust a thousand-pound animal I just met."

"See how his ears are forward?" Jenn pointed. "That means he's interested, paying attention. If they pin back flat, he's annoyed or uncomfortable."

"Is that why Noah always has his ears pinned back?" I asked, loud enough for Noah to hear me.

Jenn chuckled, but Noah ignored me. "See? His head's relaxed, nostrils soft. Good signs." Jenn ran her hand down Biscuit's neck. "Horses are like people. They put up walls when they're scared or threatened. The trick is showing them they don't need those defenses."

I caught the pointed look Jenn gave Noah. "Are we still talking about horses?"

"Just saying, fear's a natural response to the unknown. But sometimes ..." She guided my hand to rest on Biscuit's shoulder. "You have to trust that what's on the other side of that wall is worth the risk."

The horse's coat felt warm and smooth under my palm. His steady breathing had a calming effect, and I found my own shoulders relaxing.

"He's telling you he's ready when you are." Jenn stepped back. "No rush, no pressure. Just two beings learning to trust each other."

I kept my hand on Biscuit's shoulder, absorbing his quiet strength. For the first time since arriving at the stables, the knot of anxiety in my chest loosened.

"Ready to mount up?" Jenn patted the saddle.

I looked at the stirrup hanging at Biscuit's side, then at the considerable distance to the ground. The last time I'd tried to get on something this tall, I'd face-planted into a climbing wall. "I suppose."

"Foot here." Jenn pointed to the stirrup. "Hand here."

With Jenn guiding me, I grabbed the stirrup and pushed off the ground. Just as my foot left the ground, Biscuit shifted, throwing off my balance, and I slid back down.

"Maybe try jumping higher?" Jenn suggested.

"Right, because jumping is my specialty." I tried again, getting my foot in the stirrup. My arms trembled as I pulled myself up.

"You've got it," Jenn encouraged. "Just swing your leg over."

I hung there, suspended halfway up, my right leg flailing uselessly. Biscuit chose that moment to take a step forward.

"No, no, no." I clutched the saddle tighter.

"For crying out loud." Noah's footsteps crunched in the grass behind me. Two large hands planted themselves firmly on my bottom and shoved upward.

I yelped as I flopped across the saddle. Clinging to the horse's neck, I wiggled my way into the saddle. Once I was set, Noah adjusted the stirrups and checked the straps. The familiar scent of him, pine and coffee, reminded me again of how close we'd been the previous night.

"There."

"I'm not going to fall off, am I?"

"Better hope not." Noah didn't seem as concerned as I thought he should be. "Sorry, we don't have any saddles with a seatbelt."

As soon as Noah stepped back over to Duke, Biscuit decided he'd had enough of standing around and started trotting toward the trailhead.

"Whoa!" I bounced in the saddle, yanking on the reins. "Stop! Halt! Whatever the horse word for stop and turn around!" Biscuit angled toward a tree, forcing me to lean in the opposite direction to keep from being scraped off his back by its trunk.

"Pull back harder!" Jenn called after me.

"I'm trying!" Biscuit ignored my increasingly desperate commands. Remembering Jenn's lessons, I pulled the reins to the right, trying to turn the horse around.

Biscuit turned right, all right, a hard right into the trees. I ducked just in time to avoid having my head taken off by a tree branch.

Noah whistled, and Biscuit stopped immediately. Noah's second whistle must have activated the horse's reverse setting because Biscuit shuffled backward into the clearing.

"Oh my God, he's moonwalking. My horse is literally moonwalking."

Noah pulled Duke up alongside us, looking very much at home in the saddle. "Let's just hurry up and get this over with. Then you can go back to taking pictures of chocolate truffles or something. Hyah!" He dug his heels into Duke's side and they trotted off down a dirt path that disappeared into the forest. Yeti chased after them, tongue lolling out in a wolfish grin.

"Okay," I told Biscuit, squeezing my legs like Jenn had taught me. "Follow them. Go. Hyah!"

Biscuit stood motionless.

"Biscuit, come on, move!"

The horse swished its tail and started walking ... sideways?

"What are you doing?" I grabbed the saddle horn as Biscuit drifted left, then right, like a drunk uncle at a wedding.

"Biscuit, go. Move! Hyah!"

The horse responded by pawing at the ground like it was auditioning for "Horses Got Talent." Then he kept shifting his hooves, like he was dancing the salsa.

"Maybe Diego should take *you* kayaking."

Jenn marched over. "Come on, Biscuit, stop messing around. You know the routine."

Eventually, we caught up.

Noah pointed to my phone, which I was using to create a "HorseCam" video. "Keep that thing in your saddlebag. This trail gets bumpy. One good jostle and you can kiss your phone goodbye."

"Yes, sir, Mr. Grumpy Cowboy Face." I slipped my phone into the leather pouch.

"I thought it was Grumpy Mountain Face."

"Well, you're on a horse now, so ..." He really did look like he belonged on the set of *Yellowstone*.

His lips softened, and once again, I wondered exactly how soft those lips might feel on my own. We rode in silence for a moment. I decided to go for it. "We need to talk about last night."

"What's there to talk about?"

"No," I said. "Let's not do this."

"Do what?"

"That. That right there. Pretend like you don't know what's going on."

I Burned My Tongue in Colorado

"But I don't know what's going on."

I pressed my lips together, biting back the words that almost came out of my mouth. I had to take a deep breath to rally my patience. "Something happened between us last night. And we're not going to just pretend it didn't happen."

"You're imagining things."

"I told you we're not playing that game."

"What game?"

"The whole ... enemies to friends, friends to enemies trope. This isn't one of your Bigfoot mountain virgin romance novels."

"Pretty sure she wasn't a virgin."

I refused to let him distract me. "I'm not going to sit here in this saddle on this horse for the rest of the day and let you go back to being the grumpy mountain man just because two otherwise intelligent, mature adults aren't capable of having an honest conversation. It's a cliché. And we're not doing it."

The stubborn mountain man stayed stubbornly silent, staring out at the distant mountains, as if he was trying to figure out a way to teleport himself over there, as far away as possible from me. Finally, he turned back to look me in the eye. "Fine. You want to talk about last night?"

"Yes, yes, I do."

"Honest talk?"

"Please."

"Fine. Here's the truth. I like you. I think you like me. We were having a good time."

In other circumstances, my brain would have screeched to a hard stop when Noah said, "I like you." My heart beat faster. The breath in my lungs came in short, shallow bursts. *He liked me. He really liked me! Even better, he admitted it!*

"In another world, yes, maybe there could be something between us," Noah admitted. Duke snorted again, as if to put an exclamation on Noah's point. "But in our world, the *real* world, you're the LuxeLife hired gun and I'm the one being blackmailed to help you."

"I don't know that I'd call it blackmail ..."

"We're being honest, remember?"

I gave him a nod, even though my eyes fell to Biscuit's mane.

"That's what this is. You and I never would have started any of this if Victoria hadn't forced it and we both know it. We were stuck together. You pursuing your dream job and me trying to save the only life I've ever known."

"Noah ..."

"You wanted me to talk? Then let me talk. Please." His tone was not unkind. More desperate. More pleading. "Come on, Sam, you know the score. This is a business arrangement. That's all this is. And that's all it should be." His eyes drifted off to the mountains. "Maybe we just forgot that for a minute. That's all."

I swallowed down the emotion bubbling up from my throat. The raw emotion in his voice caught me completely off guard.

"Even if it wasn't just business, when this thing is over, win or lose, the big-city girl is going back to the big city. And the grumpy mountain dude, or whatever it was you called me, is going to stay put where he belongs. Goodbye. The end."

When Noah spoke, it was more like he was talking to himself than talking to me. He stared off at the mountains, and when he finally turned back, his eyes weren't angry. If anything, they were sad.

"That honest enough for you?" I barely heard him over the clomping of the hooves.

"Actually, that was ... maybe a little too honest." At first, the bluntness of his response left me dumbfounded. But what was even more dumbfounding was ... he was exactly right.

"I meant what I said, Sam. I do like you. I hope one day we

can be friends. But that's about as much as we're gonna get out of this little Colorado adventure."

"Okay," I said. I didn't know what else to say. What else *could* I say? "So, what do we do now?"

Noah thought about it for a moment. "I think the best thing we can do right now is get through Victoria's little ..." He waved at Yeti, then gestured at Biscuit. "Victoria's little dog and pony show and then we go our separate ways. You can go take pictures of yourself with cucumbers on your face at the resort, and I can go back to trying to save the jobs of me and my friends. No hard feelings, okay?"

"Okay." I nodded. And it was okay. There were no hard feelings, at least on my part, because I didn't have any feeling left at all.

"Hee-yah," Noah nudged Duke's flanks with his legs and the big horse surged forward, Biscuit falling in line behind him.

Chapter Twenty-Five

As the horses plodded further along the trail, the world moved in slow motion. Birds chirped overhead, their songs mixing with the soft clopping of hooves against packed dirt and the occasional snort from Duke and Biscuit. The scent of wildflowers fused with pine trees and meadow grass in the mountain air. Noah and I rode in silence, pretending to enjoy the peace and tranquility of the forest.

He was better at pretending than I was, though. The silence was suffocating.

"I like you too, by the way!" I shouted toward Noah's back, a couple dozen yards in front of me.

At first, he ignored me.

"Did you hear me, Mr. Grouchy Mc'Grumpy Grinch? I said I like you too!"

Noah pulled back on the reins, and Duke shuffled to a stop, kicking up trail dust. "What are you talking about?"

I somehow veered Biscuit alongside him. "You said, and I quote, I like you. I think you like me. Remember? During our honest talk?"

"I remember."

"What I'm saying is, you were right. I do like you."

"You've been spending this whole time replaying that conversation in your head over and over, haven't you?"

"Well, not the entire time. I thought about how much better this horse ride would be if there were muffins involved, too."

As he stared back at me, I could see the war playing out on his face. His blue eyes darted away, as if he was looking for an escape, then flickered back to mine. His lips parted as if he were going to speak, then pressed hard back together.

Noah looked down at Duke's mane one more time, but when he looked back up, I caught the hint of mischief twinkling in his eye. "Question for you."

"This sounds serious."

The look Noah gave me suggested all his questions were serious, and he wouldn't be asking them if they weren't. "On a scale of one to ten, how much do you hate this?"

"This?" I took a moment to consider what he meant by "this." The horseback riding? The whole being-stuck-in-authentic-Colorado-adventures situation? The whole being-stuck-in-authentic-Colorado-adventures situation with him?

"I suppose it depends," I answered, trying to keep my voice neutral.

Truth be told, despite our brutally honest conversation, followed by the traumatically awkward silence, and the fact that my butt felt like an overly enthusiastic meat mallet had tenderized it, I wasn't hating the other parts. At least it had given me more time to spend with Noah.

Before we parted ways permanently.

"Why are you asking?"

"Because your answer will determine what happens next. Scale of one to ten."

"What happens if I say one?" I asked.

"If you say one, and you really hate this, we turn around and go back. I drop you off at the resort where you get some sort of spa thingy and eat fancy snacks."

"I do enjoy spa thingies," I admitted. "And fancy snacks. Especially since I didn't get any muffins today. But we still have Victoria's video to shoot."

"Fuck Victoria's video," said Noah. "Did you actually think I was going to do that shit for even one second?"

"No." I puffed out my chest in my best tough-girl impression. "Did you actually think I was?"

"You were absolutely going to do Victoria's video."

Biscuit stumbled over a muddy pothole, and I yelped as I grabbed the pommel with both hands. "Fine. I probably was."

Noah raised an eyebrow.

"I absolutely was."

Noah pulled back on the reins, then turned Duke around, prepared to head back to the stable. "It's fine. I don't blame you. You were hired to do a job, and you're committed to doing it. No shame in that." Sinking his heels into Duke's sides, he began heading back down the trail.

"Wait." Biscuit started to turn around as well, but I pulled back on the reins to stop him from following. "What if I say ten?" I called after Noah.

Noah held Duke in place, turned back toward me. "Remember that spot at the end of Dawn Patrol? At the top of the trail, looking out over the mountains?"

"The place where we ate muffins," I said.

Noah nodded. "I know a place even better than that."

As miserable as that hike was, I couldn't imagine a place more beautiful than the mountain overlook at sunrise at the end of it. The view had made all the torture and suffering worth it.

I Burned My Tongue in Colorado

"There's this spot up near Thunder Basin," said Noah. "Not on any of the maps."

"A secret trail then."

Noah pressed his finger to his lips. "Shhh."

"Does this secret trail lead to muffins?" I asked.

"You really have a thing about muffins, don't you?"

I shrugged. "What can I say? They were delicious. I've decided to name my firstborn child Huckleberry."

"Is that a boy name or a girl name?"

"Either," I said. "Both."

Noah just shook his head, another grin forming on his perfectly shaped lips. Lips that looked incredibly kissable in the filtered light coming down through the pine trees.

"If this trail is such a secret, how come you know about it?"

"My dad and I would camp up there when I was a kid." For a few moments, it was like Noah's head was already there. "There's this old pine on the edge of the cliff that's been struck by lightning maybe three, four times. Should've died, but it keeps growing, all twisted and beautiful. During sunset, the light hits these crystal formations in the rock face behind it, and the whole cliff lights up like it's on fire."

"Ten," I said, without giving it another thought. "My answer is ten. I want to go to *that* place. The place with the lightning tree. The place you went as a kid."

The intensity of my voice surprised me. But what was even more surprising was how badly I really wanted to go there. And not just for an amazing photo op. I wanted to go to this secret place for a little peek into Noah's past. I wanted to see what kind of place could have such an impact on him. Even if I had to hike mountains, raft rivers, and ride wild horses to get there.

* * *

It was no wonder that Noah's secret trail was a secret. The trees were as dense as the floor space at a Taylor Swift concert, and the trail got even narrower the further we went. I ducked as Biscuit tried to dislodge me from my saddle with another low-hanging tree branch. "Did you train him to do this on purpose?" I asked.

"He's not usually like this," Noah called from somewhere behind me. "Must be feeling playful today."

"Playful? More like homicidal." I spat out a mouthful of leaves as I looked for the drive shaft so I could shift Biscuit into reverse.

Biscuit snorted, spraying horse snot and veering off the trail again toward a particularly nasty-looking thicket.

"Maybe I should take the lead from here on out," said Noah.

I swatted another branch out of my face as Noah and Duke squeezed past us on the trail. "How far is this place, anyway?" I asked.

"It's a bit of a ride," Noah admitted. "About an hour and a half just to get there, then another hour and a half to get back. You okay with that?"

Let's see, I thought, spending a couple of hours watching Noah's denim-wrapped butt sway back and forth on the rear end of a horse ... yeah, I thought. I can deal.

"I'm okay with that," I said out loud, keeping the part about the butt viewing to myself.

The secret trail zigzagged up the mountainside, each turn bringing another postcard-perfect vista into view. Snow-capped peaks pierced cotton-candy clouds while golden aspens dotted the slopes like confetti.

My fingers itched to pull out my phone. Victoria wanted beautifully authentic Colorado content? This was it.

Raw, untamed, breathtaking.

I Burned My Tongue in Colorado

The kind of beauty that would drive follower counts and engagement rates into overdrive. My hand crept toward the saddlebag.

"Everything okay back there?" Noah called without turning around.

"Other than my horse attempting arboreal homicide, everything's great."

"We should hydrate," Noah said from ahead of me. "You about ready for a break?"

"Yes!"

"Follow me."

Clenching my thighs around the saddle, I used the reins to guide Biscuit off the side of the trail, through the slalom of pine trees, around a jagged boulder, and then into an open meadow where we stopped on cue with both grace and precision. I was now an expert equestrian. Or ... Biscuit was simply following the swish of Duke's tail, which was about three feet in front of his nose.

"So when you said the word hydrate, were you thinking Pinot Grigio or Chardonnay?"

"I was thinking lukewarm water from a canteen." Noah jumped out of the saddle and approached Biscuit on foot. "Here, let me help you get off."

Both our eyes went wide as we simultaneously realized what he had said. I felt my cheeks flush hot as I tried to banish the inappropriate thoughts suddenly racing through my mind.

"I mean, ah, let me help you down from your horse." Noah's deep voice sent another shiver down my spine.

When Noah reached up to help me dismount, his muscular hands caught my waist, and I slid down against his solid chest. For one charged moment, I was hyper-aware of everywhere he touched. His fingers at my sides, the warmth radiating through his flannel shirt, the woodsy scent of pine needles clinging to every inch of his body. My feet touched the ground, but my heart kept racing long after he stepped away.

Noah bobbed his head toward the view, a fever dream of purple columbines and yellow glacier lilies. The vibrant flowers seemed to stretch for miles, a kaleidoscope of colors swaying gently in the mountain breeze. "So, what do you think?"

"It's beautiful," I said, careful not to say out loud what was going through my head.

"Yeti, here girl!" Noah shouted at the trees. When Yeti came running, Noah pulled the canteen hooked by a carabiner to the saddle and filled a collapsible dog bowl with water. Once Yeti had her fill, Noah reached over to hand the canteen to me.

"I guess I know where I stand in the favorites order." I took a step and suddenly realized I was now permanently bowlegged. For the rest of my life, instead of walking anywhere, I was going to have to mosey. "As soon as I get back to the resort, I'm getting a hot stone butt massage at the spa. These leather saddles aren't exactly made of memory foam.

"Hot stone butt massage? Is that even a thing?"

"If it isn't, it should be."

"You see that boulder over there?" Noah pointed at a large rock. "It's been sitting all day in the sun. Should be hot enough for you."

"Ha ha, Mr. Mountain Grumpy Dude. Ha ha."

Noah tended to the horses, then laid out a saddle blanket so we could sit.

"You guys should do a Saddle and Straddle package," I said as I made myself comfortable on the blanket. "Or the Trot and Knot."

The look on Noah's face suggested he didn't think my idea was as brilliant as I did.

"It would be a horseback riding and massage bundle. Victoria would love it. Except for the horseback riding part."

"I'll think on it." He paused for two seconds. "Yeah, no."

He handed me the canteen. I took a sip. It was warm. It was stale. It was water.

While we drank, Yeti frolicked in the meadow. I hadn't realized wolf-dogs were capable of frolicking, but she looked like she was having the time of her life. She rolled through a patch of wild iris then played tag with a butterfly.

"I should be filming this." I moseyed over to Biscuit, bowlegged, then grabbed my phone from the saddlebag. "Yeti! Here girl!"

"Just to warn you, she's not had any dog model training," said Noah as he watched us skeptically.

"That's okay. She's a natural." Yeti snapped her jaws at a flying bug buzzing around her ears. "Yeti, can you just ..." I patted the ground next to a particularly photogenic cluster of flowers.

Camera rolling, Yeti flopped onto her back, paws waving in the air, rolling in the dirt.

"No, Yeti, like this." I demonstrated what I wanted, crawling through the grass. Noah didn't bother to suppress a snort. "Don't judge. This is art."

"This is ridiculous," he muttered, but I caught the smile tugging at his lips.

"Yeti, look majestic!" I snapped another dozen shots. "Channel your inner wolf."

Yeti responded by rolling deeper into the flowers, crushing several beneath her furry bulk.

"Work with me here." I army-crawled to a better angle. "Noah, can you get her to look more ... mountain-y?"

"Mountain-y?"

"You know, like she's contemplating the profound mysteries of nature or something."

"She's probably contemplating whether she should bite you."

I switched to video mode. "Yeti, run through the flowers! Be free! Be wild!"

Yeti wagged her tail and stayed exactly where she was.

"Fine." I flopped onto my back beside her. "We'll go for the lazy mountain dog aesthetic. Very relatable." I took a selfie with the two of us side-by-side.

Noah's face appeared above me, blocking my view of the gathering clouds. "You done playing Wild Kingdom? We need to get moving if we're going to get there and back before dark." I followed Noah's eyes as he looked up at the sky, fixed on some of the darker clouds off in the distance.

"You mentioned there was a chance of rain ..."

"Not until later tonight." Noah tilted his head as if he were a professional windsock, assessing the speed and direction of the breeze. "We should be okay."

"Should be?"

"Worst case, we get a little drizzle on our way back. You won't melt if you get wet, will you?"

"Is that some kind of wicked witch reference?"

"You're the one who said it, not me. We can turn around now if you want."

"No, I want to keep going."

"You sure?"

"Positive." I would not let the chance of a little rain stop me from seeing Noah's secret place. It would take a monsoon to stop me. Or muffins. I would have been easily distracted by muffins too.

"Then let's go.

I stuck my phone in my back pocket, then waddled over to Biscuit to continue onward.

Chapter Twenty-Six

The trees parted, and Biscuit stepped into a clearing, Duke and Noah right behind us. I opened my mouth to say something, but the words died in my throat. The valley appeared so suddenly it stole my breath away. One moment we were climbing through dense forest, and the next ... paradise.

It was the kind of view that made you believe in magic, or at least in whatever supernatural power was responsible for landscape design. Jagged peaks pierced a canvas of swirling clouds, their snow-capped summits gleaming silver in the afternoon light. A crystalline lake stretched below, its surface like glass.

I just sat there, drinking in the raw beauty of it all.

As Noah hopped off Duke, I slid off Biscuit, legs wobbling like I was walking the plank on a pirate ship. At the edge of the clearing, I spotted what had to be the lightning tree, a massive old oak split right down the middle, its halves curving away from each other like two mythical serpents reaching for the sky.

The bark was scorched black in places, but somehow the tree had survived and thrived.

"You were right," I admitted. "So you came out here a lot as a kid?"

Noah took a deep breath of the crisp mountain air. "Every summer. Dad would pack up the Jeep with camping gear, and we'd spend weeks exploring these mountains. No phones, no TV. Just us."

"You really love it up here, don't you?"

His eyes fixed on the distant peaks. "It's not about loving it. It's about respecting it. Understanding it." He glanced at me. "Some things aren't meant to be packaged and sold, Sam. They're just meant to be experienced."

Noah grabbed the canteen and gave Yeti another bowl of water, then offered it to me.

"You know, my dad built the original adventure program with nothing but local knowledge and respect for these mountains. Both of which he got from my grandfather, who got them from his father before that. Now corporate suits who've never spent a night under the stars want to package and sell what took generations to learn." I followed his eyes to the LuxeLife-branded cooler. "Just because Victoria calls it authentic doesn't make it real."

"What does authentic even mean anymore?" I asked, more to myself than Noah. "Is it only authentic if it stays exactly the same forever? Or can something evolve and still keep its soul?"

Noah was quiet for a moment. "Maybe authentic just means being honest about what you are. Not pretending to be something you're not."

I thought about my perfectly posed photos, the careful captions, the strategic hashtags. "I'm not sure I even know who I am anymore."

"Seems to me like you're someone who actually cares about

getting it right." Noah's eyes met mine. "That counts for something."

"Does it?" I asked, shaking my head. "I used to review these tiny Mexican restaurants. You saw."

"I did."

"Places where abuelitas made tortillas by hand and refused to write down recipes. It was real, you know?"

"What changed?"

"Money," I said simply. "Paying bills. Trying to survive. Sponsors pay contracts for luxury content. Not hole-in-the-wall taco joints."

"Or hole-in-the-wall Adventure Centers. Apparently."

I nodded. "I guess I adapted."

"I guess we all do," agreed Noah.

We stared back over the valley, each lost in our own world.

"So all this camping with your dad, that's where you learned your badass wilderness ninja skills?"

His hands stilled on the blade of grass he'd been twirling between his fingers. "Dad taught me how to read weather patterns, find edible plants. He showed me how to tie proper knots when I was six. By eight, I could start a fire in the rain."

In the distance, a rumble of thunder rolled across the Colorado sky, as if Mother Nature was accepting Noah's challenge. "Dad used to say you could read the mountains like a book. Each track, broken twig, or scattered feather tells a story." I watched his face as he spoke, his usual guardedness melting away.

"I wish my dad taught me cool stuff like that. The only thing my dad taught me was how to fold dumplings. Well, he tried to teach me. They always come out weird-looking and lumpy. Like little mutant Buddha statues."

"I'm sure they tasted good."

"That's what Mom said. She'd tell me it didn't matter how they looked, as long as they were made with love."

"That's what my mom used to say about pie crusts." Noah's smile was bittersweet.

Across the clearing, we watched Yeti sniffing the grass like she was hunting something. Perhaps an attempt to show that her owner wasn't the only one with superior wilderness skills.

"So, your parents still cook a lot?"

"They own a dim sum restaurant in Chinatown."

"That must have been interesting growing up."

"That's one word for it. Other words are loud. Intense. Chaotic. I grew up doing homework surrounded by the sounds of broccoli chopping and sizzling woks. The smell of five-spice powder still takes me right back there."

Staring out over the mountains, soaking in the views, it seemed Noah wasn't in a hurry to leave. Which was good, because I wasn't in a hurry either. It was one of those moments you want to remember for the rest of your life, and you make a conscious effort to make sure you commit every detail to memory.

"It's not that hard, you know," said Noah, breaking the spell.

"Have you tried making dumplings?"

"Not dumplings. I meant reading tracks."

"Maybe not for you, it isn't. Or natural born predator over there." I thumbed toward Yeti.

"Anybody can do it."

I could only assume that by "anybody", he didn't mean me.

"Here, let me show you." He scanned the ground. "Elk come through here all the time." It took only a few minutes of searching for him to find something. "See, come over here."

I wobbled over, still bowlegged and saddle sore, then crouched down beside him. Noah traced his finger along the edge of what looked like a dent in the dirt to me, but clearly held volumes of information to his trained eye.

"This is an elk track," he explained, his voice dropping into a wilderness professor tone. "See the heart shape? And how it's split at the top like this?" He traced the outline. "Each animal leaves a distinct print. Deer tracks are smaller, more pointed. Moose are huge, like dinner plates."

I leaned closer, genuinely fascinated by how animated he became when sharing his knowledge.

"But tracking isn't just about footprints." Noah pointed at a broken twig. "It's about reading the entire story. Direction, speed, how recently they passed by."

"How can you tell all that from a footprint?"

"The depth tells you weight and speed. See how this one pushes deeper at the front? The elk was moving at a trot, not walking." He gestured to a nearby pine. "And look at the bark here, see the rub marks? That's a bull elk marking his territory."

He looked up, catching me staring at him rather than the track. "What?"

"Nothing," I blurted. "Just ... I'm impressed." I looked down at the tracks with new appreciation, seeing not just dents in the dirt but a narrative hidden in plain sight, waiting for someone with the right knowledge to decode it.

"First time I tracked an elk, I was maybe seven. Dad had me crawling through the mud, pointing out bent grass blades and half-eaten leaves. When she finally led us to the herd, I was so excited I stood up and scared them all away."

"Did he get angry?"

"Nah. Just laughed. Sometimes the chase is better than the catch." Noah's eyes were on me like a hunter stalking prey.

"I guess that depends on what you're chasing," I said. "And what she does after you catch her."

Noah didn't even try to hide his grin this time. "I guess so."

"Can I ask you something?"

"Shoot."

"How long ... how long have your parents been gone?"

"Long time." The way his eyes glazed over suggested it felt like yesterday. "They were setting up a new route. Something went wrong with the anchor point."

"A climbing accident ..."

He nodded. "I'd just graduated from high school.

"Noah, I'm so sorry."

"Like I said, it was a long time ago."

"But you were so young."

"Brie had it worse than me. She was only fourteen."

"So wait ... you raised her?"

"Someone had to."

I watched him stare out at the mountains, his jaw tight.

"Thank you for sharing this place with me," I said.

Another rumble of thunder rolled in from the horizon, this time accompanied by a flash of distant lightning that lit up the sky. Noah's face darkened with the clouds. "We should get back before that storm hits. Yeti, come!"

He stood, then helped me to my feet. We worked together to fold up the blanket as another rumble of thunder boomed in the distance. That storm was coming in hot, and a lot sooner than expected.

Noah's jaw tightened. "Remember how I said we might get a little wet on the way back?"

"Yes." I watched as the dark clouds swirled in the sky.

"Might be more that a little."

"Let me just grab a couple of photos for my feed." It was clear Noah didn't love the idea, but he didn't protest, either. It would have been a shame to go all the way out there and not come away with at least a few pictures.

As Noah went to gather the horses, I reached for my phone.

I Burned My Tongue in Colorado

My hand patted an empty back pocket.

"Oh, my God. No, no, no. This can't be happening." I spun in a circle, scanning the ground. "My phone's gone."

"You put it in your saddlebag like I told you, right?"

"I was taking pictures of Yeti in the meadow. I must've ..."

Thunder growled in the distance, and Noah glanced up at the darkening sky. "We need to head back now. Phone or no phone."

"We have to look for it!" The idea of being without my phone for even five minutes was almost paralyzing. The thought of leaving it behind, alone, lost in the wilderness, was simply unimaginable. My heartbeat shifted into a higher gear, and beads of sweat erupted from the pores on my forehead. "Everything we did today will be worthless without it!"

Noah's face hardened. "Worthless?"

"You know what I mean." From the look on his face, I wasn't sure that he did. But I couldn't worry about Noah's hurt feelings; I had a crisis to deal with. I had to find my phone. "It's not just today's pictures that are on there. It's everything I took the entire week. Dawn patrol. The river. All the stuff back at the resort. This entire trip would be for nothing."

"Yeah," Noah said, his voice low and cold. "I heard you the first time."

"Noah, don't."

Noah slid one boot into a stirrup and launched himself into Duke's saddle. "It probably bounced out of your pocket somewhere between here and the meadow. We'll keep our eyes open on the way back down the trail."

"That phone is my entire life."

Noah shook his head, the pity clear in his eyes. "We're too exposed up here when the lightning comes. We have to go now, phone or no phone. So either you get on your own horse or I throw you over mine."

The first fat raindrops began falling about ten minutes later. Noah dug his heels into Duke's side and the big horse surged forward, Biscuit right behind him. Thunder roared and lightning crackled across the sky.

Noah pulled a pair of flashlights from his saddlebag once the sun disappeared behind the mountains. Our light beams swayed across the rocky terrain in desperate search of my phone, but each flash of lightning made our efforts seem increasingly futile.

Another electric bolt split the sky, this one close enough to make the tiny hairs on my arms stand at attention. Yeti howled, then bolted down the trail. Even the fearless wolf-dog was terrified, which did absolutely nothing for my rapidly deteriorating confidence.

"Is Yeti going to be okay?" I yelled, trying to make my voice heard over the wind's howl.

"She'll be fine," Noah shouted back as a sudden gust whipped my hair across my face.

In the distance, sheets of rain advanced across the valley.

"We can't stay out here. It's too dangerous." Noah squinted at the sky as if he could intimidate the weather into submission. "But even more dangerous is what Jenn will do to me if something happens to the horses. We can't have one of them slip and break a leg. We need shelter. Now."

"Where are we going to find shelter in this?" Thunder boomed and lightning flashed.

The raindrops somehow got bigger. Wetter. Colder. Suddenly, finding my phone became much less of a life and death situation, at least compared to the real life or death situation we were in.

"Follow me," Noah commanded. Not waiting for my reaction, he shifted Duke into reverse, grabbed Biscuit's reins, and looped them around his own saddle horn. "Let's go!"

Chapter Twenty-Seven

With Noah driving Duke faster and leading Biscuit by the reins, we surged down the trail like we were riding a water flume ride, twisting and turning down the mud slicked trail. The rain came down in buckets now, turning the world into a gray blur.

I could barely make out Noah's shape ahead, trusting Biscuit to follow Duke's lead. My hair hung in wet ropes around my face, and my clothes clung to me like I'd been thrown into the middle of the ocean.

I didn't even see the opening, but Noah expertly guided both horses down an alternate route that appeared out of nowhere. The descent steepened, and I had to lean back to avoid somersaulting over Biscuit's head. I clutched the saddle tighter, fingers numbed, as the wind picked up, whipping the pine branches into a frenzy.

"Hang on!" Noah reached out and grabbed my arm when a sudden drop almost sent me tumbling down the mountain.

"I'm hanging, I'm hanging!" I screamed over the whistle of

the wind, which bent the tree branches at impossible angles. Each raindrop felt like a tiny ice dagger against my skin.

As the path flattened, I stretched forward to wrap my arms around Biscuit's neck, using his bulk to shield my face from the rain. "Good boy, Biscuit, good boy. I'll owe you a whole orchard of apples if you get me home safe." Biscuit must have softened his opinion of me because, for once, it didn't feel like he was plotting to launch me into space.

When a flash of lightning illuminated everything in stark black and white, I caught sight of Yeti ahead of us, leading the way down the trail. Despite the cold, the rain, and the fact that the heavens were using us for lightning bolt target practice, Yeti never wavered in her wolf-dog duty, though she did splash into every passing mud puddle with an enthusiasm that suggested she wasn't totally hating the adventure.

"There!" Noah pointed ahead, raindrops pelting my face. I squinted through the gloom, barely making out a wooden structure tucked against the rocky face of the mountain. Noah loosened the reins, and both Duke and Biscuit surged forward, hooves churning through the mud as the end times raged.

"Stay close and hold on!" Noah called over his shoulder. Duke moved with confident ease across the increasingly treacherous ground as our destination grew larger, one of the fishing cabins we'd spotted on our hike.

Almost there.

Just a few seconds longer.

Another bolt of lightning crackled overhead, and I swore I could feel the electricity buzz through my molars.

Biscuit churned forward, just as motivated as I was to get out of the storm.

* * *

I Burned My Tongue in Colorado

The door burst open with a sharp crack as Noah's shoulder connected with the ancient wood. He stumbled inside, dragging me and our saddlebags with him. Yeti raced past us, shaking water like a furry garden sprinkler.

"Stay here." Noah squeezed my shoulder, his hand warm despite everything. "I need to get the horses settled." He disappeared back into the storm before I could protest, leaving me dripping on the worn floorboards.

The cabin was dark except for the occasional flash of lightning through a single grimy window. As my eyes adjusted, I made out the sparse interior. Calling it "primitive" would've been a compliment. Water pooled around my feet as I wrapped my arms around my shoulders in a futile attempt to get warm, teeth chattering like one of those windup toys.

"I'm guessing this won't be one of those glamping experiences," I told Yeti, wringing out my hair. She gave her fur another good shaking.

A sad, bare mattress lay directly on the floor in one corner, its springs probably older than the mountains. One wall featured a cold, empty stone fireplace, with a few moldy logs beside it. No electricity. No running water. No Egyptian cotton sheets with ethically sourced goose down pillows.

The sound of rain hammering the roof was deafening. Another flash of lightning illuminated rough wooden walls, a few rusty hooks for gear, and absolutely nothing that could qualify as a modern comfort. Worst of all, I didn't have my phone to document this misery. I could only imagine the sympathy likes I would've harvested.

I peeled off my soaked jacket, hanging it on one of the hooks just as Noah stumbled back inside. Rivers of water trickled down his body, joining the growing puddle on the floor.

"You know when I said I wanted authentic Colorado

content, I was thinking more 'rustic charm' and less *Blair Witch Project*."

"Blair what?"

"Witch Project. You know, the low-budget horror movie that made everybody motion sick. The one with the girl and the snot running down her nose?"

Noah shook his head.

"Well, it's a classic, so I'm making you watch it with me if we survive this."

Noah raised an eyebrow. "If we survive this ... then sure." He stripped off his jacket and hung it beside mine. The wet fabric of his shirt clung to his torso, outlining every ridge and plane with the textured detail of a topographical map.

A steady drip-drip-drip from above made me look up. "Um, Noah? I think your roof has a leak. Make that leaks plural. An entire leak convention, actually."

Water trickled through multiple spots in the ceiling, creating an indoor rain shower that would have made the spa shower in my luxury suite jealous. Then, a gust of wind yanked the door open, slamming it against the wall with a bang even louder than the thunder. Rain and leaves whipped inside as Noah lunged for the handle and shouldered it closed.

"Here." I slipped the Gucci belt from my waist and looped it around the handle. "We can use this to tie it shut." At Noah's questioning look, I shrugged. "What? I grew up in California. You learn to get creative during earthquakes."

I wrapped the other end of my belt around a nearby hook, creating a makeshift latch.

"Not bad, city girl."

I spotted an old cooking pot in the corner and grabbed it, positioning it under the worst leak, then strategically arranged a couple of dented metal cups under the other leaks.

"Bob the Builder would be proud."

I Burned My Tongue in Colorado

"Please. Bob wishes he had my skills." I rolled up a dusty floor mat and stuffed it against the crack in the door, stopping the flow of water seeping underneath and blocking a bit of the chill from the wind. "I didn't figure you for a big Bob the Builder fan."

"Not me. Brie. She loved that show. Couldn't get enough of it. Had the lunchbox and everything."

I spotted another leak and used another cup to collect it. It seemed the rate of dripping had accelerated. "You sure Duke and Biscuit are going to be okay out there?" I could picture the poor horses huddled together, wet and miserable. Despite everything Biscuit had done to make my life difficult, he'd kind of rubbed off on me.

"They're fine. Tied them up under a thick clump of oak trees where the cliff blocks most of the wind and the rain." His eyes traced over me, from my dripping hair to my water-logged boots. "It's you I'm more worried about."

Noah dug into the dry bag he'd brought from his saddle, pulling out a thick wool blanket. "You need to get out of those wet clothes before you catch pneumonia."

My eyes went wide. "Excuse me?"

"Don't worry, I won't look." He handed me the blanket, then turned around and made a show of covering his eyes with both hands. "I'm a gentleman."

"You said you *weren't* a gentleman."

"Just don't tell anybody else." Noah still hadn't moved, back turned and eyes closed. "Seriously, you're going to get sick if you stay in those soaked clothes."

"Fine." I glanced at Yeti, watching me like a prison guard. "You too, girl. No peeking."

Yeti gave one final dramatic shake, sending water droplets everywhere. She flopped down in the corner as if to say, "Humans. So dramatic about nudity."

My fingers trembled as I peeled off my soaked pullover, letting it fall to the floor with a wet slap.

"A lot of guys have tried to get me naked before," I said, making sure Noah hadn't moved. "But you win first prize for most creative." My shirt followed, then my sports bra, both of them clinging to my frozen skin.

"A lot of guys?" Noah cocked his head, but kept his eyes shut and his back turned.

"You sound surprised." My wet pants felt like they weighed a hundred pounds as I struggled to yank them off my legs.

Noah didn't answer. Probably the wise choice.

"For the record, it hasn't *actually* been a lot." I kept glancing at Noah's back, but he kept facing the wall. "Only some. And by some, I mean a few." I removed my underwear, another red G-string from Brief Encounters. "And by a few, I mean one."

"Pilates guy?"

"Yeah." Completely naked now, I wrapped the blanket tightly around myself like a cocoon, acutely aware of every inch of skin against the rough fabric.

"It was serious?"

"I thought so."

Another streak of lightning ripped across the sky, momentarily lighting up the entire inside of the cabin. I pulled the blanket tighter as the shadows took back control.

"Okay," I said, my voice just a whisper in the storm. "I'm decent. Well, as decent as I can be while wearing nothing but a scratchy wool blanket."

Noah turned around, his face unreadable, like an ancient scroll found in a hidden tomb, covered in hieroglyphics that no one had deciphered for centuries.

"What about you?" I asked. While Noah wasn't visibly shivering, his clothes were still dripping, and I could tell he was cold by the bluish tinge to his lips. Like a Smurf. Grumpy Mountain Man Smurf.

"Just need to get the fire going first." Noah strode to a small wooden table in the corner, its surface warped from years of moisture. He grabbed one of the legs and yanked. The table splintered with a sharp crack. He broke the pieces into smaller chunks, arranging them in the stone fireplace. "This wood's been inside, so it should be dry enough to catch."

Next, he gathered the moldy logs beside the hearth, examining each one before adding it to his pile. Finally, he collected twigs and bits of bark that had blown in through the doorway, creating a careful structure.

He pointed to his saddlebags. "Can you look in there for the waterproof matches?"

Pulling the wool blanket tighter around my body, I crouched down to search his bags for the matches. Wrapping the blanket around me even tighter still, I brought them over and handed them to him.

Three tries later, a small flame caught the splintered table pieces. Noah nursed it carefully, adding larger pieces as the fire grew. The orange glow spread across his face, highlighting the sharp angles of his cheekbones, the determined set of his jaw.

"Come closer," he said, gesturing to the spot right in front of the hearth. "You need to warm up."

The firelight danced across the cabin walls, creating shifting shadows that made the space feel alive. I scooted forward on the dusty floor, drawn to the growing warmth like a marshmallow to a s'more.

Sitting in front of the fire, the heat thawed my frozen limbs one painful prickle at a time. I hadn't realized just how cold I'd been until I snuggled up next to the flames. Making sure the blanket would not slip off my shoulders, I held my hands out toward the fire, feeling sensation return to my numb fingers in waves of pins and needles.

"Better?"

I nodded, letting out a soft sigh as the warmth spread through my body. I was grateful for fire, shelter, and the mountain man who knew how to provide both.

"Okay, my turn."

When I looked over my shoulder, Noah twirled his finger, motioning for me to turn back around. "You know the drill."

I kept my eyes fixed on the crackling fire, listening to the rustle of wet fabric behind me. Each sound made my heart race a little faster, the soft thud of boots hitting the floor, the wet slap of clothes being laid out, the whisper of fabric against skin. My imagination filled in the visuals with far too much enthusiasm.

A flash of lightning illuminated the cabin's grimy window, and there in its reflection, I caught sight of Noah's bare back, all lean muscle and sharp angles sculpted by years of whatever mountainy things mountain men do.

All the air whooshed out of my lungs, and the horde of butterflies returned.

I should have looked away, should have focused on the fire or closed my eyes or done literally anything else. But I couldn't tear my gaze from that window.

The storm cast another electric flash across the glass. Noah turned slightly, giving me a glimpse of his torso, a roadmap of scars and stories I found myself desperate to know. My fingers itched to trace his lines, to learn their history.

A sharp ripping sound broke my trance. Noah yanked one of the dusty curtains from the window, tearing it in two swift motions. He wrapped half around his waist, the fabric settling low on his hips like the world's most tantalizing loincloth.

I Burned My Tongue in Colorado

"Coast is clear," he said, his voice a low rumble that seemed to vibrate through the floorboards.

I turned, trying to school my expression into something innocent, but my eyes betrayed me, traveling across the planes of his chest, following the cut lines of muscle down to where the makeshift curtain-towel rode dangerously low on his hips. A droplet of water traced the same path my eyes took.

"Feel better?" Swallowing a gasp, I bit my lip hard enough to taste the metallic tang of blood.

"How do I look?" His tone was playful, but the effect was deadly serious.

"You know what they say. Only real men wear skirts."

"Who says that?"

"Probably someone at one of those Scottish Highlands games festivals."

"We have those," said Noah. "Every spring."

"Let me guess, you do the one where they throw boulders."

"Caber toss, actually."

"Even better."

If I thought his reflection was hypnotizing, the full frontal view was a thousand times worse. Or better, depending on one's commitment to suppressing lustful thoughts. Years of mountain living had carved his body into something that belonged on the cover of *Grumpy Mountain Man Review*. Evil thoughts of evil deeds peppered the cavewoman part of my brain. The damp chill of the cabin was completely consumed by the inferno in my nether regions.

"Better lay out our clothes by the fire so they can dry out."

"Mm-hmm." I snuck quick peeks as Noah arranged and rearranged articles of clothing around the perimeter of the fire for optimal drying. I was so distracted I forgot all about my red lacy thong. My heart stopped when he picked up the thin strand of fabric. Definitely not outdoor-adventure appropriate.

He held it between two fingers as if it were a snake poised to strike.

"Don't ask," I said, pulling the wool blanket tighter over my chest. My cheeks burned, and it had nothing to do with the heat of the fire. My nipples were as hard as calcified rock, poking out against the thick wool like little stalactites in a cave.

"I don't even want to know." Noah placed it carefully on the edge of a broken chair, as far from himself as possible.

The fire popped and crackled, drawing our attention back to the now roaring flames. Noah stood up, surveying his handi-work of neatly arranged clothing. His reflection caught in the window, and he froze. Those broad shoulders tensed, and I knew exactly what he'd realized. That same window had given me quite a show earlier. Our eyes met in the reflection, and both of us knew exactly what the other was thinking.

Noah turned slowly, his eyes finding mine in the firelight. The intensity in his gaze made my stomach drop. There was something raw and electric between us now, crackling even fiercer than the storm outside.

Chapter Twenty-Eight

S o there I was. Trapped in a cabin.

      With Noah Barrett.

      In the middle of nowhere. Miles from civilization.

With Noah Barrett.

Naked.

With Noah Barrett.

As he turned away from the reflection in the window, I forced myself to look back at the flames, pretending to be fascinated by the way they licked at the wood. He said nothing, but we both knew what I'd seen in the window's reflection.

"Your fire-building skills are impressive," I said, scrambling for something to fill the void.

"Told you I could start a fire in the rain." Noah crouched down to throw another moldy log on the fire. I tried not to stare, failing miserably.

I hugged the blanket closer. It felt like there was electricity buzzing throughout the entire cabin, burning hotter than the lightning bolts filling the sky.

Noah sat beside me, trying to warm himself, with the curtain barely covering his thighs. "You doing okay?"

Surprisingly, I was. "Yeah. Not bad, considering."

"You know, for someone who spends her life curating perfection, you handle imperfect pretty well." The compliment was unexpected, offered without his usual sarcasm.

"My life is filled with imperfection," I said. "You already know about my love life. My dumpling-folding skills. All you have to do now is see my apartment in Los Angeles."

The look on his face suggested it was an invitation he might actually accept. Before I could stop myself, I let out a little laugh.

"What's so funny?"

The cold, the rain, and the exhaustion must have rattled my brain. "Nothing," I lied, clearing my throat. "I was just thinking about ..."

... taking you back home to LA

... showing you around my apartment

... giving you a hands-on tour of my bedroom furniture

"I was just thinking about what Victoria would think if I added this to my Instagram story." I waved my hand around the cabin. "I suspect a rustic cabin sleepover isn't what she had in mind when she demanded luxurious authenticity."

Noah chuckled, the sound deep and warm. "I don't know. This might be the most authentic Colorado experience you've had yet."

"Well, authentic doesn't always photograph well," I admitted.

"Maybe some things aren't meant to be captured." Noah stared into the flames. "Maybe they're just meant to be experienced. By the people who are there actually experiencing them."

Our eyes met across the fire, and something shifted

between us. The air felt suddenly thick, charged with possibility.

A deafening crack of thunder shook the cabin, wooden boards rattling like during a magnitude ten earthquake. I yelped, grabbing Noah's arm. He didn't flinch.

"Sorry," I whispered, trying to pull away, but Noah caught my hand.

"Not a fan of storms?"

I shook my head. "When I was six, lightning struck a tree outside my window. The whole thing exploded. I've been terrified ever since."

Noah's thumb traced circles on my palm. "Everyone's scared of something."

"Noah Barrett, was that *another* confession?"

He looked up from staring at my hand. "A confession?"

"You just said everyone's scared of something. Everyone includes you. So spill it. A worldwide flannel shortage? Public speeches while wearing a curtain toga? Clowns? If it's clowns, I won't judge you. Clowns are terrifying. With their creepy painted eyes. Those red noses. And big red shoes. You ever consider what gross, fungus-infested toenails they're hiding in those big red shoes?" I shuddered. "Go on. Spill it."

Noah sighed, using a long stick to poke at the fire. "Spiders."

"Spiders? Cute little furry spiders? That's what scares you?"

"Spiders scare the crap out of me. All those legs. And bulgy eyes."

"You know what would be absolutely terrifying?" I asked. "A spider dressed up as a clown."

"Has anyone ever told you how weird you are?"

"Many people."

Another thunderclap made me flinch. Noah shifted closer, his shoulder pressing against mine.

"What else scares you?" I asked.

"Public speaking actually does terrify me," Noah admitted. "Give me a mountain lion over a microphone any day." His admission made me laugh. "What else are *you* scared of?"

"Well, let's see. Where do we start?" I ticked off my many fears on my fingers. "Failure. Disappointing people. Disappointing my parents. Which I constantly do. Ending up alone." The words tumbled out before I could stop them.

Noah's hand tightened around mine. "Yeah. Those are definitely scarier than any storm."

I squeezed his hand back.

"Spiders are still the scariest, though," said Noah. "Way scarier."

"Especially clown spiders." I looked around the barren cabin built from rotting wood, with enough holes and gaps to admit an entire forest full of insect life. "You realize there are probably spiders in here with us right now, don't you?"

"Oh, I'm aware. Very aware. Just trying not to think about it."

I patted his arm, his muscle firm under my palm. "Well, I tell you what, if a spider jumps out and tries to get us, you can hide behind me."

"You'd battle a ferocious spider for me?"

"Unless it's dressed as a clown, of course.

"Of course."

"But if it isn't dressed as a clown, then yes. Might be nice to get a chance to protect you for once."

By that time, the fire had done a marvelous job of warming up the entire cabin. So nice, in fact, I let the wool blanket drift off my shoulders.

I Burned My Tongue in Colorado

Noah's eyes swept over my bare skin until another crescendo of thunder snapped him from his daze.

"You think this rain is ever going to stop?" Out the window, I saw another flash of lightning.

"Even if it does, the trails will be a mess. Can't risk the horses in the dark when everything's this slick. Looks like we might be here for the night."

My lungs stopped processing oxygen as the implications sank in. The cabin suddenly felt a lot smaller. We stared at the sad excuse for a threadbare mattress, pushed against the far wall, its springs poking through the worn fabric like skeleton fingers out of a grave. The kind of space that would force two people to get very, very cozy.

My throat went dry as I pictured lying next to Noah, feeling the heat of his skin, listening to his breathing in the dark. The blanket suddenly felt way too warm, and I had to fight the urge to cast it off.

"I'll take the floor," said Noah, swiping a clump of damp hair out of his eyes.

"Don't be ridiculous." I gestured at the cold wooden planks. "You'll freeze."

"I've slept in worse places. Besides, Yeti makes an excellent pillow." Yeti whined, expressing her opinion about that.

Another crack of thunder rattled the window. As if sensing we needed an independent third party to mediate, Yeti popped down in the middle of the mattress and claimed it for herself.

"At least you'll be warm," said Noah. "That dog puts off more heat than a blast furnace."

The silence stretched for a long time, interrupted only by the snap of burning wood from the fireplace.

"Don't move." Abruptly, without another word, Noah hopped to his feet, unwound the belt latch on the front door, then dashed out into the dark, stormy night. The wooden door slammed shut with a bang.

"Did he just abandon us?"

Yeti and I looked at each other, considering the possibility.

"Was the thought of spending the night with me really that horrible?"

Yeti cocked her head. "Definitely a possibility" seemed to be her conclusion.

When Noah burst back through the front door, wind swirling and raindrops spraying, he held up the no-longer-quite-so-white LuxeLife logo'd cooler bag in one hand, triumphant. "At least Victoria is good for something," he announced.

I joined him on the damp wooden floor as he huddled over the cooler, tugging open the zippered top. His muscles flexed as he searched, and I couldn't tear my eyes away from watching his shoulders work. The torn curtain had slipped even lower, barely hanging onto his hips.

"Bingo." He pulled a champagne bottle out by the neck, something very expensive, judging by the fanciness of the label. Then he dug out two champagne flutes.

Also in the cooler, there were nuts, berries, crackers, and cheese.

"I could kiss you right now," I declared.

The look in Noah's eyes suggested he wouldn't stop me if I did. "Wait, it gets better." Noah pulled out a handful of foil-wrapped mounds. He peeled back the gold wrapping from one of them, revealing something dark. Something cocoa brown. Something decadent and chocolaty.

"WHAT. ARE. THOSE?"

"Looks like chocolate truffles." He held one up to the light of the fire. "Dusted with cocoa powder."

Noah was roughly twice my size. Infinitely stronger. Probably the victor of several dozen fist fights over the course of his grumpy mountain man's life. But if this had been some sort of *Hunger Games* fight-to-the-death dystopian murder contest, I would have totally kicked his ass for one of those truffles.

I wiped the puddle of drool off my chin as Noah tossed one over. As soon as I took a bite, rich chocolate flooded my mouth. Dark, complex, with hints of something smoky and a touch of sea salt.

"Well? Are they any good?"

I couldn't answer at first because my brain was skipping down a chocolate bar paved lane alongside a chocolate milk river, through a chocolate-covered peppermint forest filled with chocolate unicorns. The flavor was so intense I couldn't help the small moan that escaped me, a sound that would have made an adult film star blush.

"I'll take that as a yes." Noah popped one of the truffles into his mouth too.

Working together, we spread the cooler bag feast over the included white cloth napkins, which we laid out on the floor.

"Well, this is fancy," I said, selecting a seasoned pistachio from the nut pile. "But I'm guessing this isn't the authentic, luxurious backdrop Victoria had in mind."

"Too bad you don't have your phone," said Noah. "Can you imagine her reaction if you posted our champagne toast from here?"

"Her head would have exploded." I placed a raspberry on my tongue. It was good ... but not as good as the berries we got at the festival from Mrs. Miller.

"Speaking of champagne." Noah popped the top off the bottle and poured us each a glass. "To unexpected adventures." He held up his glass, hitching the curtain toga back up his hips with his other hand.

"To adventurous expectations," I toasted back, pulling my

blanket tighter, very much aware that it was the only thing separating Noah's eyes from full frontal nudity.

I took a long sip, hoping to douse the fire burning inside my body. The champagne was crisp and bright, with notes of citrus and minerals that danced across my tongue like tiny bubbles of sunshine. Before I knew it, half my glass was gone.

"Careful now." Noah topped me off with another generous pour from the bottle. "Better keep our wits about us."

"Oh, I think my wits left me a long time ago." I pressed the glass to my lips.

Outside, the storm raged on, but in the cabin, beside the fire, sipping champagne and nibbling on truffles, a different kind of storm was brewing, one just as wild but infinitely more inviting.

As I looked again at the single bare mattress, I couldn't help but laugh, perhaps the champagne starting to have an effect. "This really isn't how I imagined my luxury resort gig turning out."

Noah set his glass on the floor and leaned back, arms propped behind him. The bottom of his curtain skirt had hiked up one leg. "It's not that bad, is it?"

I looked over, watching the reflection of the flames dance in his eyes. "Could be worse." I hitched my blanket back over my shoulders. "Maybe I'm just not cut out for this authentic luxury influencer stuff."

"I think you're cut out for anything you set your mind to," said Noah.

"Stop."

"I'm serious, Sam. You've got ... grit." Noah took another drink of his champagne. "You surprised me. You're not the person I thought you were when I first met you."

"Is that a good thing? Or a bad thing?"

"It's a good thing."

I Burned My Tongue in Colorado

Noah must have been sitting too close to the fire, because a bead of sweat had formed just beneath his collarbone. It tracked down between the muscles in his chest, weaved through the hard lines of his abdomen ... then ... lower still.

I forced my eyes back to my glass, downing the rest of it in one gulp. Before I could tell him no thank you, Noah refilled it.

"Like I said, this whole thing started off as a side project."

"Seems to have worked out."

I shrugged. "Yet here I am, drinking champagne in a cabin in the woods. Naked. Questioning my life choices."

The wool blanket was starting to chafe my side boob, and between the fire and the heavy material, I began breaking out in a sweat too. "Maybe Mom was right. The responsible thing is to just go back to school, perfect my dim sum making, and settle down with Edgar."

Noah paused mid-sip. "Edgar? That's not the Pilates guy ..."

"No, Edgar's just a family friend. We went to Stanford together, except Edgar actually graduated and got his MBA. Now he runs his family's business, the bakery next to my parents' restaurant. He's ..." I paused, picturing Edgar's perfectly pressed suits and manicured nails. "He's very put-together. The kind of guy who color-codes his closet and has a ten-step skincare routine."

Noah's mouth twitched. "Sounds organized."

"His apartment looks like a West Elm catalog."

"So you've seen his apartment ..."

"Many times." I paused, giving Noah's mind time to wander. "He drives a BMW and prefers cold-pressed juice." I wrapped the blanket tighter. "He sends my mom pictures of his latest pastry creations. She probably frames them."

"Sounds like a great guy." Noah's voice was carefully neutral.

"He is. Really. He donates to charity, remembers every-one's birthdays, loves his parents ... loves my parents." I sighed. "He's just..."

Outside, a distant rumble of thunder rolled across the night sky.

"Just?"

I couldn't tell if Noah's eyes were flaming, or it was simply the reflection of the fire. "Not what I'm looking for." The cham-pagne made my head fuzzy. Or maybe it was the way Noah looked at me.

He was quiet for a long time, studying me in that intense way of his. "What are you looking for, Sam?"

I met his gaze across the flickering firelight, my heart thun-dering even louder than the real thunder booming in the sky. The question lingered, heavy with possibility.

Noah's eyes dropped to my lips, and I found myself wanting to lean forward, as if drawn by some magnetic force.

"Well, Sam?" Noah asked again. "What is it you want?"

I stared into the fire, surprised to find I didn't have a ready answer. "I used to know. I wanted to tell stories. Real stories. About real people. People like my parents. Not just what looks good on a plate, but the hands that made it, the traditions behind it." I sighed. "Somewhere along the way, I got caught up in the filters and follower counts. And now my apartment is full of crap no real person would ever really want."

"You could still do that," Noah said. "Tell those stories."

"Maybe." I forced a laugh, then busied myself with arranging the remaining food, very aware of how the blanket slipped on my shoulder. "Right now? I'm looking for a man with dry socks and underwear." I helped myself to another truf-fle, needing a distraction.

"You've got a little ..." He gestured to my mouth.

"Where?" I swiped at my lips with the back of my hand.

"No, here." Noah leaned forward, his thumb brushing softly across my bottom lip to wipe away a smudge of chocolate. His touch lingered for just a moment too long.

My breath caught in my throat. Even in the dim firelight, I could see the intensity in his eyes as Noah's gaze dropped to my lips, and the air between us seemed to thicken. He leaned forward slightly, the movement so subtle I might have imagined it.

"Sam," he said, my name barely more than a breath.

The blanket slipped slightly from my shoulder. Noah's eyes followed the movement, darkening as more skin was revealed. His hand reached out, fingers hovering just above my collarbone, not quite touching.

"Maybe I should check on the horses," he said, but made no move to get up.

Time seemed to stretch in slow motion. My heart hammered so hard that I was sure he could hear it over the storm. I leaned forward, closing the distance between us by the smallest fraction, a question in the movement.

Noah's hand finally made contact with my skin, his fingers tracing the curve of my shoulder. Soft. Gentle. The touch sent electricity racing through me.

"This is a bad idea," he murmured, even as his hand slid to the nape of my neck.

"Definitely," I agreed, tilting my face up toward his. "Terrible idea."

"We hardly know each other." His fingers tangled in my damp hair.

"Practically strangers," I whispered against his lips.

And then he was kissing me.

Chapter Twenty-Nine

Noah's lips were softer than I'd imagined, but the pressure was firm. He tasted of chocolate and rain and something wild I couldn't name. My hands found their way to his chest, palms pressing against warm skin and hard muscle.

The kiss deepened, his tongue sliding against mine in a dance that made me forget about storms and lost phones and everything else in the universe. Noah's arm wrapped around my waist, pulling me closer until I was practically in his lap, the blanket barely staying in place between us.

His hand slid up my bare back beneath the blanket, leaving a trail of heat in its wake. I gasped against his mouth, and he swallowed the sound, kissing me harder, more urgently.

We broke apart, breathless, foreheads touching. Noah's eyes were dark, pupils dilated in the firelight.

"Still think this is a bad idea?" I whispered.

"Definitely." Noah's thumb traced across my lip one more time before his hand slid to cup my cheek. His lips met mine again, and I melted into him, my fingers tangling in his damp hair. His powerful arms wrapped around me, pulling me closer as the kiss deepened. The rough wool of the blanket scratched against my breasts as he drew me closer. I breathed in his scent, pine needles and wood-smoke and mountain rain. A small sound escaped my throat as his tongue traced my bottom lip.

The wool blanket drifted further down my shoulders, exposing the top curve of my breasts.

Noah's curtain cover loosened around his waist, falling open almost wide enough to ...

WOOF!

Noah jerked back, startled, grabbing the end of the curtain to cover himself. We both turned to see Yeti smiling at us from on top of the mattress.

"Yeti, no," Noah growled, almost as fierce as a wolf himself. "Lay back down."

Turning back to face one another, Noah leaned in again, his lips finding mine. His hand slid down my spine, leaving trails of fire down to my ...

WOOF!

"Seriously?" Noah broke away with a frustrated groan. "We're fine. Go to sleep."

WOOF! WOOF!

Yeti jumped down from the mattress and shoved her wet nose between us, tail wagging furiously and rubbing her damp fur all over our skin. I tried to push her away from me, but she used her wet, furry body to drive me back instead.

"Seems we have a chaperone." Noah growled. "Thanks, Yeti."

My body screamed in protest as I pulled further away, hiking the blanket back over my shoulders, immediately missing Noah's warmth. "Maybe she's right?"

No, she's not right. Bad Yeti. Bad wolf-dog. Bad.

"Yeah ..." Noah cleared his throat. "We should get some sleep. Early start tomorrow to beat any mudslides on the trails."

I glanced at the narrow mattress in the corner, which was now empty since Yeti had moved between us.

"We could share? Just to sleep," I added quickly. "Maybe pool our body heat."

Noah shook his head. "I'll take the floor." His tone left no room for argument.

He grabbed Yeti by the collar and tugged her toward the other side of the small room, as far away from the mattress as possible. "Come here. You're my pillow tonight as punishment."

Yeti flopped down next to Noah with a dramatic huff, clearly unimpressed about being evicted from her spot on the mattress. Noah stretched out on the wooden floor, using Yeti's furry side as a cushion.

I wrapped my blanket tighter and curled up on the mattress, stealing quick peeks of Noah on the other side of the room. The fire crackled, casting dancing shadows on the walls as I tried to slow my racing thoughts.

"Goodnight, Sam," Noah's voice came softly through the darkness.

"Goodnight, Noah," I whispered back, touching my fingers to my still-tingling lips.

It didn't take long for the fire's warmth to lull me into a hazy dreamland. I don't know what time it was when my eyes fluttered open, but it was still dark outside, and a sky full of stars had replaced the angry storm clouds.

Peering into the shadows, I saw the cabin had transformed, no longer a dilapidated shelter but a cocoon of warmth, the fire casting golden light. My rough wool blanket had fallen away in my sleep, leaving me naked, totally exposed. I wasn't cold, though. It felt ... right.

I Burned My Tongue in Colorado

"You're awake." His voice came from the darkness.

When I looked up, Noah stood over me, eyes dark and intense as he gazed down at my uncovered body. He wasn't wearing the tattered curtain anymore. He was naked too, his muscular form sculpted in the firelight.

"Am I dreaming?"

He didn't answer. Instead, a slow smile spread across his lips as he reached out, fingers tracing the curve of my hip, sending shivers up my spine.

"Is it okay if I touch you?"

"Yes." It wasn't just okay. By that point, it was critical to my sanity.

Noah lowered himself onto the mattress, his body hovering over mine. I arched my back, pressing myself against him as his lips found mine. The kiss was slow, deliberate, building a fire within me that burned hotter than any hearth.

His hands explored my body, his touch sending waves of pleasure through me. Every caress, every kiss felt like a dream, a fantasy I never wanted to wake from. The world outside the cabin faded away, replaced by the sensation of Noah's body against mine, his breath hot on my skin.

Noah's mouth traveled down my neck, across my collarbone, lower…

My fingers tangled in his hair, pulling him closer. His hands worked magic along my sides. He moved over me, his weight pressing me into the mattress. I wrapped my legs around his waist, pulling him closer.

Time seemed to stop as our bodies moved together, intertwined. I cried out his name, my breathless voice shattering the dreamlike silence as his weight settled between my thighs.

The firelight gilded his skin as he moved back up to kiss me again, his lips soft but insistent. I lost myself in the sensation, in the weight of him pressing me into the mattress, in the heat building between my legs.

Noah's mouth grew more insistent, more ... wet? Surprisingly wet. And ... rough?

Wait.

This wasn't right.

The texture was all wrong, like someone was dragging sandpaper across my face. And the smell ... Noah smelled like pine and rain and mountain air, not like ... dog breath and wet fur?

I cracked one eye open and found myself staring into Yeti's soulful gaze as she enthusiastically licked my cheek, her tongue leaving a trail of slobber from my chin to my forehead.

"Ugh, Yeti, no," I groaned, pushing her furry head away. "That is NOT the kind of kiss I was dreaming about."

Sitting up, I peered across the room to spot Noah still asleep on the floorboards in the shadows, the empty LuxeLife cooler bag now serving as his pillow. The sound of gentle snoring confirmed he was still fast asleep, thankfully undisturbed by the very vivid dreams of his cabin mate.

I laid back down, heart still racing, and waited for my breathing to steady. Flopping her considerable weight half on top of me, Yeti pinned me to the mattress in a far less romantic way than Dream Noah had. She radiated heat like a furry furnace.

"Fine," I mumbled, wrapping an arm around her thick neck. "You're better than no cuddles at all."

I buried my face in her surprisingly soft fur, the steady rhythm of her breathing lulling me back toward sleep.

* * *

KA-CAW ... KA-CAW ... KA-CAW

I Burned My Tongue in Colorado

I jolted awake to a crow perched on the windowsill, staring at me with beady-eyed judgment. Sunlight stabbed through the grimy window behind it, and the fire in the hearth was now dead and cold. My brain struggled to reconcile the lingering heat of my dream with the very real chill of the cabin.

"Noah?" My voice emerged as a croak, scraping against a throat parched from sleep and ... other recent activities. The cabin responded with nothing but the creak of old wood and a scurrying noise that sounded far too rodent-like.

I sat up, wincing as my vertebrae cracked like bubble wrap being stomped on by a vindictive grizzly bear. My neck felt as if someone had twisted it into a fancy balloon animal shape.

"Yeti?" I called out, hoping for at least the wolf-dog's company. "Anyone?"

I was alone. No Yeti. No Noah.

I hauled myself upright, clutching the wool blanket around me like a scratchy protective shield. The cabin looked smaller in daylight, every cobweb and crack visible in authentically distressed detail. Outside, the world glistened after the storm, dew-dropped and sparkling.

But no Noah. No footprints. No horses tied to the tree. No wolf-dog. Just mountains and trees, stretching to infinity. They'd probably seen thousands of abandoned women over the centuries, left to fend for themselves in rustic cabins. In a million years, I'd just be another layer of sediment in their geological history.

"Here lies Samantha Li," I said to the sky above. "Influencer. Died after losing her iPhone. And almost her virginity." One of the clouds in the sky resembled a fluffy white question mark. "At least as far as her parents are concerned," I amended.

Back inside, I surveyed the evidence. The fireplace held nothing but cold ashes, a sad reminder of last night's warmth. My clothes lay spread carefully across a chair, completely dry.

Each piece had been smoothed meticulously, like someone had painstakingly removed every wrinkle without the benefit of an iron. Except for my inappropriate underwear. Those were still dangling on the chair. At least they were dry, though.

Noah's clothes were gone. His boots, his saddlebag, and all trace of his presence had vanished with him.

My brain conjured multiple disaster scenarios simultaneously, each more catastrophic than the last. Was this some twisted mountain version of revenge for making him show me the authentic Colorado? Or worse, had he regretted our kiss so much that he'd literally ridden off into the sunrise rather than face me?

The thought made my stomach sink as if someone had tied a boulder to my ankle, then thrown me in the lake. I pictured myself years from now, wild-haired and feral, wearing nothing but the wool blanket and whatever I could fashion from pine cones, reduced to talking to rocks I'd named after reality TV stars.

I had a thought. Maybe Noah was out gathering breakfast? Maybe he was out there right now, picking fresh berries for muffins? Maybe he'd found a birch tree and was sapping it for syrup?

Clinging to this newfound hope, I let the wool blanket drop from my shoulders and reached for my underwear. The red lace looked so ridiculously out of place against the rustic setting that I laughed out loud. I held it up, remembering Noah's expression when he'd placed it drying by the fire, a mixture of embarrassment and something darker, more heated. The same look he'd given me when ...

The door creaked open behind me.

"Look what I ..."

I whipped around, heart leaping into my throat.

I Burned My Tongue in Colorado

Noah stood frozen in the doorway, eyes wide as saucers, mouth hanging open, and halted mid-sentence. "... found."

For one eternal moment, we both remained perfectly still, like someone had hit pause on the universe. Me, completely naked, holding nothing but a scrap of red lace. Him, clutching something in one outstretched hand.

One Mississippi.

Two Mississippi.

Three Mississippi.

My brain finally caught up with reality, and I attempted to cover myself with the only thing within reach, the very underwear I'd been holding. Which, given its minimalist design philosophy, covered approximately nothing.

We both spun around simultaneously, backs to each other, me scrambling to locate my clothes, Noah apparently developing a sudden, intense interest in the leaky cabin ceiling above him.

I yanked on my clothes at world championship speed-dressing pace, almost putting both legs through the same pant leg in my haste.

When I turned back around, no longer distracted by mortified embarrassment, I finally saw what Noah was holding in his hand.

My phone.

"I found it on the trail," Noah said to the wall. He held my phone up over his shoulder, still not turning around. "About halfway between the overlook and the meadow."

As soon as my essential parts were covered, I lunged for the phone like it was the most important thing on Earth. I wiped mud from the screen with my shirt hem, examining it from every angle for cracks or water damage. When pressing the power button yielded nothing but a black screen, my heart sank.

"Is it going to be okay?" Noah asked, finally turning around now that I was decent. A flush still colored his neck, creeping up toward his ears.

"I think so," I said, cradling the device like a wounded baby bird. "Just a dead battery, I hope. And the screen has a couple of small cracks."

Noah's shoulders relaxed slightly. "You can charge it when you get back to your room." He finally dropped his hand from his eyes, though he seemed to look everywhere but at me. "I'll bring the horses around front and we can head back."

The memory of the kiss lingered between us, unacknowledged but impossible to ignore.

"Get back to my room? What, no more authentic adventures today?" I attempted to recapture our normal banter. "I figured you'd want to take me mountain lion wrestling. Or cliff jumping in one of those wing suit things. Ooh, or maybe we can go raft down a waterfall."

Noah's smile was bittersweet. "I think we've both had enough adventure for a while."

Chapter Thirty

We rode into view of the Adventure Center after what felt like a lifetime of crotch torture via horse's saddle. My thighs had declared open rebellion, my spine had filed for divorce from the rest of my body, and parts of me that shall remain nameless were sending distress signals. Biscuit, clearly as eager to end our journey as I was, picked up speed as we approached the stables.

For almost the entire journey, Noah and I had maintained enough silence to get nominated for some sort of librarian's best behavior award. The one time I'd gathered the courage to reference what had happened between us, you know, the whole mind-blowing, universe-altering kiss situation, Noah had suddenly remembered an urgent need to "check the trail for storm damage" and trotted ahead, leaving me and my emotional vulnerability eating his dust.

"The thing about last night ..." I'd started.

"Hmm, better check that washout ahead," he'd muttered, spurring Duke forward like I'd announced the trail behind us was on fire.

Subtle, Barrett. Real subtle.

I gripped Biscuit's reins with white knuckles as we approached the paddock. After surviving rapids, lightning storms, and the emotional whiplash of Noah's hot-and-cold routine, it would be tragically on-brand for me to face-plant in the mud five feet from safety.

Jenn stood at the gate, her eyes widening as she took in our disheveled state. My hair resembled a bird's nest built by a bird with no design training and poor eyesight. My clothes looked like I'd participated in a spring break mud-wrestling competition, and lost badly.

Noah, infuriatingly, looked like he'd just stepped off the set of a rugged outdoor clothing commercial. Even his dirt smudges appeared artfully placed.

"Well, well, well." Jenn's lips curved into a smile full of unspoken observations. "You two look like you've had quite the adventure."

"Got caught in the storm," Noah grunted. "Had to wait it out in one of the old fishing cabins."

"Did you now?" Jenn's eyebrows waggled as she took Biscuit's reins and helped steady me for dismount. "Must have been cozy."

"Cozy isn't the first word that comes to mind," I said, legs turning to huckleberry jelly the moment they touched solid ground.

Noah dismounted with effortless grace, but everything changed when his boots hit the ground. His face contorted into a grimace that suggested someone had just stabbed him in the lower back with a sharp branch.

"You okay there, mountain man?" Jenn asked, leading Biscuit toward the stable with one hand while keeping me from collapsing with the other.

"Back seized up," Noah muttered through clenched teeth,

stretching with another wince. "Slept on a cabin floor last night."

I watched him attempt to straighten, each tiny movement clearly sending spasms of pain through his body. The memory of him curled on those rough wooden planks all night, refusing to share the mattress because of one little kiss (okay, one earth-shattering, toe-curling kiss), made something twist in my chest.

"The resort has a full spa," I said, a lightbulb of inspiration flickering on in my exhausted brain. "I could ask Maya to set up a couple of massage appointments."

Noah's head whipped up so fast he probably gave himself whiplash on top of his back spasms. "Hard pass."

"I bet they have amazing massage therapists." I pictured hands working on Noah's knotted muscles, my hands, preferably, and felt a flush creeping up my neck. "Then after the massage, we could get a pedicure." I pressed, unable to resist poking the bear. "And then a facial."

"I don't do spas." He practically spat the last word.

"But you'll let your back get so knotted you can barely stand upright?" asked Jenn, giving me a wink.

"Have you ever had a professional massage?" I asked, already knowing the answer.

"I'm not letting strangers touch my feet and put goop on my face," Noah declared with the stubborn determination of someone who would rather chew glass than admit weakness. "I'll work it out."

"Come on, tough guy. I did all your things."

"*My* things?"

"Hiking. Rafting. Climbing ... horse trying-to-buck-me-offing." The word riding didn't really seem to cover it. "Now you have to try one of mine."

Noah tried to ignore me by escaping toward the stable, but

his back seized again, and he doubled over in pain. "Goddamn it."

"One massage," I pressed. "If you hate it, you can go back to your all-natural regimen of suffering silently while your spine takes on the shape of a fishing hook."

"She's got a point," said Jenn. "If Sam here was brave enough to let you drag her up mountains and into the wilderness during a biblical-level storm, seems only fair you try something from her world."

I shot Jenn a grateful look. "Exactly. And unlike your activities, I can guarantee no risk of broken bones, drowning, or death by a wildlife encounter. The worst thing that happens at the spa is occasionally they run out of cucumber water. Or cucumber facial cream. Or cucumber sandwiches."

Noah rubbed his neck, another wince flickering across his face. "I have to tend to the horses."

"I'll take care of the horses," Jenn cut him off. "The resort shuttle will be here any minute with a fresh batch of rafters for Diego's morning run. Sam can catch a ride back with them while you go clean yourself up. You smell like wet dog and cabin mold."

We both fixed him with identical stern looks. Noah's eyes darted between us with the panicked expression of a trapped animal calculating escape routes and finding none. For a moment, it appeared as if he was about to turn and run, but then another wave of pain must have hit him because his face twisted up like a climbing knot. It looked like it took every ounce of will just to stay upright.

"Fine," he hissed through clenched teeth. "One massage. That's it."

"And lunch," I added, seizing the advantage while he was still vulnerable. "The spa menu mentioned something about a rub-and-grub package with fancy little pimento cheese sandwiches and a pasta salad made with couscous and chickpeas."

The mention of chickpeas appeared to be the final straw. Noah's eyes rolled so hard I worried they might pop out of his head. "I should have abandoned you in the wilderness," he grumbled.

"After you get cleaned up, come find me at the resort." I gave him a critical once-over. "And wear something nice."

"Define nice."

"No hiking boots," Jenn and I said in perfect unison, then exchanged a high-five.

Noah muttered something that sounded suspiciously like a promise to feed us both to bears at his earliest opportunity.

* * *

Every one of my leg muscles protested as I staggered out of the resort shuttle, attempting to remember how walking worked. It seemed after two days on horseback, my body had forgotten it was designed for bipedal movement.

The gleaming glass doors of the grand entrance reflected my apocalyptic appearance in high definition. "Good Lord," I gasped. I looked like I'd been dragged backward through a briar patch infested with wolverines, then thrown into a tornado.

The same fresh-faced bellhop who'd greeted me on my first day stood at attention by the entrance, his uniform so crisp and pristine it triggered a primal urge to run over and rub my forest-marinated body all over him just to mitigate the contrast.

His eyes widened as I approached, taking in my mud-splattered clothes and wild hair. "Miss Li? Are you okay?"

"Just peachy," I croaked, attempting to smooth down what felt like a family of squirrels nesting in my hair. "That's why they call it the great outdoors. Nothing says authentic Colorado like returning with half the forest lodged in your underwear, right?"

"Um ..." He held the door open as wide as possible, as though worried whatever I had might be contagious.

The resort lobby hit me with a wave of civilization so intense it was like landing on an alien planet. The marble floor gleamed. The massive stone fireplace radiated toasty warmth. The signature scent of sage and lavender wafted through the air conditioning, nearly masking the musky cabin stench that I was afraid had stuck to me permanently.

"Back to civilization," I sighed. "Where I belong."

My stomach growled when I caught a whiff of something sizzling from one of the resort's restaurants, reminding me that chocolate truffles and charcuterie board fare weren't sufficient sustenance after a *Dante's Inferno*-esque trek through the wilderness.

Images of the restaurant's lunch menu flashed through my mind like a slideshow of culinary pornography. Truffle fries. Seven-bean Colorado chili with extra cheese and sour cream. A big plate of loaded Mountain nachos. All of it washed down with a pitcher of huckleberry jalapeño margaritas the size of a small mountain lake.

"First order of business, a rent payment worth of room service," I said to myself. But then I remembered ... I couldn't ruin my appetite for my spa date with Noah.

Date?

Is that what it was going to be? A date? An actual date? Or did Noah only agree to meet me because his back was in horrible pain?

I shuffled toward the elevator, leaving a trail of forest debris in my wake. Date or not, I at least had to be presentable if I was going to be near another human being. Plus, I needed to call down to the front desk to see if they could send up a priest to perform an exorcism to remove whatever had taken up residence in my hair.

"Sam?" I froze mid-step, then turned to find Maya power-walking across the lobby. She waved frantically, heels clicking against the marble at a pace just shy of "jog." A warning bell sounded in my mind, but I was too exhausted and my legs were too traumatized to run.

"Sam! Thank goodness I found you," Maya said, out of breath as she reached me. "I've been trying to call since yesterday."

I held up my phone, black-screened, cracked, and lifeless. "Dead battery."

Maya's mouth dropped open, apparently really looking at me for the first time. "What happened to you?"

"Long story involving rain, horses, lightning, and a cabin in the middle of a time warp."

Maya's eyes performed a comprehensive scan of my disheveled appearance. "And why do you smell like wet wool and ..." She leaned in and took a delicate sniff, then recoiled. "... feral buffalo?"

"That would be Yeti, I'm guessing. She used my face as a pillow." I attempted to finger-comb my hair, dislodging what appeared to be part of a sap-covered pine cone. "I promise I'll tell you the whole epic tale later, but right now?" I gestured at my general state of disarray. "I need the world's hottest shower, clean clothes, and enough perfume to fill the Colorado River."

Maya opened her mouth to protest, but I held up a mud-caked hand. "After that, Noah and I plan to try every single treatment on your spa menu."

Her mouth dropped even further. "Noah agreed to everything on the spa menu?"

"Basically. Sort of."

"Even the Alpine wax?" Maya's eyes were a lot bigger than normal.

"Okay, maybe not that one. But once he realizes how much better his back feels after a nice massage, I'm hopeful his mood will be supple enough to at least try a manicure. And then after a few mimosas, we'll see where we can go from there."

"But Sam." Maya gently took my hand. "You don't have time ..."

I held up my mud-caked hand again, then grimaced as a clump of something brown and sticky detached from my sleeve and hit the pristine floor with a thunk. "The only thing I can't do is be around other humans. I have pine needles in places pine needles should never be. Give me an hour and unlimited hot water, and I'll be somewhat presentable again. Maybe even capable of complete sentences."

"You don't have an hour," Maya said, glancing at her watch. "You have about four minutes."

"Four minutes for what?"

"Victoria. She scheduled a meeting."

"In four minutes?"

Maya checked her watch again. "Now it's three minutes and twenty-eight seconds."

The room began to spin, forcing me to grab the nearest decorative bear statue for support. I gestured at my disaster of a body. "I can't do a Zoom call like this."

"It's ah ... not a Zoom call. It's in person. Victoria flew in this morning."

"No. No no no. I can't meet Victoria looking like this." I caught another whiff of wet dog mixed with what I could only describe as 'eau de flatulent horse.' "Or smelling like this."

"Sam ..."

"I have leaves in my hair, Maya. Actual leaves."

"Sam ..."

I Burned My Tongue in Colorado

"Possibly small insects building a tiny civilization." I pressed my palms against my temples, trying to contain the panic. "Tell her I'm sick. Tell her I'm missing in the forest. Tell her I got kidnapped by Bigfoot."

"Sam," repeated Maya, her tone sharpening with urgency.

"Please, Maya, I can't do this right now. Just tell Victoria ..."

"Tell me what, Samantha?"

Slowly, I turned. Victoria stood right behind me. Marcus was on one side of her. Parker on the other.

As Parker and I locked eyes, I wasn't sure which of us was more shellshocked — me at seeing him here, or him at witnessing what a few days in authentic Colorado had done to his previously polished mentor. "Sam? Are you okay?"

"I've been better," I admitted, fighting the urge to dive behind the bear statue and hide. "What are you doing here?" From the deer-in-the-headlights expression on Parker's face, I got the distinct impression he didn't quite know why he was there either.

"I asked him to come," said Marcus, his voice as cold as an abandoned cabin in the wilderness.

"We figured you were going to need the help," Victoria added, her eyes performing a comprehensive inventory of my wilderness-ravaged appearance.

"Help with what?" I asked.

Marcus smiled his shark smile. "Fixing everything you broke."

Chapter Thirty-One

Click. There I was, face-planting into the river, mouth open in a scream.

Click. Yeti and I, in a mountain meadow selfie, our tongues out like fools.

Click. Me, sweat-soaked after a hike, mascara streaking down my face like I'd auditioned for the raccoon role in a woodland creature musical.

The fluorescent lights hummed overhead, their flat, artificial glow draining all the color from the LuxeLife conference room as I sank lower in my chair. The sterile white walls felt suffocating after a day of endless mountain horizons.

"What exactly were you trying to convey here?" Victoria pointed at the screen where I hung upside down from my safety harness, hair a vertical waterfall of tangles.

"Um..."

I sat and watched as Marcus scrolled through my content from the past few days, each new image flashing on the massive screen like evidence at a trial. Every click felt like another jury member holding up a little sign that read, "GUILTY."

I Burned My Tongue in Colorado

"And this sequence?" Marcus paused on a candid shot of Noah from behind, bending over to tie his hiking boot. *Click.* Another shot of Noah bending over to collect muffin wraps. *Click.* Another, Noah, bent over to shoo a caterpillar before it got smushed on the trail.

"How exactly do these align with our luxury brand messaging?"

"I was going for authenticity?"

Even Parker closed his eyes and bowed his head.

I glanced over at my phone, plugged in to the conference room's AV equipment so it could download the past week's content and recharge. I briefly considered snatching it back and running out of the room.

"Authenticity." Victoria spat the word like a rotten huckleberry. "Looks like a completely uncontrolled narrative to me."

"After that whole sordid osprey episode, your numbers have flatlined." Marcus opened a series of charts and graphs. "Which means booking rates haven't budged." The line on the screen looked like the heartbeat of a corpse, which is basically what my career was about to be.

Marcus leaned over toward Victoria. "If we don't see a boost soon, the board is going to ..."

"Be very disappointed that you couldn't deliver what I promised them, Samantha," Victoria finished.

Maya cleared her throat. "If I may ..." She stood, commanding the room's attention. "Mother Nature isn't something we can control. These experiences? They're unpredictable by definition."

"I can verify that," I added.

Maya turned toward the head of the table. "Victoria, you said you wanted authentic Colorado experiences. The authentic Colorado *is* unexpected adventure. The authentic Colorado *is* the thrill of the unknown." Her voice grew stronger with each word, confidence building like a river approaching a rapid.

I sat back and watched Maya work her magic, feeling a surge of hope as Marcus and Victoria hung on her every word.

"Look at these engagement numbers." Maya pointed to the screen. "Sure, the total views have stabilized, but Sam's authentic moments are generating three times the interaction of her standard luxury posts. Look at the comment counts."

"It's true," said Parker. "Sam flipping over in the kayak is one of our most viewed livestreams ever. And the part where her pants got snagged on a branch is now a meme."

"It is?" I asked.

"And this helps our brand how?" Victoria arched her perfectly sculpted eyebrows.

"Because it makes luxury adventure accessible," Maya said, her passion infectious. "Not everyone wants to see another perfect person doing a perfect yoga pose on a perfect mountain-top. They want to see someone real trying something new, maybe failing, but getting back up and trying again. And again. And again."

Maya's gaze swept across the room, landing finally on me. "Real adventure isn't perfect," she said as she settled back into her chair. "It's messy and challenging, and sometimes you end up hanging on for dear life on the back of a flatulent horse. But that's what makes it authentic. That's what makes it into the memory of a lifetime."

It was the perfect moment for a slow clap. But when no one else moved, I discreetly sat back down and slipped my hands under the table.

Marcus leaned forward, pressing his elbows against the polished wood. "The posts may be popular, but how does that translate to sales? Are booking inquiries up?" he asked. "Revenues per room?"

I Burned My Tongue in Colorado

"Well," Maya hesitated, her confidence wavering. "I mean, not yet, but ..."

"What about the Adventure Center business?" asked Victoria, "Are they seeing any revenue boost?"

"The demographics aren't exactly ..." Maya trailed off, her professional facade cracking. "These things take time ..."

"Time we don't have," said Marcus.

Victoria leaned back in her chair. "So what you're basically telling me is that there are a bunch of people out there watching Sam make a fool of herself, but none of those people are spending money at my resort."

The silence stretched longer than a horseback ride to hell and back. Maya and Parker both turned to me with identical expressions of desperate hope, like I might suddenly pull a magical solution out of thin air. But the only things in the surrounding air were the smell of horse and wet dog fur.

I swiveled my chair toward Victoria. "You are a luxury brand," I said. "You offer curated perfection to perfection-minded guests."

"Yes," said Victoria. "And the sky is blue and water is wet."

"Are you suggesting curated perfection is a problem, Samantha?" Marcus raised an eyebrow.

"No, curated perfection isn't the problem. The problem is you're asking for curated *authenticity*. But curated authenticity doesn't exist."

Marcus started to respond, but Victoria cut him off with a wave of her hand. "You know what, Marcus? She's right."

"She is?" Marcus looked confused. As did everyone else.

Victoria's expression shifted to something more calculated, more dangerous. "Curated authenticity doesn't exist. But it should." Victoria tapped her manicured nails against the table, the rhythmic click-click-click like the timer on a bomb. "See, Marcus? I told you we shouldn't fire her just yet."

Parker and I exchanged a nervous look. I hadn't realized how precarious my situation really was. I'd been too distracted by a certain grumpy mountain man to pay attention to what I was supposed to be paying attention to — my job.

"Samantha is right. Authenticity *is* too unpredictable," said Victoria. "We can't risk the LuxeLife reputation on whatever Mother Nature decides to throw at our exquisitely curated guest experiences."

At that moment, an artificial room deodorizer pumped the chemical equivalent of pine throughout the room. After inhaling real pine forest the past few days, the fake smell made me want to throw up.

"So, what do we do?" asked Marcus. "Just give up?"

"I never give up," said Victoria. "I adapt."

"Adapt how?" asked Maya.

"We pivot to Samantha's idea. Effective immediately."

"My idea?" I asked. "Which was what, exactly?"

Victoria waved me off with her manicured hand. "Don't be shy, Samantha. You don't give yourself enough credit. You know the folly of trying to tame the wilderness better than anybody."

She had a point.

"Okay, people, let's ideate on Samantha's curated authenticity concept." Victoria's voice took on the enthusiastic edge of someone who'd just discovered a new tax loophole. "This is transformative thinking, Samantha. Well done. Paradigm-shifting."

"What's a paradigm?" I whispered to Parker.

"We'll do a mind-mapping exercise," Victoria commanded. "Marcus. Curated authenticity. Go." She gestured at him like a conductor cueing an orchestra section playing the "March of Doom."

Marcus seemed to know what a paradigm was because he

didn't miss a beat. "Instead of whitewater rafting, we build a lazy river behind the infinity pool."

My growing sense of fear at what I'd accidentally unleashed started to build. The rushing river that had tossed me like a rag doll was terrifying, yes, but also exhilarating and real. Was Marcus actually proposing that a glorified bathtub with strategically placed bubble jets would replace it?

"Excellent, Marcus." Victoria tapped her chin with a pointed nail. "We'll put up a barbed wire fence to keep all the real wild animals off the property and put in some more of those stuffed dead ones for people to take selfies with. We can dress them up in LuxeLife branded hats and scarves too."

My growing fear turned to growing horror.

"Maya, you go now." Victoria leveled Maya with a pointed stare.

"Well, I guess ... for people who don't want to do horseback riding, we could do e-bike tours? Still outdoors, but more ... controlled?"

"I love the electrification of the outdoor experience," Victoria said. "We'll tear down some trees and put in paved bike paths everywhere. Well done, Maya. Well done." She pointed at Parker next. "You. Asian man-child. What do you have for me? Curated authenticity. Go."

"You could put in a virtual reality arcade," said Parker. "They have these hyper-realistic fishing simulation games, hook sensitivity, weather variations, everything."

"We'll have to workshop that one." Finally, Victoria turned to me. "Samantha, your turn. Dazzle me with your curated authenticity vision."

With each suggestion, the real Colorado I'd experienced with Noah seemed to dissolve like froth bubbles in a piping hot latte. The mountains, the storms, the wildlife, all replaced with sanitized copies that wouldn't dare inconvenience a paying guest with something as unpredictable as actual nature.

"Well, Samantha?"

Across the table, Marcus shook his head, giving Victoria one of those "I told you so" looks. I could see him drafting the contract termination papers in his head.

I never intended to abandon the idea of Colorado authenticity. But with everyone staring at me, waiting, I felt as exposed as I had standing naked in that cabin, wrapped in nothing but a scratchy wool blanket. If this was the direction Victoria was determined to go, maybe I could at least preserve some tiny bit of the original vision.

"Samantha?"

My mind flashed to Brie, at the dance, at the festival, telling me about Noah's Girl Scout project, building a boardwalk with a wheelchair ramp so people with mobility challenges could still enjoy the view of the lake.

Maybe ...

"Um ... we could ... ah ..." I swallowed hard, the taste of betrayal on my tongue. "We could put in a boardwalk, with ramps. All around the perimeter with little signs about the native flowers and animals and trees."

"Yes, yes, the safe version of a hike." Victoria nodded, her enthusiasm growing like a forest fire consuming everything authentic in its path. "That way, people don't have to risk getting mud on their Ferragamos. Nice work, Samantha. Well done." I could almost see the dollar signs replacing her pupils as she mentally calculated the profit margins of the "curated authenticity" ideas.

Maya cleared her throat, teeth gnawing on a corporately branded pen. "What about the Adventure Center though? We'll still need them for the guests who want natural experiences."

I Burned My Tongue in Colorado

"And you said you would renew Noah's contract if he played along," I reminded her.

Victoria picked a piece of lint off her blazer, then slowly shook her head. "I told you I would consider renewing Mr. Barrett's contract if he helped our numbers improve." Her eyes never left mine. "Have they, Marcus? Have our numbers improved?"

Marcus shook his head, smiling as he did it.

I stared at my mud-caked fingernails and calloused hands, still bearing traces of the forest. "But the engagement numbers ..."

"Engagement without conversion is just noise," Victoria cut in.

"This isn't just business to Noah," I blurted. "This is his life. He loves these mountains more than anything." Noah's love for Colorado wasn't just something he talked about; it was something he lived, breathed, embodied with every step he took on those trails. He didn't just work in those mountains; he belonged to them.

"Maya can explore alternative employment opportunities for Barrett and his team," said Victoria. "Guest services, maintenance supervision." She paused, and for a split second something flickered across her face. "We're not in the business of destroying livelihoods. But we are in the business of sustainable profit models."

"Noah won't go down without a fight," I said, my voice sharper than intended. "The Adventure Center is his family's legacy."

Victoria's posture shifted. "Well then, perhaps you should be the one to tell him."

The temperature in the room dropped to "wilderness cabin" range. "Me?"

"You've established rapport with Mr. Barrett," Victoria

continued. "You understand both perspectives. His attachment to tradition and our need for fiscal responsibility. You're uniquely positioned to help him see that adaptation doesn't have to mean abandonment."

"Ms. Sterling ... I don't think I can ..."

Her eyebrows rose a fraction of an inch. "Unless that's going to complicate things for you personally?"

"Complicate things for me personally?"

"No. Of course not. Surely you and Noah have maintained appropriate professional boundaries, correct? Mixing personal feelings with business decisions creates casualties on all sides. That's why we have the ethics clause in your contract. To protect you."

"Ethics clause?" The words felt foreign in my mouth, though I already suspected I was about to get a very expensive education in corporate fine print.

"Yes," said Marcus, his smile spreading wider. "The ethics clause. The one that explicitly prohibits personal relationships with other LuxeLife contractors or employees."

Marcus's fingers punched buttons on the remote control, and suddenly the conference room screen lit up with images. Guest snapshots tagged on social media, all my pictures and videos and posts. An entire collection of digital breadcrumbs documenting my time with Noah.

Each image was a frozen moment that looked startlingly intimate when viewed through an outsider's lens, but I knew the truth. These weren't evidence of unprofessional conduct. They were evidence of my becoming a real person instead of a performing one.

"So all these shots of the two of you together?" Marcus let the question hang in the air, with an eyebrow raised in wait.

Victoria rested her chin on her interlaced fingers. "She was simply playing a part. Isn't that right, Samantha?"

I Burned My Tongue in Colorado

I knew that whatever I said next would determine not just my career, but who I was going to be for the rest of my life. "Yes," I heard myself say, the word hollow in my chest. "Of course. Just business. I was only playing a part. Everything we did together was strictly to generate content for the job."

The lies fell from my mouth like mountain rocks, each one landing with a sickening thud in the chasm of my stomach.

"Good." Victoria sat back, content. "Glad to hear it." She examined her nails, buffing them slightly against her silk blouse.

"Well, I for one am glad we had this little talk," said Marcus. "And I'm especially glad you, Samantha, told us that there was nothing between you and Noah. That you were simply using him to finish the job we hired you to do. Involving the legal team creates so much paperwork."

"Yes, I really don't like paperwork," said Victoria.

"Look on the bright side, Samantha." For some reason, Marcus was still smiling. "This will make it so much easier to tell Noah the Adventure Center is finished once and for all."

"You still expect me to tell him?"

"Of course. In fact, why don't you tell him right now?"

I followed Marcus's gaze to the conference room door, which sat open behind me.

Noah stood frozen in the threshold, his tall frame filling the entire doorway. But it was the details that made my chest constrict with something far worse than guilt.

He was freshly showered, hair still damp and carefully combed in a way I'd never seen before. Usually it was tousled from wind and work, but now it looked like he'd actually spent time trying to tame it. The button-down shirt was clearly new, still carrying the crisp lines of recent creases, chosen in a deep blue that brought out his eyes.

And he was wearing loafers. Actual loafers without a speck of dirt.

"Noah ..."

He'd transformed himself. Cleaned up and dressed up for an afternoon with me. The grumpy, frumpy mountain man going on an afternoon spa date he'd clearly been looking forward to.

Only to walk in just in time to hear me reduce everything between us to a business transaction.

To hear me dismiss everything we shared the past week as nothing more than content generation for my Instagram feed.

Chapter Thirty-Two

Noah stared at me from the doorway. It wasn't just hurt in his blue eyes; it was the systematic dismantling of trust, and I watched it happen in real time.

"Noah," I whispered, rising halfway from my chair.

But even as I spoke, I watched him retreat back behind his walls. His jaw, that telltale muscle that ticked when he was annoyed, now clenched with the force of someone who'd learned to swallow pain without flinching. The way he stood in that doorway, perfectly still except for the almost imperceptible rise and fall of his chest.

"I can explain."

"Don't bother." What struck me wasn't his anger; it was his sudden, terrible calm. "I get it now. All of it."

"No, you don't." But even as I said it, I saw Noah Barrett cutting his losses.

Clean. Quick. Final.

"Just business." I watched him survey the room, taking in Victoria's calculating expression, Marcus's curious smile, Maya's uncomfortable avoidance of eye contact.

When his gaze finally returned to me, it was like he'd been waiting for this exact thing to happen, and now that it had, he could finally relax. "Actually, this makes perfect sense."

He glanced down at his carefully chosen outfit, the button-down shirt instead of flannel, the loafers instead of hiking boots. "Even this." His tone was both casual and devastating. "I'm probably going to end up as a before-and-after story, aren't I? 'How I Turned the Grumpy Mountain Man into Spa-Date Material.'"

"Noah, please."

"Congratulations on your career move, Miss Li. Hope it was worth it." He turned and left.

I half-stood, torn between chasing after him and remaining in my corporate-assigned seat, playing the role I'd just reaffirmed.

"Noah, wait ..." I called after him, but he was already gone, nothing left but the faint scent of pine trees and coffee, which was quickly overwhelmed by the chemical pine scent pumped in through the air vents.

The conference room door drifted closed with a soft click that somehow sounded more final than if he'd slammed it. I sank back into my chair, aware of Marcus's satisfied smirk, of Victoria's calculating gaze, of Maya's poorly concealed sympathy, of Parker's awkward bewilderment.

"Well, that's settled then," Marcus said, as if we'd just concluded a routine budget meeting instead of witnessing the destruction of everything that mattered.

I'd spent my adult life building a career around pretending to have things I never earned, to be someone that I wasn't. And when finally given the chance to be someone real, my first real test of authentic living, I'd chosen to pretend.

Marcus and Victoria started talking about implementation timelines and rollout strategies, but their words washed over me like white noise. All I could think about was the look in Noah's eyes. Not anger, which I could have handled, but disappointment. I'd worked so hard to earn his respect. And I'd thrown it away for a contract with people who'd been using me just as surely as I was using them.

"I have to go after him."

Victoria paused mid-speech, her rant about unfiltered mountain air triggering allergies fading into silence. All eyes turned to me.

"Excuse me?" Victoria's eyebrows glowered on her face.

"I have to go after him. I have to talk to Noah."

"Samantha, think about your contract," said Marcus.

But I was already out of my chair and heading for the door. For the first time since arriving in Colorado, I knew exactly what I wanted, what I needed, what mattered most. And I'd just watched him disappear down the hallway, believing I'd played him for a fool.

Likes or love.

I made my choice.

* * *

I burst out of the conference room. The hallway stretched before me, empty except for a bewildered resort worker who jumped aside as I barreled past.

"Noah!" I called down the empty hallway. "Noah, wait!"

Barreling into the lobby, I saw a maze of potted ferns and overstuffed leather chairs, but no grumpy mountain man in sight. Just pampered tourists in pristine mountain gear that had never seen an actual mountain.

I spun in a circle, searching for any sign of him, a glimpse of those broad shoulders, that confident stride, even the scowl I'd grown oddly fond of.

Nothing.

"Sam?" Maya's voice came from behind me, slightly breathless. She'd chased after me.

"I have to find him," I pleaded. "I have to explain."

"He probably went back to the Adventure Center." Maya placed a gentle hand on my arm. "I bet you'll find him there." She glanced back toward the conference room, lowering her voice. "Marcus is pissed. He started yelling something about contract termination and blacklisting you from every luxury brand on three continents."

"I don't care." And remarkably, I didn't. The thought of never photographing another overpriced organic facial cream or saltwater infinity pool didn't bother me half as much as the memory of Noah's face when he'd heard me reduce everything between us to "just business."

"You really like him, don't you?"

"I ..." The words stuck in my throat.

Did I like Noah Barrett?

The man who'd abandoned me at the airport, but then turned around and came back.

The man who made fun of my hiking boots, but then gave me new ones to protect my feet.

The man who made me raft down a raging river, then saved me when I fell in.

Did I like Noah Barrett?

The man who baked huckleberry muffins with orange zest.

The man who let me win at axe-throwing.

The man who, when he held me, made me wish he'd never let go.

"Yes," I said. "I like him. But I think it's even more than that."

Maya dug into her pocket, pressing a lump of jangled keys with a LuxeLife logo keychain in my palm. I recognized them as the ones that operated the resort's four-wheel-drive golf carts.

"Take the service road," Maya said. "It's faster than the main drive, and Victoria won't see you leave."

"But you'll get in trouble ..."

"Some things are worth getting in trouble for." She gave me a gentle push toward the back entrance. "Now go. Tell that stubborn mountain man how you really feel before he disappears into the wilderness for good."

"What if he doesn't want to hear it? What if I'm too late?"

"Sam." Maya planted her hands on my shoulders, looking me straight in the eyes. "I've known Noah Barrett for a long time. Trust me when I say that man has never looked at anyone the way he looks at you."

Something warm bloomed in my chest, pushing back against the icy dread that had settled there in the conference room. "I'm going to find him. And then I'm going to tell him ..." I paused, searching for the right words. "Tell him everything."

With one last grateful look at Maya, I turned and headed for the service entrance, keys clutched in hand. If there was one thing Colorado had taught me, it was that real adventure, the kind worth having, never followed a perfectly curated path.

As I rushed through the back doors of the LuxeLife Resort service exit, I nearly collided with the same bellhop who'd witnessed my mud-splattered arrival earlier. He must have been used to my usual state of dishevelment, because he didn't even blink. He leaned against a wall, smoking a cigarette.

"Miss Li." He smiled. "You're still alive."

"More than ever," I answered. "Where are the four-wheelers?"

He pointed toward a row of gleaming black vehicles parked under a cedar awning. "But we don't allow guests to..." He stopped himself mid-sentence. Probably saw the fire in my eyes and decided he didn't want to tangle with the kind of person who'd survived whatever I'd been through. He took another long, slow drag on his cigarette. "The one at the end got some modifications."

"What does that mean, exactly?"

The bellhop smiled. "Means you might want to wear a helmet."

* * *

The four-wheel-drive golf cart launched airborne as I crested the top of a small hill, then bounced back down the dirt and gravel road toward the Adventure Center. I jammed down on the accelerator, the electric motor whining in protest.

The vehicle handled with all the control and stability of a shopping cart with a wobbly wheel in the slick gravel. Yanking the steering wheel back and forth, I bounced over a series of ruts, each jolt sending shocks through my wilderness-battered body. But physical discomfort was nothing compared to the ache in my chest, the desperate need to fix what I'd broken.

Whipping around the turn from the service road to the main road, the golf cart tipped sideways onto two wheels, *Dukes of Hazard* style. I threw my weight in the opposite direction and the vehicle rebalanced, all four wheels making solid contact with the ground. It should have been a warning sign to slow down.

I stomped down on the accelerator even harder. Pine trees flashed past in a blur of green as I pushed the vehicle to its battery-powered limits.

"Stupid, stupid, stupid," I said to myself, slamming my palm against the steering wheel. "I'm an idiot," I announced to a particularly judgmental-looking boulder as I swerved around it. "A complete and total idiot."

I Burned My Tongue in Colorado

The cart bounced over another pothole, sending me airborne again for another heart-stopping moment before I crashed back down onto the seat. Luckily my butt was numb, already tenderized by a day and a half of saddle torture.

"Please let him be there," I whispered to the universe, to the mountains, to whatever forest spirits might be spying on me, plotting their next catastrophe. "Please let me fix this."

I glanced one last time in the rearview mirror. Behind me, the resort receded into the distance, the infinity pools, the spa treatments, the perfectly curated luxury that had once seemed so important. Ahead lay something far less certain but infinitely more valuable.

If I was lucky, a second chance with the grumpiest, most authentic man I'd ever met.

The golf cart rattled down the mountain path, tires spitting gravel as I took each curve like I was a stunt double in *Fast and Furious: Colorado Drift*. The trail narrowed as it descended toward the lodge's outer grounds.

Aspen trees blurred past, their white trunks a strobe effect in my peripheral vision, the afternoon sun filtering through leafy branches in dappled patterns across the dirt road. The cart's tires skidded on loose gravel as I took another turn, the back end fishtailing dangerously close to a steep drop-off.

My mind raced faster than the golf cart, replaying every moment. "What if I'm too late?" The thought sent a chill through me despite the sweat beading over multiple parts of my body. What if he'd already disappeared into the wilderness, swearing off civilization forever, leaving nothing but mountain and memory between us? What if ...

A blur of motion snapped me back to reality. There in the middle of the path stood a plump, mottled bird, strutting back and forth, bouncing rhythmically. Its feathers formed a ridiculous mohawk-like crown, and its expression could only be described as aggressively observant.

The disco chicken.

Time slowed as my brain attempted to process the absurdity before me. The very creature I'd encountered on my first night, performing its bizarre mating dance in the darkness.

"MOVE!" I screamed, twisting the wheel hard to the right. The creature stood its ground, wings spreading in what appeared to be a territorial display, completely unmoved by the impending collision with two hundred pounds of pimped-out golf cart and one slow-reacting driver.

The cart lurched sideways, tires losing their grip on the gravel path. I skidded, the world tilting at an impossible angle as the vehicle left the trail entirely. Pine branches slapped against the windshield, needles raining down as I careened between tree trunks.

"Oh no. No, no, no, no ..."

The front tire caught on a rock, and the cart pitched forward. Through the windshield, I could see nothing but air and the yawning mouth of a steep drainage ditch.

Pure instinct took over. I flung myself sideways, tumbling from the vehicle an instant before it flipped. I hit the ground with bone-jarring force, rolling through pine needles and dirt, roots and branches scraping my skin as I tumbled downhill.

A thunderous crash echoed through the forest as the cart landed upside down in the ditch, electronic motor wheezing, wheels spinning in the air like the legs of an overturned beetle.

"Ouch." I lay sprawled among the pine needles, staring up at the trees. Branches swayed gently in the breeze, forming a natural cathedral ceiling against the perfect Colorado blue sky. At least it was a beautiful place to die.

I tried to sit up. Pain bloomed in various parts of my body, sharp in my left ankle, dull and throbbing across my ribcage, hot and wet along my forehead from a cut above my eyebrow.

"This is it," I said to a nearby chipmunk, who paused its acorn-gathering to stare at me, pity in its beady little eyes. "I hope you and your woodland friends enjoy the feast. Just wait until I'm gone before you start eating me, okay? Professional courtesy."

The chipmunk twitched its nose.

I imagined my obituary. "Here lies Sam Li, social media influencer and failed human being. Betrayer of mountain men. Disappointer of parents. Abandoner of authentic experiences. She died as she lived, in over her head and making questionable life choices."

My vision began to blur, the pain and probable concussion taking their toll.

"If I die here," I told the chipmunk, too battered to even name him. "Tell Noah I'm sorry. Tell him it wasn't just business. Tell him ..." The world began to fade, darkness creeping in from the corners of my vision. "Tell him I was falling in love with him."

The trees melted into a swirling kaleidoscope of green and blue. My life didn't exactly flash before my eyes, more like a blooper reel of my most embarrassing moments: spilling coffee on Noah at the airport, spilling coffee on Noah at the resort, Noah fishing me out of the river, Noah rescuing me as I dangled from the climbing wall.

A sharp rustling in the nearby bushes snapped me back to reality. My eyes flew open, head whipping toward the sound, sending fresh jabs of pain shooting through my temples.

"Hello?" My voice came out as a croak. "Is someone there?"

The rustling grew louder, branches parting as something pushed its way through the underbrush. My mind raced through the wildlife catalog Noah had drilled into me. Was it a bear? Mountain lion? Something worse?

My fingers scrabbled in the dirt, searching for a stick, a rock, anything I could use as a weapon against whatever was about to emerge from those bushes and finish what the golf cart crash had started.

The branches parted.

I held my breath.

Waiting for Death to appear in a form full of claws and teeth.

Chapter Thirty-Three

I braced myself as the leaves rustled, waiting for certain doom.

But instead of a mountain lion or a bear, it was the bizarre bird again, strutting just a few feet away, completely unfazed by the near-death experience. Its chest inflated to an impossible size, like a feathered balloon animal, the white ruff around its neck jiggling as it performed what looked like the world's strangest chicken dance.

"Are you real?" I asked, my voice a rasp in the sudden silence. "Or are you a death vision? Because if you're a sign from the afterlife, I have some serious questions about God's aesthetic choices."

The bird continued its mesmerizing dance, puffing and deflating, bouncing on stick-like legs.

"If I'm dead, and you're my spirit guide, I feel like I should at least know what you are."

The bird responded by turning in a perfect circle, its tail feathers fanned out as if it were taking a bow.

With tremendous effort, I extracted my phone from my

pocket. If I were hallucinating, I needed proof. And if I wasn't hallucinating, I needed documentation of whatever wilderness fever dream I was currently experiencing. My thumb left a smear of blood across the cracked screen as I opened the camera app. Luckily, there was enough juice left after the recharge from the conference room.

"Just in case I survive this," I explained to the bird, which continued its performance with dedicated focus. "I need evidence you exist. No one's going to believe this otherwise."

The bird strutted closer, clearly not camera-shy.

Bounce. Puff. Strut.

Bounce. Puff. Strut.

The bird tilted its head, tiny eyes fixed on me. It took two steps forward, then continued its bizarre routine, like the bird equivalent of a TikTok dance challenge.

"You're not trying to mate with me, are you?"

It was the most bizarre, authentic Colorado moment I'd experienced, lying in a ditch while being propositioned by a disco chicken.

Suddenly, the bird froze, head jerking toward some distant sound. It deflated its bizarre air sacs and disappeared into the underbrush, leaving me alone with the smoking wreckage of the golf cart, a growing collection of bruises, and the sobering realization that I was now stranded.

"Thanks for nothing!" I called after it. "Not even dinner first?"

With a groan that likely scared off any remaining wildlife within a half-mile radius, I rolled onto my side and pushed myself up to a standing position. Pain shot through my ankle when I tried to put weight on it.

"Great," I muttered. "Just perfect."

Using a nearby tree for support, I hauled myself upright, testing how much weight my injured ankle could bear. I fashioned a makeshift walking stick from a fallen branch and slowly made my way back to the road.

To my right lay the path back to the resort. To safety, to comfort, to perfectly heated infinity pools and room service.

To my left, the path continued toward the Adventure Center, toward Noah, or so I hoped. My ankle throbbed at the mere thought of walking in either direction.

But then something caught my eye, a narrow dirt track branching off from the main path, almost hidden by over-hanging branches. Fresh tire marks cut through the dirt, the distinctive tread pattern I recognized from Noah's Jeep. They veered off the main road, heading deeper into the forest.

Noah's tracking lesson echoed in my brain.

"... tracking isn't just about footprints..."

"... it's about reading the whole story ... direction, speed, how recently they passed by ..."

I looked closer, tracing my hand over the dirt. The tire prints were still fresh, the edges still sharp where the tires had cut through the soft earth. Noah had come this way, and recently.

I glanced back toward the resort, its lights just visible through the trees. Then I looked down the overgrown path, with its uneven ground and low-hanging branches. There were thorns spiking out of a nasty-looking vine curled around a rotten stump. At least a dozen creepy, crawly insects were within jumping distance of my head.

With one final glance up the road, perhaps my last glimpse of civilization, I followed the tracks of the mountain man into the unknown.

* * *

I hobbled down the brush-shrouded path, my makeshift walking stick sinking into the soft earth, still damp from the storm. The pain in my ankle had settled into a dull throb, manageable if I gritted my teeth and pictured Noah's scowl every time I was tempted to turn back. Like a drill sergeant who pushed new recruits to their maximum limit, and then beyond.

"Follow the tracks," I said to myself, examining the distinctive tread pattern Noah's Jeep left in the dirt. "Just like he told you."

The trees thinned ahead, sunlight breaking through the canopy to illuminate a clearing nestled at the base of a towering cliff face. And there, parked in a patch of wildflowers near the trailhead, sat Noah's battered Jeep.

"Noah?" I approached cautiously, leaning on my walking stick to support my weight.

No answer.

I limped toward the vehicle, hope and dread wrestling in my chest. The driver's door was unlocked, keys dangling from the ignition. In the backseat were the clothes he'd been wearing for our spa date, the button-down shirt, a pair of new-looking jeans and the loafers. Now tossed aside and discarded in a tangled ball. My heart hurt just looking at them. He had to be close. But where?

My eyes scanned the open space, then settled on the towering wall of rock forming the back edge of the clearing. A thin climbing rope caught my eye, hanging down from the top. I squinted upward, following its length. The rope disappeared over a jutting ledge about thirty feet up. I couldn't see anything beyond it.

"Noah! Are you up there?" Only silence answered me in return.

The rope swayed slightly in the mountain breeze. I knew Noah must be up there somewhere, probably working out his frustrations with LuxeLife, his frustrations with me. Not a surprise that he would use extreme adventure sports as an anger management technique.

The sun glinted off something metal, a carabiner maybe? But I couldn't make out a human figure against the mottled gray stone.

"Great. I followed him all the way out here, nearly got killed, and he's off communing with rocks instead of answering me."

A flicker of movement caught my eye, not from above me, but beside me, a shadow shifting at the edge of my vision. I turned, hopefully expecting to see Noah's tall frame emerging from the woods.

It wasn't Noah.

Instead, I found myself staring at approximately 1,000 pounds of irritated moose.

"Oh, oh."

The animal stood perfectly still, its massive body blocking my way back to the Jeep. Its dark eyes fixed on me as I held up my hands in a gesture of peace. Which in moose language must have meant something else entirely because it snorted, now even more pissed off.

"Nice moose," I whispered, trying to convince the creature I wasn't worth trampling into human pâté. "Good moose. Pretty moose."

The animal's nostrils flared, its ears swiveling forward. It took one deliberate step toward me, crushing a clump of wildflowers beneath its massive hoof. There was nowhere to run, nowhere to hide.

A soft snuffling sound from the opposite direction drew my attention. I turned my head slowly, careful not to make any sudden movements that might trigger the moose's "stomp the city girl" instinct.

On the far side of the clearing stood a smaller moose, with gangly legs and a proportionally larger head. It watched me while chewing lazily on a mouthful of leaves.

The realization hit me like a thousand-pound hoofed mammal. I was standing between a mother moose and her baby. The exact thing Noah warned me I should never let happen.

"Well, this isn't good." My mind raced through every wilderness survival show I'd ever half-watched while scrolling through TikTok. Don't run from predators. Was a moose a predator? Make yourself look big. No, that was for bears. Play dead? That was for ... something else. Not mooses. Meese? Whatever.

"Stay calm." The irony of giving myself advice I was incapable of following wasn't lost on me. "Just back away very slowly."

I took one tentative step backward, and the mother moose pawed at the ground, lowering her head. "Bad move. Very bad move."

The calf took a few steps toward its mother, which would have been heartwarming if it didn't require crossing the invisible line that connected me to certain death. Mama Moose's eyes narrowed, her massive body tensing like a furry locomotive preparing to charge.

I'd come to Colorado to create curated content about luxury wilderness experiences. Instead, I was about to become content for the moose's feed: #CityGirlSquish #NoFilter #AuthenticWildlife.

"Noah," I called, a prayer more than a call for help. "Where are you?"

The moose lowered its head further, eyes locked on mine. The message was clear. This would be my last authentic Colorado experience.

I Burned My Tongue in Colorado

"Don't. Move." The voice came from above, barely a whisper on the breeze. Every muscle in my body froze, except for my eyes, which darted upward.

Noah hung from the cliff face above me, suspended by climbing ropes and carabiners, his body pressed against the stone.

"Noah?" I'd never felt so relieved in my life.

"What are you doing here?" He kept his voice low.

"Me? What are YOU doing?" I hissed back, my neck craned to maintain eye contact.

"Climbing helps me think."

The moose snorted, drawing my attention back to the thousand-pound problem at hand. Its massive head swayed, hooves pawing at the dirt as its baby watched from the safety of the tree line.

"Don't make any sudden movements," said Noah, his voice still quiet.

The moose took another step forward, lowering its head toward my vital organs. I could practically feel its hot breath from fifteen feet away.

"Um ... can you come down here, please? Like now?"

"Not even I can make it all the way down there in time."

"I think it's going to charge."

"She's definitely going to charge." Noah's voice was impossibly calm. "But we're going to get you out of this. I need you to listen carefully."

My heart was beating so fast and so loud I wasn't sure I could listen to anything, but I nodded, eyes still fixed on the moose's flaring nostrils.

"See the rope hanging on your left? About three feet from the rock face?"

I glanced sideways, careful not to move my head. The

braided climbing rope I'd seen earlier still dangled from above, its end coiled on the ground.

"I see it," I whispered.

"When I tell you, not before, you're going to run and grab the rope."

The moose pawing intensified, dirt flying behind its massive hooves.

"Noah, I don't think ..."

"Trust me." His calm certainty steadied my rising panic. "You're going to climb, and I'm going to pull. But we have to time this perfectly."

"I busted my ankle trying to find you." I winced when I tried to put my weight on it.

"That moose is going to bust a lot more than your ankle if you don't get out of its range."

"Noah ... I don't think I can do this."

"You *can* do this, Sam, and you will. Just like we practiced on the climbing wall. Just like when you saved that osprey. Get to the rope. Start climbing. And hold on." He shifted his position slightly, bracing himself against the cliff. "The moose's first charge will be a feint. A warning. But she'll stop short. That's when you move. Not even a second early. Definitely not a second late."

The mother moose lowered her head further, muscles bunching beneath her thick hide.

"Get ready," Noah murmured. "When she charges, count to three, then dive for the rope."

The clearing fell silent, even the birds holding their breath as the standoff continued. The moose's eyes, dark pools of primal ferocity, locked with mine.

Everything stopped.

"Wait for it ..."

Time froze.

"Get ready ..."

The moose charged.

My brain screamed for me to run, to climb, to do anything but stand there counting.

"One," I forced out between clenched teeth.

The distance between us halved in an instant. Her massive head lowered like a battering ram.

"Two." My voice cracked.

The moose kept coming. I could see the individual hairs on her muzzle now.

"THREE!" Noah and I shouted in unison.

The ground shook beneath her thundering hooves as the moose skidded to a stop, her feint complete. Just like Noah said.

I dove for the rope, fingers wrapping around the rough nylon, yanking it toward me.

The moose bellowed in frustration and wheeled around for a second charge, one that would NOT be a warning.

"Climb! Now!" Noah called, his voice sharp.

With shaking hands, I fumbled with the rope. The angry moose pawed the ground again, preparing for round two.

"There's a foothold to your left!" Noah instructed, his voice urgent and patient as the moose began her second charge. This one didn't look like a practice run.

"Noah, I can't ..."

"Remember the climbing wall? The tree with the osprey? Same exact thing!"

The memory of the Adventure Center's practice wall flashed through my mind, then Noah's patient instructions at the lake, the triumph when I'd finally cut the osprey free from the fishing line.

"Put your hand in that crevice," Noah called down. "Just like we practiced."

The moose closed in, but instead of freezing, I forced my

attention to the rock face. There! A small ledge just within reach. I stretched my fingers to grip it.

"That's it," said Noah. "Now, get your foot on that outcropping to your right."

I pressed my good foot against the small jut of rock, testing it before putting my weight on it. The moose closed the final few yards between us. I could smell her wild musk, feel the ground trembling beneath her hooves.

"CLIMB!"

I pushed upward with my good leg, pulling with my arms just as the moose barreled through the space where I'd been standing. Her massive body swiped the rock face inches below my dangling foot.

The rope went taut, not jerking me up but supporting my weight as I found the next handhold. My injured ankle screamed in protest, but I gritted my teeth and kept moving.

"Don't look down, just keep going!"

While I was climbing, Noah was pulling. With his legs still braced against the floor of the ledge, the only leverage he had was from his arms. His biceps bulged so swollen they looked like they would pop.

Below, the moose passed under me, stuttering to a halt, hooves kicking up a cloud of dust. She turned to make another run.

"There's a handhold at your two o'clock," Noah called.

I reached for it, fingers closing around the rough stone.

"That's it, you got this!"

Except ... I didn't.

My foot slipped, sending a shower of rock fragments tumbling down the cliff.

"Sam!"

Without my leg to support me, my body dropped, fingers wrapped around the rope, coarse fibers cutting into my palm.

I Burned My Tongue in Colorado

"Hold on!"

But I couldn't. A muscle in my shoulder felt like it tore in half, my rope hand on fire. Above me, Noah sprang into action, moving toward me, arm extended to grab my hand.

"Sam, grab my hand!"

I tried. Our fingers were just inches apart.

Inches too far apart.

The rope slipped from my sweat-slicked grip.

The cliff face raced skyward in a blur.

WHAM!

I hit the ground hard; the breath knocked right out of me, busted ankle screaming. Luckily, I'd only scaled part of the way up, so it could have been worse. And for once, getting tangled up in a climbing rope actually helped me, slowing my descent.

I was alive.

But not for long.

The wind had been knocked right out of me, and I couldn't even feel my injured foot. It took everything I had just to sit up.

The moose finished its turn. She looked right at me, eyes on fire, nostrils blazing.

She lowered her head.

She charged.

Chapter Thirty-Four

The moose charged right at me, its hooves accelerating over the rocky ground.

Noah was screaming something, but I couldn't hear him, my attention consumed by the massive animal who had just been given another chance to end me. From the look in her eye, this time she didn't intend to miss.

I closed my eyes.

But not before I caught a flash of white and grey out of the corner of my eye.

My eyelids sprang back open as I turned.

It was YETI!

Exploding onto the scene in a flurry of fur and a ferocious howl that would have sent any other animal running. Channeling her inner wolf just in time.

She positioned herself between me and the moose. Fur standing on end. Baring her teeth. She didn't just bark; she growled and roared in a show of protective intimidation that would have made an entire wolf pack proud.

The moose didn't need to be told twice. She slid to a halt,

then quickly backed away several strides. Keeping her black eyes on the still snarling Yeti, she turned and lumbered over to the tree line where her baby waited.

With one last look over her shoulder, mommy moose and baby moose scampered off into the trees.

"Yeti?" I sat on the ground, watching it all unfold in shock. Partially from the fall. Mostly from bearing witness to Noah's wolf dog literally saving my life.

When the coast was clear, Yeti jumped into my arms, her tongue slathering my cheek as if she was checking to make sure I wasn't hurt.

"Yeti, you saved me!" I wrapped both my arms in her fur and kissed her right back, barely noticing the slobber on my lips. "Okay, okay, just to be clear, I don't need mouth-to-mouth."

Noah wasn't far behind her, rappelling down the cliff like an action hero, then racing to my side to examine me. "Sam! Are you hurt?" His hands were everywhere. Okay, not EVERYwhere. But he checked my head, my ankle, my shoulder. He looked even more scared than I did. "Sam, talk to me. Are you okay?"

"Yeah." Adrenaline coursed through my veins, giving me a momentary reprieve from the pain. "Thanks to her."

Yeti sat back, tongue sticking out, tail wagging, her smile showing her teeth. The perfect picture of a proud rescue hero.

"I guess you don't hate me, Yeti. You saved my life."

Yeti barked.

"She never hated you," said Noah, rubbing the fur between Yeti's ears. He let out a long breath, as if he'd just now remembered to breathe. "If I'm being honest, I think she kinda liked you from the start."

"She did?"

Noah kept his eyes on his wolf dog, stroking her fur. "Yeah.

She did." He was quiet for a moment, and I couldn't help but wonder if Noah's words applied to more than just Yeti.

"I'm starting to think near-death experiences might be my authentic Colorado specialty."

Noah's expression became guarded again, as if remembering why we were in this situation at all. "What were you thinking? You shouldn't be out here all alone."

"I was looking for you."

Noah's expression shifted, as if he were trying to erase all emotion there. "Why?"

"So I could explain." A jolt of pain shot through my foot when I tried to move.

"We should get you back to the resort's medical clinic. That ankle needs to be looked at." His voice was distant, all business, a clear indication of what I'd done to his trust in me.

He offered his hand to help me up. "No." I crossed my arms instead of taking it. "Not until you hear me out."

"You got something to say?" He planted a knee on the ground, now face-to-face. "Then just say it."

"I was lying to them. Back there in the conference room. Lying to myself, actually." What I saw in his eyes made my chest ache.

"Sounded pretty convincing to me. Just business. Generating content. Your words, right?" Each of my own words repeated back to me landed like a knife in the back.

"Yes, but ..."

"Marcus made it very clear what your priorities are, Sam. Sharing beautiful things so they can sell their beautiful lies. And I get it. I do. Your career is important to you. LuxeLife is important for your career. I'm just the local color to make it look convincing."

"That's not true."

Noah stood back up and walked away, gathering his climbing gear.

"Okay, fine," I yelled after him. "You're right. I was scared and trying to save my job, but I realized ..."

"Realized what?" Noah whipped back to me, and for just a moment, his carefully maintained mask slipped, his words laced with something that sounded dangerously close to hope. "What exactly did you realize, Sam?"

Words piled up in my throat, a traffic jam of emotions I couldn't untangle under the weight of his careful attention. "I ..." My voice faltered. "I don't know."

Noah laughed, shaking his head. "You don't know? Unbelievable." He turned back to his ropes, yanking them off the ground and coiling them in his arms like he was strangling something.

I struggled to my feet, then stumbled closer to him. "What I do know is that when I heard Victoria talking about replacing the Adventure Center, erasing your family's legacy ..."

Noah's hands stilled, a length of rope clutched in his hand like a vise.

"I couldn't be part of it." I hopped a couple of steps more on my good leg. "And when you walked away thinking I'd been using you ..."

The piece of rope he'd been coiling fell loose, unfurled to the ground.

I gestured helplessly between us. "Look, I don't know what this is. Or what it could be. But I know I had to find you. To tell you what happened in that cabin, it wasn't just content generation. That wasn't business. That was real." I took a deep breath. "So I came after you. A romantic grand gesture. That's got to count for something, right?"

"You almost got yourself killed," said Noah, pointing toward the spot where the moose disappeared into the trees.

"That's not a grand gesture, Sam. That's reckless. Do you have any idea what would have happened if Yeti hadn't been here? If you'd faced that moose alone?"

Something snapped.

"You don't give me enough credit," I said, limping closer through the pain. "I'm not helpless, Noah." Three days of being treated like a helpless city girl, of being underestimated and overprotected, finally boiled over.

His mouth opened to counter, but I wasn't finished. "I walked out on Victoria Sterling, the woman who will probably now destroy my career. I stole a golf cart, and when it crashed, I didn't give up. I kept going. On a sprained ankle. And a head wound dripping blood down my face." I ticked each point off on my fingers. "I followed your Jeep tracks like you taught me about animal tracking. And yes, I almost got trampled by a moose. Which would have really sucked. But I also survived a bizarre mating ritual from a disco chicken, so ..."

"A what?" Noah's expression went from stern to confused.

"The disco chicken. That weird bird that puffs out its chest and does the bouncy dance." I tried imitating the dance, but it was hard to do with a busted ankle.

"How hard did you hit your head when you crashed?"

"I know what I saw. The first one nearly got me killed on my hike to the resort. The second one caused me to crash the golf cart."

"Sam, there are no chickens in these mountains."

"Not an actual chicken. It was *like* a chicken. With these weird inflatable chest pouches, or something. It danced and made popping sounds." I imitated the popping sounds I'd heard, which in hindsight probably did more to hurt than to help my credibility.

Noah looked more skeptical the more I described it. "A dancing bird with inflatable pouches?"

I Burned My Tongue in Colorado

"And popping sounds." I made the sounds again.

"It almost sounds like ..." Noah had a faraway look in his eyes, but then shook his head. "But that would be impossible."

"Here, I can show you." I held up my phone so he could see.

Noah's eyes flicked over my screen, then widened like he'd seen a ghost. "Wait." His eyes fixed on the video. "Play that again."

I played it again.

Noah pointed to a specific moment when the bird turned, revealing a distinctive pattern on its neck feathers. "I can't believe it." His entire demeanor changed, anger and hurt wiped away by wonder. "Where exactly did you see this?"

"Coming from the resort. Near the Adventure Center."

For such a serious man, I'd never seen Noah more serious.

"Close to where I saw the one my first night. Except that one was smaller and not quite as animated. I think one was a girl and the one today is a boy."

Noah ran a hand through his hair, his eyes never leaving my phone screen. "Sam, do you have any idea what that is?" He looked at me like he actually expected me to come up with an answer.

"Not a disco chicken?" I ventured.

"It's a Gunnison sage grouse," said Noah, voice hushed with awe. "They're critically endangered. And you've seen two different ones? In the same area?"

"It's like they're targeting me specifically."

"Researchers have been trying to document their mating grounds for years. The population's been declining so rapidly that finding an active lek is rare."

"Lek?"

"Their mating grounds."

For some reason, my mind flashed back to the old cabin.

"So, me finding them is a good thing? Even if I did it recklessly?"

Noah couldn't fully suppress a smile. "We have to show the others. This changes everything."

With a renewed sense of urgency, Noah dumped his climbing gear in his Jeep, then whistled for Yeti.

"Um ... a little help, please?"

I stood on one leg while Noah considered me for a moment, then made a decisive nod. "Put your arms around my neck.

"What?"

"I'll carry you."

"I thought you said you'd never carry me." I wrapped my arms around his shoulders as Noah scooped me off the ground.

"That was before you discovered an endangered species' mating ground." He held me as if I weighed next to nothing.

I clung to Noah like I never planned to let him go. His body was warm against mine, his muscles tense as he checked to make sure I was secured. "You okay?" he asked, breath tickling my ear.

"I am now."

Chapter Thirty-Five

"Got it!" Parker fiddled with some cords, and the portable projector sputtered to life.

The hastily converted Adventure Center was now command central for Operation Save the Grouse. The room buzzed with energy — part tension, part excitement, part "we're all going to get fired, but at least we'll go down in a blaze of glory."

"Holy shit," said Jenn, leaning forward in her chair. "That really is a Gunnison sage grouse."

The cinematography wouldn't win me any awards, shot one-handed while I was woozy from blood loss, possibly concussed, but its subject commanded everyone's full attention. The bizarre bird strutted across the frame, chest puffed to improbable proportions, air sacs inflating and deflating like tiny built-in party balloons.

Diego stopped eating his pastrami sandwich mid-bite. Brie was so distracted she poured coffee all over the counter when her mug overflowed.

The bird continued its ridiculous dance, bouncing across

the frame. When it unleashed that strange popping sound, Maya gasped.

Noah had been pacing so much he'd probably worn down the treads of his hiking boots. When our eyes met, an electric tingle sizzled up my spine. I shifted on my plastic folding chair, wincing as my ankle reminded me I was lucky to still be alive.

He brought me a fresh ice pack, gingerly removing the other one, which had melted into my sock. "Does it feel any better?"

I nodded. "I think the swelling's gone down. Thanks."

"Look at the tail pattern," Jenn pointed at the screen. "And that distinctive white ruff. This is definitely a mature male in full display."

When the video ended, the room remained silent for several heartbeats, the significance of what I'd captured fully sinking in. Then came the questions.

"How many did you see?" asked Diego.

"Where exactly was this taken?" asked Brie.

"Did you notice any females nearby?" asked Maya.

Noah held up his hands, quieting the chaos. "This isn't just about us anymore." He pointed to the grouse, now frozen on the screen. "We're also fighting for him." He cued Jenn, who moved to the front of our makeshift war room.

"The Gunnison sage grouse is one of North America's most endangered birds. Once common throughout the Gunnison Basin, their population has declined by over ninety percent in the last century."

Jenn signaled Parker, who changed the view on his laptop to a map. "Development, roads, and recreation have fragmented their habitat." She paused, nodding at me and smiling. "What Sam discovered appears to be an active lek. Their mating ground."

"Like the bird equivalent of a singles bar," said Diego.

"Something you know well." Maya gave him a friendly punch in the arm.

"These leks are critical to their survival," Jenn continued. "Males return to the exact same spot year after year, generation after generation, to perform these mating displays. If a lek is destroyed, the birds don't just find another location. The whole breeding cycle collapses. And then they're gone."

"Diego, you're up." Noah thumbed toward the front.

Standing in front of the row of folding chairs, Diego's usually playful demeanor gave way to something fiercer. "And it's not just the grouse," he said, pointing to some of the framed wildlife posters on the walls. "This area supports an interconnected ecosystem that includes elk migration routes, beaver habitats, and some of the last uninterrupted sagebrush landscapes in the state."

Parker, media whiz and master showman, hit the power button on the connected speaker system, and dramatic music played. The projector switched to a series of high-definition photographs. Mountain vistas. Bubbling streams. Wildflower meadows. Native animals in their natural habitats.

"LuxeLife's expansion plans would cut right through critical winter range for elk and mule deer," continued Diego.

Parker switched the view to drone footage of the entire area, including both the resort and the Adventure Center, juxtaposed with a 3D rendering of LuxeLife blueprints he'd found in shareholder reports on the corporate website.

"Victoria's curated authenticity program would involve clearing old-growth forest for its boardwalks and viewing platforms."

"Not to mention the light pollution," Jenn added.

"The noise. The increased traffic," said Maya.

"Tourists trampling wildflowers for the perfect selfie shot." Brie looked pointedly at me.

"Hey, I'm a reformed trampler," I protested, earning a small smile from Noah.

Maya cleared her throat, stepping to the front. "There are laws protecting endangered species habitat," she said, signaling Parker to bring a list of rules and regulations on screen. "The Endangered Species Act specifically prohibits any action that results in the 'taking' of a protected species, which includes significant habitat modification."

She met each of our eyes in turn. "If we can prove this is an active lek for the Gunnison sage grouse, we can trigger a mandatory environmental impact assessment before any development can continue."

"Which would delay Victoria's plans by months, if not years," Noah added.

"But laws and regulations aren't enough," said Maya. "Victoria has an army of corporate lawyers who specialize in finding loopholes. They'll argue the lek is abandoned, or that their development won't significantly impact the habitat."

Noah stopped pacing directly in front of my chair. I fought the urge to reach out for him. "That's why we need the community behind us," he said. "We need to make this so public, so visible, that it would be a PR nightmare for LuxeLife to harm one feather on this bird's head."

"He's right," said Maya. "We need visibility, public pressure, and a whole lot of noise."

"But we only have a few days," said Jenn. "And how much noise can the few of us here even make?"

I stood up, ignoring the protest from my battered body. Noah stayed close, probably worried he'd have to catch me if I fell.

"That," I said. "Is where I come in."

"Let me guess." Diego pointed at the screen. "You're going to make it into a TikTok dance."

I Burned My Tongue in Colorado

"I can do better than a TikTok dance."

"Better how?"

I looked over at Noah, and he gave me a little nod. "Grouse-apalooza," I announced.

A lot of blank faces stared back at me.

"Grouse-a-pa-what-za?" Diego frowned.

"Grouseapalooza," I repeated. "A festival. A celebration. A community event centered around saving our feathered friend. We'll create specific hashtags, #SaveTheGrouseDance and #GrouseapaloozaColorado. I'll reach out to my network of influencers, get them to amplify. We can livestream the whole event."

"You realize 99.9% of the population has never heard of the Gunnison Sage Grouse, right?" Jenn didn't seem convinced.

"That's the beauty of it. First rule of social media: people can't care about what they don't know about." My influencer's brain kicked into high gear. "We host a festival, just like the ones they hold downtown. Music, vendor booths, educational displays. We showcase the grouse in all its disco glory. And most importantly, we make it Instagram-worthy, TikTok-friendly, and hashtag-ready."

My audience still looked dubious at best, except for Parker, whose eyes had taken on that calculating gleam he got when evaluating the viral potential of a concept.

"People care about things they feel connected to," I explained, settling into my comfort zone. "Right now, this is just a weird bird doing a weird dance that nobody's ever seen. But once people come to Grouseapalooza, once they learn about it, once they post about it and tag their friends, suddenly it's their weird bird doing their weird dance."

"And then they'll care if Victoria tries to bulldoze its habitat," Maya finished for me.

"Precisely." I pointed at her like she'd just won the bonus

round on a game show. "We create a movement around this bird, and suddenly LuxeLife isn't just fighting some obscure environmental regulation, they're fighting public opinion. And trust me, as someone who lives and dies by the court of public opinion, that's a battle they don't want to get into. Once people get to know this bird ..."

"Gary," Noah interrupted.

We all turned his way.

"Who's Gary?" asked Diego.

"He is." Noah pointed at the screen. "Gary the Grouse."

"You gave the grouse a name?" Jenn looked like she was about to make an appointment for Noah to get his head examined.

"Nobody cares about a random bird. Everybody loves Gary." Noah looked back at me and smiled. It seemed the stubborn mountain man had been paying more attention to me than I thought.

"Gary the Grouse," Maya repeated. "I like it."

"It's kinda adorable," said Brie.

"It does have a nice ring to it," Diego admitted.

"Fine," said Jenn. "Gary it is. But a cute name isn't going to solve the problem of putting together an entire festival last minute."

"I can coordinate with the other vendors from the festival circuit," said Brie. "Most of them would love a chance to earn a little extra business on a weekend off."

"But it's too late to get permits for downtown," Maya cautioned.

"We'll use the Adventure Center," said Noah. "Set up tents in the parking lot. Use the main building for displays."

Maya nodded. "We could probably get away with an 'educational event' here with minimal paperwork. Since this is private property."

"LuxeLife property," Diego pointed out.

"LuxeLife property leased to us," countered Jenn. All eyes settled on the big calendar hanging on the wall — the last day of the month circled in red Sharpie. "At least for the next few days, it is."

"I mean, if they're not renewing the lease, what are they going to do?" asked Brie.

Everyone looked at Maya. "Not much they can do, as far as I can tell."

"You really think we can pull all this together in a few days?"

"A few days is forever for a social media campaign," said Parker.

"He's organized viral flash mobs on shorter notice," I added.

"I'll set up a multimedia presentation," Parker continued, fingers tapping at his laptop. "Project the grouse footage between music sets, maybe create some interactive displays where people can learn about the habitat."

Jenn drummed her fingers on the back of a chair. "I know some wildlife photographers who'd donate images. We could create a photo exhibit showing all the species affected if Luxe-Life expands."

The energy in the room had shifted, trepidation transformed into triumph. Noah watched it happen, his eyes seeking mine across the room with a look that made my heart skip a beat or two.

"Music," I said, forcing my attention back to the plan. "We need live music to draw people in."

Diego's smile went from rebellious to mischievous. "Maya should be able to help with that."

Maya immediately shook her head. "No. No way."

"Come on, Maya. It's for the grouse."

"For Gary," Noah reminded them.

"No grouse is worth that." Maya held her hand up. "Even one named Gary."

"I'll call him for you then," offered Jenn.

"Don't you dare."

"Call who?" I asked.

Maya, Diego, and Jenn all exchanged suspicious looks. Even Noah seemed to be in on whatever the big secret was.

"Maya's ex is a singer in a rock band," said Diego. "A pretty good one, too."

"Pretty good?" Noah crossed his arms. "I'd say average at best."

"Are the rumors about the piercings true?" asked Brie.

"Not going there," said Maya.

"What about the tattoos?" asked Diego.

"We're not going there either. Not now. Not ever." The look on her face made it clear the topic was closed.

There was a story worth telling though; I was sure of it. How did a good girl like Maya end up with a bad boy like ... whoever they were talking about. I promised myself I would follow up later.

We spent the rest of the day brainstorming. The momentum built as everyone contributed; the room buzzed with collaborative energy. One by one, all the details fell into place.

"Wait, wait a second, hold up!" Noah held his hands up in the center of the room. "There's a problem. A big one." Everyone got quiet. If anyone was going to rain on our grouse parade, naturally it had to be the grumpy mountain man.

"Food," he said grimly. "Can't have a festival without food."

"He's right." Brie nodded. "All the food trucks will be at that festival in Denver. I can bring my coffee cart, maybe rustle up some muffins, but feeding hundreds of people? No way."

An uncomfortable silence fell over the room as our perfect

plan hit its first major roadblock. Then Parker cleared his throat. "I know how we could feed hundreds of people," said Parker. I immediately noticed he wouldn't look me in the eye.

"How?" asked Maya.

"Sam's parents. They feed hundreds of people every day."

"No," I said immediately. "No, no, no, no, no."

"But Sam ..." Parker handed me back my phone. "Do it for the grouse."

"For Gary," Noah reminded again.

"There is no way in hell I'm letting my parents anywhere near the state of Colorado." Now, for once, I was the grumpy one.

Chapter Thirty-Six

Mom's feet hit the tarmac. She rushed right past me and scooped up Noah in a giant hug. "You must be Noah! I've heard so much about you!"

"So much for a dignified entrance." Dad patted my shoulder with the weary solidarity of someone who'd spent thirty years married to a human tornado.

Meanwhile, Noah stood frozen in my mother's embrace, his arms hanging awkwardly at his sides like he wasn't sure what to do with them. For a man who scaled cliffs for fun and stared down angry moose, he looked utterly terrified by my five-foot-nothing mother and her enthusiastic welcome.

"Mrs. Li, it's so nice to meet you too."

Mom finally released him, then moved back a few steps to conduct her inspection. Her critical gaze traveled from his freshly trimmed hair down to his, wait, were those new boots? When had Noah Barrett acquired footwear that wasn't held together by duct tape and stubbornness?

"So handsome!" Mom declared, patting his cheek like he was

a particularly adorable toddler instead of a fully grown mountain man. "Much better than those dating app pictures Samantha shows me. Those men all look like they're afraid of sunshine."

"Mom," I hissed, mortification spreading like wildfire. "I never showed you my dating app pictures!"

"I know the password for your phone when you visit," she replied with a dismissive wave. "Bensongirl71305."

"Mom!"

Dad stepped forward, extending his hand. "Henry Li, thank you for looking after our daughter." His voice carried its usual stoic reserve, but I also caught the genuine gratitude.

"Noah Barrett. And it's actually the other way around, sir. Sam's the one rescuing endangered wildlife and rallying the community."

I caught a smile tugging at Noah's lips as he reached for Mom's suitcase, which appeared large enough to transport a small family across three thousand miles of shark-infested waters. "Let me help with your bags."

"So strong!" Mom exclaimed, beaming at me over Noah's shoulder with a not-so-subtle thumbs up. "A mountain man with mountain muscles!"

Dad cleared his throat. "Helen, let the poor guy breathe. He's turning the color of your chili oil."

"I'm fine, really," Noah insisted, though the tips of his ears had indeed gone suspiciously red. He hoisted both my parents' suitcases with ease, the muscles in his forearms flexing beneath his rolled-up sleeves.

Not that I was looking. Or noticing. Or mentally photographing for later appreciation.

As Noah led us toward the airport exit, Mom linked her arm through mine, squeezing with both tenderness and intensity. "He is very handsome," she whispered at a volume that could probably be heard in Denver. "Good shoulders for carrying grand babies."

"Mom!" I said. "We're organizing an environmental festival, not planning a wedding."

"Why not both?" She waggled her eyebrows with exaggerated meaning.

Noah's Jeep sat in the pickup lane. Once again, I almost had to pinch myself to make sure what I was seeing was real. When he'd picked me up that morning, I'd almost fainted. The vehicle I'd come to associate with mud and mechanical failure had undergone a miraculous transformation. The exterior gleamed in the morning sun, windows crystal clear, even the dent in the passenger-side door somehow hammered back into place. Not a single splatter of mud.

"This is your vehicle?" Mom ran an appreciative hand over the hood. "Not nearly as bad as Samantha described. What did she call it again, Henry? Death trap on wheels?"

"Something like that," Dad mumbled, trying not to get sucked into it.

Noah glanced at me, eyebrow raised.

"Well, like its owner, it cleans up pretty nicely when it wants to," I said.

"So you washed it special for us?" Mom clapped her hands in delight. "So thoughtful!"

Noah loaded the suitcases in the back, then held the passenger door open for Mom with a gallantry that made her positively beam. "Such a gentleman, too."

Noah looked at me pointedly. "Thank you. I *always* try to be."

"Where's Yeti?" asked Dad, who climbed into the back with surprising agility for a man who claimed knee pain whenever it was his turn to take out the trash.

Noah turned the key in the ignition, starting up the Jeep. "I left Yeti back home," he answered, carefully navigating back toward the main road. "Didn't want her getting fur and drool all over you."

Mom waved away his concern. "Nothing scares us. Samantha once brought home a frog from the school pond. Kept it in a soup pot for three days before we found it."

"Mom, please."

"She named it Soup."

"She was a very practical child," said Dad.

"She was a very messy child," said Mom.

"Stop talking, Mom."

"Bossy too." Mom patted Noah's arm like they were co-conspirators in the "Embarrass Sam" club. "Even as a baby. She used to scream and cry if I didn't carry her everywhere."

"Some things never change," Noah replied, shooting me a sidelong smirk.

"I must say, Noah." I braced myself for whatever was about to come next. "You're not nearly as mean as Samantha said you were."

"She said I was mean, did she?"

"Oh yeah. Every night when she called us from her fancy hotel room."

"Mom."

"Every night. Noah did this. Noah did that. Noah, Noah, Noah."

"Mom."

"Sounds like she talked about me a lot."

"You have no idea," Dad grumbled.

Mom patted Noah's arm again. "You're pretty much the only thing she's talked about since she landed in Colorado."

Chapter Thirty-Seven

It was the morning of the festival. We'd spent every waking moment over the past three days planning, preparing, and strategizing. I'd moved out of my suite at the resort and moved into one of the old lodge cabins with my parents. One without holes in the roof and with a still-functioning outhouse nearby. Noah even let me borrow a surprisingly comfortable sleeping bag and loaned my parents a couple of fold-out cots.

The Adventure Center parking lot had transformed into a bustling hive of activity, with enthusiastic volunteers, busy vendors, wildlife photographers, and one very determined Chinese-American family wielding woks and fryers like they were about to take on the Mongol hordes all by themselves.

"No, absolutely not!" Mom waved her special wooden spoon, the one she claimed could detect dishonesty in both dumplings and daughters, at the portable kitchen setup. "This burner is far too weak! How are we supposed to get proper wok heat with a camp stove? We need fire!"

Dad nodded sagely beside her. "The restaurant burner

gives ten thousand BTUs. This gives maybe ten. It's like trying to get a tan with a flashlight."

Diego, who had somehow appointed himself my parents' personal assistant, portable kitchen fixer, and taste tester, crawled out from under the makeshift cooking station with grease smudged across his forehead. "Try it now, Mrs. Li."

Mom turned the knob, and flames leapt up with enough ferocity to singe her eyebrows. She cackled with delight, the kind of laugh that usually preceded culinary magic. Or minor kitchen disasters. "Now we can cook proper food!"

"Let me know when you need more taste testing," said Diego.

"That boy is skinny, but he eats like a teenage bear," Mom observed, already mincing ginger at a speed that rivaled a commercial-grade blender.

I turned back to the makeshift fusion menu Noah and Dad developed. They'd spent the previous evening gathered around the Adventure Center's old wooden table, sipping Colorado craft beer, snacking on dumplings, and brainstorming dishes that would merge Colorado mountain cuisine with Chinese influences.

"So we've got Disco Chicken Dumplings," I read off our list, "which, to be clear, are made with regular chicken and absolutely no trace of endangered sage grouse."

"And High-Altitude Har Gow," Noah added, pointing to the next item. "With trout instead of shrimp."

"Sage Grouse Sage Buns," I continued, choosing to ignore the hastily brainstormed pun. "Also not containing any actual grouse ingredients."

"Mountain Mating Dance Momos." Noah gave me a satisfied smile, clearly pleased with himself for that one.

"And for dessert, Huckleberry Egg Tarts and Migration

Moon Cakes." I chewed my lower lip, surveying the ambitious menu. "You think we can pull this off?"

Noah leaned closer, his shoulder brushing mine as he studied the list. "With your mom's motivational techniques? Absolutely."

"Yes, I'm familiar with Mom's motivational tactics. Speaking of motivation," I said, nodding toward the far side of the parking lot where Brie presided over a growing village of pop-up tents and tables. "Your sister has somehow transformed this place into a festival grounds overnight."

Brie moved between vendors with clipboard in hand, directing traffic with the casual authority of someone born to organize chaos.

Local artisans who'd been left with a free weekend by the cancellation of the downtown festival had rallied to our cause, setting up booths to sell everything from hand-carved wooden grouse sculptures to "Save the Disco Dance" t-shirts that Parker had designed and rush-ordered from an eco-friendly printer in Boulder.

"Mrs. Miller's bringing extra berries for your moon cakes," Noah said, checking his phone. "And Al's bringing over a taxi-full of flapjacks and syrups from Mabel's Diner. Insisted he would be doing the syrup-making demonstration himself."

The way the community mobilized made something warm unfurl in my chest. This wasn't the carefully curated support of paid sponsorships and strategic partnerships I was used to. This was real people showing up because they cared.

"I still can't believe we pulled this together so quickly," I admitted, watching Jenn stride purposefully toward us, her muck-stained stable overalls exchanged for jeans and a t-shirt bearing a stylized grouse silhouette.

"Got an update," said Jenn. "Local news is sending a crew.

I Burned My Tongue in Colorado

Nothing major, just the affiliate station from Grand Junction, but it's something."

"Every bit helps," Noah said, his gaze drifting toward the large screen Parker set up at our main stage area.

Parker stood on a ladder, directing two volunteers with the authority of a Hollywood director. "The projector needs to be angled three degrees higher. And make sure those speakers are positioned for maximum acoustic dispersion!"

For someone who usually spent his days taking artful photos of anime figurines, Parker had morphed into a surprisingly competent technical director. He'd created a multimedia presentation that would showcase the grouse footage between music sets, complete with infographics about habitat loss and conservation efforts.

"Marketing update!" Parker called, spotting us. He scrambled down from his ladder perch and jogged over, tablet in hand. "We're trending regionally on all platforms. The hashtag #SaveTheGrouseDance has been used over ten thousand times since yesterday."

"And the crowdfunding campaign?" I asked.

"Just hit twenty thousand. People are donating from all over the country." Parker swiped through analytics on his tablet. "Your original video has been viewed over half a million times, and we've got commitments from influencers with a combined following of twelve million to share content from today's event."

The sound of a guitar being tuned drew my attention to the makeshift stage. Jenn and Diego had eventually convinced Maya to go to Denver to convince the mystery man she had apparently dated once to join forces with the Wayward Sons at our festival, a story worthy of its own someday.

I watched as Maya led the leather-clad man with tattoo

sleeves and artfully disheveled hair toward the microphone stand set in the middle of the stage. "Is that ..."

"Yup," said Jenn. "The one and only." I found myself unable ... perhaps unwilling ... to pull my eyes away from his colorfully tattooed, sleeveless shoulders.

"This was a bad idea," Noah growled. "I told him if he ever came back here, I'd kick his ass."

"Wait," I said. "You know Axel Ryder? Like, personally?"

"You could say that," Jenn answered for Noah.

Everyone knew Axel Ryder from the music charts. And the tabloids. And on the evening news. He was one of those stereotypical bad boy rock stars. Money. Fame. And the appetites that came with them.

"Well, I think Axel Ryder is watching you," I noted, nudging Noah with my elbow. "Or more like glaring at you."

Noah grimaced. "Let him glare. As long as he stays away from me."

"Is there a story I should know about?" I asked, curiosity piqued.

"Oh, there's definitely a story," said Jenn. "But whether you'd want to know about it ... that's up for debate."

Before I could press Noah or Jenn to elaborate, Axel hopped off stage and started coming toward us. As Noah curled both hands into fists, Axel scooped Jenn up in a hug, which I noticed she didn't seem to mind. "Hey there, mountain girl! Still hanging out with this mountain hermit?"

"He's kind of like a bad habit," said Jenn. "Hard to get rid of, I guess."

Axel met Noah's gaze with a challenging grin. "Speaking of bad habits, you ever dust off that Martin guitar of yours, Barrett? Or is it collecting cobwebs like your social skills?"

Noah's posture shifted at the mention of the guitar. Like Axel had just pressed on an old wound.

"You told me you didn't play guitar." I gave Noah a curious look.

"I don't know that 'play' is the right word," said Axel with a smirk that carried more history than humor.

"The guitar's fine, Ryder," said Noah. "Unlike your ego."

Axel twirled a guitar pick between his fingers, then clapped Noah on the shoulder with a familiarity that suggested their antagonism masked something deeper. "Good to see you, too."

"And who's this?" There was a twinkle in Axel's eye as he seemed to notice me for the first time.

"Someone smart enough to stay away from you," Noah answered.

"Samantha Li," I said, ignoring Noah. "My friends call me Sam."

"Nice to meet you, Sam." Axel took my hand in his, then lifted it to his lips. When I glanced over at Noah, he stared at Axel's hand like he was planning to break every bone in Axel's fingers.

Axel let go just in time. "Any friend of Noah's is ... well ... I'm not sure because he doesn't have any friends, so we're in uncharted waters here. Good to see you again, buddy." Axel gave Noah a good-natured jab in the arm. Noah looked like he wanted to give Axel a different kind of jab. In the face.

As Axel strode back to the stage, Noah watched him go with an expression that mingled irritation with something else I couldn't quite place.

"You two friends?"

"No." Noah's tone left no room for debate, but I caught the way his hands unconsciously flexed. "Not anymore."

Looking back toward the stage, I saw Maya laughing at something Axel said, tucking a strand of hair behind her ear in a gesture I'd never seen from our normally composed resort manager. She looked like a backstage groupie. As we watched,

Axel handed Maya his guitar, and she slung it over her shoulder like she'd done it a million times before.

"Maya plays?" I asked, watching her fingers move confidently across the strings.

"Maya has all kinds of secrets," Noah replied cryptically.

The opening chords of "Landslide" drifted across the parking lot as Maya and Axel leaned toward the same microphone, their voices blending in harmonious counterpoint.

"They seem good together." On stage, Maya and Axel shared a smile that definitely wasn't just about music.

Noah grunted, but when his eyes met mine, they softened in a way that made my breath catch. For just a moment, his walls were down completely.

Something warm and unexplored passed between us.

"Noah!" Dad called from the cooking station. "We need your mountain man muscles to move these propane tanks!"

"Be right there!" Noah answered, but his gaze lingered on mine for a heartbeat longer. "We'll talk," he said, like he could read my mind. "After the festival."

"Yeah," I agreed, a mixture of anticipation and anxiety warring in my stomach. "After the festival."

When Noah went over to help Dad, I surveyed the transformed parking lot, taking in the cumulative efforts of our unlikely coalition. Booths lined the perimeter, colorful banners announcing everything from wildlife photography exhibits to conservation education stations. A small army of volunteers in matching t-shirts moved between stations, hanging signs and distributing flyers.

But as if they had a mind of their own, my eyes drifted back to Noah, where I was treated to a nice view of him bending over to pick up a propane tank.

"That mountain man is a very hard worker." Mom appeared at my elbow, somehow having navigated the crowd without me noticing. She had an uncanny parental ability to materialize exactly when you were thinking inappropriate thoughts.

"More important, he's a good man," she said, nodding approvingly toward Noah, who was now efficiently directing the placement of picnic tables. "Strong hands, too."

"Mom."

"What? I see how you look at him. The same way I look at a perfect batch of fresh xiao long bao." She made a slurping gesture and a sucking motion with her lips that I desperately hoped Noah couldn't see from his position across the lot.

"I'm not looking at him like anything," I protested. Weakly.

Mom's expression turned unexpectedly serious, her hand tightening on my arm. "Samantha. For many years, you've shown me pictures of fancy food, fancy hotels, fancy everything. All pretty, no substance." She waved her free hand dismissively. "But here? With these mountain birds and this mountain man? You have purpose in your eyes. This is not nothing."

Her words hit me hard. For the first time, Mom wasn't criticizing my career choice or questioning my life decisions. She was seeing something in me that I'd only just started to see myself.

"I'm just trying to help a good cause."

"Mm-hmm." Mom's skeptical hum contained multitudes of disbelief. "And I just make hundreds of dumplings because I'm hungry."

Luckily, a commotion near the entrance caught our attention before I lost it completely. I wiped away the one tear that dribbled down my cheek.

"They're here!" Brie called, waving frantically. "First festivalgoers are arriving!"

A small crowd had already gathered at the parking lot

entrance, carrying homemade signs with slogans like "Let the Grouse Get Down" and "Dance Like Nobody's Bulldozing Your Home."

"Showtime," I murmured, a mixture of nervousness and excitement bubbling in my chest.

Mom squeezed my arm once more before releasing me. "Go. Save birds. Win hearts. Multitask like a true Li woman."

As I moved toward the entrance to greet our first supporters, I caught Noah's eye across the crowded lot. He gave me a thumbs up, that rare genuine smile transforming his face from brooding mountain man to something that made my heart stutter in my chest.

Whatever happened next with Victoria, with LuxeLife, with Noah, at least we'd created something real together. Something authentic.

Chapter Thirty-Eight

No longer the quiet wilderness outpost I'd first encountered, the Adventure Center now crackled with raw, vibrant energy. Festival-goers packed every available space, moving between vendor stalls, conservation booths, and the main stage area where Axel Ryder, backed by the Wayward Sons, were delivering their third set of the day.

I wove through the crowd, stopping to pose for selfies with fans who recognized me from my viral grouse video, now lovingly dubbed "The Disco Chicken Dance" across multiple social media platforms. The genuine enthusiasm on their faces, not just for meeting me, but for the cause we were championing, sent a surge of pride through me, unlike anything I'd felt from posting perfectly filtered breakfast photos.

Parker materialized at my elbow, an iPad in one hand and his laptop in the other. "The numbers are insane," he announced, falling into step beside me. "We've blown past all projections."

"Details, Parker. Feed me details."

He flipped the tablet around, revealing a dashboard of analytics that made my social media marketer heart skip a beat. "Over two thousand attendees so far, and they're still coming. The petition has over five thousand signatures. The livestream has viewers from thirty-seven states and twelve countries."

"And the hashtag?"

"Trending nationally." His grin widened. "And 'Chinese Mountain Cuisine' is now trending in three major metropolitan areas. Your parents' fusion menu is generating its own buzz; we've got food bloggers from Denver who left the festival there to come here just to try it."

I glanced toward the food tent, where my parents presided over a line that snaked around the parking lot. Possibly all the way back to Los Angeles. Mom wielded her ladle like a conductor's baton, directing Dad and three hastily recruited local volunteers through a synchronized cooking dance. The Disco Chicken Dumplings had sold out twice already, with patrons returning for seconds of the Migration Moon Cakes. Al even had to make a second flapjack run.

"I'd better get back to the main stage. The timing of the Kevin the Goshawk and Gary the Grouse mashup gets tricky, so I prefer to handle that one myself."

As Parker returned to the AV equipment command center, I wove between booths, just soaking up the scene. Near the conservation education area, children gathered in an excited semicircle, their attention focused not on the impressive wildlife displays or interactive exhibits, but on Yeti.

Noah's wolf-dog had become the festival's unofficial mascot, sporting a handmade bandana emblazoned with a disco-dancing grouse that Brie had crafted the night before.

"Now remember," Diego instructed the wide-eyed kids as Yeti sat with regal patience, "wilderness creatures aren't pets. They're wild animals that deserve our respect and space."

I Burned My Tongue in Colorado

Understanding her role in this demonstration, Yeti offered a paw to a small girl in pigtails, who giggled with delight at the contradiction.

The "Pet the Wolf-Dog, Save Her Home" attraction was Brie's idea, with a suggested donation that already filled three five-gallon jars. Each child received a "Junior Conservation Ranger" badge, complete with Yeti's paw print stamp of approval. When the demonstration ended, Yeti wagged her tail with such enthusiasm her entire rear end swayed.

My attention shifted back to the stage when a cheer rose from the crowd. The band finished their song, and Axel leaned into the microphone, voice carrying across the festival grounds.

"We've got a special surprise for you all," he announced, prompting another round of cheers. "Someone who's been essential to protecting the wilderness we all love is going to join us for our next number."

My stomach dropped as Axel's gaze settled on Noah. "Ladies and gentlemen, give it up for Aster Park's very own mountain guardian, Noah Barrett!"

The crowd erupted, and I couldn't suppress a chuckle at the look of pure horror that crossed Noah's face. He shook his head vehemently, trying to back away as Jenn and Diego each grabbed an arm and shoed him toward the stage.

"No way." I watched in disbelief as Noah reluctantly mounted the steps, looking like a man approaching his own execution. "Noah Barrett sings?"

"Not in a long time," said Brie, stepping up beside me. She hit record on her phone. "This is going to be gold."

Noah stood awkwardly at center stage, accepting a guitar with the enthusiasm of someone being handed a live snake. For a minute, it was touch and go whether Noah was going to hit Axel over the head with the guitar, or flee the stage entirely.

But as soon as his fingers made contact with the instrument, his entire body went still. For a split second, his face calmed, even that hard jaw relaxed.

The crowd's roar intensified, and a chant began to build: "No-ah! No-ah!" But he didn't seem to hear them, somewhere else entirely, his thumb unconsciously running along the guitar's worn edge.

"I can't believe he's actually doing this." Brie seemed as mesmerized as I was.

I leaned forward, desperate to watch what came next.

"Some of you locals might remember," Axel continued into the microphone. "That before Noah was your friendly neighborhood wilderness guide, he and I used to play a bit of music back in high school."

The ripple of surprise that moved through the audience was nothing compared to what I was seeing play out on Noah's face.

"This next song is an old one," Axel continued, "but it feels right for today. It's about finding something real in a world of illusions. Something authentic when everything else is just for show." His eyes flicked briefly toward me, then back to Noah. "It's called 'Seeing Clear.'"

When the drummer counted them in, Noah's fingers moved across the strings. The opening notes rang crisp and clear, but I was watching Noah's face, seeing the exact moment when he finally let go. Like he'd forgotten where he was, and who was watching.

And then something amazing happened.

Noah began to sing.

His voice wasn't polished. Wasn't perfect. It carried a rough-edge that matched the rugged contours of his face. Every note carried weight. And as his voice filled the festival grounds, I watched something extraordinary happen. The weight of the world drifted off his shoulders and floated away on the breeze.

I Burned My Tongue in Colorado

"Through all the filters, past all the lies,
I finally see you with unclouded eyes.
What looks like chaos might be a dance,
in wilderness wisdom I found my chance."

As Noah sang, his gaze swept the crowd, finding mine. The air between us seemed to vibrate as the chorus built. Noah never took his eyes off me.

"I'm seeing clear for the first time,
mountains rising in my mind.
What once was distant now feels near,
I'm finally, finally seeing clear."

Brie nudged me, a smile on her lips. "You do realize he's singing about you, right?"

I didn't have the breath to form any words. My heart beat faster with every note. The lyrics washed over me, each verse peeling back another layer of whatever had built up between us.

On stage, Noah seemed transformed, the reluctance melting away as the music took over. He leaned into the microphone for the bridge, his voice dropping to an intimate rasp that somehow cut through the ambient noise of the festival.

"City lights can't outshine the stars,
authentic hearts leave the deepest scars.
What seemed so foreign now feels like home,
in your reflection, I'm not alone."

The realization hit me with the subtlety of a mountain avalanche.

"Oh, no."

"What?" asked Brie.

It wasn't just attraction or chemistry or the adrenaline rush of shared adventures that was forming between Noah and me. It was something deeper. Something that had been building since our first hike together. Since he'd rescued me from the rapids. Since we'd sheltered together in that storm-swept cabin in the middle of nowhere, just the two of us all alone.

"I think I'm falling in love with your brother."

Brie smiled. "And you're just now figuring that out?"

The thought should have terrified me. I, Samantha Li, aspiring social media maven and dedicated city girl, fell for a grumpy mountain man whose flip phone was not only not Wi-Fi enabled but also held together with duct tape.

But instead of terrifying me, it settled in my chest with the comfortable weight of something that had been there all along.

Just waiting for me to notice it.

As the song built toward its final chorus, Parker switched the massive screen behind the stage to the grouse footage.

The ridiculous bird appeared in all its glory, chest puffed, performing its bizarre mating dance in perfect synchronization with the music's rhythm.

The crowd roared their approval, phones raised to capture the unlikely combination of wilderness conservation, live music, and disco-dancing wildlife.

Noah's voice rose for the final chorus, his eyes finding mine again across the sea of upturned faces. The connection between us felt almost tangible, like a tether pulling us together despite time and space.

> *"I'm seeing clear for the first time,*
> *Mountains rising in my mind,*
> *What once was distant now feels near,*
> *Are we finally seeing clear?"*

I Burned My Tongue in Colorado

The song ended, and the silence that followed lasted only a heartbeat before the crowd erupted. Noah looked momentarily stunned by the reaction, then offered an awkward half-bow before attempting to escape the stage. Axel caught him by the arm, forcing him to stay for another round of applause.

I stood frozen, the revelation of my feelings rendering me temporarily incapable of movement.

Noah Barrett.

I was falling in love with Noah Barrett.

As Noah finally extracted himself from Axel's embrace and descended from the stage, a commotion at the festival entrance broke through my emotional epiphany. Heads turned toward the source of the disturbance, conversations faltering as a familiar four-wheel-drive golf cart careened into the parking lot.

The vehicle still bore the scars of my crash, dented front bumper, cracked windshield, one headlight dangling.

Marcus and Victoria stepped out, and like someone flipping off a light switch, the energy of the entire festival changed.

Chapter Thirty-Nine

Marcus stepped out of the driver's side of the LuxeLife golf cart, surveying the scene like an aristocrat who'd accidentally wandered into a peasant uprising.

Victoria stepped out of the passenger seat; her pristine white pantsuit remained immaculate despite the surrounding wilderness. Her gaze moved systematically across the scene: conservation booths, fusion food tent, the massive screen displaying Gary the Grouse dance videos, crowds wearing "Save Gary" t-shirts.

Then, Victoria's eyes found me.

"Oh, oh," said Brie. "She doesn't look happy."

Marcus scrambled to keep up with Victoria's measured pace as she marched toward me, flinching whenever he made accidental eye contact with anyone wearing tie-dye.

Victoria pressed her perfectly painted lips into a thin line, her eyes boring into me. My newfound emotional clarity about Noah would have to wait. Because right now, Victoria Sterling was bearing down on me with the momentum of an avalanche, and I had the sinking feeling that no amount of social media savvy was going to deflect what was coming.

From my peripheral vision, I caught both Noah and my mother converging on my position from opposite sides of the festival grounds, each wearing identical expressions of protective determination.

"I've got this," I said quietly as they reached me, holding up a hand to stop them both. Noah hesitated, concern etched across his features, while Mom's eyes narrowed with the protective instinct of a woman who once chased a crooked health inspector out of her restaurant with a meat cleaver.

"You sure?" Noah asked, his voice still carrying the husky quality from his song.

"I'm sure." Our eyes met, and I found strength in his steady gaze. "This is my mess to clean up."

Victoria came to a stop before me, her heels sinking slightly into the graveled parking lot. Her perfect features contorted with barely contained fury as she surveyed the surrounding festival. I watched as she watched the video display above the stage. I saw her take in the signs. "Save the Grouse!" "Stop LuxeLife!" "No More Corporate Expansions!"

"What exactly do you think you're doing?" Victoria demanded, each word as sharp as a scalpel. "Besides violating approximately eighteen clauses in your contract?"

I tilted my chin up, refusing to be intimidated. "Saving an endangered species. Protecting a community landmark. Oh, and generating the most authentic content this resort has ever seen."

Victoria's laugh echoed off the mountains. "This little ..." she waved a manicured hand dismissively at the festival, "... freak show won't change anything. The development plans are already in motion. The board has approved the budget."

"You have obligations, Samantha," said Marcus. "Contractual ones. With very specific penalty clauses for breach."

Victoria stared at the video screen, frowning. "What is that, exactly? A bird? Dancing? It looks like the chicken version of Barry Gibb." She looked at the faces of the crowd gathering around us, most of whom were much younger than she was. "That's a Bee Gees reference for all you millennials, by the way. Greatest disco band of the 70s. Look them up."

"We know who the Bee Gees are," said Brie.

Victoria's eyes narrowed as she turned back to me. "This little stunt of yours could end your career. One call from me, and you'll never work with another luxury brand again. Is that what you want, Samantha?"

I took a deep breath, drawing strength from the friends around me. From the community that had come together over the past few days. From Noah's song, still echoing in my heart.

"What I want," I said, my voice growing stronger with each word, "is to do work that matters. The Adventure Center matters. The grouse matters. This community matters."

Victoria's perfectly shaped eyebrow arched. "Does it really? Do you honestly believe people care about this beyond a few earthy-crunchy wackadoos?" She gestured to the festival-goers around us.

"Did she just call us wackadoos?" asked Diego.

"I think so," answered Jenn.

"This is a momentary distraction," said Marcus. "I know it. You know it too. Next week they'll all be obsessing over some new TikTok dance or one of those stupid challenge things where they dump a bucket of ice water on their heads."

"People might surprise you," I said, not backing down. I knew that for a fact because I had even surprised myself.

"Yes, well, the numbers don't support your confidence," said Marcus. "Our projections for the curated authenticity expansion are quite clear. Thirty-eight million in first-year revenue alone. Do you really think we're going to just give that up because of some half-baked festival?"

Victoria stepped closer, lowering her voice. "Samantha, you realize LuxeLife has an entire army of lawyers at our disposal. We will use the full resources of our corporation to push this development through. The Adventure Center will be gone, and no one will even care or notice."

Victoria stepped back and smiled, letting the weight of her threats settle in. She was right, of course. LuxeLife had more money, more lawyers, more corporate resources than we could ever hope to fight against.

But then, as if on cue, Parker's massive screen shifted from the grouse footage to a comment feed from the event's livestream. Messages scrolled past too quickly to read them all, but certain phrases jumped out:

"Does the resort offer grouse viewing tours? Trying to book now!"

"Tried to reserve a room for next month but the website says you're sold out??"

"My daughter has a school project on endangered species. Can we visit the disco chicken???"

Victoria's head whipped toward the screen. "What is that? Where are those comments coming from and what exactly are they talking about?"

Marcus frowned at his phone, fingers flying across the screen. "This can't be right. The booking system shows we're at capacity for the next three months. That's impossible."

"Not impossible," Parker said, stepping forward with his

iPad. He turned the screen toward Victoria, displaying graphs and analytics. "The festival livestream has driven over a thousand unique visitors to the booking portal in the last three hours alone."

Maya moved to stand beside me, her professional manager's smile locked in place. "If I recall correctly, Victoria, you promised to extend the Adventure Center's contract if Sam and Noah increased revenue and helped you make your booking targets."

"Yes, but they didn't," Victoria snapped. "After their little osprey rescue, they never budged."

"Until now," Parker interjected, swiping to a new screen on his tablet, "and the numbers are still climbing."

Marcus's expression soured as he consulted his phone. "He's right."

"What exactly is going on?" asked Victoria.

Marcus shook his head. "I don't know."

Maya scratched hers. "Well ...

The crowd fell silent all around us. Blank stares all around.

"Can anybody tell me what's happening right now?" shouted Victoria.

Realization dawned on me like the sunrise breaking over the mountains. "I can."

"Can what, Samantha?" Up until that point, the way Victoria was staring at me would have made me crumble. But this time when I looked her in the eyes, I noticed something I didn't think was even possible. There it was, on her forehead. A tiny bead of sweat. "Tell me, Samantha. What the hell is going on?"

"We missed it," I said, gesturing at the scrolling comments from the livestream. The festivalgoers all stared at me, nervous chatter grinding to a halt. "We all did."

I Burned My Tongue in Colorado

"What are you talking about?" Another bead rolled down Victoria's forehead.

"We had the *what* and the *how*," I said. "What we didn't have was the *why*."

Noah looked confused. "I don't understand, Sam."

From the looks on all the faces, neither did anyone else.

"The *what* is the luxurious resort experience," I explained, gesturing toward the LuxeLife property up the mountain. "The *how* is the authenticity, the real Colorado experience you, and Jenn, and Diego provide. But the *why* was missing." I turned to Victoria and Marcus. "Why should people pay premium prices to go on an authentic Colorado adventure at a LuxeLife resort?"

"Your job was to figure that out," said Marcus. I noticed he was sweating too. But a lot more than Victoria.

"We have to give them a purpose first. That's the why."

Understanding dawned on Maya's face. "Ecotourism," she said, nodding slowly. "It's been one of the fastest-growing sectors in travel for years. People want to feel their vacation dollars are making a positive impact."

"Exactly!" I pointed to the comment feed still scrolling on the massive screen. "These people aren't just booking rooms because they want luxury amenities. And they're not all looking for Colorado adventures either. They're booking because they want to see Gary the Grouse, to be part of something meaningful."

Maya nodded. "Studies show ecotourists spend up to thirty percent more per trip than traditional tourists," said Maya, backing me up yet again.

I watched as Victoria's eyes scanned the festival. Dollar bills being exchanged for Gary the Grouse t-shirts. The see-through plastic donation bins filled to the brim with wrinkled bills and shiny coins. The vendors and food tables and merch tents.

"And they stay longer," Maya added. "More nights, more meals, more activities."

Victoria's expression shifted from skepticism to calculation as she ran the numbers in her head.

"The data doesn't lie," said Parker, flashing more numbers and graphs on his iPad.

"Ecotourism?" Victoria frowned. "People pay money to ... help things?"

"Think about that new property you bought in Alaska," said Maya. "The one between the brown bear sanctuary and the whale migration route."

"That place is a money pit," said Marcus. "Should have shut it down months ago."

"Unless ..." Maya waited for Victoria to connect the dots.

"They have bears there. And whales. People like those, right?"

"People love bears and whales," Brie confirmed.

"And the new acquisition in Florida, too," said Maya. "Think about it."

"The one near Miami right next to the swamp?" Marcus shook his head. "The whole thing needs renovated."

"Yes," said Victoria. "But the permits keep getting held up by those stupid sea cows."

"You mean manatees?" asked Diego.

Overlooking all of us, the massive video screen above the stage shifted back to the grouse footage. Gary strutted and bounced, air sacs inflating, his distinctive mating calls broadcast from the loudspeakers over the entire forest.

That's when the miracle happened.

"Look! Over there!" One of the girl scouts pointed to something beyond the stage, her hand trembling. All heads turned to follow her hand.

At the edge of the festival grounds, where the parking lot met the tree line, a mottled brown bird emerged from the underbrush. She moved cautiously, head tilting as the recorded calls of her species were amplified through the festival speakers.

"Is that..." Marcus began, his corporate cynicism momentarily forgotten.

"A female grouse," Noah whispered, his voice filled with awe. "Here? Now?"

We'd spent days planning this festival to save a bird we'd captured on video, and now the bird itself had shown up to the party. As if the universe was finally ready to stop messing with me and start helping instead.

The best part? Noah stood right there beside me.

The festival crowd froze in collective astonishment. Phones raised and recording as people instinctively understood the gravity of the moment.

For several moments, nobody spoke. Nobody moved. Nobody breathed.

Then, impossibly, another movement at the tree line. The male grouse, the same one from my video, identifiable by the distinctive pattern on his neck, strutted into view. His chest inflated as he began his courtship dance in real time, just yards away from hundreds of star-struck festivalgoers.

"It's him," I said, clutching Noah's arm. "Gary has returned!"

Victoria and Marcus stood transfixed alongside everyone else, corporate strategizing momentarily forgotten as nature delivered its own perfect presentation.

The male grouse bounced and strutted, popping sounds

emerging from his air sacs in perfect sync with the recording playing on the speakers.

The female watched with what I could only interpret as avian skepticism, making the male work harder, his movements becoming more elaborate, more desperate for her approval.

Jenn looked like she might faint from the significance of the moment. "This confirms it. This is an active lek. Their ancestral mating ground. They're still using it."

For several magical minutes, the entire festival stood witness to a courtship ritual millions of years in the making. Then, with the same mysterious impulse that had brought them, the grouse pair retreated back into the forest, leaving behind a stunned silence.

For a long time, nobody breathed, nobody spoke, nobody moved.

Then ...

"Bye, Gary!" Noah waved at the spot where they'd vanished into the trees.

"Bye Mary!" I waved too.

A smile twitched on Noah's lips. "You named her Mary?"

"Yes. Mary. Seemed like a good fit."

"I guess we'll see."

In addition to his smirk, I couldn't help but notice the twinkle in Noah's eye.

Chapter Forty

Excited crowd chatter erupted all around us as Noah pulled me aside. "So, did you see all that male grouse had to go through? All that dancing, all that effort, just to get her attention?"

"I did. Seemed like a lot of work." My heart was suddenly racing. "Almost as much work as rescuing someone from rapids. Or building a fire with moldy logs in a storm-swept cabin. Or carrying them to their Jeep after a moose attack."

"Don't forget baking muffins before dawn," he added, the smile spreading over his face. Or scraping all the mud off a Jeep that hasn't been washed in ... well, ever. Just to impress someone's mom."

"You definitely made an impression, that's for sure."

"With your mom? Or with you?"

I considered. "Both."

Noah's hand found mine, his fingers intertwining with my own. "We should probably finish that conversation we started by the cliff," he began. "The one where you were going to tell me how you ..."

I figured actions were stronger than words. If the sage grouse could put himself out there like that, putting on a public display for all the world to see, risking rejection, looking foolish, dancing his heart out for love, the least I could do was show a little public display of affection myself.

I cut Noah off by rising on tiptoe and pressing my lips against his. The kiss was everything a kiss in front of hundreds of people should be, slightly clumsy, unexpectedly soft, and absolutely electric.

But more than that, it was honest. Here I was choosing love in front of half of Colorado and my parents and a very judgmental-looking wolf-dog.

Noah froze for a heartbeat, then his arms wrapped around me, lifting me slightly off the ground as he deepened the kiss.

Sinking into Noah's embrace, the noise of the festival faded away, replaced by the thundering of my heart and the certainty that had been building since that first disastrous meeting at the airport. This, us, was authentic in a way no curated content could ever be. Every spilled coffee, every airport abandonment, every eye roll, every grumpy growl, every reluctant compliment had been leading us here, to this moment of perfect clarity.

When we finally broke apart, I laughed at the pure joy bubbling in my chest, the kind of laugh that comes from genuine happiness.

"I am falling in love with you, Noah Barrett," I admitted, the words tumbling out before I could second-guess them. "Which is completely ridiculous and makes no logical sense and will probably end in disaster."

"Possibly," he agreed, his smile wide enough to reveal that hidden dimple. "But I'm willing to risk it if you are."

But even as I'd said it, I knew it wasn't ridiculous at all. Falling in love with Noah made perfect sense. Sometimes the best content was just life, lived honestly, with someone who saw you clearly and loved you anyway.

"I lied to Victoria," I added, because if we were doing honesty, we might as well do it completely. "About us being just business. About everything being for content. I lied because I was scared of losing my career, but I ended up losing something much more important."

The words felt like stepping off a cliff, but Noah's smile caught me before I could fall.

A low growl, followed by a bark, drew our attention back to the world still happening all around us. Yeti watched us like a protective parent, tongue rolling out of her mouth. The entire festival had shifted focus from the departed grouse to our impromptu romantic scene.

My parents stood nearby, Mom looking smugly vindicated while Dad pretended to study the cloud patterns. Brie was openly collecting cash from Jenn, Maya, and Diego, apparently settling some sort of wager at our expense.

The crowd burst into another round of cheers, this one even louder than the last. Even Axel was clapping. But I didn't miss his quick glance toward Maya afterward.

As the applause continued, Noah's ears turned an endearing shade of red, but he kept his arm firmly around my waist, as if afraid I might vanish if he let go.

Marcus observed our embrace with all the warmth of a corporate restructuring announcement. "Well," he said, straightening his tie and brushing a leaf from his pressed shirt. "It's fortunate you two are on good terms again, because we're going to be doing quite a lot of work together if we're all going to spin this ecotourism angle. I have some thoughts."

It was a career opportunity of a lifetime. Travel, adventure, authentic content creation with someone I loved. Six months ago, I would have seen it as a vindication of everything I'd worked for. But now I recognized Marcus's offer for what it was, another way for him to sell what didn't belong to him.

"That's a generous offer," I said, Noah's arm tightening around my waist. "But I think we might have our own ideas about how to move forward."

I was done with the manipulation. I'd spent the past few years trying to influence other people, when the only person I'd really needed to influence was myself.

But before I could fully process my own character development breakthrough, Victoria was already moving into her true element, seizing opportunities as the strategic landscape evolved. Her eyes fixed on the giant video screen where a replay of the sage grouse's elaborate dance was playing.

"They are pretty remarkable, if I'm being honest. All that effort, all that performance, just hoping someone will notice." She paused, caught up in the footage. "Kind of reminds me of Felix."

"Felix?" I noticed her corporate composure soften; something almost like fondness in her eyes.

"Who's Felix?" Maya asked.

The moment she realized she'd spoken aloud, Victoria's hand moved instinctively to smooth her already-perfect hair. "Felix was my pet chicken. When I was a little girl."

"You had a pet chicken?" I asked.

"And a pet piglet. And a pet donkey. And a pet goat. My parents had a small family farm in Wisconsin. Felix used to follow me around everywhere. To the barn, to the market, even to school sometimes when I could get away with it."

Victoria's jaw tightened, the memories playing out behind her eyes. "Until the family farm went bankrupt and Consolidated Agricultural bought my parents out." She stared at the video of the grouse for a few moments longer. If I didn't know better, I'd have sworn the bead of sweat wasn't the only moisture forming on her face.

"Guess you could say I learned early that if you can't beat them, you'd better become them." Whatever moment of humanity Victoria had experienced, she snapped out of it quickly. "And if you're going to become them, you'd better be the best one in the room. Especially if you're the only one wearing a skirt." She looked back at me. "Isn't that right, Samantha?"

The revelation re-contextualized everything I thought I knew about Victoria Sterling. Not a corporate ice queen, but a farm girl who'd weaponized competence to ensure she'd never be powerless again. I could see both versions of her now, the little girl who'd loved a pet chicken and the executive who'd built an empire on strategic emotional avoidance.

As her polished shield clamped back down into place, Victoria's gaze moved between Noah and me. "What if you had complete operational control? Full decision-making authority. Complete creative and strategic autonomy."

"Victoria ..." Marcus started, but Victoria cut him off.

"I've been watching the engagement metrics, the guest satisfaction scores. The traditional luxury model shows diminishing returns across all our properties."

Her mental gears were turning, a strategic mind that had built an empire now pivoting to protect and expand it.

"We have resorts across the world. All operating on the same tired luxury model, several struggling with the same engagement challenges we were facing here. All sitting on authentic cultural and environmental resources we've been systematically ignoring in favor of generic amenities."

We all gathered round. Noah, Jenn, Maya, Diego, and Brie.

"For this to work, I need partners who understand authentic engagement isn't just better ethics, it's better business. People who can help transform LuxeLife from a luxury accommodation company into an authentic experience designer."

The mountain air was still cool, but Marcus was sweating bullets. "Victoria, I really don't think ..."

"That's right, Marcus. You don't think. Which is why we're in this predicament to begin with."

Victoria shifted her attention back to Noah. "And we'll need your wilderness friends to help conduct site visits, I imagine. Environmental assessments, activity development, staff training." She smiled. A real one. I think. "So instead of one Adventure Center, you'll have to figure out how to run several. Think of it as a promotion."

"That sounds like a lot of travel," said Noah, and I could practically see him recalculating Victoria from "corporate threat" to "complicated ally with a pet chicken in her past."

"For both of you," Victoria confirmed. "I'll have legal draw up the contracts immediately." But then she paused. "Unless, of course, you prefer to go back to Los Angeles, Samantha. And you, Mr. Barrett, would rather stay up here on your mountain."

"We're open to new possibilities," I answered for both of us.

"Excellent," said Victoria. "I feel good about this. I think it could work out very nicely for all." She snapped her fingers, and Marcus scurried after her like a chastised intern, his perfect white teeth no longer quite so intimidating when his ego was deflating faster than a sage grouse's air sacs when it was done with its show.

As Victoria and Marcus moved away to continue their number crunching, Noah's expression was a mixture of hope and uncertainty. "So, are you sure you're okay with mountains in Alaska? Swamps in Florida?"

I pretended to consider, tapping my finger against my chin. "I don't know. Are there moose there too?"

I Burned My Tongue in Colorado

"In Alaska? Even more than here. And bears. Lots of bears. Big bears. Not so much in Florida though. There, it's just the snakes and the alligators. And spiders." Noah shuddered.

"But will there be muffins?" I asked.

His smile brightened. "Possibly."

"Then I'm in." I rose on tiptoe again to place another quick kiss on his lips. "But you should know, I'm still not hiking without frequent rest breaks. And I expect to be carried at least forty percent of the time."

Noah laughed. "Only when you're actively bleeding or being chased by wildlife."

"I'm sure that won't be a problem for me," I said.

"Deal." He sealed our agreement with another kiss, this one drawing a fresh round of cheers from our audience.

Around us, the festival continued, the crowd now buzzing with talk of grouse sightings and eco-adventures and the unlikely romance between a city influencer and a grumpy mountain guide.

Parker was already coordinating with the livestream team to capitalize on the magical moment, while my parents had returned to their cooking station, Mom no doubt already planning wedding venues and Dad calculating how he was going to afford wedding bills in addition to the student loans.

I thought to myself, maybe I could convince Victoria to let me take a business trip, with a few special guests of course, to the Copenhagen resort to ease the sting a bit.

But in that moment, with Noah's arms around me and the mountains rising in the distance, plans for the future would have to wait. I was too busy enjoying the present.

Living in the moment.

And I didn't need to curate anything to make it perfect.

Epilogue

Sunlight painted the mountaintop in a palette of molten gold and crimson. One year since my first disastrous trek up this mountain, my quads barely burned as I followed Noah along the familiar trail, the strength in my legs a physical reminder of how much had changed.

"Almost there," Noah called over his shoulder, the corner of his mouth quirking up in that half-smile that still made my heart beat just a bit faster.

"You said that twenty minutes ago." I jabbed a finger into his ribs as I caught up. "And don't think I haven't noticed that suspiciously heavy backpack. If there aren't muffins in there, I'm going back to LA without you this time. Leave you in the woods with all the meese by yourself."

Noah's laugh echoed against the mountainside. "Always the drama queen."

We crested the final ridge, and there it stood, the lightning tree, its trunk twisted and split. It looked exactly the same as we'd left it.

Noah dropped to one knee ...

I Burned My Tongue in Colorado

ha

... and began unpacking what could only be described as a five-star picnic. Fresh sourdough from the local bakery, Mrs. Miller's special reserve cheeses that never made it to her market stall, and the pièce de résistance, huckleberry muffins, still warm and fragrant.

"You remembered." I snatched one immediately, the buttery deliciousness melting on my tongue, the burst of wild berries still as surprising as that first Dawn Patrol breakfast.

"Hard to forget when you complained about being hungry or tired every five minutes that day." Noah's eyes sparked.

"I did not! It was every ten minutes at most."

He pulled out two ceramic mugs and poured something that definitely wasn't coffee. The liquid caught the light, shimmering golden in the waning glow of sunset.

"Is that the same champagne from our cabin adventure?" I accepted the cup, breathing in the mineral bouquet.

"Maya helped me track down a bottle." Noah settled beside me on the blanket, his shoulder warm against mine. "Though personally, I still think whiskey pairs better with huckleberry."

"Such a purist." I took a sip, letting the champagne and the moment wash over me.

Below us, the valley stretched like a patchwork quilt of forest and meadow, shadows gradually claiming the landscape as the sun sank lower. A red-tailed hawk circled, effortlessly soaring without a single wingbeat. The breeze carried the scent of pine and wildflowers.

"This is perfect," I said, leaning into Noah's solid warmth.

His arm slid around me, gentle hand resting on my hip. "Better than Victoria's infinity pools and diamond dust facials?"

"So much better." I broke off another chunk of muffin. "Though I still maintain these would sell for ten dollars each in

LA. Twenty if we ask Parker to do an endorsement. You know, his follower count is now higher than mine."

Noah snorted. "I'll stick to my mountain prices, thanks."

The past year had been like living in a fever dream, except the calluses on my hands and the firm curves of my leg muscles proved it had all been real. From social media darling to eco-adventure entrepreneur, from city girl to mountain woman. I finally realized that not just one thing defined me.

"Remember when you made me climb that tree to rescue the osprey?"

"You mean when you couldn't stop staring at my abs instead of focusing on the rescue?"

"I was perfectly focused on the mission." My cheeks blushed at the memory. "That bird made a full recovery, by the way. Dr. Martinez spotted her nesting with a mate last spring."

Noah's thumb traced lazy circles on my palm as we watched alpenglow paint the peaks in rose and violet.

What a year it had been, turning Victoria's "curated authenticity" concept into something genuine instead. Our Authentic Adventures network now spanned four wilderness regions, with more to come.

Diego's Everglades Center had taken off like crazy, his swamp tours and airboat safaris booked solid months in advance. The photos he sent last week, of him leading a night-time expedition, headlamp illuminating the ruby-red eye shine of alligators, had sparked another wave of bookings.

"Did you see Jenn's latest update from Kodiak?" I asked, thinking of our friend and partner who'd led the charge in Alaska. "Three coastal brown bears in one frame, and not through a telephoto lens."

"Speaking of updates," Noah said, "Brie called again this morning from Costa Rica."

"How's the coffee farm adventure going?"

Noah shook his head, suppressing a smile. "That girl's determined to revolutionize sustainable coffee production single-handedly. Though between you and me, I think she's more interested in the farmer than the farming."

"I knew there was a reason she kept extending her 'research trip.'" I made air quotes with my fingers.

"Who would've thought our authentic Colorado adventures would evolve into this?" I gestured at the wild landscape around us.

Dark clouds rolled over the distant peaks, and a cool breeze ruffled my hair, carrying the electric scent of approaching rain. "We should probably head back soon," I said, eyeing the storm front. "Those clouds look mean, and I'm still traumatized after dodging all those lightning bolts the last time we were up here."

Noah's eyes sparkled with mischief as he stood up. "Just need to do one more thing before we go. Yeti! Come here, girl!"

Our wolf-dog lounged in a patch of wildflowers a few yards away, pretending not to hear. Something metallic glinted on her collar, a carabiner that definitely hadn't been there when we started our hike.

"Yeti, come!" Noah's voice took on that authoritative tone he used with tourists who wandered too close to a cliff.

Yeti rolled onto her back, exposing her belly to the sky, the very picture of canine insubordination.

"Yeti! Come!" Noah tried again.

The wolf-dog stretched lazily, her gaping yawn showing off a mouth full of teeth.

"For heaven's sake," Noah muttered. "You're messing up my surprise!"

"Surprise?" My heart rate kicked up a notch.

Finally, with theatrical reluctance, Yeti trotted over and dropped her massive head in my lap, completely ignoring Noah's commands.

I bit back a laugh. "Yeti, sit."

She immediately planted her furry bottom on the ground, fixing me with those ice-blue eyes.

"Lie down," I said.

Yeti flopped onto her side, still watching me adoringly, while Noah threw his hands up in exasperation. "At what point did she become the boss?" he asked the dog. "After all these years, this is how you repay me?"

"What's that on her collar?" I reached for the metal glint, but Yeti rolled away, tail wagging in excitement.

"Come here, you furry menace." I grabbed her collar, and my breath caught in my throat. A ring dangled from the carabiner, delicate yet rugged, with tiny mountains etched into the silver band.

My heart hammered in my chest as I turned around. Noah knelt in the wildflowers, his usual confident smirk replaced by a raw vulnerability that made my chest ache.

"Sam." His voice cracked on my name. "You changed everything. My life. This place." He shot Yeti a wry look. "Even my dog's loyalty, apparently."

The setting sun gilded his features, highlighting the laugh lines I'd grown to love, the tiny scar above his eyebrow, the slight curl of dark hair at his temple where it was getting too long.

"I thought I had it all figured out up here in my mountains, but you showed me what was missing." Noah swallowed hard. "You're the adventure I never knew I needed. Will you marry me?"

"Yes." The word burst out before he finished asking. "Of course, yes!" Tears blurred my vision.

I stepped forward to kiss him, but Yeti wedged between us, nearly knocking Noah backwards. The dog's tail whipped back and forth like a furry windshield wiper as she covered Noah's face in slobbery kisses.

"Down!" Noah commanded, laughing. "Let me kiss my fiancée!"

Yeti ignored him, continuing her enthusiastic face-washing.

I grabbed Noah's hand and pulled him up. "Come here."

Before Yeti could intervene again, I pressed my lips to Noah's. His arms wrapped around me, lifting me off my feet as he deepened the kiss. The taste of huckleberries and champagne mingled on our tongues as the first wet raindrops fell.

"You taste like dog slobber," I murmured against his mouth.

"Does that mean you're changing your mind?"

"Never." I pressed my forehead to his as rain pattered around us. "But we'd better get moving before this storm hits full force. I've already had my 'trapped in a cabin with Noah Barrett' adventure."

"That's a shame." Noah's fingers tangled with mine as he slipped the ring onto my finger. "I was rather hoping for a sequel. Except this time, maybe we can share the bed."

"I don't know," I said. "You'd better take that up with her." I nodded my head toward Yeti.

The heavens opened above us, but neither of us moved to pack up. Some adventures were worth getting soaked for.

Behind us, Yeti barked joyfully at the sky, as if claiming credit for bringing us together. And maybe she deserved it. She did save me from that moose, after all.

Noah's lips found mine again as lightning flashed across the valley, illuminating the beginning of our greatest adventure yet.

Love can be messy... but finding your next great read doesn't have to be!

Join the FoxJam Books newsletter for exclusive updates, behind-the-scenes peeks at upcoming novels, and special subscriber-only content.

Visit foxjambooks.com to sign up and stay connected.

FoxJam Books